JOE DALLAS

MW00681220

Unforgiven Sins

HARVEST HOUSE PUBLISHERS
Eugene, Oregon 97402

The Scripture quotations in this book are taken from the King James Version of the Bible.

The story *Unforgiven Sins* and its characters are fictitious. However, certain true-life events and public figures have been included as reference points. These known figures have played pivotal roles in the ongoing controversy over gay rights, and the mention of each is made with the most respectful of intentions.

UNFORGIVEN SINS

Copyright © 1995 by Harvest House Publishers
Eugene, Oregon 97402

Cover photo ©1988 Regis Lefebure/Third Coast Stock Source Inc.

Library of Congress Cataloging-in-Publication Data

Dallas, Joe, 1954-
    Unforgiven sins / Joe Dallas.
      p.   cm.
    ISBN 1-56507-167-0
    1. Gay men—California—Crimes against—Fiction. 2. Hazing—
California—Fiction. 3. Revenge—Fiction. I. Title.
PS3554.A4337U5   1994   93-23527
813′.54—dc20   CIP

Printed in the United States of America.

95 96 97 98 99 00 01 — 10 9 8 7 6 5 4 3 2 1

For Jody.
May he never live in fear.

PROLOGUE

*E*ither we'll kill a fag or we'll freeze to death."

Desmond was whispering, which wasn't a good idea, considering the location. The Long Beach cliffs were seldom quiet; conditions that night made any communication other than shouting a waste of time. Between the waves crashing a hundred yards ahead, the traffic on Ocean Boulevard twenty feet behind, and the November wind whipping through his T-shirt, Greg could barely hear his soon-to-be fraternity brother.

No matter. Desmond's tone of voice said they had more in common than the status of lowly freshman: They were both scared.

"I'm not killing anybody!" Greg shot back.

"Hey!" Curt Ramsey screamed at Greg's back while delivering a hefty kick to his rear. "No talking, Bishop! No talking, no stopping, no looking around!"

No dignity, either. That was annulled when Greg decided to join the Argonauts, California State-Long Beach's most elite fraternity. Dignity was replaced by six months of groveling, swats with a nine-foot wooden paddle, and unbridled abuse at the hands of postadolescent sadists. The humiliating pledging ritual was justified by fraternity members with the old "*I*-had-to-take-it-when-I-was-a-pledge-and-*I*-didn't-whine!" routine.

Ramsey's kick threw Greg a couple of feet headlong. Desmond caught him around the waist to steady him, and of course Master Ramsey couldn't let it pass.

"Looks cute, you two. Gonna meet some of your boyfriends out there?" Argonaut laughter roared across the beach.

Desmond and Greg couldn't answer, of course, or even look back to acknowledge the insult. But they'd been the fraternity's prey for half a year, and had learned to absorb their masters' abuse.

They could smell them, too. The members had gone through at least two cases of beer and the night was still young. Some were still finishing off cans of Budweiser, gulping, belching, and relishing this most sacred of annual events.

Black Tuesday.

All twenty-seven of the Argonauts had turned out for the orgy of violence second only to Hell Night in the terror it held for pledges. As usual, they walked in front of the members, eyes straight ahead, while every move their trembling bodies made was scrutinized and taunted. And tonight they were headed toward a strip of beach known as Boystown, where on any given night homosexual men carried out their liaisons.

Or, where they "queer up to each other," as Damon Boswell would say. Boswell was president of the Argonauts, and as such it was his responsibility to come up with new and improved rituals for Black Tuesday. His effectiveness as president was determined, in fact, by the ingenuity of the festivities. Each Black Tuesday had to be more horrific than the last, and in this challenge he had stiff competition indeed. Pledges in '67 had to drink a pint of Tabasco sauce mixed with lighter fluid and cologne; '68's boys were forced to sprint across the Long Beach freeway seven times while holding hands. How do you top that?

By making the pledges of '69 pay a visit to Boystown, find a homosexual, and beat him to a pulp.

"Hey, you guys are getting off easy this year!" Boswell jeered when he announced the plan. "Any normal Argonaut would pay for a chance to do it." Then he paused, emphasizing each word with his finger: "And anyone who refuses probably has a few problems himself, if you know what I mean."

They reached the shoreline, the pledges wondering if they were going to be marched right into the ocean, when Boswell barked out the order to halt.

The area was pitch-dark except for a light from the lifeguard station some thirty feet to the left.

Feet planted in the sand, the pledges glanced at each other and waited. Besides Desmond and Greg, there were four other pledges waiting to prove their manhood: Lars Freidman, a sophomore track star who'd already distinguished himself as a title holder in the quarter mile, Jim and Jeff Billhart, twins who played baseball and football respectively, and Rick Mosley, a baseball player and president of the Drama Club, which was unusual for a jock. Desmond played tight end on the football team; Bishop played quarterback. Both were second-string, which was respectable as long as it was temporary. Argonauts were, after all, athletes. Wimps and hippies need not apply.

Greg tried guessing the other pledges' feelings. Lars was pale and wide-eyed. The Billhart twins shifted nervously. Only Mosley seemed calm, almost relaxed. He wore a slight smile, his eyes communicating something like...anticipation?

The surf crashed, the icy wind bit into their chests.

"All right, boys, show time." Boswell's low voice caught their attention. "Face left, shut up, and listen."

They pivoted. Boswell and Ramsey stood in front, arms crossed, authority intact. "That's where they meet," Boswell said, jerking his head toward the lifeguard station. "One of them just stands there until another comes along."

"And says, 'Ooh, I love your new hairdo,'" Ramsey cooed.

"So here's the plan," Boswell continued. "One of you is gonna stand in front of the station and be the queer bait." He noticed their puzzlement.

"Don't you idiots know what queer bait is?"

"I do, sir," Mosley piped up.

"Educate your fellow scumbags, Mosley."

Mosley stepped out of the line and faced front. "Queer bait is a guy who baits queers," he recited. "He sits there waiting for one to try and pick him up while his friends hide, then he and his friends jump the guy." He looked to Boswell for approval.

"Didn't know you had a brain, Mosley!" Boswell pushed him back in line. "So the bait waits under the lifeguard station. The rest of you crouch down and stay low till the bait gets the queer talking. Then when you hear me say 'Now,' you jump him. And here's how you do it."

They held their breath.

"Ten punches each. You take turns. Each of you gives him ten punches in the face or the stomach while the rest of you hold him down and count out loud."

"That's 'cause we know some of you can't count for yourselves," Ramsey chimed in.

"No pussyfooting around, either," Boswell warned. "You take him one at a time, throw your punches, then when everyone is finished you split back to the car."

"Unless we get inspired and just can't stop." It was Mosley again, staring intensely at his president.

"You stop once you've thrown ten punches, idiot! Wanna go to San Quentin?"

Mosley just shrugged. Boswell shook his head then turned to the rest.

"Got the game plan?"

They nodded, but Greg had already decided not to play. Not quite, anyway. If there were going to be any punches thrown, he'd let the others throw them while standing close enough to look like he was joining in. Fighting wasn't the issue; he'd been in, and won, quite a few rounds. But this was different. He couldn't do it.

But neither could he prevent it. Correction: Neither *would* he prevent it. He was too decent to hit a man who'd done nothing to him, but too frightened to stop his friends from doing the same. Or to speak out against this thing they were planning.

Boswell was looking them over now. "Okay, who's the bait?"

Silence.

"Hey, Ramsey, choose. Who's the best-looking?"

"They're all uglier than dirt, but I guess Bishop's the least ugly."

They looked at Greg.

"I—I don't think I can," Greg stammered. "I mean, what do I say?"

"You say, 'Hi, big boy,'" Ramsey sang out in falsetto, wiggling his hips while the others chortled.

"I'm serious. I don't know what to do!" Greg's voice was so high and panicked he barely recognized it as his own.

Boswell grabbed the front of his T-shirt and shoved him toward the station. "Move it."

He stumbled a few feet ahead.

"And look pretty," Boswell yelled.

He reached the station, faced the ocean, then looked to the right. They were still there, crouched and watching, barely visible.

Nobody to the left, nobody behind or in front. He waited, then looked at his watch. It said he'd been waiting three minutes.

Then five, then eleven. Nothing.

Thank You, Lord. I'm so sorry I'm here. Please don't let anyone come and I swear I'll never do anything like this again. Just please keep anyone from coming here, okay?

Two minutes later Greg got an answer. The wrong one.

Someone was walking toward him from the cliffs separating the boulevard from the beach. Greg turned his back on him and looked toward the water, hoping he'd get the hint, until he heard a "Pssst, look!" from Ramsey's hiding place, and knew he was trapped. He turned back to the cliffs.

The guy was closer now, maybe fifteen yards. He was still obscured by the dark, so Greg couldn't see his face.

Another few steps and he could make him out more clearly. Tall, thin, much younger than Greg thought he'd be. Weren't all these guys supposed to be older?

His fists tightened. He came as close to shaking his head at the stranger as he dared, but the guy didn't catch it. Closer now, he could see him plainly. Blue jeans, windbreaker, sneakers, baseball cap.

A kid, for God's sake! His own age or maybe even younger. He stopped a few feet in front of Greg, cleared his throat, offered a soft "Hi," and waited for a response.

No pussyfooting around.

Greg looked down and fought tears.

Anyone who refuses probably has a few problems himself—

Greg swallowed hard and looked back up, then to his left to where they were waiting.

Ten punches each.

"No!" It came out of Greg suddenly.

"What?" The stranger stepped back, startled.

"Nothing." Greg glanced left, then made a quick decision. "Just go away. Please. This is—"

The kid was staring hard into his face.

"Greg Bishop?"

Greg looked closer and was stunned.

"Bennie?"

They locked eyes. They'd locked arms before, too, seeing who was the strongest arm wrestler in the second grade. Or who was the fastest runner, or who could hold his breath the longest underwater. Bennie Hudson, his best friend by default because there weren't any other kids on the block. Since kindergarten, Bennie Hudson had meant daily companionship, baseball after school, spending the night on weekends watching scary movies, and swapping details of first crushes. Then junior-high football, experiments with cigarettes, and pressing cut fingers together because they were blood brothers until death, or at least until ninth grade, when the Bishops moved to a separate school district, which meant, of course, separate lives.

Until now.

"Bennie, what are you doing here?" he asked, not wanting to know. *Bennie couldn't be a... He'd always seemed so...so normal.*

Bennie's expression said he was thinking the same thing about Greg.

"Greg, are you—"

"*NOW!!!*"

Boswell's shout boomed across the sand like a war cry. It was answered by an echo then a crashing wave. Greg pushed Bennie in the chest as hard as he could. "Get outta here. Run!"

No good. He'd pushed too hard. Bennie was on his back, dazed and confused, when the Argonaut pledges swarmed him. Jeff Billhart was first, grabbing his arms and pinning him to the sand. Lars was next. He went for Bennie's legs, which were kicking and flailing wildly, and wrapped his arms around them in a wrestler's lock. He and Jeff stretched their prey, held him fast, then Lars yelled behind him at the others. "Who's first?"

Bennie was trapped, spread-eagled on the sand when Mosley jogged up to him, followed by Desmond and Jim.

"Me first," Mosley announced.

Greg's mouth opened. Nothing came out.

The Argonauts moved in to watch the kill, hooting, laughing, shouting encouragement. Someone threw an empty beer can at Bennie's head.

"Me first," Mosley repeated, crushing the boy's chest with one foot.

Greg tried moving again. Nothing. Legs, feet, and hands were stone.

"Hello, sweetheart," Mosley crooned, leaning into Bennie's face. "I'm your blind date." He spit on his eyes, then slapped him.

"One!" the pledges shouted in unison.

"That doesn't count!" Mosley sneered. "That wasn't a punch! I'll show you a punch!" He was drawing his fist back full force when Greg found his voice.

"Hold it!"

Mosley's fist hung midair. He turned to Greg quizzically; the others did the same. Bennie, who'd been paralyzed till now, spoke up.

"Greg, what is this? What are they doing?"

Mosley loosened his fist, stepped off Bennie, and stared at Greg, astonished. The others stepped back a few feet, and Lars and Jeff nearly let go of Bennie for a moment. All of them looked at Greg, openmouthed, thinking the same thing in unison: *He knows Bishop. The queer knows Bishop.*

Ramsey pointed at him.

"Bishop! Is this guy your *friend?*"

Everyone froze, hanging on his answer.

He wanted to say yes. He wanted to tell them to lay off or pick a fair fight. Then he wanted to grab Bennie, haul him up the cliffs to safety, and tell the Argonauts to kiss off.

But what he wanted was secondary to a realization too threatening for his seventeen-year-old mind to handle:

If they think this guy's my friend, they'll think I'm one of THOSE!

"No."

Bennie raised his chest off the sand, eyes bulging. "What?"

"No," Greg repeated, "I told him my name just now, but I don't know him." He looked at the ground while he said it.

"Then let's do it!" Mosley cheered. The pledges turned back to their duty.

"Greg?" Bennie wailed as they closed in on him again. "Greg, *please!"*

He looked away. Mosley straddled Bennie while the others took their places. Greg clamped his eyes shut.

But that didn't stop him from hearing Mosley throw his first punch into Bennie's jaw, the crunch of bone punctuated by the chorus shouting, "One!" More screams followed, higher and desperate, blending with the laughter of twenty-seven drunk boys egging their pledges on. Boswell called him.

"Bishop! Get over here!"

He turned back around in time to see them grab Bennie, pull him off the ground, throw him an incredible seven feet into the air, then slam him back onto the wet sand.

They were, as Mosley predicted, getting inspired. He pummeled Bennie's face, then Lars hammered ten punches into his torso—punches that had to have broken several ribs. Jeff was next, throwing his fist into whatever body parts were left to injure. Thirty blows and it was just beginning.

They formed a circle around him as he crawled back and forth, pleading and sobbing. When he came to the edge he was greeted with a kick and another round of laughter and name-calling.

"Who's next?" someone yelled.

"Bishop! Get in here, Bishop. It's your turn!" Mosley was yelling from the circle while Greg's ex-blood brother quivered at his feet.

He barely heard.

"Bishop! He's waiting for you." And with that, Mosley picked the boy up by the hair and turned his face toward Greg.

Only the eyes were recognizable, peering at him through blood and bruises. They were less afraid now, softened, looking at Greg with a strange sort of understanding. And something else.

Pity. Greg looked closer, astonished. Then believing, then incredibly ashamed. Bennie pitied him.

That did it. He was sprinting toward the cliffs before he realized it, away from the beach and up the wooden stairs, running and sobbing and covering his ears all at once.

Thirty more yards and he'd be away from the Argonauts, whom he wanted nothing more to do with, and their stupid pledges who would never forgive him for dropping out of the club. And away from Bennie, whom he suddenly hated for no particular reason except that he was a victim and a homosexual and Greg could do nothing to change either fact. Maybe someone else could.

He reached the top of the stairs, caught his breath, and noticed a sailor with his girlfriend. They were necking on a bench facing the water.

"Hey!" Greg yelled, running toward them. "Hey, can you help me? There's a guy down there getting beat up!" He barely got the words out through his huffing and panting.

The sailor looked at him, then at the beach. "Down there?"

"Right. Right down there." Greg pointed to the spot.

A scream floated up from the shoreline.

The sailor smirked, took his arm from around his girl's shoulders and lit a cigarette. "That's Boystown. Didn't you know that?"

Greg bent over, held his stomach, and took a few breaths. "Yeah, I know. Can you help?"

"Don't you know what kind of guys hang around down there?"

"Yeah!" he yelled, straightening up, "and one of them's getting killed!"

"So?"

"So can you help him?"

The sailor exhaled some smoke, then flicked an ash toward the beach. "Forget it. You can't help guys like that."

ONE

*T*he sound jerked Dr. Bishop awake like the clock radio usually did, so on impulse he leaned across the bed and pounded the top of the snooze button. But that didn't stop the sound.

Beep-beep-beep-beep-beep-beep-beep.

Louder now. Not the radio, of course; the radio woke him up to light jazz, not *beep*, but since it was nearly midnight it took a few seconds to connect sounds with meaning: light jazz meant "good morning," *beep* meant "emergency, move fast." He clicked the lamp on and looked around.

Beep-beep-beep-beep-beep-beep-beep.

Christine sat up and groaned.

"Sorry, honey, I can't find it," he mumbled.

"Left side by your watch," she slurred, pointing at the dresser.

He jumped across the room, grabbed the pager, and hit the button. The beep died and the answering service's number came up on the screen.

"Who is it?" His wife was fully awake now.

"It's the exchange." He flicked the lamp off. "Sleep. I'll take it in the kitchen."

It took about nine large steps to get there, every one of them sending a scream from his calves to his brain. He'd just started a new leg routine at the gym—double the amount of weight and exercises he was used to—and the onset of soreness made him want to take as few steps as possible. *Sometimes you can actually thank God for a small house,* he thought while punching the number in, *even though it's not your typical Orange County dwelling.*

"Dr. Bishop's exchange," came the answer.

"It's me," he yawned. "What's up?"

"Dr. Bishop? We've got a man on hold who says he needs to speak with you immediately, but he won't give his name or number. Should I connect you?"

"Did he say it was an emergency?"

"He said it's a matter of life and death." The operator paused. "Yours, not his."

"*What?*"

"That's what he said. Do you want the call?"

"Put him through."

"Go ahead, please," she told the caller.

Static came over the line; someone was calling from a phone booth. Or a portable phone? Greg couldn't tell.

"Hello, this is Greg Bishop."

"Quick response," a low, groggy voice answered. "Shows concern. I like that." The man spoke slowly and his words were slurred, indicating booze, drugs, or both.

"I'm responding to your page. Did you just—"

"Yes I did. And you're Dr. Gregory Bishop and you're quick and concerned. I would have liked you."

Intoxicated or not, he sounded cultured. And familiar. Not a friend, but familiar.

"Who's speaking, please?"

"I would have liked you," the caller repeated softly.

Patience wasn't Greg's strong suit; patience with drunks who called late at night was out of the question. Even if they were cultured ones.

"You paged me on the emergency line, sir, so if this *is* an emergency, please tell me who you are and what you need."

"I don't need *anything* from you," the caller retorted. "My emergency is over. Now it's *your* emergency, so I called to tell you what *you* need—"

"More sleep and less phone calls like this, buddy," Greg murmured under his breath.

"—and to clue you in on some fascinating events that are about to take place."

"Pardon?"

"Taxing your patience, aren't I? But this conversation is going to mean quite a bit to you in the not-too-distant future."

Long pause.

"Still there, Dr. Bishop?"

"Still here."

"You'll be in your office tomorrow?"

"Right."

"Counseling people?"

"Sure."

"Before two o'clock?"

Strange question, but what the heck—

"Before two? No, not tomorrow." Tomorrow was Wednesday, and Wednesday mornings were reserved for administrative work. No appointments were scheduled until two. "Why do you ask?"

"Because you'll be receiving a hand-delivered package in the morning." The slurring was getting worse; *package* came out *packash*. "It'll arrive by eleven at the latest. Promise me you'll read it before your two o'clock appointment. Then you'll understand the emergency, and you'll have some time to decide what to do. Or what not to do."

"Sounds like a lot to handle."

"I'll be watching from the other side to see if you can do it."

Greg's irritation faded. This was either a suicide speech or a cry for help. He had to assume the former; he'd been trained not to take chances.

"You sound as though you've been drinking," he said, hoping to keep the man talking.

"What an ear for detail."

"And are you on any medication, or have you taken any drugs in the last forty-eight hours?"

"Are you reading these questions off a suicide hotline brochure?" Long pauses between his words—not a good sign. "Sorry, that was rude. To answer your question, yes. I am on medication. I'm not feeling well, so I took medication."

"What did you take?"

"Enough. I took enough."

"Is anyone with you?"

The man chuckled softly. "Nobody's been with me for a long time."

"Okay, I can hear you've got a lot on your mind, and I'd really like to talk to you about it. Maybe I could drop by?"

"I'm not up to it. I've got a splitting life ache. Anyway, this call is for you, not me, remember? So please don't interrupt me again."

"But we'd do so much better face-to-face—"

"No interruptions!" the caller exploded, catching a second wind. "No more 'save the crazy old man routine' or I'm hanging up. Okay?"

"Okay, sure." Greg's right leg cramped, and his feet were chilled on the hardwood floor. But he was alert by now, mentally working out the next moves: Let the man talk, establish trust by listening, keep him talking till he wears down and states his location, then call the paramedics. "So, what about this emergency? Can you tell me a little more about it?"

"Not now. I'll be telling you more later. This is the start of a beautiful friendship."

The more he talked, the more familiar he sounded.

"Have we met? At least tell me that much," Greg urged.

"In a sense. Sounds like I said *innocence,* doesn't it? But I didn't say *innocence,* believe me. I dropped that word years ago. I said 'in a *sense,*' because yes, we've met, but only in a sense, old friend."

"I'm glad to hear we're friends. Friends talk about their problems. So tell me about yours."

"Trying to keep me talking? Good effort, doctor. Nice tone, too. Very earnest. You should have been a radio shrink."

"It's Greg, okay? Call me Greg." *Call me anything as long as you keep talking, mister.* He heard more static, then a gulping sound on the other end, then a long sigh.

"I have a request, Greg."

"Yes?"

"Say NO to them. Somebody's got to say NO to them!"

"Tell me who you're talking about and I'll tell you if I can."

No answer.

"Come on, I'm completely in the dark here!" Greg said, his voice rising.

"Then you're in good company." The man giggled softly. "Divine retribution, that's what it is. I sniffed out the awful truth and put it on display, and they loved it. People always love it, until it's done to them."

"What's that got to do with—"

"Now everyone's going to think they know the awful truth about me. But guess what, Greg?"

"Hmm?"

"There's more awful truth to find out. And not just about me. There are plenty of others. But I'll let you in on something, Greg."

"Yes?"

"They can't win—unless we become what they *want* us to become. Now, good night."

"NO!" Greg scrambled for another tactic. Polite conversation wasn't working; maybe anger would.

"Your game-playing is very arrogant, you know that?" He feigned irritation. "You call me in the middle of the night, you say we're old friends, but you won't even tell me who you are!"

No response—just soft, slow breathing. Then the voice returned, thin and fading. "No more. I'm so tired, Greg. Don't ever get tired. You've got work to do. And tell Robbie how sorry I am. I'm so unbelievably sorry. Tell him."

"Robbie? Who's Robbie?"

"Good night."

Click, dial tone.

He held the phone at arm's length, shaking his head at it, then dialed his service.

"Dr. Bishop's exchange."

"It's me again. Did that man tell you where he was calling from?"

"No, but it sounded like a cellular phone to me."

"Me, too. Can you remember exactly what he said?"

"Let's see. He asked to speak to you. I told him he could leave a number and I'd page you and have you return the call, but he said he couldn't do that. Then I asked if he was in crisis, and he said, 'No, but this is a matter of life and death. Dr. Bishop's, not mine.'"

"That's it?"

"Sorry. That's all he said."

"Thanks. Good night."

His legs cramped up again, protesting yesterday's torture session. Greg locked his knees, touched the floor and held the stretch for a full minute, then limped back to bed.

Christine stirred. "What happened?"

He eased in beside her, snuggling his face into her hair. "Nothing, I hope."

The driver placed the phone back into its cradle, then stroked it and sat motionless in the midnight silence. There was nothing left to do but wait.

He would be dead before morning if no one interfered, and interference wasn't likely. That's why he chose this spot. The Orange Hills were secluded, pedestrians were nonexistent at this hour, and the cul-de-sac where he'd parked his Mercedes was heavily landscaped with trees and shrubbery. He was certain to go unnoticed by any of the residents until they wandered out at dawn for the morning paper. By then it wouldn't matter.

Thirty minutes before making the call he had parked, loosened his tie, then drawn three bottles out of the briefcase he kept on the passenger's seat. Two were filled with Phynothal, prescribed by his physician for nerves and insomnia with strict warnings about overdose. The other bottle contained a half-pint of whiskey. After emptying the contents of the first two into his mouth, he washed them down with the third. The effects were almost immediate, making it difficult for him to finish his conversation with the doctor.

He taped a brief note to his wife onto the dashboard. "And that," he mumbled, "concludes our broadcast." His head rolled back on the seat. "Thanks for joining us."

The drugs kicked in full-force just before 12:30. Despair had killed his appetite, leaving his stomach conveniently empty, and the whiskey hurried things along.

He'd anticipated some last-minute panic, maybe a change of heart once the severity of his actions set in. But the sensation overtaking him was rather nice, really—like floating on a raft down a gentle current.

The first jolt came at 12:35—a sudden dip as though the raft hit a small waterfall and was sinking downward. Another came within minutes, sharper and longer. Now the raft was an elevator, dropping a hundred floors a minute.

This is it? he wondered. *No final profound thoughts? No flashing of my illustrious life before my eyes? Might have been a good movie, you know, maybe even a miniseries.* He tried to smile at the thought but couldn't find the strength. Instead he sighed and surrendered, letting the tide take him down, down, down.

TWO

*G*reg's usual morning jog was unthinkable, so he opted instead for a brisk two-mile walk—the maximum his rubbery legs could take. It wasn't much of a strain, but he worked up a respectable sweat. The radio alarm had gone off at 6:30 as always, and even without a decent night's sleep he welcomed the idea of being outside. Mornings were the only time he had to himself.

Christine was sipping coffee in bed when he got back. She was browsing through the paper while listening to the morning news at the same time—a custom she observed as religiously as he did his morning jaunts. Both were exercise buffs; she would attend her aerobics class later, preferring dance and rhythm to the monotony of jogging.

He stood in the doorway smiling, waiting for her to look up and blush when she noticed him staring. It was a favorite game of theirs: He'd stare, she'd blush, and for a moment they were teenagers.

She was listening intently to the radio news, holding the paper in front of her without reading it.

"—*alone in his car, a victim of apparent drug overdose. Police were unable to*—"

He coughed. She put a finger to her lips then looked back at the radio. No blush today.

"—*is unknown at this time, but all agreed his death contrasted dramatically with a life of remarkable accomplishments.*"

She finally looked up at him. "Josh Ferguson died."

"No! When?" Greg moved to the bed and sat beside his wife, thumbing through the paper.

"Careful, you're dripping." She pulled a Kleenex from a box on her nightstand and dabbed his forehead. "Last night. It's not in the papers." She pointed at the radio. "They just announced it. It happened around midnight, they think. It was a suicide. He overdosed in his own car. Can you believe it? They found him in Orange Hills this morning."

She noticed his shock. "Greg?"

He shook his head then looked toward the dresser. "I couldn't place his voice."

She followed his gaze to the beeper, then gasped. "You're kidding."

"Nope. I knew the voice, but I just couldn't place it."

They stared at each other, flabbergasted. Neither of them had met Ferguson, and they certainly didn't run in the same circles, so mutual friends were unlikely.

"Gregory, are you sure?"

"Positive. It was him."

"It couldn't have been someone else?"

"Break it down. He called from a cellular phone just before midnight, and he'd overdosed. He told me as much. And I knew the voice was familiar."

"He didn't tell you who he was?"

"He wouldn't budge."

"Why'd he call you? How did he get your number?"

"I can't even guess," Greg said. "Let's see. He was drinking; I could tell that much. And he knew who I was but wouldn't say how he knew."

She pushed the papers aside and pulled the bedspread over his shoulders. "You'll get chilled. Did he say anything else?"

Greg huddled under the spread. "He said there was an emergency coming up, and that I should apologize to Robbie for him."

"Who's Robbie?"

"He wouldn't say. I was trying to get him to tell me where he was, but he kept cutting me off." He took a sip of her coffee and started to warm up again. "When I get to the office I can jot down the main points, then maybe call the police."

"*Maybe* call the police?"

"Yeah, maybe. I think we've got a confidentiality problem here. Technically, he called me as a professional. He paged me on the office emergency line, which makes him my client. And client confidentiality is protected. I could get sued if I break it."

She nodded, then stared out the window. "This is weird." She looked at the clock. It was nearly seven. "When's your first appointment?"

"It's Wednesday, remember?" He pulled the spread down, jumped off the bed, and headed toward the bathroom. "No appointments till two." Then he remembered something, turned around, and blurted it out.

"Ferguson said I have a two o'clock appointment today."

"Who?"

Greg shrugged. "And he's sending me a package," he added.

"What?" she shouted, and he immediately wished he hadn't mentioned the package. He shrugged again.

"That's what he said, anyway. It's supposed to be at the office before eleven. That's when the bomb inside it will go off, don't you think?" He did an imitation of her worried face and she punched his shoulder a little too hard for it to be taken as a joke.

"It isn't funny. Neither are you."

Greg stretched, grinned, then started back toward the bathroom.

"What could you tell the police anyway?" she called after him. "You can't prove it was Ferguson, can you?"

"No, I can't." He turned on the shower and shouted to be heard over it. "But it was. I know it."

His thoughts cleared as the water poured over him, but his feelings were mixed. He felt awful about Ferguson, of course. But not entirely. In some small part of him, a tiny excitement grew. After all, it wasn't every psychologist who could say that Josh Ferguson, renowned investigative reporter, had called to deliver his last and rather cryptic "good night."

Dr. Alex Crawford unlocked his office suites overlooking Santa Monica Boulevard at 7:30 A.M. and wondered, for the thousandth time, why he didn't get another secretary. Celeste already worked a mere three-day week, since he only practiced Wednesdays through Fridays, giving them both a four-day weekend. At his age and in his health, there was no other way to go on working, or so said his physician. So if the confounded girl had four days to herself, was it too much to ask that she get in a little early on Wednesday mornings to unlock the place and have coffee ready?

The double doors to the waiting area flew open as he answered his own question. *Celeste is gorgeous, and you know you won't fire her, you old goat,* he thought, then laughed openly. To him, sixty-three was a wonderful age. You could finally relax and josh yourself a little.

He found the key to the glass door connecting the waiting area with the main office, and was just inserting it into the slot when he noticed broken glass at his feet.

And to his left, and straight in front of him. Then he realized with cold horror that the glass door had been completely shattered. Only the frame was left.

He clutched his chest, keys forgotten, then slowly stepped through what was left of the door, mindful of the glass shards crunching under his wing-tipped shoes. Walking softly to the receptionist's desk, he looked toward the restrooms on the right and the smaller offices on the left. Then he noticed the door to his private office. It was discolored.

No, not discolored. Defaced with graffiti. He moved closer to read it, and his hand instinctively made the sign of the cross as the words hit him.

Lewd, filthy greetings. Threats. Unmentionable words. And some mentionable but vicious phrases:

What concentration camp did you train in?

Dr. Baron von Frankenstein Crawford, the Butcher of Men, the Maker of Monsters!

Shock Therapy 10¢: The Homophobe Is In.

Under each slogan, a word was slashed in bright red. *BRAVO.*

He tapped his door open, started to enter the office, then checked himself. Was he alone?

"Is anyone here?" he asked, sickened at the quavering of his own voice. He was ashamed to be so afraid, but personal safety wasn't his only concern. What if—

He finished opening the door and saw his worst fears confirmed. There were no real valuables to steal in his office—no works of art, no cash or expensive equipment. Only one thing of importance was here, and it was of value only to him and his patients.

The file cabinet. A two-drawered oak piece containing the names, histories, and most intimate life details of over a hundred people.

It was smashed open, either with an ax or a sledgehammer, the drawers splintered, the files scattered across the floor in one huge manila blanket.

He was on his knees in an instant, not to clean the mess but to determine whether any files might be missing. Instinctively, he knew already. He'd known the moment he saw someone had broken in, but refused to admit it until there was concrete proof.

He had it within minutes. *Their* files were missing; all the others had been left. He eased himself onto the the floor, shaking.

Celeste arrived thirty minutes later to find him in the same spot. She knocked on his door then entered, ashen-faced, clutching a newspaper.

"Dr. Crawford, what happened?"

The doctor shook his head wordlessly. He felt weak and dizzy.

"And," she began hesitantly, "have you heard about Mr. Ferguson?"

Joshua Ferguson. One of the missing files. Pain crept up his lower back and stomach.

"What?" he croaked.

"It was just on the news. They found him dead. They're pretty sure it's suicide."

He closed his eyes and shuddered.

"No. Dear God, no."

His left arm tightened, then clenched involuntarily.

"Dr. Crawford?"

Pain slammed into his chest, and he clutched his shirt while his body spasmed. Then the room swam, his ears rang, and through the haze he could barely hear Celeste scream his name over and over.

Greg got to the Berean Counseling Center by 9:00, went straight to his office, and jotted down the main points of his conversation with Ferguson. The details were sketchy but the essentials were there.

Then he checked the American Psychological Association's law and ethics manual, and was glad he'd held off calling the police. Client confidentiality was protected, even if the client had made brief, singular contact via telephone. Greg found two cases in which lawsuits were filed, on behalf of the decedent's estate, when psychologists had volunteered information which proved damaging to the decedent's reputation.

By 10:00 he was finished.

That left some time to update file notes and catch up on administrative planning, neither of which he felt like doing but both of which were unavoidable. "Clinical director" was a nice title to have, but it carried lots of strings and endless details.

He was still reviewing progress reports an hour later when the receptionist buzzed the intercom. United Parcel had something for him.

The package was actually a large brown envelope—the kind normally used to mail books and tapes. Greg signed for it then retreated to his office, locked himself in, and tore it open.

It contained three envelopes. Two were letter-sized; the third was the large manila type used for reports and booklets. Each was numerically marked, the sender obviously intending them to be opened in a certain order.

Envelope #1 contained a cashier's check for $5000 payable to the Berean Counseling Center and signed by Joshua Ferguson. It was stapled to a typewritten note dated March 12, 1991, 2:00 P.M.

Yesterday. Ten hours before he phoned.

Dr. Bishop:

The enclosed check has been made out to your organization. It's for Robbie's treatment, which I pray he'll accept from you. At your rate, which I've already checked, this should cover about two years' worth of counseling. If for any reason he refuses counseling, then accept this as a donation.

Robbie will see you this afternoon at 2:00. Before then, please review the enclosed material carefully and decide how best to proceed.

Greg put the note down and checked the appointment book. No "Robbie" was scheduled, but a new client named "Carl Robinson" was listed for a 2:00 session.

"Robinson." "Robbie." An alias? Why?

He picked the note up again.

>I was referred to you by Alex Crawford, who's been treating me for over a year now and who, I have learned, assisted you in your training. You have his highest recommendation. Unfortunately, Dr. Crawford will soon be retiring. I'd look for another psychologist—even you, perhaps—but as you'll see in letter #2, my situation has become quite hopeless and further therapy would be a waste of time.

Greg frowned. Crawford hadn't mentioned any of this to him. They hadn't spoken in months.

>Robbie is another matter. This needn't be the end of the road for him. That's where you come in. After reading this material, I'm asking you to do three things:

>1. Accept Robbie as a patient. He has no family, and I've no one else to entrust him to. Your services are paid for in advance, so you've no good reason to refuse. Besides, I've done enough background checking on you to know this is a case you shouldn't refuse.

>2. Decide when and how to tell Robbie about the information contained in letter #2. Please remember that, should you refuse to tell him, others will—in the worst possible way.

>3. Review the videotape in the third envelope. It represents a year's worth of painstaking research—Dr. Crawford will attest to that. It also includes information that will be useful to you. I transferred it onto video just this morning and destroyed the original reels. This is the only copy, and it's meant only for your eyes.

>Remind Robbie of my love. This is a small way of trying to express it and alleviate the problem I've caused for him.

I'll call you tonight to ensure you'll be at your office to receive this package.

Yours,

Joshua Ferguson

A brief, businesslike note from a man planning to wrap it all up. Ferguson had been thinking more clearly when he wrote it than when he made his last phone call. Greg tried to do the same, but it wasn't easy. Too many questions.

Ferguson knew who he was and had taken the time to run a background check on him. Why?

The connection with Crawford was puzzling, too, but Ferguson was right about his assistance in Greg's training. Greg favored him above all his university professors, and the relationship between the two—mentor to student—thrived long after his graduation.

Dr. Crawford had also been an avowed enemy of the gay activist community since 1988. Prior to then he'd specialized in the treatment of developmental disorders, but for reasons Greg never fully understood, he adopted homosexuality as a cause. Lately, in fact, he'd stepped up his efforts, giving radio interviews and public lectures more and more frequently. It was an unnatural but treatable condition, he insisted. Therefore, America had no business sanctioning it. Hated by the gays and ridiculed in the press, Crawford denounced the gay rights movement before school boards, legislative meetings, and anyone else who would listen. The country was in grave danger, he warned, if its trend toward legitimizing sexual perversion continued.

Josh Ferguson was one of Crawford's patients. He must have shared his views; his remarks on the phone indicated that he did.

"Somebody's got to say NO to them!"

The gays? Possibly. They certainly were gaining power, and no one seemed willing to stand up to them. Did Ferguson expect Greg to?

And Robbie? Whoever he was, he'd clearly been a high priority to Josh Ferguson. Greg had never heard of anyone advancing a psychologist $5000 to treat a patient he'd never met.

He tore open envelope #2. It contained a faxed copy of a handwritten note addressed to Josh Ferguson.

It resembled an assault more than a message, printed in

thick black slashes, like graffiti on paper. If it was meant to be intimidating, it succeeded handsomely.

March 11, 1991

Mr. Ferguson, this is your wake-up call.

You are gay, sir, gay and in the closet, which is a precarious position indeed. Records from your so-called therapy sessions with homophobe Dr. Alex Crawford are in our possession, detailing your sexual activities and your unrequited love for Robbie Carlton. According to your own words, documented in these records, Mr. Carlton is also gay. He, too, will be hearing from us.

With homophobia rampant, right-wing politicians promoting the destruction of lesbians and gays, and religious zealots condemning us to hell and beyond, our survival depends on our willingness to fight bigotry by openly declaring ourselves and showing society just how many of us there really are. In this you have failed. We're going to help you rectify your failure.

You have until March 30 to come out publicly and declare yourself gay. Surely it will be better for all concerned, your family especially, if you do this willingly and with dignity. The many young gays who see you weekly on television are entitled to view you as a role model. Coming out is your responsibility.

We prefer you to do this on your own! We take no pleasure in exposing anyone, and our rights are better served when gay citizens voluntarily acknowledge their true selves to society. Accept your responsibility with dignity by coming out on your own, and there will be no need for our interference.

Neglect your responsibility, and you will find yourself outed, publicly exposed as a homosexual with Dr. Crawford's records on display for verification. Do not underestimate our resources or our commitment.

Until March 30

BRAVO
(Bent on Removing All Vestiges of Oppression)

He read the note three times, his anger escalating with each reading. "Act now," he said out loud. Plenty of time to react later.

First he checked the Rolodex for Dr. Crawford's number in Santa Monica, then dialed. The line was busy, so he set the phone on automatic redial. It would call the number again every thirty seconds.

Greg had three hours to absorb what he'd read, then decide what, if anything, to do.

At least Ferguson's death made sense now. He preferred suicide to humiliation.

That was ironic, because he'd raised humiliation to an art form. In Southern California, his name was a curse to anyone in public life with anything to hide, and there were few who didn't have. Those unfortunate enough to have been the subjects of his investigative stories might never repair the damage to their careers and reputations. His weekly series, "Limelight," had been the downfall of corporate executives, political candidates, and an occasional televangelist. He was dreaded, respected, sometimes funny, and always without remorse.

Professionally, that is. Apparently he was very remorseful about his personal life, his sexual dark side in particular. He was in treatment for it with Crawford, no doubt hoping to keep his family intact while battling private demons.

Then public demons found out. BRAVO. Greg knew the name well, as did anyone who read the newspaper. Like other militant homosexual groups, they specialized in terrorism and intimidation of anyone who resisted the gay rights agenda. But what set them apart was their emphasis on "outing." To "out" someone meant to expose and publicize their homosexuality, and though many gays found the practice deplorable, plenty of others reveled in it. Chapters of BRAVO thrived in metropolitan areas were there were enough gays committed to the cause of destroying lives to further their purposes.

If Ferguson was on their hit list, he had good reason to despair.

He wasn't alone. Someone named Robbie Carlton was involved. *"He, too, will be hearing from us."*

The phone on his desk clicked and whirred. Automatic redial had finally gotten through.

"Dr. Crawford's office."

"Is Dr. Crawford in?"

"I'm sorry, he's not. Can I take a message?" The woman's voice was strained.

"Yes, this is Greg Bishop, and I'm calling regarding—"

"Greg Bishop, the psychologist? In Irvine?"

"Well, yes. Do we—"

"Greg, how are you?" The voice brightened and went up a notch. "It's Celeste. Celeste Bolton, remember?"

Did he! Getting over Celeste had been enough of a chore; he certainly couldn't forget her. Both had studied counseling psychology at the University of California–Irvine, both were Christians, both studied under Dr. Crawford. A romance developed, but whereas Greg saw Celeste as the one and only, Celeste viewed Greg as no more than a boyfriend/steady date. She became an obsession to him, while he became a straitjacket to her: possessive, smothering, a bit too serious, and far too eager to please. The relationship fizzled and, at her request, ended. Greg met Christine on the rebound.

He grinned into the phone. "Yeah, I guess I remember you, Celeste. How'd you know I work in Irvine?"

"I have friends who've gone to you for counseling. In fact, I referred them to you, but don't even try to get their names out of me."

"Good for you. What are you doing working for Crawford? I thought you'd be a licensed therapist by now."

"Forget it, no license for me. I'm a married mom now." A pause. "I'm waiting."

"For what?"

"For congratulations!"

Greg leaned back and put his feet on the desk. "Congratulations and all my best, old friend. Can't kiss the bride over the phone, can I?"

"Just try it and see how long you live. I'm married to a green-eyed Rambo; he goes bonkers if even a cocker spaniel looks at me."

"Tell him I'm safe. I'm an old married man myself."

"I heard. Anyway, I starting working for Dr. Alex—ooh, he hates it when I call him that, don't repeat it—when my kid turned four and started kindergarten. Mitch—that's my husband—said it was okay because I was getting bored and we needed extra cash, so here I am. He thinks the world of you, you know."

"Mitch the green-eyed Rambo?"

"Crawford, smart aleck."

Greg's eyes wandered back to Ferguson's notes. "Speaking of which, Celeste, I need to talk to him ASAP. I've got a major problem here."

She lowered her voice. "Greg, there's been trouble here, too. Ever hear of BRAVO?"

His feet fell off the desk. "BRAVO?"

"It's a gay terrorist group. They broke in here yesterday and trashed the place. I mean, you wouldn't believe it. Graffiti spray-painted on the walls, furniture ripped up, everything. They've been attacking Dr. Alex in the press for years, and we've gotten some hate calls, but we never thought they'd do anything like this."

"There's nothing a group like that won't do," he said, piecing together facts he didn't want to believe.

"But Greg, do you want to hear the worst of it?"

"They broke into the files," he guessed aloud.

She drew a quick breath. "How'd you know?"

"Celeste, get me in touch with Crawford. Do it any way you can, right now, okay?"

"Can't do it. He's in the hospital."

"NO!"

"Yeah. He had a heart attack this morning. His health has been pretty shaky lately. But this morning, besides the break-in, he found out one of his patients killed himself. One of the nicest ones, too. A celebrity. Dr. Crawford thinks it's his fault; don't ask me why. Anyway, when I told him about his patient, it was too much for him, I guess."

"What hospital is he in?"

"Santa Monica General, but he's not taking visitors. Or phone calls. I'm still trying to put the place back together, field calls, and cancel his appointments. Now come on, Greg, tell me what's happening."

"I don't know. Just tell me this: Does he have a patient named Robbie Carlton?"

"Robbie Carlton the singer?"

"The what?"

"The singer. No, he's not a patient here. Believe me, I'd know if he was. Don't you know him? Don't you ever listen to Christian radio?"

"Sometimes. Why, is he a gospel artist?"

"Greg, you're out of touch! He took the Grammy last year for best gospel artist. He's singing for the pro-life benefit at the Irvine Meadows Amphitheater in April, right in your own back-yard. I'm really surprised you haven't heard of him."

"I'm an old fogy. I just listen to Handel these days." He frowned. "Celeste, help me out here. I can't give you any details right now, but please get word to Dr. Crawford that I need to speak with him as soon as he's able."

"This is scaring me."

"Me, too. Do that for me, okay, Celeste?"

"I'll call you as soon as I tell him. By the way, you can always call to see how he's doing."

"Right. I will. Thanks, Celeste. Really nice talking to you. And congratulations—I mean that."

"I'll bet."

"What?"

"Oh, I'm sorry," she answered. "That was dumb. 'Bye, Greg."

He lost track of time, sitting with the phone in his hand, remembering Celeste, his early training, simpler times...

His wristwatch beeped him back to reality. It was nearly 1:00. Robbie Carlton, *aka* Carl Robinson, would arrive in an hour. Most likely it *was* the singer, though the name wasn't so unique it couldn't have been someone else. But he'd made his appointment under an alias—a gesture unlikely for the average person to make.

He took out a legal pad and began to jot down some main points, trying to make sense of it all.

Point One: BRAVO had broken into Crawford's office, prob-ably as an act of terrorism, possibly to get information on some of his patients. They'd gotten more than they bargained for when they found Josh Ferguson's file.

The image of them dancing around the office—"Look what we've found! Josh Ferguson and Robbie Carlton are gay, hee hee hee!"—filled Greg with the kind of rage Christians aren't sup-posed to have.

He shook it off.

So they intended to expose both Ferguson and Robbie Carlton. They sent a note to Ferguson. Another was on its way to Carlton.

Point Two: Ferguson panicked, then despaired. He decided to end it, but not before trying to cushion the blow for Robbie by finding him a psychologist who could break the news to him gently (if that was possible, which it wasn't) that he was soon to be "outed" and help him through the crisis.

So he found a psychologist, put together a package, mailed it, and phoned at midnight to be sure it would be received before Robbie's appointment.

And something else. Greg hadn't seen envelope #3 yet.

He fished around the desk, grabbed the envelope, and tore it open.

A videotape fell out. The plain white label on the front was marked:

"Unforgiven Sins"
A Special Report
The Effects of Gay Militancy on American Religion

A future project for the "Limelight" program? Probably. Maybe Ferguson sent him the copy to educate him about homosexuality. He'd look at it when he had some free time.

His watch said it was twenty-five minutes until 2:00.

He put the video back in the envelope for later viewing. After resharpening the pencil, he started writing again.

Point Three: The relationship between Josh Ferguson and Robbie Carlton was pretty deep. Ferguson obviously loved the young singer—at least, Greg assumed he was young if he was, as Celeste said, a well-known gospel artist. They tended to be young, anyway.

Were they lovers?

No. BRAVO's note to Ferguson mentioned his "unrequited love" for Robbie, suggesting Ferguson had feelings for Robbie that were unreturned—at least physically.

Nancy buzzed again. "Carl Robinson, your 2:00 appointment, is here. He's a bit early. Should I have him wait?"

Greg closed his eyes.

"Have him fill out an intake form, Nancy. I'll be right out."

He put the papers and tape in the third file drawer, locked it (and vowed to get better locks on the files), then stood up and prayed for wisdom and for the right words. And for the gospel singer waiting in the front who was about to get some shattering news.

Another buzz on the intercom. "Greg, Pastor Mike also wants to see you. I told him you've got 3:00 open. He asked if you'd come by his office afterward."

"Sure. Thanks, Nancy." He turned toward the door. Pastor Michael Cain, who not only shepherded the three-thousand-plus-member congregation of Berean Community Church but also oversaw the counseling center, was not an easy man to see. Not because he was aloof, but because he was terminally busy.

If Mike wants to see me during office hours, he thought, *something's up. Maybe an emergency.*

"My emergency is over. Now it's *your* emergency, so I called to tell you—"

The thought stopped Greg as he grabbed the doorknob. Ferguson's voice. Drunk, but emphatic. A dead man's warning.

"—and to clue you in on some fascinating events that are about to take place."

He pulled open the door and started down the hall to meet Robbie Carlton.

THREE

*C*hristine couldn't focus. She forced her eyes back to the illustration she'd been starting and stopping since Greg kissed her good-bye five hours earlier, but concentration wouldn't come. She dropped her pen. The job wasn't due for another few days; why push it? Working out of her home was part of the convenience of being a freelance graphic artist; setting her own hours was another.

Getting up from the drawing table, she considered fixing herself a sandwich, then vetoed the idea. The ache in her stomach was worry, not hunger.

She flopped onto the living room couch and punched the small decorative pillow Greg's mother had embroidered for them the previous Christmas. "Doesn't he ever worry?" she'd asked her mother-in-law over lunch years ago.

"He's too dense for that," Mrs. Bishop replied frankly. "He sees adventures where the rest of us see disasters. If there's any worrying to be done in your home, you'll have to do it for the two of you."

Christine was doing her share. Greg was taking this too lightly; she was certain of that. Ferguson's call shocked him at first, but by the time he dressed for work he'd seemed almost enthused over the whole mess. *Adventures where the rest of us see disasters—could he possibly be enjoying this?*

She tucked her feet under her and hugged the pillow, trying to reason with herself.

Of course he's not enjoying this, idiot. Remember the way he looked when he heard Ferguson was dead? He couldn't talk the man out of killing himself—do you really think your husband's so callous as to call that an adventure?

She reproached herself. Greg was a good man; everyone knew that. A little boyish at times, but wasn't that part of his charm?

But the light in his eyes when he left for work! He might

have been sad about Ferguson, but he was also flattered, remarking, three times at least, how amazing it was for Josh Ferguson to call him, of all people.

And didn't he swagger just a bit when he walked out? That worried her.

She noticed the time and thought about dinner, suddenly missing Greg and wishing he'd come home early. Fat chance—he never left work before 5:00, some nights he was gone until 9:00. She went to the icebox and pulled out a package of chicken breasts to defrost, then remembered the flowers she'd been wanting to plant in the front. They'd provide a nice distraction from her brooding.

After changing into shorts, she grabbed the old sweatshirt of Greg's she used when gardening, then headed for the front yard. Her mood lifted a bit as she started to work the flower bed—but only a bit.

"Four key phases define the relationship between psychologist and patient," Dr. Crawford used to lecture. "The initial meeting when they assess each other, the honeymoon period when the patient idolizes the psychologist, the rocky moment when the patient devalues the psychologist and knocks him off his pedestal, and the resolution, when the patient assumes more independence and no longer needs counseling."

When meeting new patients, Greg liked to rehash his mentor's insights. "Four key phases," he reminded himself on the way to the waiting room, "assessment, idealization, disappointment, and resolution."

For him, phase one was the toughest. Competent though he was, Gregory Bishop was a man of a thousand insecurities. Much prayer and personal counseling had been invested to build his confidence, but ghosts of decades-old rejection loomed over him like Scrooge's Christmas visitors. He battled them by quoting Scripture when he was in a better frame of mind; other times he employed less spiritual means to defend himself. Rather than let people judge him, he'd beat them to the punch by judging them first: their looks, intelligence, and class were all scrutinized and compared to his own. If he came out ahead (and he usually did), then he could relax. If not—well, that's why phase one was the toughest. He always feared he'd come out behind.

So, as he stepped into the waiting room, his defenses were already up. When he turned the corner and saw his new client, they crashed through the ceiling.

At six-foot-one with a gymnast's physique, the young man would have looked at home in a Greek statuary. His abundantly thick brown hair framed a photographer's dream: emerald-green eyes, thick brows, square jaw, Roman nose. He was dressed casually in tan slacks, brown loafers, and a dark-green polo shirt revealing a chiseled torso and long, muscular forearms.

Greg made a mental note to double his upper-body workout.

"Mr., uh, Robinson? I'm Greg Bishop."

Mr. Robinson, *aka* Robbie Carlton, put down his magazine and rose off the couch, extending his hand.

"How are you, doctor?" Greg checked Carlton's left hand while shaking his right one. No wedding ring.

"I filled these forms out," he was saying. "Do I give them to you?"

"Nancy will take them," Greg answered, turning to the receptionist's desk in time to see her fussing with her hair and straightening her blouse. Carlton evidently had that effect on people. Greg couldn't resist seizing the moment.

"Why, Nancy, what's the matter? You look a bit flushed!"

She stiffened her back. "I'm just fine, *doctor.* I'll take the forms." Robbie put them in her outthrust hands. She bayoneted Greg with her eyes and he smiled innocently at his new client. "My office is right this way."

"Thanks," Robbie smiled back, and Greg noted that if the kid lost his music career he could always do Pepsodent commercials.

Greg took a deep breath, then plunged in as soon as the door was shut. "I need to cut to the chase."

Robbie's eyes widened at the blunt remark. "Pardon me?" He had seated himself on the couch, leaning forward and twisting his hands together nervously. Clients were prone to do that on the first visit.

"I said, I need to cut to the chase." Greg felt like an executioner and he hated it, but he'd already decided to be direct. "We've got a lot to talk about." He sat down in one of the two wingback chairs facing the couch.

Robbie unlocked his hands. "Do you recognize me? I feel like a jerk saying that, but sometimes people do."

Greg wasn't about to say he'd never heard his name until this afternoon. "I know who you are," he said truthfully, "and I understand why you used a phony name when you made your appointment."

"I didn't want to take a chance on your secretary. If I made the appointment under my name, well, you never know. She might mention it to a friend or somebody. I've got to be careful."

"Grammy winners usually should. May I call you Robbie?"

"Please do."

"And I'm Greg, okay? Not 'Dr. Bishop,' just Greg."

"Got it."

"What brings you here?"

"Josh asked me to come."

There was pure desolation in the way he said "Josh."

"You're here because of Josh?"

"Uh-huh. He called yesterday and begged me to see you today. Said you'd have something to tell me, and that it couldn't wait." He looked at Greg expectantly.

He decided to drop the bomb, but in slow motion.

"Have you gotten a letter recently? A disturbing letter?"

"No." He squinted. "Why?"

"Robbie," Greg said carefully, "I already know more about you than you realize—"

Amazing how wide his eyes could get. Greg's defenses had already melted; the other man's vulnerability touched him.

"—and I want you to believe I'm on your side, because you need help. You may even need legal counsel. Do you understand what I'm saying?"

"No. What exactly are you saying?"

"Brace yourself. Last night Josh Ferguson called me. He told me you'd be coming in today, and insisted I see you. He also sent me a package of information. Scary information, I'm afraid, some of it about you."

The singer looked like a terrified kid about to be punished.

"You know he's dead, don't you?" Greg asked gently.

Robbie closed his eyes, nodded, and a single tear fell on his tanned cheek. Then his eyes flew open again as something hit him.

"He *called* you?" He sat up, ramrod-straight. "He called you about *me?* What did he say? I don't know why he didn't call me. What did he tell you?"

Greg remembered the first axiom about a suicide victim's loved ones: They need reassurance.

"What he said about you, Robbie, was that he loved you. He was thinking of you in a very positive way," Greg stressed, hoping to quench any notions of guilt Robbie might have. "Josh made up his mind; no one could have stopped it. He gave up. Even so, he was thinking about you. 'Tell Robbie I'm sorry,' he kept saying."

He spoke quietly and slowly. Robbie's face contorted; Greg could tell he was suppressing an explosion of grief—grief that needed to be expressed. He moved forward and touched Robbie's shoulder, looking for words that would give him permission to let go.

"You must have meant so much to him, Robbie, for him to have gone to all the trouble to call me. You must have meant so very much."

Robbie responded with a low moan that escalated into a wail, then fell back onto the couch and sobbed, grabbing his head with both hands. "Oh my God, Josh, oh, Josh." The words choked out for a few minutes, muffled by Robbie's hands which had moved to his face, covering and clutching it at the same time. Greg sat quietly, watching and nodding.

"Oh my God," he groaned one last time after a few minutes of weeping. His hands came down from his face (which was no longer a photographer's dream, Greg noted with some triumph, then mentally slapped himself), and he looked around the office. "Got any Kleenex?"

Greg kept the standard equipment on an end table: pen, writing pad, and tissues. He handed the box to Robbie, who fished out a tissue, wiped, blew his nose, then wiped again. "I can't believe it," he said to the floor. "Josh called you. I just can't believe it."

"Neither can I. I never knew him, but he'd heard of me, somehow."

Carlton nodded, still eyeing the floor.

"Robbie?"

He looked up.

"I have a lot of questions to ask you. Do you feel up to answering them? Because there's more. I hate to tell you that, but there's more."

"More?"

"I'm sorry."

Robbie went limp, then extended his legs in front of him and leaned back wearily.

"You've had a shock, I know," Greg went on. "How did you find out about Ferguson?"

"I heard it on the news."

"Did you talk to anyone about it?"

"I called and left a message for Alma. That's his wife; we've been friends for years. But she hasn't called back yet. In fact, I almost canceled my appointment with you, but then I figured this was as good a time as any to see someone like you—" He broke into another round of sobs.

When the crying subsided, Robbie wiped his eyes with his hand, composed himself, then looked steadily at Greg. He had another step to take, something to say which he'd only told one other person—someone who was gone forever. He debated whether or not he should, and in the silence Greg knew he was being appraised again.

Can I trust you? the singer asked with his eyes.

Can you afford not to? the doctor replied silently.

Robbie sighed and went ahead.

"I have a—uh—personal struggle. Did Josh tell you?"

Greg nodded.

"Did he tell you what *kind* of struggle I have?"

"I think so."

"I'm not gay." He said it too quickly; Greg's eyebrows arched.

"I mean, I don't have sex with men or anything like that. But I've got these feelings, these attractions to men. Does that make me gay?"

"Not necessarily."

Greg noticed a hint of relief.

"Well, those feelings are there. And sometimes—"

"Sometimes?"

Robbie was about to take another step, but first he asked the question public figures always posed during counseling.

"You can't tell anybody about this, can you?"

"No, I can't repeat anything you tell me. I can't even tell anyone you've come here."

"Good." He hesitated, then let it out. "Sometimes I come so close to giving in to it that I swear I'll just disappear, go find a lover, and say 'drop dead' to God, the church, everything."

He waited for a shocked response from Greg but, to his relief, he only got a nod.

"You're the only person I've ever told, other than Joshua. Nobody else knows."

"I'm glad you told me."

"That's probably why Josh wanted me to see you."

"It's not the only reason."

That shook him. "Then what's this all about?"

Greg drew a deep breath; time to deliver the next blow. "What this is about is 'outing.' Do you know what that means?"

He didn't. Greg explained the term, then continued. "Josh Ferguson was going to be outed. That's probably why he committed suicide. And someone's planning to out you, too."

He said the fatal words carefully, monitoring Robbie's response. So far it was nothing more than a blank gaze. "Have you ever heard of BRAVO?" Greg asked.

"Of what?"

"Not what, who. BRAVO. It's a gay terrorist group. They specialize in exposing public figures who might be gay."

"BRAVO." Carlton repeated the name softly, remembering something. "Right. Josh was doing a report on them."

"He sent me a tape of it," Greg replied. "I haven't watched it yet, but I'm sure you're right. They found out about him, and about you."

"About him and me?" His eyes flew up. "But we never—"

"I know, I know. But they broke into his psychologist's office and stole his files. Most psychologists keep notes on what their patients say during their sessions, and I guess Josh mentioned you during one of his."

Robbie flinched.

"I have a copy of a letter BRAVO sent him saying he had until the end of March to publicly admit he was gay. And they said you'd be hearing from them, too."

Instead of the panicked reaction Greg had expected, Robbie just stared straight ahead, lost in some private thought. Then he nodded, his expression resigned. "Can I have a glass of water?"

Greg complied without comment. It took two minutes to go to the kitchen, fill a glass, and bring it back to the office. Robbie was frozen in the same upright position when he returned.

"Thanks." He took two gulps. "So, I got my answer."

"What answer?"

Robbie stammered. "This is hard. It's hard to know where to start."

"Start anywhere."

"Well, I've prayed about this for years."

"This?"

"These feelings."

"Homosexual feelings?"

"Yeah."

"How long have you had them?"

"Since I was twelve, maybe longer."

"And you never told anyone?"

"Only Josh."

"That's quite a difficult secret you've been carrying."

"That didn't stop me from trying."

"Trying what?"

"Everything," he began, his words spilling out in a rapid, frustrated staccato. "Prayer. Fasting. Going to the church elders. Asking for prayer without telling them what I wanted prayer for. Dating." He threw back his head and laughed derisively. "Oh, yes, dating! Girls are crazy about me. Sound egotistical? They are! You should hear what they say. 'Robbie, you're so *sensitive!* You're so *different* from other guys! You *understand* me so well!' Not a one of them ever stopped to figure out why. And none of them could understand why it didn't work out, why it *couldn't* work out!" Tears welled up again. "I've left a trail of beautiful girls behind who thought there was something wrong with *them,* not me."

Robbie's story, and his way of relating it—lyrical, impassioned, and rhythmic—was fascinating.

"Have you ever known anyone like me? Anyone with this problem?" Carlton asked.

Greg squirmed and cleared his throat as memories welled up inside him; memories of a night, a beach, and brutality he was unable to prevent. "Yes. A long time ago."

"Were you able to help him?"

A long silence.

"No," Greg said quietly.

"Maybe you'll have better luck with me."

"I hope so."

"It's been hard," Robbie continued, oblivious to Greg's inner turmoil. "I thought I'd learned to live with it."

Greg pulled himself back into a professional frame of mind. "You learned to live with it," he repeated, "until?"

"Until I got into the music business and the pressure started. People think you're God if they see you on stage! I started feeling like the biggest hypocrite on the planet."

"Why?"

"*Why?* Because here I was, Mr. Christian Singer, having sexual feelings for men! And everyone thinks I'm so stable."

"From what you've told me so far, I'd agree with them. You have a weakness, sure, but you haven't given in to it."

"I've come too close, though. Last year I was on the road in Nashville and went to a gay bar."

"Why?"

"The stupidest reason you can imagine."

"Which was?"

"I wanted to be with people who understood me."

"Nothing stupid about that."

"But going there was crazy! I didn't go home with anyone or do anything like that. I didn't even talk to anyone! I just sat in the corner for an hour, scared to death. Then I went back to my hotel room and started wondering."

"About what?"

"About whether or not I should stay in gospel music. I don't want to be gay, but I don't want to be a hypocrite, either. Besides, if even one person who knew me had seen me go into that bar, it would have been the end of everything."

"Are you afraid you'll do it again?"

"Who knows? I might, only next time I might do something really stupid. So, I've been thinking about quitting while I'm ahead. That's what I meant when I said I finally got my answer."

"If you quit singing, what would you do?"

"The royalties should be coming in for a while. And I've got a master's degree in vocal performance—I can teach. Or direct a choir. Or wait tables, I don't care." He threw up his hands. "I just can't go on like this. So you see? This business of being exposed is my answer. And the answer is, Get out. Now."

Greg noticed the hour was almost up. "Robbie, I've got to know a few things before we run out of time here."

Robbie looked at the clock on the wall. "That went fast."

"It's not quite over. How did Ferguson know about your problem? And how did you know about his?"

Robbie leaned back and sighed.

"Well, you've got to understand that Josh and I were real close. He helped launch my career, in fact."

"Oh?"

"It's a long story. But he didn't know anything about—about *this,* not for a long time."

Greg's curiosity about the relationship between a Christian musician and an investigative reporter was aroused, but he let it pass.

"One night we were alone at a restaurant having a late dinner. I'd moved to Orange County by then, and Josh was covering a convention in Anaheim, so we got together. He was a big drinker, and that night he'd had more than usual. That's when he told me."

"That—"

"That he was in love with me."

Greg nodded.

"He was so ashamed afterward. It wasn't a proposition, just a confession. Josh was married, you know, but sometimes he'd go out and find partners. That's what he told me, anyway, although he swore he'd never felt anything emotionally for a man until he met me. He said he'd loved me from the night he first heard me sing, that he hated himself for having those feelings, and that sometimes it tore him apart just being around me."

"How'd you handle that?"

"I was floored. I never knew. Never even suspected!" He sighed again. "But I should have figured it out. Since when does a famous guy like him take such an interest in somebody like me who's half his age?"

"So you told him about yourself?"

"I had to. He looked so pitiful, spilling his guts like that. I wanted him to know I could relate, even though I didn't feel that way about him."

"What did you tell him?"

"I said I couldn't judge him because I had those tendencies, too. And if he'd keep my secret, I'd keep his. Then he said something else."

"Yes?"

"'Swear to me that you'll never give in to it.' That's what he said. And I did. And so far I've kept that promise."

"You've never—"

"Never. I've been tempted, but I've never actually done it."

"Okay. One more question. Did you know Ferguson was seeing a psychologist?"

"Dr. Crawford? Sure, I knew. I think he started seeing him about a year ago. And he was making some real progress, too. No more sex with strangers, his marriage improved, and he even quit drinking. He begged me to see the guy, but I've always been skeptical of psychologists. No offense."

"None taken." Greg got up, unlocked the file drawer, took out BRAVO's letter to Crawford, and read it aloud to Robbie. Then he explained as much as he knew about the break-in at Crawford's office.

"You'll be getting one of these letters too, and soon. So even if you decide to retire, you'll have to deal with this."

"What should I do?"

"For now, nothing. BRAVO hasn't contacted you yet, so I'd suggest you wait until you hear from them. Then we'll know what they want. And when they want it."

Robbie stood up. "In the meantime, where do we go from here? Seems like we just got started. Can I see you again?"

"I'd like you to. It's certainly what Josh wanted. I've got this 2:00 slot open on Wednesdays. We could meet weekly."

"I'd like that."

"We've got a lot of work to do. You've got some major decisions to make."

"I want to change," Robbie said abruptly.

"Change what?"

"I don't *want* to be gay. No matter what happens, I want to change. Can you help me?"

Greg had never heard of a homosexual who wanted to do that. His human sexuality professors had scoffed at the very idea.

"I don't know," he admitted. "Truthfully, I still don't understand why Josh Ferguson referred you to me."

He saw a flicker of hurt on Robbie's face.

"Don't misunderstand," Greg emphasized. "I'd very much like to work with you, whether Ferguson referred you or not. It just isn't clear to me *why* he referred you, that's all. And I can't make any promises about changing your homosexuality. But if that's what you want, I'll do everything in my power to help you."

"Fair enough. And thanks for being honest. That makes me trust you all the more." He put out his hand, then withdrew before Greg could shake it. "I almost forgot. What do you charge?"

"It's paid for. Your old friend sent me a check for at least two years' worth of counseling."

"Thanks," he murmured.

"You're very welcome."

"I wasn't thanking you."

FOUR

*C*alvin Blanchard wasn't looking forward to this broadcast. The topic was Christian dating, and his guest was a youth pastor promoting his latest book on the subject. Calvin didn't begrudge the man some airtime; the book was worthwhile and relevant. But his mood was somber, and the news today somehow warranted a more serious show. He had decided to vent his feelings with his opening commentary.

"And good afternoon," he began as the "Open Heart" theme music faded, "I'm Calvin Blanchard and this is 'Open Heart,' coming to you weekdays at three on KLVE Orange County. We'll be with you till five o'clock, sharing thoughts and conversations with our in-studio guest, and we hope you'll share a few thoughts of your own with us. Our lines are open between four and five, so call in with any questions or comments you might have for me or my guest."

Calvin reviewed his notes on the guest in question.

"Today we'll be tackling the subject of Christian dating with Pastor Jim Reese, Youth Minister at Trinity Assembly of God and author of the new book, *Date or Wait?* Wait for what, I wonder? I'm not getting any younger, are you? Well, maybe Pastor Reese can enlighten us, but first, some commentary on the headlines."

He shifted his papers and swallowed. This wouldn't be easy; he was too close to the subject.

"A note of sadness, today. California has lost a respected figure in the field of television news, and I've lost a personal friend and colleague as well. Worse yet, we've lost him in the most senseless of ways. Joshua Ferguson has died, evidently at his own hands. Speculation on his motives will no doubt continue for years, but in the wake of the gossip and innuendo that will certainly surround his death, let me focus for a moment on his life, and what it can teach us about true success."

The engineer pointed at the clock; Calvin was cutting into a scheduled station break. He ignored the signal and plunged ahead.

"As some of you know, I've worked in television production for years, and have had the pleasure of working as Josh's production assistant for numerous Limelight specials.

"Josh's investigative reports served a valuable purpose beyond sensationalism or scandal. Yes, he was a tough reporter. Some might rightfully call him an inquisitor. But he never tackled an issue unless he sincerely believed that doing so would benefit all of us. He hated hypocrisy and corruption, and when he exposed it, as rough as it may have been on some people, justice was usually served. How many corporations cleaned up their acts after a visit from Ferguson and his camera crew? How many get-rich-quick schemes were exposed, and how many phony manufacturers were dissuaded from peddling false promises to the public after Josh got their number and brought it to the public's attention? Love him or hate him, we owe the man a debt of gratitude for his tenacity."

The word *tenacity* stuck in his throat. *Oh, Josh, where was your tenacity when you really needed it?*

"His success was of the All-American variety," he continued. "He pulled himself from childhood poverty to begin a career in journalism before his twentieth birthday. He was fueled by a love of the facts—pretty facts or ugly ones, he didn't discriminate— which sustained innumerable journalistic and broadcasting achievements. His secret? He told me once, when I was starting out, that if I could overcome the fear of being disliked, there wasn't anywhere I couldn't go, nor anything I couldn't achieve. 'Strive to be well liked,' he said, 'and you'll be popular, but that's all you'll be.' And isn't that what Jesus meant when He said, 'Woe to you when all men speak well of you'? Hats off to Josh. His life tells us that perhaps if we were more interested in truth than in popularity, we might find more success in our own lives."

He set the papers down and smiled wanly at the engineer who pointedly did not return the smile.

"That's something to think about," he concluded, adding his trademark tag line.

The producer was bringing the guest into the studio, so Calvin put on a bright expression that belied his mood.

"So! Let's move on to our guest, Pastor Jim Reese, who's joining us in the studio to give us singles a few tips on the dating experience. Pastor Reese, it's good to have you here."

Greg realized, as he walked Robbie to the reception area, that he'd broken a basic rule of ethics: Never act beyond the scope of your own experience. He'd never treated a homosexual before, and wondered why he'd agreed to treat this one. Intrigue? Sure, that was part of it. A midnight call from a celebrity, a secret request to save a young man in crisis—who could resist that?

Still, you're out of your league, he reminded himself after he waved to his new patient then returned to his office. *Out of your league and over your head.*

"Greg, don't we have an appointment at 3:00?" Pastor Mike's voice over the intercom made him jump.

"Right. I'm on the way."

Seeing Mike was a pleasant alternative to unpleasant doubts. Greg jogged over to the main office. His legs protested, but it was already 3:05 and he knew Mike would needle him for tardiness.

By the time he burst into the pastor's office, Mike was standing beside his desk, holding a watch in front of him, and counting the seconds out loud.

"Inexcusable!" he roared. "Don't you know better than to keep God's anointed waiting?" At fifty-three, with the build of a sumo wrestler and the mind of a Greek philosopher, Reverend Michael Cain always reminded Greg of a well-read grizzly bear.

"A thousand pardons, your eminence." Greg crossed the floor, genuflected reverently, grabbed his pastor's hand, and made a sloppy attempt to kiss his ring.

"Grotesque!" Cain hissed, jerking his hand away and wiping it on his pants leg.

Greg smiled. He loved bantering with Mike almost as much as he loved Mike himself.

The pastor settled behind his desk and gestured to Greg. "Sit. So how's Freud today?"

"Quite Freudian, thank you." Greg eased into the over-stuffed chair facing Mike's desk, admiring the decor. The pastor was simple at heart, easygoing, and wonderfully down-to-earth, though he led one of Orange County's prominent megachurches. The only hint of grandeur about him was a penchant for quality— a trait reflected in his office furnishings. Desks and tables from Ethan Allen, accessories from the Antique Guild. The television set he kept to appease his addiction to news and sports was turned on, as usual, to the Orange County News Network. Mike adjusted the volume and sat down facing his clinical director.

"We've got a board meeting coming up and they're going to want to know about profit and loss over at the counseling center. How's our budget?"

Greg gave him the lowdown on current operating expenses, counseling fees and advertising costs. Mike seemed satisfied, and with that bit of business concluded, the conversation turned to sports, family problems, and light gossip. Both men enjoyed each other's company immensely; both regretted the time constraints limiting their visits. So when they met, they kept their business discussions as brief as possible, preferring to chat amiably.

The words "homosexual rights" drifted from the television, catching their attention. They both looked at the screen.

"Gay activists today demonstrated outside the capitol where AB101, the controversial bill that would prohibit discrimination in housing and employment based on sexual orientation, is expected to pass its first committee hearing and be referred to the Ways and Means Committee. Governor Wilson has indicated that, should the bill pass the State Assembly, he will sign it into law."

A crowd of demonstrators appeared, carrying signs and marching in a circle.

"Although AB101 has several committees to go through before the Assembly votes on it, gays say they're here today because they want the State Assembly and committee members to be aware of their presence during each step of the bill's process."

Standing to the left was a tall figure with a shock of white, frizzled hair. His back was turned to the camera while an OCN reporter held a microphone up to him. When he turned to face the camera as it zoomed in for a close-up, the sight of him pulled audible gasps from both Greg and Pastor Mike.

His shoulder-length bleached hair, topped with a red bandanna, framed the angriest, most menacing face Greg had ever seen. The eyes, black and deep-set, were surrounded with thick, coal-black slashes of mascara and eye shadow, giving him a raccoon-like appearance that might have been funny on another man. But not even a suggestion of humor could be found in that scowling face.

The high forehead and square jaw suggested he might be handsome without the makeup and hair, but everything about his personage declared he was more interested in intimidating than attracting. Besides the red bandanna, he sported an over-sized leather jacket with a pink triangle sewn into the lapel, a huge gold hoop earring glistening from his left ear, black leather gloves, and thick Coke-bottle glasses that emphasized, rather than obscured, his bizarre eyes and his even more bizarre way of decorating them.

Greg felt a twinge of recognition when he saw those eyes.

The man pointed at the camera and shouted in a thick Bronx accent.

"*We're not asking nicely anymore. We're demanding the same rights the rest of you have—the right to work without fear of discrimination, to love who we choose, and to be who we are without apologizing to anyone. The day of the polite homosexual is over. The state has the opportunity to secure these rights for us, but we're serving notice that we'll take them any way we can, whether by vote or by force.*"

Back to the announcer:

"*While many Californians disagree with the notion of civil protection for homosexuals, most psychologists agree that homo-sexuality is an inborn, unchangeable condition. That opinion reinforces many California legislators' commitments to gay rights.*"

Pastor Mike flicked the television off. "They never stop, do they?"

"Never," Greg replied absently. Something about the garish, angry activist had shaken him, though he couldn't say what. "But some gays really do want help. I just finished a session with one."

"Really?" Mike was visibly pleased, and would have pushed for details if he hadn't known the law forbidding Greg to discuss his cases with anyone. "Great. I wish more of them would come in for counseling. But how exactly would you counsel them?"

"I have no idea."

"I hear they're a high suicide risk."

"I don't know. Maybe."

"Hmm." Mike got up, indicating it was time to go. "Speaking of suicide," Mike added, "did you hear about Josh Ferguson?"

Greg knew how to maintain discretion, even with his pastor. "Yeah, I heard. See you tomorrow."

After two more appointments, Greg drove home at 5:30 wondering how so much excitement, sadness, frustration, and intrigue could coexist in the same body.

It was possible, his analytical side concluded, as long as there's good reason for each of them to be there.

There was. Two celebrities had asked for his help within the last twelve hours—that was exciting. But one of them had just died at his own hands, and Greg felt incredibly sad for him and his family. Robbie would probably lose his career—another reason for sadness. And frustration—so many things to be frustrated about, not the least being his own limitations. He could empathize, educate, and advise his clients, but that was never enough. What he wanted—secretly and unreasonably—was to find The Answer that would make life wonderful for each of them. An impossible task.

Especially for Robbie, he thought, jockeying for position on the eastbound freeway. No magic wands. That was his main frustration—he could do so little for a crisis requiring so much.

But intrigue overrode all other feelings. The events of the past twenty-four hours left Greg feeling singled out, chosen. He'd been made privy to astounding information with a potential for statewide (think about it!) shock waves. A scary situation, yes, but scary/fun, like a roller coaster.

Christine was watering the tiny patch of green they called a front yard when he pulled into the driveway. Their house in Garden Grove was usually a twenty-minute drive from work; tonight's traffic expanded that to a half hour.

"Hi, Gregorino," she called while he turned the ignition off and jumped out of the car. He welcomed the sight of her—most men would. "I've put some chicken on. Look at the gardenias!" she said, waving at the flower bed.

She'd been trying to make something lovely out of the little yard since they'd moved in six years ago, newly married and barely able to make a down payment on anything bigger than this two-bedroom, one-bath tract home. Her latest effort was a row of gardenias in the bricked flower bed. The lawn was a mere fifteen square feet, which seriously limited any landscaping plans. But the white flowers added some welcome cheer, and Greg told her so between several kisses.

"Dr. Bishop, we do have neighbors," she chided. She'd been watering and planting, and it showed. Her shorts were muddied and his sweatshirt, borrowed for the occasion, was half-soaked. She wore it well.

"Do they like watching you as much as I do?" he asked, nuzzling her neck.

"Well, the Martins' dog seems to like me." She broke away from his hug to turn the hose off. "He came by twice to express his approval of the flowers, but I caught him before he could— oh, honey, don't!"

He'd touched the petals on one of the gardenias. "They're really sensitive," she said, slapping his hand away.

"Yeah, so am I." He touched her cheek, then put his face close to hers.

"Good grief, what's with you today?"

"Are we in a big hurry to eat?"

"Oh, I don't know," she pouted with mock innocence. "Why?"

The odd combination of feelings in Greg faded, eclipsed by something warmer, something blessed. He pulled his wife back to him, then moved toward the house.

Two hours later they sat down to cold chicken and lukewarm peas while he filled her in on the day's events. When discussing work, they normally followed a strict policy of discretion. Speaking freely about her work as a freelance graphic artist was no problem, but Greg's was another matter. He'd tell her, in broad terms, how his day had been without giving the names or specifics about his clients. They preferred it that way.

But since she already knew about Ferguson there was no point in being coy, so he explained the details of his package, the blackmail note from BRAVO, Robbie Carlton's crisis (she'd heard of him and was amazed Greg hadn't), and the video.

Christine could tell he was still excited to be in the middle of all this, and it didn't sit well with her. She listened quietly as she ate, then put on a kettle for some after-dinner tea while Greg finished his meal.

"Some crazy stuff is coming down," he said, helping himself to more chicken. "That BRAVO group wants blood, and once they go after Robbie, his career will be history."

"What's with these people, anyway? Do they think blackmailing each other helps their cause?"

"You should see the letter they wrote to Ferguson!" Greg scraped the last spoonful of peas out of the serving bowl. "Yeah, I guess they figure if they can show how many gays there are in public life, then we'll all change our minds and say homosexuality's fine. Strange reasoning."

"They were on the news today." The kettle whistled. She went to the cupboard for tea bags.

"I know. Pastor Mike and I watched it in his office."

Christine poured two cups, sat back down, and looked across the table at him. "So."

"So?"

"So, I've been worrying all day."

"Why?"

She hoped he was kidding. "Oh, I don't know. Why worry? My husband gets midnight calls from reporters who kill themselves and old friends have heart attacks and packages come telling him stranger things are about to happen and he's supposed to do something to stop them, but hey, who doesn't have a little stress these days?"

Greg didn't appreciate the sarcasm, nor did he want cold water thrown on his adventure. "I didn't ask for this, you know," he said defensively. "But I'm trying to handle it, so a little support would go a long way."

"You sound as though you're enjoying it."

"I'm not!"

Christine's eyebrows raised.

"Okay, maybe a little," he admitted. "It's interesting. You've got to grant that."

"I want you to stay out of it."

"Too late," he said. "I was volunteered."

"It's scary. Please stay out of it."

He didn't want tension between them tonight, so he tried to close the discussion. "Well, I've got to see Robbie for treatment."

"Treatment for what?"

"Crisis. And grief. And homosexuality. He wants to change, and I want to help him."

"You've never done that before."

"But I said I'd try, so I will." Both of their voices were tightening. "Other than that, there's not much to do except watch the tape Ferguson sent me," Greg finished.

"And what did you say that's about? Gay politics?"

"Something like that. He said it would give me information I'd need in the future."

"But you're not getting involved in gay politics."

"It's not on the agenda, no. But what if I was?"

"You're not."

His dander flared again. Was she trying to tell him what to do? "No, I'm not, but what's the big deal if I did?"

They'd finished their tea, so Christine refilled both cups. "I don't know. It's just that every time someone takes on the gays his whole life goes down the tubes."

He could see she wasn't being bossy now, just protective, bless her heart. "Cheers," he said, clinking his cup against hers and trying to lighten things up.

She ignored the attempt.

"Look at Jerry Falwell. The press attacks him every which way, and the gays have sued him at least once that I know of."

"He's survived pretty nicely, I'd say."

"And what about Anita Bryant? When she fought them in Florida, they gave her a hard time."

"Honey! Are you really putting me in the same class as Anita Bryant and Jerry Falwell? Me, the little old counselor from Garden Grove? I'm flattered."

"Alex Crawford's the little old counselor from Santa Monica. Look where he wound up."

"He's got problems, that's for sure."

"So will you. So will we."

"No we won't. I'm not getting sucked into all this, believe me."

They were both quiet for a moment.

"I get scared, that's all," she murmured.

"You and me both. So let's get unscared." He looked across the living room. "Anything on TV?"

"Oh, I forgot," she exclaimed, getting up from the table. "*Casablanca* is on cable tonight; I think it starts at nine."

The perfect remedy, since they were both old movie buffs. For the next couple of hours they were happy to forget their problems and let Humphrey Bogart and Ingrid Bergman work theirs out.

FIVE

I can't GET no—
    Sa—tis-FAC-tion—

It belted out of the three-foot speakers, volume cranked, bass throbbing.

I can't GET no—
    Sa—tis—FAC—tion.

He took center stage in front of the bedroom mirror, singing over the recording of his favorite song, and thrust his hips forward.

And I try, and I try—
And I try, and I TRY—

Each *try* grew more urgent. And louder.

I can't GET NO!

He exploded, attacking imaginary guitar strings while the imaginary fans in the imaginary audience went berserk.

Hey, hey, hey.
That's what I say!

But no one heard.

The Santa Ana apartment was secluded and inaccessible, like its inhabitant. He seldom entertained at home, preferring to meet friends and associates at bars or restaurants, and a roommate was out of the question. For the time being, what more did he need than this no-frills, minor-upkeep studio? Plenty of time to settle into comfort later.

For now, there were the children to attend to. He actually thought of them as kids, though his forty-one years hardly qualified him as a father figure. But he was authoritative and controlling, a trailblazer by nature with a startling, scary appearance. When he appeared at demonstrations, people laughed. But they laughed nervously. And when he led, people followed.

The members of BRAVO were a case in point. Like most activists, they were rebels by nature, not easily led. Rare was the person who commanded their loyalty; but "rare" was an apt description of Yelsom.

An impressive mixture of dark virtues, he was both cynic and soldier, part steely businessman and part lone (some said "rabid") wolf, an impassioned advocate for humanity with unbridled contempt for ninety percent of the human race. Causes, not people, mattered to him, and even causes were valuable only as outlets for the rage he seemed to have been born with.

And he wasn't shy about expressing that rage. His nickname—the only name he was known by in the homosexual community, for that matter—referred to his noisy ways. "He sure yells some," his parents were rumored to have said of their child, and so the name *Yelsom* stuck.

In his family there were good reasons for yelling—none of Yelsom's friends or schoolmates would have guessed the turmoil he returned to every day from school. His father, a burly Long Beach hotel manager who revered his gun collection as much as he loathed Martin Luther King, had joined himself to a timid bookkeeper in her late twenties who saw him as her last chance at marriage. Yelsom was the result. "The *only* result," his father would sneer when appropriately sauced, "thank God! One of his kind is enough."

What was meant by "his kind" Yelsom never quite figured out, but whatever it was, it clearly wasn't the kind Dad wanted. And the price to pay for being "his kind" was steep. When Dad was sober, it was verbal abuse. When Dad was drunk, it was a fist in the ear, or a dinner plate smashed in the face, or a telephone cord, freshly ripped from the wall, slashed across the neck. Yelsom never took it quietly. He screamed and threatened that someday the favor would be returned, but he was never taken seriously.

Mom was too busy fending off similar attacks from her husband, so she had little to offer by way of defense. Sometimes, though, when Dad's drinking reached the danger point, she'd warn her son and sneak him out the back entrance of the Ocean Avenue hotel they managed and lived in. He hated leaving her at the mercy of his father's rage, but not as much as he hated being the object of it himself. So when Mom said, "Stay away for a while until he calms down"—which meant, "until he passes out"—he always cooperated.

Since Dad's rampages increased with time, so did the frequency of Yelsom's escapes—escapes which acquainted him with life in downtown Long Beach.

Multiple trips to the movie houses made him a devotee of films, and by the time he was twelve he could reenact entire scenes from the current hits. Long into the night, when Mom was asleep and Dad was blessedly unconscious, he retreated to the theater of his bedroom. There he became Christopher Plummer, leading his family from Nazi-occupied Austria in *The Sound of Music.* Or Paul Newman as Hud romancing Patricia Neal, or Anthony Perkins wielding a knife as the infamous Psycho.

Sometimes he even adopted roles of the opposite sex—blind Audrey Hepburn outwitting her attackers in *Wait Until Dark,* or demented Bette Davis terrorizing Joan Crawford in *Whatever Happened to Baby Jane?*

But Yelsom liked horror films the best.

He also liked the Pike, Long Beach's decades-old amusement park. Next to the movies, it became his favorite refuge. There were curio shops to browse in, penny arcades to spend quarters on, and a titanic, rickety, old roller coaster which never failed to thrill.

And there were people—fascinating, colorful, earthy people. Sailors and tourists, winos and street preachers. Men of all sorts whom he loved to sit and watch.

Some of them watched him, too. Quiet men; men with furtive, questioning eyes. Men who liked boys. And who would, he learned, pay good money to boys who were nice to them.

By the time he was fourteen he knew the ropes very, very well.

Yelsom sat on his bed, remembering. He liked to remember. It fed his anger and his sense of purpose.

It was 10:30. The meeting was at 11:00. Time to dress. He prided himself on punctuality, though they certainly couldn't start without him.

He'd come a long way.

Twenty-two years earlier he'd gladly wiped the dust of Southern California off his tennis shoes. He was an outcast by then, betrayed by old friends, beaten down, embittered, and isolated in a city that refused to understand him or his kind.

But he'd heard of other cities. Other people, too, more open-minded and reasonable. New York, for example, where he learned about a more appealing lifestyle and a new form of activism just brewing—an activism that sneered at polite discussion. An activism going straight for the jugular.

No draw could have been more powerful. So, after a brief stint of hustling and petty thefts, he scrounged the money for a one-way ticket and made connections on the East Coast.

He became known as Yelsom, dropping his real name when he left the Golden State, and soon he was immersed in protests and subversions. A demonstration in front of a church. An informal but highly committed group of university students leaving pamphlets in strategic places. Mild desecrations of the enemy's buildings. And without fail he was the undisputed captain who rose to leadership in every group he joined.

He knew this was all child's play. He and his cohorts were building steam while testing the effectiveness of their tactics. The real battle, they assured each other for two decades, was coming with the certainty of an apocalypse.

I can't GET no!

No, no, NO!

The song ended. The crowd went wild.

He bowed in front of his full-length mirror and blew a kiss to his image.

The gay nineties had arrived. He'd returned to California. The apocalypse was now.

His image smiled back admiringly.

He turned off his CD player, stifled a yawn, and decided that, despite the hour, a cup of coffee was in order. The long day wasn't over. He stepped into his closet-sized kitchen, filled the carafe, reached for filters, and scooped in three spoonfuls. High energy was required of BRAVO leaders, among whom he ranked highly. Whipping the Orange County group into shape in five months had earned him respect; he was second only to the founder in the national pecking order.

His earlier appearance at the protest in Sacramento had the desired effect. Three on-camera interviews had come from it, along with an invitation to a national talk show on CNN. His outfit was deliberately eye-catching—few reporters could resist it. And though the commuter flights to and from Northern California left him drained, the prospect of tonight's meeting revitalized him.

There would be applause, appreciation, debriefing. And plans. Terrific plans...schemes the kids would love.

The coffeemaker clicked and steamed—another two minutes to brew. Time to get ready. He'd have a cup once he was dressed.

His "half-drag" look (as he and others called it) could be put together in minutes. He laid out the standard attire—black leather jacket, red bandanna, torn Levis—then showered and got to work on his makeup. Twenty minutes later (he constantly timed himself nowadays—"staying organized," he called it) he was almost set.

The phone rang just as he was finishing his eyes. He yanked it to his ear, glaring. Yelsom didn't like interruptions.

"Some outing," the caller said flatly. Recognizing the voice, he jerked to attention.

"What are you talking about?"

"I'm talking about Joshua. Joshua Ferguson. Haven't you heard?"

Slowly he lowered the mascara brush. "Heard what?"

"He's dead. He overdosed in his car last night. Nobody's told you?"

Yelsom gasped as if he had been punched in the stomach. *This could ruin everything!*

"I've been up north," he said finally. "Now what?"

"Sit tight. We'll have to see what develops. Meanwhile, carry on as usual."

"There's a meeting tonight. What do I tell them?"

He listened to instructions from the other end, nodding and occasionally repeating "sure" in a tone uncharacteristically obedient for Yelsom. "Okay, fine," he said as the caller concluded. "That's how we'll do it. I'll let you know how it goes."

He hung up, poured himself some coffee, and sat brooding. Dead. Overdosed in his car. That wasn't the plan.

And I try, and I try—

He finished dressing. Slowly.

Casablanca ended at 11:00, just in time for the news. Greg switched the channel from cable to the ABC affiliate.

"Not tonight, Greg," Christine groaned as the station's news theme came on. "I don't feel like watching it."

"Really?"

"I'm tired of heavy subjects, that's all. How 'bout bed?"

"Just the main stories, okay? Or you can go to bed and I'll be there in a minute."

Too late. The first story was exactly the one Christine hoped to avoid.

"Mystery still surrounds the apparent suicide of investigative journalist Josh Ferguson. Ferguson, winner of countless awards for a lifetime of media achievements dating back to 1962, was spotted by the police in the City of Orange parked in his—"

Click. Christine had snatched the remote control and turned the set off. "Let's go to bed."

"I want to see this."

"It'll just upset us both again!"

"Turn it on. Please?"

Grudgingly, she complied.

"—efforts to revive him were unsuccessful and he was pronounced dead on arrival."

"Efforts to talk to him were unsuccessful, too," Greg muttered. Christine looked at him uncertainly.

"The subject of suicide was also raised at the state capitol today as gay activists gathered to demonstrate in favor of Assembly Bill 101, which, if passed, will guarantee civil protection to gays and lesbians in California. Some Californians question the need for such a bill, saying that homosexuality is a choice and therefore not entitled to the same protection as race or gender. But an activist spoke about efforts at change, and the damage done when gays try to become heterosexual."

Now Greg was suddenly tired of it all, and nearly asked Christine to turn off the set when the subject of the interview appeared.

Hello again. What was it about this guy . . .

Scowling face, bleached hair, and heavily made-up eyes. The setting was the front of the capitol, so it was obviously the same clip OCN had shown earlier. But ABC was showing more of it.

"Thousands of gays will tell you they've been to shrink after shrink who told them he could make them 'normal,' only to find that after years of hypnosis or analysis or whatever else, they're still gay. That's because they're born that way and were never meant to be anything else! Any psychologist who tries to cure homosexuals is a liar who wants to make a quick buck."

"That's it." Christine snapped it off, this time for good. "No more. Okay?"

He stared straight ahead.

"Greg?"

Nothing.

"Greg, can we pray? We're hardly ever having devotions anymore, and I think we need to."

He didn't move. "Tomorrow morning," he said, absently. "When we're more alert."

"But when you say that, then you get rushed in the morning and it doesn't get done."

"It'll get done."

"Okay, then let's go to bed. Please? Honey?"

He was still staring at the blank television screen.

"There, but by the grace of God, go I," Calvin murmured, "twice."

He flicked off the television set and thought of both men he'd just seen on the news. One was eulogized for his accomplishments; the other was spitting out defiance. Both were homosexual, but while one demanded sanction for it, the other preferred to die before letting it be known. Both had his sympathy—he might have become either.

Of course he had no proof that his late friend Joshua Ferguson was gay, but Calvin had suspected it for years. Too many unexplained absences during late-night production meetings, heavy drinking masking some inner turmoil, a marriage that tried too hard to look happy. And Robbie Carlton. You couldn't miss Josh's reaction to the kid.

He was a man tortured by passions he neither chose nor accepted. Calvin could relate.

And the activist? Wild, furious, railing against the oppression of gays and lesbians with statements that were partially true, mostly exaggerated. He was an angry man who, unlike Josh, celebrated his passions and demanded that the world do the same.

Calvin could relate to him, too. Without the support, counsel, and encouragement he'd gotten during a crucial period, who knows...?

He was sorry for the activist, but heartbroken over Josh. More than that, he was angry. And determined to find out what had really happened to his old friend.

It had given him a measure of satisfaction to praise Josh on the air, but his editorial hadn't told one-tenth of the story. Trouble was, he didn't know how much of the story could be told, or where the details might be found. But he had a solid lead.

"Unforgiven Sins." Josh's pet project, or, more accurately, his obsession.

It had begun innocently enough. Josh had asked him to come on as associate producer for a report he was doing on gay militants versus fundamentalist Christians. Calvin had co-produced a few specials with Josh by then, and they worked well together.

The assignment intrigued Calvin for reasons unknown to Josh, and so together they had conducted interviews with gay activists, psychiatrists, and professors. That was in the spring of 1990.

Six months into the project, the host of "Open Heart," KLVE's only live talk show, resigned. The station tried to fill the vacancy by offering it to some of the area's better-known radio person-alities, none of whom showed an interest. When an open call went out, Calvin interviewed for the position, made a suitable impression, and by September of 1990 he was hosting "Open Heart" during the coveted 3:00–5:00 P.M. weekday slot.

His work on Josh's project was naturally curtailed, although Ferguson insisted he retain the title of associate producer. He played a limited role in planning, editing, formatting. Then, early in January, things changed.

Josh was onto something. Something to do with a group he'd encountered.

Most of the preliminary interviews were completed when he became secretive about the report. He allowed no one to view it, not even Calvin. Josh curtailed the use of assistants, preferring to spend hours in the editing department alone, snapping the film off whenever someone entered the room. He had time for nothing but the "Unforgiven Sins" project until last Monday when, who knows why, Josh apparently decided there was no more time. For anything.

Calvin switched off the bedroom lamp and peered into the dark. *Did he have a right to know? Probably. Was there more to know? Possibly.*

No. Definitely. And he, nice little Calvin Blanchard who in his twenty-eight years had not so much as jaywalked, was about to plunge into a roomful of hostile strangers to find out.

"They're called BRAVO," Josh had said during an editing session.

"Of all the activist groups I checked on, they're the wildest. And they've just started a group in Orange County. They meet monthly, usually late into the evening."

Calvin's watch said it was eleven-fifteen.

"They wouldn't allow me to film their meeting. I could go myself without the cameras, but they'd recognize me. But not you. Maybe you could check them out for me."

He promised he would. Nobody would recognize Calvin Blanchard.

"You'll find their number in the Orange County Vine. *You'll get a recording telling you when their next meeting is, and where. Dress sloppy."*

He looked for the oldest jacket he could find. And for a casual hat, maybe a baseball cap.

"Don't get there too early. Come a little late, in fact, so you won't have to make small talk. Your conversation can give you away, and they wouldn't take kindly to infiltrators."

He never had gotten around to visiting BRAVO. The new job hosting "Open Heart" on KLVE cut down his free time considerably. That's the excuse he'd given Josh, anyway, for not going underground for the story.

The truth was, the whole idea was too scary.

"But you promised," Josh had nagged.

"I will, I will, as soon as there's time."

Then Josh began guarding the project. Then all hell broke lose.

Calvin found a gray Pendleton and a Dodgers cap, double-checked the address he'd gotten over the phone, took a deep breath, and headed into the night.

A promise was, after all, a promise.

"Expose the church, scare the church, or stop the church! That's what we're about, isn't it?"

The meeting was in high gear, and the energy in the crowded room was palpable. A casual observer might have mistaken this for a town hall meeting, with the leader in front fielding questions and comments from the crowd. But a closer inspection of this crowd would rectify the error.

In spite of their agitation, outlandish attire, and theatrical flair, one could not find a more serious group of people. They listened intently when spoken to, and spoke passionately when listened to. They were masters at planning and organizing, leaving nothing to chance. They had learned the science of force and numbers, and were determined to make it work for them. Even their most vocal opponents had to admire their fortitude.

The late hour hadn't dampened their enthusiasm. The participants tended to be night owls who could hold marathon sessions then report to their daytime jobs refreshed and capable. They were young, after all, the median age of the group hovering around thirty-two, and their zeal was ferocious. For a righteous cause, late hours meant nothing.

Lisa, an attractive, athletic-looking lesbian, was arguing a point with Yelsom.

"So if that's what we're about, why are we being so polite?"

"I didn't say be polite," he answered. "I'm saying keep things in perspective."

"But exposure is crucial! If we back down on that, what's the difference between us and every other group? We might as well close shop and join up with them."

Most of her forty or so comrades murmured in agreement. Yelsom was growing impatient.

"I'm not saying we should back down on exposure, all right?" he barked in his thick Bronx accent. "That's part of our focus. Maybe the most important part."

"It is?" a youngish male newcomer in a Dodgers cap asked hesitantly, much to the others' amusement. "I mean, I've never been sure. This is my first time here."

"It is," Yelsom pronounced solemnly, and when he adopted a solemn tone, the group listened. They were more accustomed to hearing him yell—anything less caught them off guard. He was as formidable as he was reclusive—so reclusive, in fact, that few of BRAVO's members ever socialized with him outside of meetings or official activities.

"That's why we're called BRAVO: Bent on Removing All Vestiges of Oppression." His voice rose—this was Yelsom the preacher, warming up his congregation. "You can't remove oppression against gays as long as gays are still hiding. So we give them a hand," he smiled, extending both hands and clapping them together. "And we say BRAVO!"

The room erupted into cheers, applause, and chants of *"Bravo!"* This was routine—a ritual to keep spirits high, much the way athletes hoot and shout and give each other high fives. Among this group, whenever anyone clapped their hands together and yelled *"Bravo!"* the others were expected to follow suit and chant Bra-*voh!* Bra-*voh!* Bra-*voh!*

When the noise settled, Yelsom returned his attention to Lisa. "But timing is crucial, so let's see how this method works with Robbie Carlton."

"This method is too easy on them!"

"But it's a more effective way of bringing them out of the closet."

"They'll never come out unless they feel the heat!" she countered, "and what you're proposing just makes it easier for them to hide."

"Not at all," Yelsom corrected her. "Did you read the note we're sending Carlton? We told him he's got until April 19. If he refuses, then we do the job for him."

"How?"

"He's doing a concert for the pro-lifers on April 19."

At the mention of *pro-lifers* the room filled with hisses.

"Pro-deathers is the correct term, Yelsom," someone shouted.

"Whatever you call them, they're doing a big benefit that night, and we're gonna be there."

"I'm not paying to see a bunch of bigots on stage!" Lisa protested indignantly.

"It'll be money well spent. Because if he hasn't come out by then, he'll be outed—by us—in front of his whole right-wing fan club!"

The group caught on and expressed their noisy approval.

"It'll be BRAVO's Orange County debut!" Yelsom announced loudly.

Cheers and whistles greeted the idea.

Lisa wouldn't be swayed. "But why not just show up and do it without warning him? If we give him time to do it himself, isn't that like sending him an engraved invitation? I say out him now. He doesn't deserve anything more!"

"Of course he doesn't," Yelsom agreed, "but's that's not the point. Retaliation isn't our only goal."

"Nothing's wrong with retaliation, Yelsom," a bearded man called out from the back of the room. "It intimidates them and it's good for morale!"

"But does it really help us or does it just make us feel better?" Yelsom snapped, his patience ebbing again.

The room quieted.

"Remember the plan. Lisa said it herself earlier—expose the church, scare the church, or stop the church! Exposure is step one. And speaking of exposure, we got a list of closet cases from Crawford's office that'll keep us busy for a year!" With that he displayed a computer printout he referred to as the "out list" and read the names from it. Businessmen, civic leaders, entertainers, and teachers were all included.

"And there are plenty of good Christians in this bunch," he added, putting it aside.

"So are we contacting all of them at once, or what?" It was the newcomer again.

"We'll warn them one at a time, then expose the foot-draggers. Meanwhile, we move on to shock tactics. They've worked well so far. Then, when all else fails, we attack. And speaking of attack, the protest in Sacramento yielded an interesting little contact."

He paused for effect.

"BRAVO will be featured on CNN next week with Melanie Stone!"

The mood had been festive so far; now it turned riotous. Yelsom basked in the roar of approval. They knew, as he did, that an appearance on CNN was another step toward credibility. And an interview with Melanie Stone could be taken as a stamp of approval from one of the country's foremost television hosts.

"You'll notice, folks, that Melanie has yet to let anyone from the religious right come on her show. What does that tell you? Who's in the back of the bus now?"

Pandemonium, cheers, hand clapping, and the BRAVO chant broke out.

Yelsom held his hands up (after enjoying the din for a few minutes) and called for quiet. "We've got more to discuss. Josh Ferguson is the next order of business."

Boos and hisses emanated from the crowd, none of whom noticed the blood draining from the newcomer's face.

"He didn't sabotage our plans as much as you might think," Yelsom shouted over the noise. "The man was a coward, but he's still going to be useful to us."

"Isn't he a good example of why we shouldn't warn them first?" Lisa spoke up again.

"Like I said before," Yelsom insisted, "we've got to give this method a chance. And remember, you can out the dead as well as you can the living."

"Didn't somebody do that to Rock Hudson?" a voice in the crowd called out.

"Yeah," a woman responded, "but they did it in a book and made money for it! We just do it out of the goodness of our hearts." Everyone laughed.

Yelsom asked for their attention again, knowing the next topic would bring down the house.

"Let's talk about the living for a bit, shall we? Let's begin with a member of the 'near living but not doing so well' club." Yelsom paused, then announced the name as if he were Ed McMahon. "A-A-A-A-l-l-e-e-e-x CRAWFORD!"

It worked. Few were as hated among the gay community as Dr. Crawford. His name conjured up images of shock treatment, repression, and right-wing supremacy. By now all of them knew about his heart attack, since news traveled through this group like greased lightning, and Yelsom's mention of the archenemy signaled a chance to officially rejoice. And rejoice they did. Not even Yelsom could quench their glee as they stood with a triumphant roar. They'd managed to incite a heart attack in one of their most reviled foes, and no one was going to take the moment from them.

Yelsom went with the flow of hooting and clapping. When it passed, he was ready.

"The good doctor is under the weather," he observed.

"Anybody sending him a get-well bullet?" Whoever said it earned the biggest laugh that night.

"Well, let's not hate him too much," Yelsom chuckled, "because he was kind enough to supply us with a list of Who's Who in Closetland. Which brings us back to the subject of Robbie Carlton. Do you know what a catch he is? One closet fundamentalist celebrity is worth twenty heathens."

"I'll take the heathens, thanks," Lisa said.

"So would I, personally. But if we can expose fundamentalist Christians we can weaken the last bastion of resistance, don't you see? So the name of the game is to target the church for future prospects. We don't just want to smash closets anymore. We want to smash stained-glass closets!"

"But do you really think you'll find that many gays in the church?" the young man asked from the front row. The members of BRAVO let out a collective howl.

"Any Catholics here tonight?" Yelsom shouted. Hands shot up everywhere.

"How about some Baptists?" More hands. "And some Pentecostals? Come on, we've got to have some holy rollers in the crowd." A few timid hands found their way up. "Look around," Yelsom instructed the young man. "Where do you think all these people were before they came out?"

The newcomer was educated and humbled.

"Enough said. So! The church is our target, beginning with Robbie Carlton. He gets his note tomorrow. April 19 is his coming-out deadline, so let's see if he's made of stronger stuff than his friend. And, while we're on the subject, let's not forget our unfinished business with Ferguson."

He set the list down and clasped his hands together, imitating a pious clergyman. "Dearly beloved, we'll soon be gathering to pay our respects to our dear, departed brother. I assume you all have something suitable in basic black?"

He laid out the plan. They loved it.

They were officially adjourned with a reminder to watch Melanie Stone on CNN next Tuesday.

Clusters of excited BRAVO members started forming throughout the huge theater basement that served as their meeting ground. If true to form, they'd chat and joke for at least another hour, reveling in like-minded company. Yelsom grabbed his black leather jacket and started to make a quiet exit, pausing only long enough to scan the room and reflect on how curious it was that these people looked up to him.

Calvin Blanchard made a beeline for the parking lot once the meeting broke up and was waiting for Yelsom when he came out.

"Uh, excuse me?" he ventured, stopping Yelsom mid-stride.

Yelsom whirled and regarded him coldly. *Impudent pup! Doesn't he know better than to accost me?* He lowered his glasses and peered.

The new kid, of course. The dumb one. Other BRAVO members wouldn't have dared interrupt him. "Well?" he barked.

"I just want to say I appreciate what you're doing for all of us. Like I said, this was my first time here, and I really—"

"Who'd you come with?" Yelsom snapped, stepping forward to get a better look.

"I got the number from the paper," Calvin volunteered, holding the man's gaze and fighting to keep a steady voice while ransacking his memory for the name of the gay newspaper he'd gotten the number from.

"From the *Vine*?"

"Right."

He stepped forward again; Calvin held his ground. "Who told you to come?" Yelsom demanded.

"Wayne. My friend Wayne. You'd know him if you saw him." Calvin was sure his attempts at looking casual were failing; couldn't this man see his legs shaking? "You don't know him, but he knows you. He hangs out at that same bar you do."

Yelsom drew back and squinted.

Idiot! Calvin's brain screamed. *What made you say that? What if he asks which bar you're talking about?*

"You mean The Shaft?" the man asked.

Calvin exhaled. "Yeah, The Shaft. Well, anyway, I just wanted to say I really admire you. I'm kinda shy, and I guess I'm making a fool out of myself." He backed away from the lot and toward the street.

Yelsom found himself enjoying the attentions of this wimp, who was obviously so impressed with him that he stammered and sweated in his presence. "What's your name?" he asked softly, putting out a hand and standing still.

Calvin hesitantly stepped forward to shake it. "Jeremy." At least he had that part down. "Jeremy Rolfing."

"I'm Yelsom." He smiled paternally, sizing the kid up and deciding he needed someone like this who was so intimidated, so easily led. "Join us again, Jeremy."

The smile sickened Calvin. "I will," he promised. "I need to be more involved. Anyway, sorry if I bothered you. Good night."

Yelsom pointed at him and winked, which was his way of ending a conversation, then strutted off to his car whistling an old Rolling Stones song. Calvin recognized it but couldn't remember the title.

He turned and walked toward the street.

Then he turned around again to see where Yelsom's car was. And in which direction he drove.

SIX

Good morning, Gateway Ministries."

"Hi, I'm calling from Orange County, and I was wondering if you had any materials on how to start a ministry?"

"Sure do. We've got a tape series on getting a ministry going, and we've also got a handbook that sort of walks you through the process. State regulations, forming a board of directors, that sort of thing. It also tells you some dos and don'ts we've learned over the years. Are you interested in getting a group started in your area?"

"I'm thinking about it."

"Terrific! I don't think there are any groups in Orange County, and I know there's a need. We get calls from your area almost weekly. Can I ask if you've ever been a part of a Gateway ministry yourself?"

"A long time ago."

"Which one?"

"The San Francisco chapter."

"You're kidding! When?"

"Back in '81."

Pause. "Can I ask your name?"

"Calvin Blanchard."

"*Calvin!* It's Paul Kaplan!"

"Paul!" he shouted back. "Paul, I don't believe it! I've meant to get in touch with you for so long, but I didn't know where you were living!"

Still shaken from last night's adventure, Calvin was glad to connect with a friendly voice from the past.

They babbled into the phone, interrupting each other, punctuating every sentence with *I-don't-believe-its* and trying to spell out the details of each other's lives for the past ten years. Calvin was too excited to hear most of what his old friend said, but the words *wife* and *married* caught his attention.

"Paul, you're married?"

"That's what I've been trying to tell you! I got married in '86. I moved back to Kansas after I left the program, got an insurance job, then fell in love."

"Kids?"

"One. One more next year, hopefully. Anyway, I got a job transfer out to San Francisco. True irony, huh? So we moved out here, then I started doing some volunteer work for the Gateway office. They hired me full-time just last March. I'm basically the office manager now."

A success story. Calvin heard so few of them. Since finishing his year at Gateway he'd learned of so many others that had gone "through the program" then gone right back into the gay lifestyle. They tended to become Gateway's loudest critics, blasting the ministry for what was often their own failure. The success stories just quietly lived their lives; you seldom heard about them.

"So, Calvin! How about you? I hear you went into broadcasting."

"I've got my own radio show now."

"You?" Paul sounded incredulous.

"Thanks a lot for the vote of confidence," Calvin responded with mild sarcasm. "But yeah, that's my line."

"I'd have never guessed it of you. What's your address? I'll send you the ministry manual."

Calvin recited the information, told Paul how good it was to talk with him, and promised to call back with an interview date. They hung up after another minute of mutual well-wishing.

So far, so good.

By hook or crook he'd find out what pushed Josh over the edge. He had to know.

Meanwhile, he'd also work on doing something more redemptive. God had been good to him lately—exciting career, good friends, good life. It was time to give something back.

It's happening, he told himself. *It's finally happening.*

Greg and Christine had devotions at 7:00, after Greg finished his walk. They recommitted to prayer and at least two Bible chapters a day, starting in 1 Samuel, where they left off a month earlier. After scanning the papers, they sipped coffee and gulped down a quick breakfast.

Christine had two brochures to design with a four-day deadline, so her worktable was spread out in the kitchen by the time Greg was ready to leave. "Is this a late work night for you?" she asked while he threw his jacket on.

"My last client is at 8:00." It was Thursday; Mondays and Thursdays he worked until 9:00 P.M. He grabbed a cup of coffee for the road.

"Let's try to get to bed early, then. You haven't slept much the past couple of nights."

"Tell me." He kissed her. "Good-bye. Draw pretty today."

"Counsel brilliantly."

His first client (he preferred calling them "clients" instead of "patients") was pacing the waiting room when he strode through the glass doors of the counseling center.

"Morning, Albert."

"I thought you weren't coming."

Same ritual, every week.

"Am I late?" Greg wasn't and he knew it.

Albert checked his watch and was visibly disappointed. "No, I guess not. I just thought you'd be here by now."

Nancy was typing across the room and didn't look up, still pretending to be irritated with him for teasing her yesterday in front of the good-looking new client.

"Morning, Nancy," he said, cautiously.

"Good morning," she said with icicles in her voice.

He caught the gleam in her eye and knew everything was fine. Then he glanced at Albert, who'd stopped pacing and was watching them. "I'll be ready in a minute, Albert," he said, leaving the reception area.

"God bless Albert," he murmured while unlocking his office. Albert was a tough client to work with: edgy, mildly compulsive, suspicious. Certain clients were irritating, and this one topped the list. Greg had confessed this once to Pastor Mike, who encouraged him to bless Albert whenever the irritation flared. Greg found himself "God blessing" Albert at least twice a week.

The appointment book was already opened to Thursday, March 14, telling him what he didn't want to see: seven clients today, no cancellations. Two free hours in the morning for paperwork; three hours in the afternoon for lunch and a workout.

Yes, a workout, he lectured his tired body. The new client's young physique had reminded him how quickly an older model would fade without proper care.

Robbie. How is he doing today?

He shook it off. Time to focus on today's clients. No fair playing favorites. He buzzed the intercom.

"Please send Albert in."

The Berean Counseling Center was open for business.

The center was Pastor Mike's brainchild, conceived in 1979 when he noticed how many of his parishioners were going outside the church for psychological help. He never discouraged them. "But why," he asked his board, "should our people have to look elsewhere for counseling when we could provide it right here?"

He was right about that. The Berean Community Church was well-endowed, supported by an upper-middle-class congregation with the means and desire to see it thrive. And so, three months after its board of directors gave approval, the church added the center to its growing list of resources.

Dr. Bob Evashwick was the original clinical director, and under his supervision a staff of two licensed therapists and one secretary manned the organization during its growth and expansion. Within five years it established credibility in both religious and secular circles, which was nothing to sneeze at in Orange County, where professional competition was stiff indeed.

In October of 1984, Greg joined Berean's membership rolls after being taken with both the pastor and the raven-haired Italian girl on the worship team. A married couple he'd known since the seventies had invited him to Berean, and when he remarked on Christine's talent, they caught his drift, introduced the two, and conveniently invited them both to a party they were giving the following month.

It took Greg less than three months to pop the question. He knew what he wanted. They were married the following August.

Meanwhile, there was training to complete at St. Joseph's Hospital, finals to pass, a dissertation to write, and state exams to endure before becoming a licensed psychologist. Greg cleared the hurdles with no small amount of help from Christine, and in June of '86 she officially changed his name from "Honey" to "Dr. Honey." His license was granted and the ability to make a decent living was secured.

The frosting on the cake was offered him later the same year, when Dr. Evashwick announced his retirement plans and the board of Berean Community Church unanimously voted Dr. Gregory Bishop into the position of clinical director. Both Dr. and Mrs. Bishop agreed that he had arrived.

After his session with Albert, Greg got more coffee from the kitchen, then rested at his desk, sipping and gazing around the office. It was generously furnished, courtesy of Berean's budget and Christine's taste. Burgundy wing chairs, large overstuffed couch, and a mammoth oak bookcase with a matching desk and file cabinet.

His gaze stopped at the file cabinet.

Third drawer. "Unforgiven Sins."

He'd almost forgotten the tape. With two hours until the next appointment, there was time to watch at least some of it. He opened the cabinet, reminding himself about stronger locks, and pulled out the manila envelope marked #3.

The intercom buzzed.

"Greg?"

"Nancy?"

"You got a call from a Mrs. Ferguson while you were in session."

"You're kidding."

"What?"

"Did she leave a message?"

"Just that she'd call you back. I told her she might catch you before 11:00."

He didn't want to wait until then—not if it was the Mrs. Ferguson he thought it was. He grabbed a pen. "What's her number?"

"She didn't leave it. She said she preferred not to, but she wanted you to know she's trying to get in touch with you, and she'll call back."

"Thanks. Oh, Nancy?"

"Yes."

"Is anyone using the conference room?"

"Let me see. No, nobody's scheduled to use it until 3:00."

"Okay, then I'll be in there for a couple of hours. I've got a video I need to watch. By the way, how did Mrs. Ferguson sound?"

"Tired. Not too stressed out, though, if that's what you mean. It didn't sound like a crisis."

"Thanks."

Maybe it wasn't Josh's wife, he thought. *Ferguson is a common enough name. Maybe a client or an old associate?* He thumbed through the Rolodex: Feinstein, Felton, Fenswick, Finley. No Ferguson.

Alma Ferguson, Josh's widow, was calling to either tell Greg something or get him to tell her something.

Back to the tape. He picked it up, locked his door, and headed for the conference room.

This was the center of activity at Berean Counseling, where staff meetings were held, corporate decisions made, and group therapy conducted. It also served as a break room for weary counselors, and a classroom for viewing videotapes and audio presentations. The furnishings were plain and functional: huge oak table, oval-shaped and capable of seating fifteen, one medium-sized beige couch, a counter and sink, and an entertainment center equipped with television, VCR, cassette player, and rows of audio- and videotapes.

Greg closed the door, switched on the VCR, and was about to slip in the tape when he got an urge to lock the door. After doing so, he inserted the video, grabbed the remote control, and settled into the couch.

Josh Ferguson appeared on screen, without introduction or credits, seated behind a desk in a small den. His cardigan sweater was light blue, buttoned tightly over a white sports shirt. His eyes were intense; his expression was haggard.

For nearly a minute he stared silently into the camera, then leaned forward, as though ready to share a confidence.

"Hello, Dr. Bishop."

Greg jumped off the couch.

"Surprised? Don't be. By now you've gotten a phone call from me and a package. Have you met Robbie yet? You may have, if there wasn't time to watch this before your appointment with him."

Greg jammed the pause button on the remote. His pulse was racing.

Getting a dying man's phone call had been unsettling; being addressed by a dead man on videotape was too much. He crossed the room to stand directly in front of the reporter's image.

"Cat and mouse, huh?" Greg asked the image on the screen. "Why'd you pick this mouse?" He looked hard at Ferguson's face, sizing him up as though they were about to box. And the longer he looked, the harder it was to tell whether his opponent's eyes were sinister or heartbroken.

He decided they were heartbroken, which relaxed him somewhat.

"What the heck, Josh—" he said, ending the staredown and backing into the couch again. "You don't mind if I call you Josh, do you?" He released the pause button. "Let the games begin."

SEVEN

*T*he relationship between patient and psychologist is both friendly and adversarial. Friendly because the psychologist dispenses information the patient needs; adversarial because it's not always information the patient wants to hear.' Remember saying that, Greg?"

Ferguson was holding a notebook up to the camera.

"It's from your paper on the doctor/patient relationship. You wrote this in '85 for your finals at UC–Irvine. It's still in the research library, so they must have liked it. Interesting stuff, although you borrowed a little too heavily from Freud. I thought Christian counselors didn't rely on his theories. Didn't he think religion was a just a defense mechanism?"

He put the notebook down.

"Anyway, you pretty well described the relationship you and I are going to have. I'm going to give you information that's helpful, but you may hate me for it in the end."

Greg's brows furrowed. Ferguson smiled back at him.

"You see, I really did run a background check on you. Do you think I'd have sent Robbie to you otherwise? I've gotten to know you, Greg, and I like what I know."

That lowered Greg's guard a bit.

"I'm sure you're wondering why I singled you out, so before you view this report—oh, that's what most of this tape is, by the way. A report. I've been working on it for months. It was scheduled for airing this spring, but as you'll see, it was never finished. Most of it consists of interviews, though, and all of them are included on this tape. This is the only copy and it's for your eyes only. But before you view it, let me give you some background on me. Fair exchange, don't you think?"

He stood up and pointed behind him. "See these? Pictures, trophies, and certificates." Now he was moving along the wall, tapping first one award then another. "There's an Emmy. And here's a plaque from NBC. News awards, which I find humorous, because news was never really my passion."

He paused.

"News is about what people *do*. My passion is uncovering what people are trying to *hide*."

After resuming his seat behind the desk, he folded his arms.

"Did you know I was raised to be a churchgoer like you, Greg? A Pentecostal, no less, born and raised in Kentucky. That's the buckle on the Bible Belt, if you didn't know."

Greg suddenly remembered that once, during a "Limelight" special on televangelists, Ferguson mentioned that Christianity was a part of his own early culture.

"Get comfortable. I'm going to tell you a love story," Ferguson was saying.

Greg leaned back on the couch.

"My father was a deacon in the Claremont Church of Prophecy," Ferguson began, "and in Claremont, that meant high, high status, which he loved. Not that he was vain. He was just a dear, simple man who served God and enjoyed the public's respect. I was proud of Daddy, more so than he would have been of me."

His voice cracked, then he continued.

"And Daddy revered our pastor, with good reason. He was a bold man, an independent thinker. Pastor Clark also had a social conscience. He hated bigotry and preached racial equality. That's an interesting trait for a Pentecostal preacher in the forties, don't you think? It probably cost him his life."

Ferguson looked down, shook his head, then looked back into the camera.

"We held Pastor Clark in high esteem. In our home you no more questioned him than you questioned the Bible itself. When he said, 'Thus saith the Lord,' it was as good as getting a telegram from on high. That's the environment I grew up in, and it was a predictable one until my seventeenth birthday, when *she* entered the picture."

With that, he pulled a worn, pocket-sized photo from his wallet and stared at it. The same instinct telling Greg the girl in the photo wasn't Ferguson's wife also told him Ferguson's wife had no idea he'd kept that photo.

"You can't see this picture, of course," Ferguson was saying, "but believe me, this girl was beautiful. Shining dark hair. Sparkling eyes... and strong. Strong will, clear mind. You didn't mess with her."

She almost sounds like Christine, Greg thought.

"Her family had moved in from Tennessee, and they were known to be a tough bunch. Rumor had it, in fact, that her father was with the Ku Klux Klan, but I didn't believe it. I was sitting in the left-front row of the church the first day she walked in with her family. The congregation was right in the middle of singing 'Happy Birthday' to me, as our custom was, when she strode down the aisle with her folks, and I nearly broke into the most heartfelt doxology you ever heard! We had lunch after the service and hit it off in an instant. Within weeks I'd fallen in love. And it was mutual."

Greg was thoroughly caught up in the story.

"I wasn't the only one who noticed her, though. Brother Clark was interested in her, too, but for different reasons. He knew, as did others in Claremont, that her family background was questionable. There was talk of her father having a hand in lynchings, cross-burnings, that sort of thing. I never believed it, and when I brought it up to her she laughed it off. But Pastor Clark didn't laugh it off. He couldn't.

"You see, she and her folks had just moved up from Lexington, and already they were consorting with some of the local Klan. Mind you, this was the South of the 1940s. Plenty of respected citizens were active in the Klan back then, and sheets or no sheets, it wasn't much of a secret who did or didn't belong to that bunch. So Pastor Clark had no trouble tracking the rumors down to their source."

Greg checked his watch and was glad to see he had another ninety minutes to spare. This was getting good.

"Now, her family's involvement with the KKK, and her involvement with me, presented two problems to our pastor. First, his church's reputation. He fancied himself a godly rebel— one of the few preachers with the guts to criticize the mistreatment of blacks. The church wasn't integrated, of course; we didn't go that far. But give the man credit: He spoke out when so few Christians and even fewer pastors lifted a finger for justice. So a deacon's son hooking up with a KKK daughter flew in the face of all he stood for.

"The second problem was a bit more personal. Pastor Clark doted on me, plain and simple. He was worried, bless his heart."

Josh's voice cracked again, and his face was etched with regret.

"So Pastor Clark went on a one-man crusade to break us up. Good intentions, bad methods, I guess. He warned me about her. I got defensive, and for the first time ever I rebelled against a man of the cloth."

A smirk played on his lips.

"But as I got to know her family, I had to admit to a few doubts of my own. During one dinner at their house, they asked many questions about my background. That was okay to a point. But they gave me the third degree about my ancestry. When I asked why they wanted to know about my past generations, they said they were particular about the sort of lineage their daughter associated with. Lineage—can you believe it? She squirmed; I knew they were embarrassing her. Later on when we were alone I confronted her. She admitted that yes, her family believed in 'all that stuff,' but she herself thought it was silly and never had anything to do with it. I was naive and believed her. What can I say? I was seventeen and in love."

Greg found it hard to believe such people existed.

"I proposed to her a few months later. I figured that marrying into a crazy family was a small price to pay for a bride like her. Of course, word of the engagement spread quickly. So Pastor Clark paid a visit to my father and told him his son was yoking himself with evil. He said that if I should be persuaded to adopt her family's ways, the blood would be on my father's hands."

An off-camera sound caught Ferguson's attention and he jerked his head to the left. Greg could tell this was unrehearsed and, for the first time, realized he was watching a home video. From Ferguson's home.

"Joshua, are you working?" a woman's voice asked. Her words were muffled, as if spoken through a door.

"You know I am. No more interruptions! *Please!*"

Josh said it with the same brutal tone he had used on Greg two nights ago. *"No more interruptions, no more saving the crazy old man—"*

Ferguson composed himself and continued.

"My father gave me an ultimatum: Break off the relationship or move out. In his eyes, my engagement was an act of defiance and a disgrace to my church and family. Now, I could have lived with being thrown out; we planned on living in another town anyway because of her reputation. But then Daddy pulled his trump card, and I was buffaloed."

The memory was bitter, and it showed.

"My college trust fund. The one dream I'd held onto was a career in broadcasting, which was impossible in those days without a degree. The money was still mine, he assured me, as long as I submitted to Pastor Clark's judgment. If not, then I could take my bride and forget my ambition."

And, Greg thought, there would have been no Emmy, no "Limelight," no investigative career. The end of the story was already clear.

"So, in essence, I sold my soul. That Sunday, at Pastor Clark's insistence, I denounced her in front of the entire congregation."

It was a miserable confession, made in miserable tones.

"Simply breaking it off wasn't good enough for Pastor Clark. I had publicly defied him, so I'd have to publicly come back to the fold. People were already wondering how he would handle the situation, and he was determined to deal with it in a way that would prove he wouldn't tolerate intolerance in his church. He had lots of zeal, that man. But not much sensitivity."

Ferguson took out the girl's picture again, then told the rest of the story—half to Greg, and half to her.

"I yielded to Daddy and Pastor. I told them I would break it off; just give me time. But I dragged my feet; I couldn't bring myself to tell her I'd chosen college over her. Pastor sensed I was stalling so he helped me along. One Sunday morning we were sitting together, as usual, when he began his sermon by calling me up in front of the congregation. I was terrified but obedient. He stood me up in front of the people and told them I'd bound myself in an unholy alliance and was ready to loose myself again.

"I barely heard the words, Greg; I was so stunned. Then he turned to her and said, 'Daughter, you have one chance now to denounce your family and their ways!' Well, what seventeen-year-old girl could do that? Of course, she said nothing. She just stared at me, scared and vulnerable. So Pastor said, 'Joshua, this young woman is hereby to be shunned by you and by this church, and we turn her over now to Satan for the destruction of the flesh as the apostle Paul enjoined us to. Denounce her now, son, and spare yourself.'

"I couldn't speak. I just watched her and tried to say how sorry I was with my eyes, but words wouldn't come. 'Make your statement, son!' Pastor said. 'You're ready to denounce her, aren't you?'"

Greg shuddered; why did the story sound so familiar?

"She stood up from the pew, called my name, then waited. 'Make your statement!' Pastor kept saying. 'I turn her over to Satan for the destruction of the flesh! Just say it!' Everyone else, Mom and Dad included, waited for me to say it. I couldn't. I barely got out the words, 'I turn her over'; that was all. Then I looked down and started to cry. 'Finish your statement: to Satan for the destruction of the flesh. Come on, Joshua!' he kept saying, but that was all I could manage. My eyes were glued to the floor, so I didn't even see her when she ran out of the church, back home, and out of Claremont. We never heard from her or her family again. But they sent us a message."

Josh nodded slowly.

"Two weeks later the church was burned down. So was the parsonage. With Pastor Clark in it."

Greg winced. Ferguson said nothing for a minute.

He pointed back at his awards on the wall.

"I got my education, Greg. And I succeeded. But I've re-played that Sunday morning in my mind nearly every day since."

He waved at the wall and the room around him. "After that, I never loved—oh, forgive the melodrama, but I never loved any-one like that again. And other things started to happen to me. Other feelings, other relationships that weren't so normal. Maybe they'd have happened anyway. I'll never know."

Greg knew what he meant.

"And Greg? I've never forgiven myself." He paused. "Can you understand that?"

Ferguson eyed him knowingly.

"I think you can."

Greg's breathing stopped.

"Twenty-two years isn't long enough to forget, is it, Greg?"

Greg's body responded before his mind did. He flew at the set, froze the tape again, and held onto the frame of the en-tertainment center, thoughts and questions jumbling together.

Josh Ferguson knew about Bennie. How?

He scrambled across the room toward the phone while his dead tormentor watched him quietly from the entertainment center.

Christine answered.

"Honey?" he gasped.

"What's the matter?"

"That tape? The one Ferguson sent me?"

"Yes?"

"It's too much," he panted. Hyperventilation was only a notch away. Greg pointed across the room. "He knew—he knew an awful lot about me."

"What's to know?"

"Bennie."

His Achilles' heel, the sin he never forgave himself for. She knew she'd better say something quick—something perfect.

"I'm sure you're wrong. Nobody knows about that."

"He just told me so."

"Greg!"

"On the tape. He recorded a message just for me."

"Impossible!" she exclaimed.

"Oh, baby, I wish it were."

She calmed down. One of them had to. "That," she began slowly, "helped make you what you are today. It was horrible, but it taught you what happens when you compromise. Some people never learn that lesson."

It worked. His breathing began to slow.

"So if he knew about Bennie," she continued, "then he knew what made you sensitive and strong at the same time. Is that so bad?"

She could make anything right, he marveled.

"I needed to hear your voice, I guess."

"So what's going on? How did he know all this?"

"Yes," he said absently, staring at the TV screen. "I mean—" Greg realized he was anxious to get back to the tape. "I don't know, that's what I mean. Just let me watch the rest of this, then I'll call. I'm fine now, really. I'll call you as soon as I finish."

She sighed. "Okay. Call me."

He hung up then hit the button, resurrecting Ferguson.

"You watched them drag away someone you loved too, didn't you?" Ferguson was commiserating, not accusing. "And you said nothing. After you scurried away from the Argonauts that night, word got around that you refused to join the club."

Ferguson held up a notebook to check his facts.

"You were ostracized after that. They called you a 'queer lover.' They even insinuated you might be one yourself. No college parties for you, Gregory. Your grades went down right along with your social life, and it looked like you were going nowhere fast. Then you got caught up in the Jesus movement. All those Christian hippies singing love songs to each other must have been a nice break after being shunned for so long. You dropped out of college after that. Thought the Lord was coming in a week, didn't you? And you didn't return to your studies until 1982 when you decided to be a psychologist."

Accurate to the last detail, Greg marveled.

"And what about the friend you betrayed? He disappeared, just like the girl I betrayed. He ran away after your buddies damaged him."

He checked the record again.

"Damaged him badly, I'd say. Five broken ribs, moderate concussion, multiple lacerations, broken blood vessels—oh, I won't go on. But he did vanish once he left the hospital. You're still not sure what he told his family. They wouldn't let you visit him in the hospital, and they refused your phone calls. And when you wrote, his mother returned your letter, unopened, with clear instructions not to contact her again."

He rattled off the horrible recital like a weather report.

"And you never forgave yourself. Never."

His voice turned suddenly gentle.

"I didn't learn this yesterday. I've been putting together a report on gay activists for over a year now. Your friend—the one whom they assaulted on the beach—moved to New York and became one of the city's foremost gay activists. I interviewed him last year and your name came up; that's how I first heard about you. You'll see it on the tape. Some other people from your past are on that tape, too. You'll be amazed at how complicated this all gets. I was planning to do an interview with you as well. That's why I'm so well-informed. I always do background checks before interviews."

He tapped his forehead. "I did this report because I wanted to understand the mind of a gay activist—not just what they do but how they think. The people that influenced their thinking, too. And I'm truly sorry I never got your side of the story. But no matter. Here's the real issue."

Greg had forgotten that Ferguson's story was supposed to have led up to something.

"I found out more than I bargained for when I did this report. More than I ever wanted to know."

Greg's heartbeat picked up again.

"I loved Robbie Carlton. You probably know that by now. And I had a serious problem which we won't get into but which you already understand, I'm sure. But in spite of the—oh, what would you call them? The unnatural affections I had for Robbie, there was also true friendship there. I wanted him to succeed, so I pulled strings to help him along. He was someone I'd invested in, so can you imagine how I feel now, knowing he's going to be thrown to the lions because of me?"

Some of Greg's pity for this man returned.

"There are only two things I can do now. The first is to get him some professional help. Dr. Crawford is retiring. He specializes in Robbie's type of problem; you don't. But you'll give him the best care available. I know that because Dr. Crawford raves about you, and he's no fool. Besides, this is your chance to atone. Robbie is everything your friend could have become. I've known them both, and I'm a pretty good judge of character. Here's your second chance to keep an innocent boy from being beaten. Save Robbie, Greg, and perhaps you'll let yourself off the hook."

Only now did Greg realize he was crying.

"By giving you Robbie I'm giving you another chance to help a confused, vulnerable young man. That makes our relationship friendly, doesn't it? But there's something else I'm doing that could make me your adversary."

Adversary? Greg thought as he wiped his eyes. *Just when I was starting to like you?*

"We created monsters, you and I. When we betrayed them, they became something malignant, something unforgiving. They have a plan. And they're coming back."

He pointed straight into Greg's face.

"So stop them without turning into a monster yourself. Here's your chance to do the exposé I never finished. This report will tell you how."

Ferguson stood.

"Do nothing, and you'll spend a lifetime fighting to ignore this. That will make me an adversary to your thoughts. If you try but don't succeed, you'll hate me for getting you into this. But if you can stop our monsters, you'll bless my memory for giving you the chance, and I swear from the grave and beyond I'll always love you."

Fade to black.

Greg stopped the tape and sat silently, not ready to hear more just yet.

Fifteen minutes later he walked to the church sanctuary, hoping it would be empty.

Pastor Mike saw him from his office, considered joining him, then thought better of it.

"And good afternoon! I'm Calvin Blanchard and this is 'Open Heart,' coming to you weekdays from three to five o'clock here at KLVE Orange County."

Another day, another show. Funny how quickly it could become routine. Not long ago, Calvin had thought the joy of broadcasting would never ebb.

"Today we're going to jump into some controversy and hit the issue of gay rights head-on. The subject on most Californians' minds these days when we talk about gay rights is, of course, Assembly Bill 101, which the state legislature is considering now and which would grant homosexuals the same civil rights status we currently afford blacks, women, and other minorities. Got your attention yet? I'm sure I do, because whenever we talk about homosexuality on this show, the phones ring off the wall. Well, you'll get a chance to join in when our guest, Pastor Ruben Anderson from Berean Community Church, talks to us about this and other related topics. But first, I get to blow my own horn with some commentary."

He arranged the notes he'd been working on all morning. He'd also arranged for a few more minutes of airtime for his commentaries, as they were becoming a meaningful part of the show.

"I've always been fascinated with the story of the Samaritan woman in John's Gospel. Remember her? Jesus approached her for a cup of water and they wound up having quite a conversation. Mind you, this was a woman with a past, so it's notable that

Jesus didn't start right off by preaching to her about her loose ways with men.

"He just wanted to talk, and talk they did. About lots of things: religion, racism, marriage. Finally He revealed Himself to her as the Messiah, and good grief, was she bowled over! She dropped her water pot and left the Lord standing right there, rushed into town, and started preaching the only way she knew: with her own testimony. 'Come see a man who told me everything I ever did!' she said. 'He's the Messiah; come on!' And, as you know, they came, saw, and believed.

"Now let's stop the story right here. This lady took one whopper of a chance! What credibility did she have? She was a Samaritan, which was pretty low status in most of Palestine, and a woman—strike two—and a loose woman, at that. She ran the risk of being laughed at and humiliated when she stuck her neck out. After all, there was a good chance people would say, 'Hey, you tramp, what right do you have to even mention the Messiah?' But she went anyway—she ran, in fact—to tell everyone about her changed life.

"The apostle Paul said we can be living epistles—letters that are alive with the good news. People read us, you know. When people read us, what do they see? A saintly, self-righteous soul who looks like he never had a problem in his life? Hey, nobody can relate to that. Perhaps we should look again at where we've been, what pit we might have come from, and let people know what things the Lord has wrought in us. Risky? You bet. But where would that little town be if that one outcast woman hadn't been willing to risk?"

Listen to yourself, Calvin, he thought.

"That's something to think about."

Calvin shook Ruben Anderson's hand and gestured for him to take a seat behind the second microphone. They had a two-minute break before the next segment.

"Good to see you again," Calvin said, vowing to remain on his best behavior. He'd worked with Anderson before, and try as he might, he found it hard to like the man. His views weren't the problem, because Calvin agreed with him on most issues, but he found Ruben to be harsh and pompous, a rather judgmental type who, in earlier times, might well have felt the Lord's whip across his fanny as He drove the moneychangers out of the temple.

The thought of that broadened Calvin's smile.

"Good to be here," Anderson said with customary stiffness. They sat in strained silence, waiting for airtime.

"We're talking now with Pastor Ruben Anderson," Calvin began, relieved when the break was over. "He's the director of social concerns at Berean Community Church in Irvine. Pastor, thanks for joining us."

"It's a pleasure."

"Tell us a little about the social concerns committee at your church, if you would."

"Gladly. We formed the social concerns committee to help organize a Christian voice in Orange County on matters that the church is, or should be, concerned about. We hold monthly meetings and invite guest speakers in to update us on legislation that will affect the church and the family, and we encourage our members to take action. We petition legislators, we attend school board meetings, we initiate letter-writing campaigns, and we keep people aware of local and state matters."

"Fantastic! I wish more of us were aware and concerned," Calvin said amiably. "Now, you've been following the progress of AB101 up in Sacramento. Tell us about this bill and why we should be concerned about it."

"Well, Calvin, the homosexuals have been pushing for an antidiscrimination bill for years, and if you know anything about homosexuals, you know they're a stubborn bunch of people! They have an agenda, and part of it is to force all of us, Christian and non-Christian alike, to accept their lifestyle. In essence, that's what this bill's about. It would deny all California businesses and homeowners the right to decide whether or not they want to hire or house avowed homosexuals. Under AB101, homosexuality would be given the same status as race, gender, religion, or physical abilities. Why should we be concerned? Because we can't afford to equate sodomy with normal traits, that's why, and we sure can't afford to treat it as something that deserves protection."

Calvin kept a neutral expression throughout the speech. He agreed with the main points, but he would have used different terms. A different tone might have helped, too, as Ruben's had a tendency toward shrillness. And something else needed to be said.

"No, we can't afford to equate homosexuality with race or religion, certainly not," Calvin agreed. He wet his lips and dove in. "But I've always wondered. Isn't there some way to show love and respect to these people even as we fight their agenda? I mean, shouldn't we also be trying to reach them?"

Pastor Anderson's expression told Calvin it was going to be a long show.

The quiet of the sanctuary helped some, though Greg could hardly pray. He spent almost an hour there, absorbing what he'd seen of the tape. He could only take so much of it at one time, so he decided to view the rest later.

A custodian came and went, reminding him of the time. He returned to handle a couple of counseling sessions, trying with limited success to concentrate on someone else's problems.

Then, after picking at a salad during his lunch break, Greg remembered the workout he'd promised himself earlier. He considered, then declined. No energy. Instead, he sat in his office, craving more solitude, then remembered a phone call he'd been putting off.

"Santa Monica General."

"Patient information, please."

"The patient's last name?"

"Crawford."

"First name?"

"Alex. You might have it under Alexander."

"Date of admission?"

"Yesterday."

"And what did you wish to know?"

"How he's doing, that's all."

"Hold. I'll transfer you to the nurses' station."

Another voice came on. "East Wing, this is Sharon."

"I'm calling about Dr. Alex Crawford. He was admitted yesterday."

"Yes, is this a family member?"

"No, a friend. Can you tell me how he is?"

"He's resting comfortably, but he's not taking calls."

"That's fine, I don't want to bother him. Would you please tell him Greg Bishop called?" He left the office phone number with her. "Tell him I'll be in touch later."

"Greg Bishop? Got it. I'll leave a message."

"Thanks. Good-bye."

Less than ten minutes passed before Nancy buzzed to tell him Alex Crawford was on the line.

"Alex?"

"Hello, Gregory."

Greg cringed. The voice he loved and respected above all others, the one that rebuked impudent students and consoled frightened interns, was barely a whimper.

"Alex, how are you? I've been worried."

The voice swelled a bit. "Don't patronize me, young man. I'm the one who should be worried, with half-wits like you running around psychoanalyzing innocent people."

Same Alex, Greg beamed. He loved it. "What do the doctors say?"

"Not much, those stooges, but enough to let me know I needn't update my will. How are you?"

"Fine. And mighty relieved to hear you're okay."

"You're not fine, and you're not much of a liar, either. Celeste told me you called, so of course you know about Joshua."

"I know. I'm so sorry, Alex."

"Never mind, I can handle it."

"When can I see you?"

"Whenever you'd like. Are you seeing patients tomorrow?"

Greg smiled. They'd fought incessantly over that word. Greg felt *patients* was a demeaning term; Crawford was from the old school which insisted they were just that: *patients.* The older man thought Greg's idea downright silly, and loved to pointedly refer to his "patients" just to irritate his former student.

"Some things never change, do they, sir? Yes, I am seeing some—"

"Patients," Alex finished for him.

"—*clients* tomorrow," Greg said, grinning. "How about Saturday?"

"Try to come in the afternoon, Greg. Then you can tell me what's troubling you, and we'll tackle it. Won't we, Dr. Bishop?"

"Of course."

There were still four more clients to see, but talking with Alex cheered him, reminding him there would always be at least two other people rooting for Greg Bishop. By late afternoon he reached the halfway stretch—just three more appointments.

His phone rang just before the next one was due.

Since Nancy had already gone home, the phone calls came directly into his office instead of to the receptionist's desk. He could choose to answer or switch to voice mail. Tonight, he preferred to answer, at least between counseling sessions.

"Good evening, Berean Counseling Center."

A thin, tired woman's voice asked if Greg Bishop was in.

"This is Greg."

"Dr. Bishop, this is Alma Ferguson, Josh Ferguson's wife."

"Yes! How are you, Mrs. Ferguson?" he asked gently.

"Not well. Dr. Bishop, I only called to ask if you might attend the services we're holding for Josh next Thursday at Waverly Chapel?"

"Well, yes." He stopped.

"You'll be getting notice by mail," she continued, "but I wanted to ask you personally to come. I was hoping I might meet you."

"Of course. When are the services?"

"Thursday the twenty-first at 1:00. Waverly Chapel in Orange. You'll get a card."

"Mrs. Ferguson, I'll be there. I'm so sorry about Mr. Ferguson. Thank you for asking me."

She hung up without answering.

He was home before 9:30, deflated and uncertain. His vulnerability always brought out the best in Christine, who fed Greg and mothered him through a hot bath, spiced tea, and cake for a snack, then an extended back rub that left him purring off to sleep before eleven.

It was Christine's turn at sleeplessness, but where her husband was prone to worry through his insomnia, she was given to prayer.

They both needed it.

EIGHT

*F*riday morning started the same way Thursday morning had—with a difficult counseling session. The husband was a recovering alcoholic, the wife was a rescuer—someone who was at her best when she was taking care of somebody else and ignoring her own problems.

Married for twelve years, they'd never hinted at divorce until he joined AA two years ago. Before then, she knew her role and played it well, hiding the bottles from him, calling in to work and making excuses for his absences, letting their friends pity her and hold her up as a martyr. Then he had to ruin it all by getting better.

Not too much better, though. In his eyes, everyone else was to blame for his mistakes, and since she'd put some weight on lately, he indicted her figure as the cause of their marital woes. She, in turn, decided now was the time to finally get angry with him for the years he'd been drinking, so they were both armed with formidable weapons: She clobbered him with the past, and he retaliated with weighty matters of the present.

Greg's interventions had been fruitless so far. Communication techniques, boundary setting, and forgiveness exercises were all met with enthusiasm, only to be dumped a week later.

"He won't let me be angry," Barbara complained. "He thinks I'm supposed to feel nothing after a thousand nights of him coming home drunk and screaming at me and the kids."

"You can be as angry as you want. I'm just sick of hearing about it," Bob groused.

"We're supposed to be communicating our feelings, aren't we? Okay, I'm feeling angry. Isn't it okay to feel angry?"

"Every twelve seconds? How do you find time to eat so much when you're a walking Godzilla?"

"Hold it." Greg was already worn down—this wasn't helping. "There's nothing wrong with being angry. It's not how you feel that counts, but how you handle the feelings. Go ahead and be angry, Barbara, but realize that you don't have to tell him every time the anger hits you."

Barbara didn't take the advice with a smile. He turned to the husband.

"And you, Bob. Cut the sarcasm. Your wife saw you through your drinking problem for ten years, so cut her a little slack on the weight business. Every time you insult her, you're just driving her back to the dessert tray."

"What do you mean 'the dessert tray'?" Barbara demanded. "I don't eat desserts! Are you agreeing with him? Are you saying every time I get mad I stuff myself? You don't know how hard I'm trying!"

"I don't think you know how hard I'm trying, either, Greg," Bob interjected. "I don't insult her half as much as I'd like to."

"Oh, great! How often would you like to?" Barbara snapped.

"Every twelve seconds. Why should you have all the fun?"

"Time out!" Greg shouted.

That stopped them cold, and Greg learned there was a slight echo in his office as his voice bounced from wall to wall.

"We're almost out of time here," he said more gently. "Listen, I want us to get back to the communication exercises we were doing. Remember the workbook I gave you? Let's get back to using it this week."

"Oh, I don't see why," Barbara answered sweetly. "I think we communicate pretty well, don't you?"

Her husband nodded.

Greg looked at the floor.

God bless Barbara and Bob.

Pastor Mike could barely conceal his amusement from his associate pastor. Much as he loved Ruben, he knew how exasperating the man could be. Intimidating, too. So when someone like Calvin Blanchard challenged him, Mike understood why.

He sat behind his desk while Ruben paced around the room. They were discussing yesterday's radio show.

"Ruben, he was only asking you some honest questions," Mike said. "That's his job. Radio hosts aren't supposed to pamper the guests; they're supposed to ask hard, thought-provoking questions."

Anderson kept the pacing up and grunted.

"I don't see why you're upset, anyway. I thought the show went very well. You sounded great and did us all proud."

Ruben stopped and looked at his senior pastor. "I hate being patronized, Mike," he muttered. "You know that. I don't need you to compliment me."

"Okay, then to be honest, you sounded like a right-wing fascist with constipation. Happy?"

Ruben smiled coldly. "I didn't appreciate the tone of his questions, or the way he insinuated I was more interested in politics than in people."

Mike leaned back thoughtfully. "Well, I don't think that's what he meant. He was trying to get you to tell him what we're doing for these people—the gays, I mean—besides fighting them, that's all. I thought the point was well taken."

"You can afford to be generous. You weren't there."

"Listening to some of your remarks to the callers, I'm not sure you were all there either, Ruben!"

"I was there, trust me. But they were rude, and Blanchard wasn't much help."

Two gay men had called during the program and challenged Pastor Anderson to prove gay rights were a threat to the state. Unaccustomed to being on the spot, he'd resorted to arguments that weren't too convincing. When the callers began shooting holes in his reasoning, even Calvin Blanchard had to agree with some of their points.

"Whose side is he on, anyway?" Ruben fumed. "That's what I asked him after the show, and you know what he said? He said, 'I'm not sure anymore.' What's that supposed to mean? We've got a Christian talk show host who isn't sure which side of the homosexual issue he's on?"

"He's on the right side, Ruben, but he doesn't sound too crazy about the way the right side is handling itself. Truth to tell, neither am I." He pulled out a chair for Anderson. "Come on, sit down, and talk to me. I want your opinion."

That smoothed at least some of Pastor Anderson's feathers.

"When he asked you if we're providing anything but criticism for gays, I got to thinking. How about social concerns doing some kind of outreach to the gay community?"

Anderson flew out the chair as though he'd sat on a wasp. "Are you crazy or just plain stupid?"

"Easy, Ruben." Mike could adopt a very intimidating tone himself, when necessary.

"Sorry. No disrespect intended, but are you serious? Do you know what these people would do to us if we let them overrun our church?"

"No, but to be honest with you, I'd like to find out. Wouldn't you like to see a few of them in church rather than at the gay bars?"

"I want to see them where they belong!" Anderson retorted, exposing his real attitude. Mike looked at him and shook his head.

"That's a shame, Ruben. A real shame. It's not what we're supposed to be about here, you know."

"We're about maintaining certain standards, Mike. Drop them and we'll lose everything."

"I wouldn't dream of dropping them. I'd just like to add a few more, that's all."

"Such as?"

"Compassion might be a nice start." He stood up; Ruben took the cue and did likewise. "I really would like to pursue the outreach idea. I don't know how, but it's worth considering."

"With all due respect, Mike, I'll fight you on this one."

"So what's new?"

With nearly two hours before his next session, Greg finally allowed himself a workout—his first since Wednesday. The gym was a convenient five-minute drive from the office, and at this hour the crowds were down. He tore into the weights gratefully. It was nice to do something physical, something that didn't require interpretation or empathy.

The shoulder press was open. He hopped in, set the weights and started to pump. His mind wandered as he counted each repetition.

Ferguson knew all about me.

One!

He thought I could kill his monster. And mine, too. I didn't know I had one, though.

Two!

Is his monster gay? My monster's gay. Are gay monsters pink, or what?

Three!

And how, pray tell, am I supposed to stop them?

Four!

With a can of Monster Away?

Five!

That's an interesting ad idea. "Got Gay Monsters Coming Your Way? Rid Those Pests with Gay Monster Away!"

Six!

Robbie's no monster, though.

Seven!

He's my second chance.

Eight!

Nine! Ten! Eleven! Twelve!

Stop. The weights clanged into place.

I'm getting a second chance.

He still wasn't sure he wanted it.

He was back in the office by 2:30, with half an hour to kill before the next session, when Nancy told him an unscheduled client was there to see him: Mr. Carlton. Did he have a few minutes to spare?

Greg walked into the waiting room, extending his hand.

"Here." Robbie thrust a paper into Greg's hand instead of shaking it. Without looking at it, Greg knew what it meant. "Come in for a few minutes, Robbie."

"Now what?" Robbie asked after seating himself on Greg's couch. He'd known this was coming, but he'd retained a small hope it would all blow over. The note was proof it wouldn't.

"When did you get this?"

"This morning's mail."

"It says you have until April 19 to come out. Now, I'm not sure how they operate, but I know they mean business. Does your manager know about this?"

"Nobody knows but you."

"You'll have to make arrangements. Notify him yourself. Your record company, too. It's better they hear this from you than from a bunch of protesters."

"Notify them of what, though? How do I put it?"

Greg had already thought this out. "Tell the truth. All of it. That they broke into a doctor's files, stole the records of one of his patients who mentioned you, and that you're being exposed because of it. Tell them you're in therapy yourself, trying to work on this problem, but stress the fact that you've done nothing wrong. Then let them decide what to do."

"What about the law?"

"Find out exactly who broke into Crawford's office and who wrote this note, and you'll have a good case. But activists, especially this kind, are hard to trace."

"How hard can they be to trace? They demonstrate in public all the time!"

"It's not illegal to belong to a group that's taken credit for a crime, that's the problem." He patted Robbie's shoulder. "See your attorney, by all means. But at this point, there's not much more you can do."

Robbie took the paper back from Greg's hand and crumpled it in his own, watching it. "You know why they chose April 19?"

"Haven't a clue."

"Because that's when I'm singing in Irvine Meadows. These people do their homework, don't they?"

Greg ransacked his brain for something to say. He came up empty, then remembered the time.

"Robbie, I've got a client coming in a few minutes. I'm sorry."

"I was hoping we could pray."

"Sure. Let's do it."

He took Robbie's hand. It was cold.

When they finished, Robbie left no cheerier than when he'd arrived. Greg couldn't blame him.

He noticed the crumpled note on the floor. Robbie must have dropped it when they prayed. He picked it up and read.

March 13, 1991

Mr. Carlton:

> Sing unto the Lord a new song, Robbie! One which we can all appreciate, especially those in the gay community who need to know that a fine Christian boy like you is one of them!

That's right, Robbie, this is your wake-up call. Respond now.

Written evidence of your homosexuality is in our possession, and we intend to use it to help liberate you and thousands of other gays in the church who live in the bondage of repression and self-denial, not allowing their true natures to come out. Your example will free them, and yourself as well.

You have until April 19 to come out publicly and declare yourself gay. Refuse and you will be thoroughly outed, exposed as a closet case. We prefer you to do this on your own, but do not underestimate our commitment. You are one of many closet cases who will no longer be allowed the luxury of keeping their true identities secret.

Until April 19,
BRAVO
(Bent on Removing All Vestiges of Oppression)

He opened the cabinet and put the note in with the new file on Robbie Carlton, then realized how easy it would be to hate these people. Their actions invited a hateful response. Was that really their goal?

His next client was waiting.

Pastor Mike buzzed Nancy just as Greg and Robbie disappeared down the hall.

"Nancy?"

"Yes."

"Is Greg back?"

"He just stepped into his office with a client, Pastor. They shouldn't be long, though, because he's got someone else scheduled for three o'clock. Can I leave a message for him?"

"I just wanted to talk to him. How's he doing? I saw him headed for the sanctuary yesterday, looking pretty forlorn."

Nancy was glad someone noticed. Something was definitely wrong with Greg, but she hadn't been sure how to approach him about it.

"Pastor, something's wrong. I'm in the dark, but if you're asking me if Greg's okay, I'd have to say no."

"Sorry to hear it."

"Was there anything else?"

Mike hesitated.

He rarely interfered with his staff members' personal lives, preferring to let them come to him if they wanted to talk. But neither was he disinterested, especially when it came to Greg Bishop. He loved the doctor, as most people did, and counted him one of Berean's finest assets. More than that, he valued Greg as a friend. If something troubled him, he wanted to know about it.

"Yes, there is. When's Greg got some free time?"

"Between four and five."

"Schedule me in, would you? Tell him the pastor's cracking up and wants an appointment."

Greg finished his last session at 3:50 and was putting his notes in place when Nancy told him his next client had arrived.

"I don't have one scheduled for four."

"You do now."

He walked toward the waiting room, irritated. Nancy knew better than to schedule someone without telling him. What was she thinking of?

"Help me, doctor, I'm so distressed!" The voice came from the waiting-room couch, where Pastor Michael Cain was curled up like a neurotic baboon with his feet tucked under his massive legs and his thumb in his mouth. The sight had Nancy in stitches; it left Greg speechless. Then he recovered and adopted a very professional tone.

"Shock treatment is this way, sir," he said, pointing down the hall. "Nancy, this guy looks dangerous. Call 911 if I'm not out in an hour."

He led Mike to his office and offered him a seat. The pastor hunkered down on the couch; Greg took his customary chair.

"I don't get down here often, Greg. I thought I might take advantage of your expertise. Can you help me?"

Greg pretended to scrutinize him, then held up an imaginary Rorschach test. "Just look at this ink blot and tell me what you see."

"Two elephants speaking in tongues."

"I see. And this?" He held up another imaginary blot.

"Two elephants doing the cha-cha on a steeple."

"Very good. And this?"

"A dear friend of mine who's troubled and is doing his best to hide it."

Greg dropped his hands into his lap. Mike looked at him. "Shall I go on or stay out of it?"

"You feel like playing Father Confessor?" Greg asked.

"If it'll get you in a better mood. You've got me worried."

"Strict confidence? Just between us?"

"Pastor/parishioner communications are privileged too, you know."

"You've got it."

"Okay. I've got lots to tell you."

Greg let it all spill out, trying to be concise: the phone call, the package, the tape, Crawford's illness. And a cold November night in 1969. Nobody but Christine had ever heard that story from him.

"Greg," Mike said over and over when it was finished, "oh, Greg. Where do you think this is heading?"

"Ask Ferguson. He's the one who says the monsters are coming."

"What's this report of his all about?"

"'Unforgiven Sins.' That's the title, anyway. I haven't looked at it yet," Greg admitted. "I'm not at all anxious to deal with it anymore. Ferguson's message at the beginning of it did me in."

"I want to watch it with you." Mike's curiosity was aroused, but his main concern was for Greg. If there were any more surprises on the tape, he wanted to be with him when they came.

"Now that you know all this, sure. How about Monday? Late afternoon?"

"Can you wait until then to see it?"

"No problem, believe me. I don't even want to think about it for a while. I've had enough shock for a few days."

"I can meet you here at three, then. We'll watch it in the conference room. And Greg?"

"Yes?"

"You didn't feel you could tell me all this before?"

"Remember our agreement? I'm not supposed to reveal the name of anyone who comes here for counseling. That's our policy, and I just broke it."

"You're safe; you know that. I won't mention it to anyone. Anything else I can do?"

Something occurred to Greg. "There is, actually. When Robbie's recording company finds out what's going on, they may release him from his contract. Or he may decide to retire."

"That's pretty drastic."

"But it's possible. His image is going to be pretty tarnished any way you cut the cake. This will probably ruin him."

"You think so? Even though he hasn't really done anything wrong?"

"I don't think it matters whether he's done anything wrong or not. As soon as the word *homosexual* is associated with him, plenty of people will turn their backs. They won't care if he's a practicing homosexual or a man with homosexual temptations. It'll all be the same to them. And remember, he's not entirely innocent. He did go to a gay bar, which wouldn't sit well with anyone."

"True. But what can I do about that?"

"Give him a bit of personal care? If he doesn't have his pastor's solid support, will you give him yours?"

"Count on it." He got up. Greg walked over and hugged him. "Thanks for being nosy."

"My specialty. So what do I owe you for your services, doc?"

"A repeat performance of that stunt you pulled in the waiting room. But let me get it on film next time. The missions board needs to see it."

That night the Bishops attended a surprise birthday party Sherry Nelson was throwing for her husband, Duane. Greg and Christine hadn't seen them in nearly a year, so they could hardly turn down the invitation. Nor did they want to. Greg's long hours kept them from too many get-togethers. Their friends were tolerant, but Greg felt perpetually guilty having to say no to them time and again. Besides, he missed them. In the not-too-distant past he and Christine saw them more regularly, but children (theirs) and careers (his) made socializing a lot tougher.

They arrived ten minutes before the surprise. Sherry had taken Duane out for dinner and let her sister decorate their house, leaving instructions for the guests to park around the corner, socialize until 6:55, then gather in the hallway with the lights turned off. Greg let Christine walk in first, always proud to have his gorgeous wife in front of him. They were greeted with the typical "It's been too long" and "I've been meaning to call you" remarks. He loved it, needed it. It reminded him there was more to life than problems.

At 7:00 on the dot, the guest of honor was appropriately shocked and the party was on, with food, milling, gossip, and charades. A few couples left before ten, but the core of the party remained late into the night, and as the evening wore on, the tiny knots of conversation merged and became a group discussion of current events.

Abortion was the first topic, which was always good for lively discourse. Education and the media followed; homosexuality couldn't be far behind. It crept into the conversations of most Christian gatherings sooner or later.

"But nobody's pushier than the gays," Duane exclaimed as they compared liberal interest groups. "They throw a tantrum anytime they don't get their way."

Most of the others agreed.

Greg was interested. "What do you mean, 'throw a tantrum'?"

"Well, take this gay rights bill they're trying to push through."

Everyone reacted. Assembly Bill 101 was already being mentioned and denounced from pulpits across California.

"What's happening with that, by the way?" Sherry asked.

"It's in the Ways and Means Committee now," Duane said. "They need time to really discuss this thing and make an intelligent decision—"

"*Can it!* That's the intelligent decision," one of the men retorted.

"Sure it is, but hey, if they *do* pass it, I want them to at least discuss it first. But the gays don't even want that. They're at the capitol every step of the way, putting pressure on the assemblymen to pass it *or else!*"

"But," Sherry countered, "not all of them are that way. A friend of mine from high school is a lesbian, and she's not pushy at all."

"You mean Camille?" Duane asked. "She's not a lesbian; she's just confused."

"Not a lesbian? Duane, she's been living with the same woman for seven years and says she's her lover. What's your definition of a lesbian?"

"I don't care. Camille's too pretty to be gay." Everyone laughed.

"It's the guys who are the pretty ones," Sherry's sister added. "Why are so many gay men such hunks?"

"Could we get off this subject?" Carl Henderson asked, looking disgusted. He coached football at El Medina High School and had three sons of his own; Greg guessed they were the cause of his discomfort. Most fathers he knew wished the homosexual issue would just go away.

"This subject won't get off us, Carl," Duane answered. "You can't get away from it. It's in your face every day, bro; you've got to deal with it."

"I've got a few ideas on that score. Deal with it by shipping them off to a tropical island where they can be as queer as they like without bothering the rest of us."

"What will you do with the ones who don't like being queer?" Greg interjected, his not-too-friendly voice startling everyone. Carl was an old friend and occasional golfing partner, but tonight his attitude rubbed Greg the wrong way. "You gonna ship them off, too?"

"Honey, I don't think that's the point," Christine volunteered nervously. She knew Greg was getting on edge, and she knew why.

"If they don't want to be queer all they have to do is stop," Carl said confidently. "And more power to them if they do."

"Fat chance of that." It was Duane again. "They're so proud of their sex life they want to shove it down our throats, that's what gets me. Ever see them on parade, marching around hollering? They make me sick."

The men concurred. Greg couldn't.

"If you found out that someone you really respected had that problem," he began.

"Then I'd send him to a fine shrink like you!" Duane cut in.

"Oh, goody! More business!" Christine sang out, trying hard to keep the conversation light.

"I'm trying to make a point here," Greg went on testily. "Just suppose a Christian brother had this problem—mind you, he wasn't marching down the street hollering about it, he just had those tendencies. And he really wanted to get over them, but he was having a hard time doing it. What would you say to him?"

"Have you got something to tell us, Greg?" Sherry asked mischievously.

"Very funny. What if I did, Sherry?"

"Greg," Christine observed, "you're getting a little heavy."

"I'm just asking a question, do you mind? What if I did have a problem like that, Carl?"

Carl met his gaze. "If you had a problem like that I'd question whether or not you were ever really a Christian."

Greg stared, openmouthed.

"Why, Greg? What did you expect me to say?"

NINE

*G*reg slept in.

A morning person by nature, he couldn't understand people who stayed in bed past 7:30, even on Saturdays. Normally he would have been up hours ago, but this week had defied everything normal. His sleep had been sparse and irregular, and emotional exhaustion had depleted him. So this morning he slept in.

Christine had been up since 7:00, straightening the house and enjoying breakfast alone.

She needed time off from Greg. Last night had been too intense. Why did he have to get so heavy? Everyone was enjoying the party until he started his sermon on homosexuality. For the first time she could remember, he'd actually been a source of embarrassment. On the way home she told him as much.

"I was just asking an honest question, babe," he'd answered tersely.

"But did you have to ask it like a preacher? You may not know it, Greg, but you were very pompous. People were put off by it."

"I was put off by them. What if Robbie—"

"I don't want to hear any more about Robbie! Greg, you've never brought your work home the way you've been doing it this week!"

"My work's never followed me home the way it has this week."

She couldn't argue with that.

"It's just that I don't want this to hang over us," she said finally. "I'm picking up a little bit of obsessiveness in you, and I don't like it."

He shrugged. She could feel him withdrawing.

"I just want us to be able to relax when we're together with friends and forget about work, okay? Everything doesn't have to be an issue."

"I agree." But his tone was a little too cool. He kept his eyes on the road, and Christine wasn't sure if he was lost in thought or punishing her by not talking. The drive home was silent after that.

Home itself was silent, too. They'd undressed for bed without a word, read separate books in bed without a word, turned out the lights and kissed good night without a word.

She definitely needed a break.

At 9:30 he stirred, checked the clock, jumped up, and headed for the kitchen. "Holy cow, lady! You let me sleep this late?"

Christine looked up from her coffee. "You needed it. So did I."

He scratched his chest and sauntered over to her, kissing her hair lightly. She melted. When Greg was rumpled she couldn't resist him. He never understood it, but when he flopped out of bed in boxer shorts, bleary-eyed and with his usually perfect hair pointing everywhere, she adored him.

"Good morning, my hairy man," she purred. "Want coffee?"

"I'll get it. Anything in the news?"

"Not really. Is it today you're going out to see Alex?"

He poured himself a cup. "Later this afternoon."

"I want to pick some roses for him. Be sure to remind me."

"And remind me to lighten up," he said, putting on a contrite, little-boy face. "I'm sorry I was a stuffy bear last night."

"You're already forgiven, only because you're so cute in the morning. Look at those deltoids!" she exclaimed, stroking his shoulder.

He flexed. "Freshly pumped, the better to boss you around with, my dear."

"I quiver in submission. Get me some more coffee."

It took forty-some minutes to drive from Garden Grove to the Santa Monica Medical Center. He dressed casually for the trip in jeans and a sweatshirt, not even bothering to shave. Once he hit the freeway, he turned the radio to KRTH 101, where music from the sixties was featured twenty-four hours a day. It was his only concession to worldliness. He and Christine were both strict about the movies and television shows they watched, but when the radio played the relatively innocent sounds of the Beach Boys and Elvis, he had few qualms about listening. When they played Motown, he had no qualms at all.

He reached the Santa Monica Boulevard off-ramp looking forward to being with Alex while dreading the thought all the same. Seeing him ill, much less with heart trouble, was frightening.

Parking took an extra five minutes and three dollars. Greg entered the main lobby with Christine's roses in hand, asked for directions to room 305 in the east wing, and wound his way through halls and ramps until he found it.

The first bed was empty. A curtain was drawn, hiding the second bed from view. Greg stood in the doorway a full minute, then stepped in and announced himself by clearing his throat.

Alex Crawford was pale and fragile-looking, but his fiery eyes were sharp as ever as they rested on his protégé.

"Do you have an appointment?" he asked dryly.

"I spent three years traveling through hallways and elevators to get to your stupid classes, and here you are, perched in a place where I have to brave hallways and elevators to get to you again! Try being a little more accessible, would you?"

The doctor smiled wickedly. "You'll work to get a piece of my time, boy, or you'll do without! Get over here."

Greg put his hand out and his teacher clutched it.

"I prepared myself to see you hooked up to machines," Greg noted. "I'm glad it wasn't necessary."

"Nonsense. I'm supposed to be on life-support systems with seven tubes up my nose, but I remembered what a panty-waist you are so I asked the nurse to remove them while you're visiting."

"*Gracias*. Here." He handed him the roses. "Fresh from the Bishop nursery."

"For me?"

"No, for the nurse. See that she gets them, will you?"

Alex placed them on the bedside table, pushed a button to raise his bed up, and pointed to a chair by the window. "Take a seat, Gregory."

Greg positioned the chair so they could face each other. "So what's the verdict?"

"Simple pulmonary failure. I won't confuse you with the medical details. They're still running tests, but I should be out within a couple of days. I'd better be. The bill I'm running up here is astronomical."

"You've got insurance, though, don't you?"

"Some help that is. I'm self-insured."

Greg sympathized. Most private practitioners had to buy their own insurance—often, they could only afford the cheapest plans, which covered a fraction of their medical costs.

"My medical bills," he continued, "will give me another heart attack before I've recovered from this one."

"Have you got enough saved up to cover it?" Greg knew it was an impertinent question, but he asked it anyway. He was concerned.

Alex's face clouded. "Hardly. What I make slips through my fingers. It always has. I'm terrible with money, Greg. It will be the death of me yet."

"What happened, anyway?"

Crawford looked for something to his right. "Hand me the water pitcher, would you?"

Greg did so and offered to pour, but Alex refused. "I need my exercise," he said, pouring half a glass for himself. "What happened? Simple. I've had heart trouble the past couple of years, and I was warned to take more time away from work. That's all it comes down to, you know. I pushed too hard, and it caught up with me."

Greg knew Alex was oversimplifying things, trying to make them sound brighter than they were.

"Tuesday, when I saw what those animals did to my office, it was too much. You know the rest."

Greg nodded and paused. "Alex, I need your help."

"With what?"

"Josh Ferguson sent me a videotape of a report he was working on. I guess it was going to be broadcast sometime soon, but he said he'd destroyed the original tapes and sent me the only copy left."

The effect of that bit of information on Dr. Crawford scared Greg so much that he wished he'd never brought it up.

"What," Crawford asked shakily, "was on it?"

"I haven't seen all of it yet. The first part was a personal message from him to me."

Alex thought it over, his eyebrows deeply furrowed. Then, with some difficulty, he pushed himself up in the bed and sipped from his water glass. "Go on."

"Let me give you some background first. Ferguson called me the night he died."

"Beautiful," the doctor said dully. "He called you but not his own psychologist."

Greg hated himself for telling him that. "But he wasn't calling me for help, believe me! He made that clear. He wouldn't even identify himself!"

Crawford smiled. "It's all right. I understand why he didn't call me. There was nothing more for him to say."

"There wasn't much to say to me, either. He just wanted to make sure I'd be in the next day to get a package he was sending me, and he made me promise to look it over before Robbie came to see me."

"Robbie Carlton." It was a statement, not a question.

"Alex," Greg begged, "tell me what's going on! How much do you know?"

Dr. Crawford sipped more water. Now he seemed more thoughtful than nervous. "I know enough to recognize the makings of an Alfred Hitchcock movie, Greg. You like Hitchcock?"

"Sometimes."

"He was paranoid. Look at his films and you'll see the same theme over and over: Something terrible happens to innocent people minding their own business."

"Is something terrible happening to me?"

The eyes flashed. "Dr. Bishop, if I thought something terrible was happening to you would I sit here guzzling water? No," he sighed, looking out the window, "terrible things are happening, but you needn't be a part of them."

"Josh Ferguson seemed to think otherwise."

Crawford kept his eyes fixed somewhere out the window. "What was his message on the tape?"

"It started with a story about a girlfriend he had when he was a kid. How his father made him break up with her because she was a—Alex! Are you okay?"

Alex had swallowed some water, then choked on it when Greg mentioned the girl. Greg moved toward him but Alex waved him away. "Just tell me the rest," he said when he finished coughing.

"It was a long story," Greg said, settling back into his chair. "But the upshot of it was that this girl was coming back. He called her a monster."

"And?"

"And he said my monster was coming back, too."

Alex, who'd been nodding as though he knew exactly what Greg was talking about so far, was suddenly puzzled. *"Your* monster?"

Greg nodded. "An old friend. Someone I really let down."

"I don't know anything about that."

Greg was anxious to get some answers. "Alex, I've got so many questions to ask you about Ferguson. I'm not asking you to talk about his treatment, but let me tell you how I got mixed up in all this and maybe you can shed some light for me."

"Tell me about the rest of the tape, first."

"I can't," Greg replied sheepishly. "I got so upset watching the first part of it, I turned it off. I haven't looked at it since. Now it's your turn. What do you know about all this?"

Alex considered where to begin. "Josh Ferguson," he finally said, "knew you well, Greg. He researched your background last year, and I don't mind telling you I bragged on you a bit myself."

"I know about his research." Greg laced his fingers behind his neck and leaned back. "He said he'd done a background check on me. It must have been pretty thorough!"

"He was an investigator; of course it was thorough. Watch the rest of the tape carefully. You'll probably see me in it."

"No!"

"That's how Joshua and I met."

Greg unlocked his hands and sat upright. "Doing that report?"

"That's right. He came to me as a reporter, months before he came to me as a patient. He'd heard about my work and wanted to get the more conservative view on the homosexual matter. We did a few interviews at my office."

"For the report? The 'Unforgiven Sins' thing?"

"That's the one. I thought he showed unusual interest in my treatment of homosexual men, so I had already pegged him when he finally asked me if I'd take him on as a patient. I agreed, but forbade any further interviews for his report once we'd established our doctor/patient roles."

That made sense to Greg, but something else didn't. "How did you know he was interested in me?"

"He told me so. He asked if I knew a psychologist named Greg Bishop, which, of course, I did. And he was anxious to know all about you. I gave him your number. That's when he told me he'd already interviewed your old friend who's a gay activist now."

"That's my 'monster,' as he put it."

"Ah. Yes. Well, he planned to interview you as well. At the time, I had no idea what direction this all would take or else I might have warned you. I'm not sure how much good that would have done, though."

"Not much. It looks as if the die was already cast."

"It was." He looked more closely at Greg. "He turned Robbie over to you, didn't he?"

"Yes. He's a client of mine now."

"He's a *patient* of yours now. Won't you ever get comfortable with your role?" He fingered his hospital gown. "I knew he'd wind up referring Robbie to you. I had first crack at him, but I don't like seeing two patients who know each other. Besides, I was planning my retirement by the time he asked, so it was out of the question. He'd been trying to get that boy into therapy for years, but he resisted. You fundamentalist types are much more afraid of mental-health care than we Catholics."

"But why did you suggest me?"

"I didn't, strictly speaking. I only said that, next to me, you were the best. I didn't make the referral. Josh must have had other reasons for choosing you."

Greg swallowed but said nothing.

"Anyway, if the patient has decided to see you, that means he's comfortable with you, so most likely he's suitable for treatment."

"But why did Ferguson send me the tape?"

"I can't say," Alex replied vaguely. "Hmmm. You're going to learn some interesting things from it, I can tell you that much."

"Like what?"

Alex held back. "Tell you what, Greg. Get back to me after you've seen it. Then I'll answer all your questions."

Greg wasn't about to settle for that. "What's wrong with answering them now?"

"Because we'll both be able to make more sense of this once you've seen everything on that report. If he sent you all of it, that is. Once you've seen it, you'll understand."

He wasn't happy with Alex's plan, but he knew the man too well to think he could change his mind. "Fine. I'll tell you as soon as I've seen it. Meanwhile, what about Robbie?"

"What about him?"

"I've never worked with a homosexual before."

Alex nodded. "Ah. So you want to know how to counsel a homosexual."

"I'd prefer to know what in blazes I've gotten myself into, but since you're not going to tell me, then yes. For a consolation prize I'll settle for learning how to counsel a homosexual."

Dr. Crawford laughed dryly. "And I'm to tell you in one hospital visit what it's taken me years to learn?"

"I'll settle for a few pointers. Anything."

"Then we'll do it together. Get Robbie's permission to discuss the case with me."

That sparked Greg's interest. "You'll supervise the case?" It was more than he'd thought to ask for.

"Why not? I've got a vested interest in it too, you know. We'll get started once I'm out of here."

Greg was delighted. "And I'll be calling you Monday as soon as I've seen the whole report."

Alex shook a long, skinny finger at him. "Concentrate on your new patient, now, not on Josh Ferguson."

"I'm concentrating on him already, believe me. I have to make sure I'm giving equal time to my other clients." Greg waited for the inevitable reaction.

"Attorneys have *clients*, psychologists have *patients*, and you have to leave," Crawford said, looking over Greg's shoulder at a nurse who'd suddenly appeared behind him.

"Oh, I'm sorry," Greg said as he noticed her and stood up. "I didn't see you."

She gestured at the bed. "We have to run some more tests, so I'll have to ask you to leave."

"No problem. Alex?"

"Greg." He held out both hands again and Greg took them. "Call and keep me posted, will you?"

"Are you kidding? You'll be hearing a lot from me."

"Then you might get a bill. God bless."

The nurse watched Greg leave, then looked at Dr. Crawford's chart.

"Nice young man, isn't he?" he asked her. "Look here, he brought you some roses..."

Greg drove home with more optimism than he'd had all week. Alex's condition was the main cause of it. There was more to it than he was letting on, but that was typical of Alex. Still, he was in much better shape than Greg expected.

Which was exactly why he'd avoided the two subjects that might have stirred the doctor up. The first was the outing BRAVO had planned for Robbie. Alex was still grieving over Ferguson, so there was no point in letting him wonder if another tragedy was in the making. Funny, now that he thought of it, Alex seemed almost guilt-ridden over Josh. But then again, he'd been the man's psychologist. Losing a client under those circumstances was a terrible blow, and it was, after all, his office where BRAVO had gotten the records from.

The second subject Greg might have brought up under different circumstances was Crawford's public position on homosexuality. Such a conservative, sedate man—Greg had always wondered what inspired him to take on the gays and endure ridicule from the press and his fellow psychologists.

Later, when Alex was on his feet, he'd ask. For now, there were other matters needing his attention.

Like the Smokey Robinson song coming over the oldies station.

TEN

Yelsom got in from The Shaft around 11:30, not too late, which was typical for a Saturday night.

There was a message waiting for him on the answering machine. He returned it immediately.

"What's happening?" he asked into the phone.

"He sent the tape out."

"The tape?"

"The report! He had it all on tape."

"We can get it from the station. I can get someone to break in."

"That's what I'm telling you! The station doesn't have it. He put it all on one video then destroyed the reels. Then he got rid of it."

"Where is it now?"

"He mailed it to a psychologist. We still don't know why, or what he had in mind."

"Who's the psychologist?"

"His name is Gregory Bishop."

"Greg Bishop?"

"From Irvine. He works with a church out there. I have both his office and home phone number."

"You're kidding! You've got to be kidding! I know that guy!"

"How?"

He explained the whole, long story.

"Anyway," he promised, "I'll get right on it. We'll send the girls again. I'll let you know how it goes."

He hung up, astounded at another of life's twists.

Greg Bishop!

He knew Greg had become a shrink of sorts; a religious one, at that. And he knew he was living in Orange County. He'd even planned on paying him a visit soon. But not this soon.

It had to be the same Greg Bishop. A confrontation was inevitable now. Was he ready?

"You've been getting ready for years," he reminded himself.

He undressed for bed, lit a cigarette, and lay smoking with the lights out.

Greg Bishop. We've got so *much catching up to do.*

He started to laugh.

The fall of '69.

His eyes blazed in the dark. He sang quietly.

I can't get no satisfaction...

"What were you driving at yesterday?"

Pastor Mike was puzzled at the question, but that was nothing new. Greg had a habit of throwing verbal curveballs; that's what made him an interesting conversationalist.

"Come again?" he asked, unlocking the door to the conference room. Monday was his day off, but he didn't mind coming in. He'd been anxious to see the video that had caused Greg so much pain.

"That business about 'alternative ministry' in your sermon yesterday. It sounded a little mysterious."

They stepped into the room together. Greg carried the tape. "I was trying to point out the stupidity of telling people what *not* to do unless you also help them do what's right," Mike explained. "Wasn't that clear?"

"Basically, but I got the feeling you were preaching more to the staff than to the congregation. You kept saying 'We in leadership need to show more compassion.' Was that 'we' as in 'we pastors at Berean'?"

"Glad somebody noticed. Got the tape?" He took it from Greg and switched the player on. "I had a conversation with Ruben last week that got me thinking." He tapped the cassette. "And this goes right along with it. Have you ever thought of starting an outreach to gays?"

"They've been reaching me lately without any encouragement," Greg sighed. "No, I don't think we're ready for that."

"My sermon didn't get through to you, either. I'm crushed."

"Nice sermon, rotten timing. I mean, I'm already up to my neck in this mess with Ferguson and Robbie. I'm doing my share, don't you think?"

Mike slid the tape in and rewound it. "I guess so. Let's talk about it more when things settle down, though. I'm feeling pressed about this whole issue."

"You and half the country."

"Oh, by the way. Nancy said a couple of students from Brea Seminary called this morning. They're looking for internships in the counseling center. I told her you're the man to send them to. Do we have any openings?"

Greg did some quick arithmetic. He was currently seeing twenty-nine regular clients—thirty now, counting Robbie. Two other staff counselors each saw about fifteen per week.

"I doubt it. We've got sixty regular clients. I'm full, but Paul and JoAnne could see a few more apiece before they're filled up. I'm not sure we have enough left over for any new counselors."

"Well, they'll be getting in touch. They'll probably give you a call this week. One's already done some work with kids, and I think the other said she's had training in depression and suicide prevention."

"Sounds good. Are we ready?"

Mike started the video, sat on the couch, and patted the cushion next to him. "Show time."

They sat together watching Ferguson's opening segment. This second viewing was less chilling for Greg; Mike was thoroughly taken aback, looking from Ferguson to Greg to Ferguson again throughout the reporter's narration. When it closed with his final admonition to Greg—"But if you can stop our monsters, you'll bless my name for giving you the chance, and I swear from the grave and beyond I'll always love you"—Mike blew out his cheeks. "Whew! That was spooky!" he offered as the screen went blank.

The scene then shifted to a crowd of protesters circling in front of a large cathedral, chanting "Stop the church!" and carrying a variety of signs. Josh Ferguson's voice come on.

"New York City, October 3, 1988, St. Patrick's Cathedral. Members of the AIDS Coalition to Unleash Power, known as ACT UP, demonstrate their anger toward Cardinal John O'Connor for his antihomosexual stand."

Mike pointed at the set. "I remember this."

The interior of the cathedral was shown now, with midday mass in session. Protesters seated throughout the congregation were jumping into the aisles, shouting, and blowing whistles while the terrified congregation froze in their pews, clutching each other. The cardinal sat quietly at the front, gazing sadly.

"Mass was disrupted," Ferguson's voice continued, "and the communion host, which had just been consecrated, was stomped on by one of the demonstrators. While members of his flock looked to him for direction in the midst of the chaos, Cardinal O'Connor encouraged them to pray for the intruders and for AIDS patients everywhere."

"How did we get here?" Ferguson's voice asked as the camera panned the outside of the cathedral, where police were arresting protesters and trying to contain the gathering crowd. "And what events have led to the escalating conflict between organized religion and America's homosexual community? That's the subject of this report, 'Unforgiven Sins.' Stay with us as we explore the effects of gay militancy on American religion."

Nancy buzzed the intercom in Greg's office. It could be heard from the conference room, but the pastor and clinical director were too engrossed in their viewing to pay attention.

Calvin didn't think the materials would arrive so soon, but here they were in Monday's mail. Paul had moved fast for his old friend.

"Gateway Ministries" was engraved on the cover of the three-ringed binder, with "Starting a Ministry" placed a few inches below. The notebook contained three sections: Preliminary Preparation, Organizational Structure, and Suggested Discussion Outlines. A cover letter came in a separate envelope:

Calvin,

So good to hear from you. Even better to know you're interested in getting a work going in your area. Call me if you have any questions.

Regards,
Paul

He flipped open to Preliminary Preparation.

"Ministry to homosexuals is perhaps the least understood and most difficult of all kinds of ministry. For that reason we suggest you spend considerable time in thought and prayer before attempting this work."

No problem—he'd been thinking and praying about it for a long time, probably longer than necessary.

"Be sure you've secured the covering and blessing of your own church leadership as well. Sponsorship by Gateway Ministries requires you to be in an ongoing relationship with your pastor, who will need to send a letter of recommendation to us before we can put you on our referral list."

Calvin gulped. He and his pastor got along, sure, but there were certain things he'd never discussed with him. Personal things that were more than a little relevant to this undertaking. He put the notebook down, grabbed the phone off his end table, dialed the church, and made an appointment to see Pastor Cox Thursday at 11:00.

Hopefully he'd approve of Calvin's plans to start a ministry. He certainly wouldn't approve of his other plans, but they'd already been set in motion last Wednesday, and Calvin had no intention of sharing them with his pastor... or anyone else.

A black-and-white photograph appeared on the screen, showing a handful of men and women. Some were obviously gay, two were transvestites, others appeared to be sympathizers. All were more sedate than those shown at St. Patrick's, mugging for the camera with expressions of quiet triumph.

"Greenwich Village, New York," Ferguson's voice explained, "June 28, 1969, the morning after a watershed event in gay history. Here at the Stonewall Inn, a gay bar, customers the night before had staged an uprising against nine plainclothes officers who were attempting to shut the bar down for operating without a liquor license. As the bartender was being led away in handcuffs, patrons began throwing bottles and bricks at the officers. When police reinforcements arrived, the uprising swelled into a mob scene, with gays inside and outside the bar cursing, resisting, and pelting the officers with any throwable objects they could find. After what they described as decades of harassment, they were, in their own words, 'finally fighting back.'"

"And they haven't stopped since," Mike remarked. Greg said nothing.

A silver-haired man in his early sixties appeared, seated in an apartment living room answering Ferguson's off-camera questions.

"The violence was justifiable?" Ferguson asked.

"Absolutely," the man replied, his voice high and slightly nasal. His posture was mildly effeminate: legs crossed at the knee, head cocked, back erect. His manner was that of a delicate aristocrat. "We'd done nothing to deserve the treatment they'd been so relentlessly dishing out. But it was 1969, you know—hardly a time of gay liberation. You could get arrested just for being in a gay bar, never mind whether or not you were breaking the law. So their harassment of us was business as usual."

"But your response wasn't."

He laughed—a lilting, tinkling sound. "Hardly. The sissies were tired of being sissies, I guess. Seriously, you know, you can only push people so far."

"But why that night?"

"Who knows? Judy Garland died that day, and a lot of us were in mourning; that might have added to the tension. I rather think, though, it was only a matter of time before an eruption like Stonewall would happen."

"Describe the eruption."

"Beautiful anger, that's the best description," he gushed, waving his hands in huge circles. "Chaos, rage, passion, a statement of our defiance!"

"I've never seen a guy do the hula while he's being interviewed," Mike chortled.

"Congratulations on your newly found compassion, Pastor Cain," Greg shot back.

"Ouch."

"Specifically, describe the scene," Ferguson was saying.

"Okay. We were lined up at the back of the bar, ready to leave since the officers had just told us to leave. And suddenly, from behind me, I saw an ashtray fly toward one of them. It barely missed his face. And then we knew, don't ask me how, that now was the time. Without even being told to, we started shouting in unison and throwing ashtrays and glasses every which way. And you should have seen New York City's Finest run for cover! We took control. The rest is history."

"Indeed. But couldn't history have been made some other way?"

The man leaned forward earnestly, his voice deadly grim. "No. There was no other way. If we had gone on being polite boys and girls, do you honestly think society would ever have paid any attention to us?"

"And indeed, society sat up and took notice," Ferguson said. He was shown now standing on a New York street, microphone in hand. "The Stonewall uprising shattered once and forever the image of the mincing, passive homosexual."

A dignified, middle-aged woman came on next, seated behind a desk in what appeared to be a den or a library. Ferguson introduced her.

"Dr. Mary Wilkerson is a professor of Women's Studies at Cornell University, where the history of lesbian and gay activism is included in her curriculum."

"Stonewall," she began, "represents collective anger, a necessary element for social change. No movement exists without it. And the rules, on occasion, have to be rewritten to accommodate this element. After all, unempowered groups, be they blacks, women, or homosexuals, remain at the mercy of the privileged majority so long as they work only within the system. So going outside the system is a mandate for revolution."

"But did Stonewall really accomplish that?"

"No, of course not. No single event accomplishes change, but it certainly did spark a new beginning. Lesbians and gays began committing themselves to exposure. Exposure of themselves and exposure of the ignorance and bigotry that was keeping them— *us*, I should say—in our place."

"She's good," Greg commented.

"Yeah, but can she preach?" Mike asked.

Greg jabbed him with his left elbow.

"So Stonewall," Ferguson said, "sparked this exposure?"

"It did. It unified us. We gradually evolved from a fringe group of outsiders into a unified voice with a purpose. And our purpose became to expose the institutions most responsible for our continued oppression."

"Which were?"

"Well, the church, of course, is the primary offender. But we knew even then that we'd never succeed if we attacked the church directly, although the prejudice against us can be directly traced to church teaching. Still, we knew we'd need the public's sympathy first, so we focused our efforts on the less venerable institution of American psychiatry."

"Why psychiatry?"

"Psychiatry and the church had much in common at the time. Both preached on the 'unnaturalness' of homosexuality, so both were our enemies. But even though people were widely influenced by psychology, they didn't revere it as they did religion. So attacking the American Psychiatric Association was far more acceptable than attacking the church. To do the latter would have made us monsters in America's eyes, whereas doing the former made us into mere social rebels. And, in those days, being a social rebel was somewhat in vogue."

"And what exactly were you trying to achieve by challenging the American Psychiatric Association?"

"We were, by their definition, mentally ill, and America took its cues from the psychiatrists. We could never convince the public we were normal unless we first persuaded psychiatrists to stop calling us abnormal."

"And how did you do that?"

"By whatever means necessary."

The scene changed abruptly.

"'Whatever means necessary,'" Josh said, standing now in front of the New York Center for Psychoanalytic Studies, "became the battle cry for gay activists in the early seventies as they organized demonstrations at the annual convention of the American Psychiatric Association. Dr. Ronald Flessing was a presenter at their 1970 gathering.

"They took over our meeting," the elderly psychiatrist said bitterly. Bearded and weary-looking, he spoke slowly and with effort, obviously not in good health but just as obviously pleased to tell his side of the story. "I was in the middle of my speech on human sexuality when a mob of gay activists crashed into the room and started shouting me down. I asked them to please give me a chance to finish, then they could have their say. But they stomped right up to the podium, grabbed the microphone from my hand, and announced a takeover of the meeting. 'You're going to listen to us now,' they kept saying when we tried to reason with them. But how do you reason with a bunch of storm troopers? Lots of us just left the meeting and went home. But the few who stuck it out had to listen to hours of these people screaming at us and calling us butchers and quacks. Don't let anyone tell me that the American Psychiatric Association voted on its own to declare homosexuality normal. They did it because the homosexuals intimidated them, not because they reached a clinical consensus."

"But not all psychiatrists agree with Dr. Flessing's assessment," Ferguson narrated. "Dr. Elizabeth Fuller gives a different account."

A tall, silver-haired woman addressed the camera.

"Of course the gays got our attention at that meeting, but we were already reconsidering whether or not homosexuals were truly impaired. In my opinion they never were, and it was only a matter of time before the long-held theories about homosexuality would face new scrutiny. I'd known many homosexuals who were perfectly normal in their day-to-day functioning, and several other clinicians had the same experience. So no, the gays didn't force us to change. They simply forced us to listen."

"And listen they did." Ferguson was back in front of the New York Center for Psychoanalytic Training. "In 1973, after three years of protesting, disruptions, and negotiations, the American Psychiatric Association voted to delete homosexuality from its list of disorders, saying, in effect, that it should no longer be considered an abnormality."

"I never knew any of this," Mike commented.

"I hate to admit it, but neither did I," Greg replied.

Dr. Flessing was back.

"Since then, every psychiatrist, psychologist, and social worker has been forced to treat homosexuality as though it was every bit as viable as heterosexuality, or face the wrath of the gays and their allies."

"What do you mean by 'wrath'?" Ferguson asked.

"Let me give you an example. I continued to lecture publicly on sexual perversions like homosexuality, but time and again gays would show up and heckle me. Pretty soon the invitations to speak at universities and conventions dwindled because nobody wanted to make the gays mad by asking me to speak. By the mid-seventies I couldn't speak anywhere in public without getting harassed, so I finally gave up the lecture circuit. That's what they had in mind all along. Not a fair debate or exchange of ideas, just censorship of anybody with views different than theirs. Nowadays we call their philosophy 'political correctness,' but what it's been all along is really fascism. Just ask my friend Alex Crawford. He's been speaking out on this for years now, and he could tell you some horror stories that would curl your hair."

Greg nudged Mike at the mention of Alex. "That's my old friend—the one Ferguson was seeing."

Dr. Crawford was shown at his office, looking twenty years younger than when Greg had last seen him. Ferguson's voice introduced him as a private practitioner in Santa Monica, and the irony of a living Josh Ferguson describing the work of a healthy Alex Crawford was not lost on Greg.

"Dr. Crawford specializes in the treatment of male homosexuality," he explained, "a form of treatment roundly criticized by many in his profession. The men who come to him are, by his description, dissatisfied with their homosexuality and willingly seek to change."

"I began this work in 1988," Crawford began, "when a male patient of mine, a married patient, no less, came to me in crisis over his sexual desires. He was attracted to men, but he didn't want to leave his wife and children, and wanted to know what to do about it. In twenty years of practice this was the first time I'd treated such a case, but I agreed to help him."

"How did you help him? Could you really change his sexual desires?"

Greg could only speculate on how important the answer must have been to the interviewer.

"Certainly. And I could help him cope with homosexual urges when they came up, and give him tools to resist them. It was a good start, at least. But then..."

"What happened?"

"He never completely broke off his relations with men. Now, a psychologist can only do so much. We can encourage a patient to resist certain urges, but a patient has to do the actual resisting."

The last line was spoken rather pointedly, or so it seemed to Greg.

"Was that the best advice you could give? I mean, if he had those feelings, didn't he have the right to pursue them?"

"In my opinion, no. He wanted to stay married, remember, and his wife knew nothing of his problem or his outside contacts. AIDS was in full bloom by then, and I told him, several times, that his behavior was very risky to himself and his wife."

"He didn't agree?"

"He agreed, but refused to do anything about it. We argued the point nearly every session, and got nowhere. So, finally he quit seeing me and took up with another psychologist who encouraged him to accept his homosexuality and indulge in it discreetly. Discreetly, mind you! And you know what happened?"

"What?"

"He contracted the AIDS virus and passed it on to his wife. She'd have never found out if it weren't for a new insurance policy they signed up for which required new applicants to take the AIDS test. Imagine how she felt."

"That's tragic, but what did it have to do with you?"

"Plenty! His wife left him, he developed full-blown AIDS, and he blamed me! He said, and his psychologist agreed, that if I had only told him to accept being gay and divorce his wife, then they'd have split up before he could pass the virus on to her. They both suggested that I should have told him to find a male lover and settle down, to minimize the risk of infection. He slapped a malpractice lawsuit on me."

"He did? Malpractice?"

"Absolutely. It took over a year to settle the case, which he lost, by the way. But in the meantime, I spent thousands of dollars on attorney fees and the case became the talk of the American Psychological Association. I was branded 'homophobic' and 'archaic' by half the profession. Then things really heated up."

"I can't imagine them getting hotter."

"Oh, they did. Because once people found out I was willing to treat homosexuals, the number of patients I saw nearly doubled. You want to know a well-kept secret? Not everyone who's gay wants to be. My practice is living proof."

"Back to things getting hotter."

"Right. Well, all the criticism I took from my peers just made me more outspoken. So I submitted an article to the *Journal of*

California Psychology stating my views on homosexuality and why homosexuals who want to change should be given every encouragement to do so. They ran it, the gay community exploded, and I became the Anita Bryant of the nineties."

Back to a shot of Ferguson, this time sitting at his own desk, holding a set of news clippings. "Dr. Crawford wasn't exaggerating. His subsequent battles with gays are legendary, and—" he held out the clippings—"he's been in the news ever since, widely regarded as one of California's most outspoken opponents of the gay rights movement."

"Was he doing that when you knew him?" Mike asked Greg.

"No. That came later."

Dr. Wilkerson was on again. "But fighting for psychiatric alliance didn't achieve all we thought it would, and our efforts have turned to several other institutions: law, education, the arts, of course. But organized religion still presents our greatest obstacle, and fundamentalist Christians are more committed than ever to frustrating all our advances."

The intercom in Greg's office sounded again, this time noticed by both men. "Should you get that?" Mike asked, his eyes still glued to the set.

"In a minute."

"So, we're again rewriting the rules of common civility and relying instead on the tactics employed by other minority groups."

Another buzz, longer, irritating.

"—is best achieved by infiltrating the religious right, gathering information—"

The buzz stubbornly continued in Greg's office. "All right, all right," he said, getting off the couch.

"—preparing an onslaught to stop them from—"

A knock crashed on the other side of the conference room door just as he reached it, sending Greg back two feet.

"Hello?" a female voice called from the other side. Greg swung the door toward him and faced a slim, studious-looking brunette with a hesitant expression.

"Dr. Bishop or Pastor Cain?"

"Greg Bishop. Can I help you?" He signaled Mike to kill the tape.

"I'm Lisa Simmons. I spoke with your secretary this morning about doing an internship here. She buzzed you a few times just now, but she couldn't get through and she said I might find you here."

Greg felt awkward starting an interview in the doorway. "Did you have an appointment?"

"No, but she told me it would be okay to just drop by."

That wasn't like Nancy. Greg looked at Mike who shrugged back at him. He turned to Lisa.

"Is this a bad time?" she asked.

"No, no, it's okay. Why don't you step in my office over here?" he directed, opening his door for her. "I'll be right in."

"And my friend?" she asked hopefully. "She's in the waiting room."

"Oh." He'd gone blank. "Oh! Right," he recovered, remembering there were two interns looking for a job. "Did Nancy give you an application?"

She handed him the completed form.

"We'll talk one at a time. Just wait inside."

He poked his head back into the conference room. "I'd better see them while they're here. It'll take an hour or so."

"No problem," Mike grunted. "Time for a bathroom break anyway. I'll be back in an hour." He sauntered into the hall.

Greg met the other girl in the waiting room—"I'm Roxanne Hamilton, thanks for seeing us," she said politely. He nodded to her, then went back to his office, where Lisa was waiting on the couch.

He took in her features while reviewing her application form. She was dressed conservatively in a brown wool skirt and white long-sleeved blouse. The skirt fell several inches below her knees—a bit longer than the current style, and it somehow didn't suit her. She seemed uncomfortable with herself, or with him. Greg chalked it up to the nervousness typical of a job applicant.

"Your resumé looks fine," he began. "Can you tell me a little about your experience?"

"I've finished my bachelor's degree in child psychology," she answered, "and was hoping to get in with a Christian organization while I worked on my master's at Brea. I'll need at least thirty hours of supervised work before I can graduate."

"What kind of work have you done so far?"

"I spent a year as a volunteer at the Novak Center in Pasadena. That's a home for abused children. I supervised some of the day activities and ran support groups for the kids and their families."

"That sounds hard. Working with abused kids, I mean."

"I loved it!" she exclaimed. "You know something? Kids like that aren't so different, not really. They have special needs, sure, but they're still just kids. But because they've been mistreated, people don't know how to relate to them. It was easy for me. I just learned to be natural around them and they responded. They trusted me. It was the best job I ever had."

Greg noticed she'd dropped her stiffness. She spoke earnestly about these kids, and he was pretty sure he knew why.

"Why was it so easy for you to relate to them?" It was none of his business but he asked anyway.

Her eyes glazed over. "Well, I just liked them, I guess."

The way she answered said it all. He dropped it.

"Any other experience?"

"No, but I have good references from the Novak Center, and I did work there a year, you know. They said I had a natural gift for doing therapy with children. I made real headway with them."

She was selling herself pretty hard; Greg could see she wanted the job badly. Well, why not? Internships were hard to find.

"Why do you want to work here, Lisa?"

The stiffness returned. She cocked her head to the left as though she was trying to remember her lines.

"Well, you're a Christian counseling center, for one thing. I want to work with Christians. The secular field is so hostile to Christians, you know."

She was more convincing when she talked about abused kids.

"Yes, but why here?"

"You have a reputation," Lisa replied after thinking it over. "You have credibility in Orange County, and to be frank with you, it looks good to have a credible organization on your resumé."

"That's flattering."

"And true."

Now came the part he wouldn't dream of omitting. "Lisa, we have a policy of only hiring Christians who are solidly grounded in a local church fellowship and are living an exemplary lifestyle." He knew the little speech by heart; he should—he carefully wrote it and committed it to memory years earlier. It contained all the right questions: Was the applicant a born-again believer, did she or he have pastoral oversight, would his or her life reflect well on Berean? Since he was responsible for hiring, he needed to know that anyone working for him met the spiritual and behavioral standards of the church.

Lisa seemed prepared to answer.

"Yes, I'm a member of First Baptist in South Pasadena. You can check with Pastor Ray Clements for a personal reference. Would you like his phone number?"

He would. She gave it. Everything looked fine, but he was still uncomfortable with this woman.

"Lisa," he said, standing up to let her know the interview was ending, "your application looks pretty good. Give me two working days to process it, okay?"

She stood up, extending her hand and giving his a firm shake. "Thanks for seeing me, Dr. Bishop," she said crisply. "I hope I'll be working under you. You really do have a good reputation and it's a pleasure to get to meet you." With that she opened the door for herself and strode down the hall.

Greg thought he saw her exchange a meaningful look with her friend Roxanne, who was already out of her seat and headed for his office without an invitation.

Roxanne Hamilton was more outgoing than her predecessor, though not nearly as attractive. She was hefty, to begin with, and square-jawed. But she had a warmth her friend could have used, and it showed in her breezy, talkative style.

"I take it you and Lisa are classmates or friends?" Greg asked while scanning her application.

"Both. We go to the same church in South Pasadena, and we're both enrolled at Brea. I love your office! Did you do it yourself? Very classy. Anyway, yeah, we're classmates. Baptists, too. Is that okay? I know Berean is a charismatic church, but I never really could see all the fuss over denominations, or tongues, or whatever. We both feel the same calling, too, so we've got a lot in common."

"Who?"

"Me and Lisa. But she's into child psychology. Me, I don't have the patience. Is that awful?"

"It's honest."

"But I've done some suicide prevention work at the local crisis center. I worked on their night shift for a couple of years;

it's all there on the resumé. And I'm interested in depression. I think people in counseling are almost always suffering some kind of depression."

"Could be." Greg liked her.

"Depressed people warm up to me. I guess that's because I'm like a great big bounce that just energizes them. At the hot line they called me the Baptist Ethel Merman, if that tells you anything."

"It tells me a lot," he chuckled.

He posed the same questions to her that he'd asked Lisa. Her answers were similar in content but delivered with a good deal less hesitation. By the time the interview was over he was sold on Roxanne and dubious about Lisa. Hiring one without the other, he knew, could get tricky, so he also gave her a two-day time limit on his decision. She took it well.

"Terrific meeting you, Dr. Bishop. Dr. Greg Bishop. You know something, that sounds like a television series. 'Dr. Greg Bishop, Therapist in Action.' Is that your real name?"

He assured her it was and showed her to the waiting room. Lisa wasn't there.

"Your friend said she'd wait in the car," Nancy told Roxanne from her desk. Roxanne thanked her, threw another smile at Greg, and left.

"Pushy, aren't they?" Nancy asked.

"What do you mean?"

"I mean, just walking in here like that without an appointment."

"You didn't tell them they could just drop by?"

"Of course not! And remember when I buzzed you earlier?"

"Yes?"

"When you didn't answer, that one girl—Lisa?—she asked where you were. I told her and she went straight to the conference room. I said I'd buzz you again, but she just stood outside the door for at least ten minutes. I really think she was eavesdropping on you and Pastor Mike!"

"Before she knocked?"

"Right. Then she went back there again while you were interviewing her friend."

"Just now?" Greg's heart began pounding.

"Just now! She walked right into the conference room without even asking me. I was about to follow her in but the phone rang. Then she came strolling out a minute later as if she owned the place and told me to tell her friend she'd be waiting in the car. If she thinks that's the way to—hey, what's up?"

Greg had already bolted to the conference room and slammed his hand into the cassette player. No tape.

He looked on top of the VCR, under the couch, over the shelves of the entertainment center. Nothing.

Pastor Mike returned and framed the doorway. "What do you think? They looked nice."

Greg waved him out of the way and sprinted out of the building in time to see a green Mazda screech out of the parking lot.

_____ ELEVEN _____

After chasing and missing the girls, Greg slammed his fist into the wall of the building in the parking lot, marched back to the office past his frightened receptionist, and into the conference room where he'd left Mike.

The explosion followed.

"How could you leave it out in the open!" Mike shouted.

"It wasn't in the open; it was in the slot. Didn't you think to take it when you went to the bathroom?"

"Why should I? It was your tape!" Mike shot back.

"But it was in here when you left it!"

And so the blame-placing continued until they moved on to more constructive actions, the first of which was to call the police.

Mike called, with Greg standing by for additional details: the information on the applications, the suspects' noticeable physical characteristics, anything said during the interviews that might be useful.

A second explosion was prompted by one of the details the police wanted, a detail Greg hadn't caught.

"You didn't get the license number?"

"It happened too fast."

"Greg, Greg, Greg! That's the first thing _anybody_ would have checked!"

"Oh, what difference does it make now?"

In six years of working together this was the closest they'd come to a bitter argument. Both were disappointed in themselves and each other; both were afraid, but for different reasons. Greg knew that Ferguson's tape, containing personal information, was privileged material. He didn't know Alma Ferguson— not yet, anyway—but he could guess her reaction if the tape was made public, which was likely, considering the tactics of the people who (probably) now had it. He smelled a lawsuit.

Mike was understandably afraid for his congregation. His fear, unspoken at that point, was that Berean Community Church might now be plunged into the sort of controversy any pastor would want to avoid.

Mike made the first conciliatory move.

"I'm sorry." He clapped a hand on Greg's shoulder. "Let's both calm down and go home, okay?"

Greg did, but not calmly. He dumped the whole mess in Christine's lap, bursting into the house and cutting her greeting off by screaming *"This is absolutely unbelievable!"*

When he gave her the details, she had to agree.

Roxanne clinked her beer bottle against Lisa's. "To a brief career in church counseling."

The Mesa Lounge was starting to fill up, as most bars did during happy hour. But they'd managed to find a small table near the dance floor.

"We can kiss Brea good-bye once they call and tell the dean about this," Roxanne sighed.

"Ask me if I care. And ask me if I'll ever wear another skirt like this again!" Lisa snorted. "I don't see how anyone can sit comfortably in these things. Every time that guy asked me a question I wanted to say, 'Would you mind if I just slipped into something more comfortable before we continue? Like a pair of Levis?'"

Roxanne choked on a mouthful of beer. "You're so stereotypical. Me, I like getting dressed up and pretty."

"You can have it."

"Hey, did he lay this on you?" Roxanne did an exaggerated imitation of Greg's deep, serious voice. 'Now, we have to make sure our counselors are living an exemplary Christian lifestyle."

Lisa was lost in giggles. "Yes, yes, I almost blew it!"

"Oh, I loved it. He's a nice guy, I guess. Misguided, but nice."

"Better than Crawford, anyway."

"Bleccch! I'm glad we never actually had to meet him."

Lisa quieted down. "That's probably why Crawford never called Brea. But this guy will call as soon as he sees the tape has been taken. And Pastor Clements will find out."

"It's worth it," her friend assured her. "We were on our way out, anyway."

"But it's sad," Lisa considered, fingering the label on her beer. "It's sad to say good-bye to the church. I know it's not for us, but I've enjoyed some good times there."

Roxanne reached over the table and took her hand. "And we'll have new good times in another church where we'll feel welcome and not ever have to hide again." She squeezed Lisa's hand.

Lisa smiled and squeezed back. "It is worth it. Of course it is. Shouldn't we call Yelsom now?" she asked, changing the subject. She'd felt slightly patronized by him at last Tuesday's meeting. There was an arrogance about him. His confidence in the others— the female others, especially—seemed limited, suggesting a notion that only he could do things right. That irritated her, so the thought of reporting a successful scam was appealing.

"Finish your beer and savor the moment." Roxanne surveyed the bar happily. "I feel like a kid with a secret she has to keep for now. I want to shout out, 'Hey people, guess what?' Oh, well," she shrugged, draining her bottle, "I guess discretion's still the better part of valor."

"I'm gonna call now before it gets too crowded and I can't hear anything over the phone." Lisa slapped a dollar on the table. "Order me another, would you?"

The pay phone was at the far end of the bar, next to a video game where several women were clustered. Lisa recognized a few friends, said hi, then edged over to the phone. After dialing she plugged a finger into her left ear to block the din.

Yelsom answered the first ring.

"We got it."

"Already?"

"Already!" She didn't try to hide her feelings. "It's incredible! We don't have to take the jobs at all. We were in the waiting area and the receptionist said they were listening to a tape in this big room. So I thought I'd see if I could hear what they were listening to, just in case. And I heard it! I waited a few minutes to make sure, but Yelsom, I'm absolutely positive this is the one. So I knocked and got them out of there before they'd have time to take the tape out, and they went for it. The counselor interviewed Roxanne while I just walked in there and got it. Piece of cake!"

"Do they know you took it?"

"I'm sure they do. Or they will the next time they want to look at it."

"You know they'll report it, maybe even to the police."

"A stolen videotape? Let them try—they can't prove anything. I didn't touch anything in the room but the tape."

"But they'll call your school, you know. And your school will take their word."

"We knew that before we agreed to do this, Yelsom. It was our decision."

"Any regrets?"

"None."

"Have you watched it?"

"The tape? No, we just left. Why?"

"I need it now. I'll come get it. Where are you?"

She was disappointed. Both women had hoped to see this video Yelsom was so worried about. "We're at the Mesa. You sure you want to come here? We could drop it off at your place or something."

"No, no! Just stay put, okay? Is it with you?"

"In my purse."

"Keep it. You didn't rewind it, did you?"

She rolled her eyes. "Why would I do that? No. I just took it and ran."

"Sit tight. I'll be right down."

"Bring some extra picture ID. I'm sure you'll be carded."

At first, Christine's reaction was much like Mike's: accusative, blaming, indignant.

Much later, when Mike, Christine, and Greg would consider the facts, they would agree no one was to blame. Greg couldn't have known they were after the tape. Mike couldn't have known they'd go into the conference room uninvited. Nancy couldn't have known why they were eavesdropping. Nobody could have known anything. On that score, finally, all parties would agree.

But for now they fought, with Greg on the defensive and Christine alternately blaming, then relenting.

Christine blamed him for getting them into this mess in the first place, then retracted when he reminded her the mess had gotten into him, not vice versa. Then she accused him of careless-ness, but backed down when he asked if she or anyone else would have known there was anything to be careless about. No, she conceded, the average person wouldn't anticipate the theft.

"Then what are you so mad at me for?"

"I don't know!" she wailed in frustration, clenching her fists. They were in the living room standing face-to-face, much as he and Mike had squared off less than an hour ago. The meat loaf she'd fixed for dinner was drying out on the stove, visible from where she stood. It reminded her again how Josh Ferguson, whom she'd never known but was growing to hate, had injected so much misery into their private life.

"Are you hungry? Dinner has been ready all along."

Greg was tired of it all, too. "Great. Let's just put this on hold and eat."

They didn't, although they both pretended to, picking at food and trying to keep the conversation on things that didn't matter. It was a bleak effort.

"So what's the worst that could happen?" Christine asked over tea, tired of avoiding the subject.

"A lawsuit." Greg admitted the worst right off the bat. "Mrs. Ferguson could go after me for letting out private information about her husband."

"It was coming out anyway."

"That wouldn't have been my responsibility. But this was. And remember, it had a lot of information on Ferguson they might not have had before."

"So you're pretty sure they'll use it?"

"It's too good not to use."

"But how did they know you had it? How'd they even know there was such a tape?"

Greg had been wondering that himself. "Maybe," he ventured, "Josh talked to Alex about it and Alex put it in his notes. That would explain how they knew about the tape, but it doesn't tell us how they knew he'd sent it to me. Unless—" He stroked his chin. "Unless he told someone else he was planning to."

"Suppose she doesn't sue you, or get mad, or whatever. What's the second worst thing that could happen?" Christine was trying to break the situation down into manageable points—a habit she and Greg shared.

"They could use it against me. It's got stuff in there about me too, you know."

"I know, but they're not outing you."

"Still, it's embarrassing."

"Okay, you could be embarrassed. What else?"

"And they could use whatever else is in the tape. I haven't seen it all, you know."

"You know something, Greg? The stuff you've told me about in that report—the interviews and all? It's nothing new. I mean, it's interesting but most people have known about gay rights and protests all along. I don't see what the big mystery is."

"He was building up to something else, though. Something that *was* a big mystery, and now they've got it. That's the problem."

"Well," she sighed, "if they've got it, they've got it. Let them use it. It doesn't have to be our problem. Does it?"

She waited. He took too long to answer.

"No, I guess not," he said, finally. "How 'bout TV?"

"Haven't you watched enough for one day?"

"How 'bout anything that will get our minds off this stuff?"

They weighed options and decided it would be nice to get out to a movie. Christine chose the film.

The few male customers who entered the Mesa Lounge were asked to show two pieces of picture ID before they were allowed inside—a harassment device that usually worked. The Mesa didn't exactly crave men's patronage.

Yelsom eyed the bouncer coldly.

"I've only got a driver's license. Why do you need so much ID?"

"Sorry, that's the policy." She was as tall as he and probably as strong. Mascara or not, he had a typical man's attitude, she told herself. It was her pleasure to have the upper hand. "Two picture IDs or I can't let you in."

The manager interrupted. "Rusty, it's okay. I know him. Hi, Yelsom," she said, taking his arm to guide him past the disappointed bouncer. She shared Rusty's dislike for the man, but Yelsom was known as a fighter for their community, and needlessly offending him could cost her. "Buy you a drink?"

"Thanks, no." He scanned the room, aware of but not acknowledging the women (and there were several) who had put their drinks down to stare at the intruder. "I'm looking for Lisa and Roxanne."

"Table by the dance floor. See?" She pointed them out, then excused herself. "Nice seeing you," she lied.

He strode through the crowd to the women who, finishing off their third round, had yet to see him. As usual, Yelsom didn't bother with a greeting.

"Got it?" he asked to Lisa's back. She jumped a little, turned around, recognized him, and set her face grimly.

"A decent greeting wouldn't hurt. You know, like 'Hello, Lisa and Roxanne, how are you?' and that sort of thing. Is that beneath you?" Downing three beers helped her speak freely.

Other customers had heard, had indeed followed his every move since he'd walked into the bar. He checked himself, swallowing the sarcastic response he was about to hit her with. No time for nonsense.

"Sorry, I wasn't thinking. I'm in a rush."

Lisa and Roxanne exchanged glances, acknowledging a small victory, then Lisa reached into her purse. "Here."

Yelsom stuffed it into his jacket without examining it. He was off on the wrong foot with these two, and he wanted to keep them in BRAVO's ranks. They were pretty sharp.

"You're phenomenal. Both of you," he boomed, changing his perpetual scowl into a very convincing grin of appreciation. "Just phenomenal." He spoke loudly enough for the others to hear which, he knew, Lisa and Roxanne would enjoy. "Thank you very, very much."

With that he found his way out, saluting the bouncer as he did.

The screen flickered to a gray mass. Yelsom contemplated it, too tired to even hit the remote button. This was his fourth viewing. Three times last night, and once again this morning. And since the women hadn't rewound the tape he knew exactly how much Greg Bishop and the pastor had already viewed when they were interrupted.

Greg Bishop!

Yelsom spat the name out viciously. How much of this had he seen? Was it his first viewing that Lisa and Roxanne interrupted, or had he already seen all of it then watched it again with the pastor?

He'd find out.

Even if Greg had seen it all, things could be worse. All America might have seen this tape if Ferguson had his way. Hundreds of thousands of viewers would have clucked their tongues and shaken their heads at the sorry state of affairs things had come to. And everything he and the others—bless them, good brothers and sisters every one of them—everything they'd worked for could have been shot down by one stupid television special. His feelings were not unlike those of other leaders of organizations subject to Josh Ferguson's scrutiny. Free press was all well and good as long as it stayed away from him.

He shut off the set and dialed the phone.

"I've seen it," he said into the receiver. "You don't know how lucky we are."

TWELVE

*T*hose with a fondness for labels would have classified Greg as a Melancholy. He felt things, absorbed and brooded over them, sometimes with an intensity bordering on the morbid. It was his strongest quality, and it helped make him a compassionate, attuned psychologist. Seldom did a client leave his office without feeling heard and consoled. One client accurately described him as "a man who enfolded you in his concern," and his sensitivity gave him a capacity to soothe and understand.

It was also a nagging thorn in his side, compelling him to flights of elation and despondency, according to the whims of circumstance. Poor Christine grew weary, much as she loved her man, of the roller coaster she'd joined in holy wedlock.

Melancholy. Definitely a Melancholy.

So his sleepless night, peppered with nightmares and groanings, was no surprise. Nor was Christine surprised at the groggy, baggy-eyed face that murmured good morning to her after oversleeping. She knew he'd be exhausted and depressed. But it would be nice, she thought as she handed him some coffee in bed, if he would also notice how upset she was over the tape (cursed thing!) and all the craziness leading up to it. He wasn't in this alone, after all.

"You don't have to be in early today. Why not go for your jog?" He was looking at the newspaper without reading it. She wanted to see him perk up a bit, and some exercise might just do it.

"You want to get rid of me," he growled.

"That's right."

"It won't work."

"I want the paper to myself."

"Too bad."

"You have terrible morning breath."

"I'm staying put."

"And love handles."

"I'm outta here."

The park was less than a minute away, and joggers were already circling it. Greg joined them, creaking along at first, then loosening his stride as the blood pumped and the muscles stretched. He was in excellent shape by most standards, especially considering his forty-one years and the sedentary work he did. None of his friends displayed a physique that could match his for muscularity and leanness, and when the shirts came off during volleyball matches between the pastoral staff and the youth ministers, he held his own quite nicely among the twenty-year-olds, thank you.

Love handles my foot, lady. He picked up the pace and determined to go at least four miles.

"Detective Bauers called me at home," Pastor Cain announced as Greg walked in.

Mike didn't look like he had slept well, either. Greg had come to his office as soon as he arrived. With no clients scheduled for the morning, there was plenty of time to talk, and a lot to talk about.

"He said," Mike went on, "that the girls we saw fit the description of two women who went to Alex Crawford's looking for a job last month. They used the same line they used on us, in fact."

Greg scowled. This was more bad news. He pictured his office being vandalized, but decided not to share his thoughts with Mike, who already had enough to worry about.

"How'd they know these women had gone to Alex?"

"When his secretary reported the break-in at his place, they asked her if anyone out of the ordinary had been in the office lately. These two were the only ones she could remember. She took their applications and said she'd forward them to Crawford, but he wasn't interested. She didn't think much of it at the time, I guess. But they pressed her for a description just in case, and it sounds like it was the same two."

"They've already talked to her, then?"

"No, but they've got her statement on file. I'm sure it's the same two, Greg."

"What about the applications? Were they legitimate?"

"Sure. They used their own names. They also used to go to First Baptist out there in Pasadena."

"How do you know?"

"I already called Ray Clements, and he knows them both. When I told him what happened, he didn't sound too surprised. He said he'd been hearing some strange things about these two. Anyway, they haven't been to his church for a few months, and the address and phone numbers they have on file at First Baptist aren't accurate anymore. I guess they both moved."

"How about the addresses on their applications?"

"They may be good, but probably not. After all, would two women planning to steal something give their correct names and addresses to their victim?"

Greg tried to figure out possible leads. "Did they get any fingerprints from Alex's office?"

"Well, there were fingerprints all over the place, but that doesn't mean much. How many people go in there every day? Besides, they're fairly sure that whoever broke in wore gloves because the only prints they found on the file cabinet were Crawford's and his secretary's."

"Have they called Alex yet?" He hoped they hadn't.

"I don't know, but they will, I'm sure. Why?"

"He's just had a heart attack, remember? He doesn't need this."

"You'd better break it to him, then. Better you than the police, right?"

Greg remembered someone else he'd have to break it to. "If you were in my position, would you tell Alma Ferguson about this?"

"I wouldn't have the slightest idea what to do," Mike admitted. "That's why I'm not in your position. But my opinion, for what it's worth, is that you should tell her sometime soon."

"I guess so, but I sure am getting tired of bearing bad news to people."

"Which reminds me," Mike said, checking his calendar, "we've got that board meeting coming up. They need to know about this, too."

"Already?" Greg didn't like the idea. "Are you sure?"

"Greg, we've been robbed. And somebody tried to sign up here under false pretenses. Yes, they have to know."

"About Ferguson? And Robbie? Do they need to know that, too?"

Mike saw the problem. "No, not for now. Maybe not ever. Tell you what. I'll downplay it. I'll tell them about the women and the tape, but not what it was about. Hopefully they won't press me, because if they do I'll have to tell them the rest."

He stood up. "By the way, Greg, have you thought any more about that outreach to gays?"

"I'm considering it."

"I'm reconsidering it."

"I don't blame you."

Greg called Santa Monica General first and was delighted to hear that Alex had been released on Monday.

He dialed his home number, knowing Crawford would be there; whether or not he'd answer the phone was questionable. He was still in recovery and wouldn't welcome calls. If there was still a Mrs. Crawford he could check with her first, ask how the doctor was feeling, and relay messages through her. But Alex's wife had died years before Greg ever met him, and the widower had lived alone ever since.

After three rings he decided there'd be no answer or a machine would come on, so Greg was surprised when Crawford answered two rings later with a weak greeting.

"Good morning."

"Alex?"

"Gregory," Doctor Crawford said, and Greg knew immediately that, for some reason, Alex wasn't a bit glad to hear from him. "How are you, Greg?"

"Doin' all right," he said uncertainly. "Did I call at a bad time?"

"No, no."

Greg didn't believe it, but went on anyway. "So how are you?"

"Resting well, enjoying all the pity I'm getting." His voice picked up. "I didn't know I had so many friends! They like me, you know."

"Really?"

"I've had phone calls from one after another telling me to hurry up and get well. 'Get back in there and fight some more!' That's what they're all telling me, Greg."

Greg laughed without humor. "Alex, do you know what happened yesterday?"

"No." It came out like a question, as in "What now?"

"Two women showed up at my office looking for intern positions. They said they were from Brea. Pastor Mike and I were watching that tape I told you about—the one you were on. Well, one of these girls stole it out of the VCR while I was interviewing her friend."

"What on earth—"

"The police say these same two women might have come to your office last month."

"Ah," Alex responded. "Those two. Celeste told me she felt funny about them."

"So you remember them?"

"No, I never met them. I don't take interns; they're a nuisance. But I do remember Celeste describing them to me as being just a little too sweet."

"That's how they struck me. Alex, I know you're probably tired, but can you tell me as much as you know about this video?"

"Not much, really," he said faintly.

"What *can* you tell me?"

"Oh, I don't know." He paused. "Greg, can this wait?"

He knew he shouldn't have called. Alex was too sick to be going over all this on the phone. "Of course it can. I'm sorry. I shouldn't have bothered you with it. But when we called the police, they made a connection with the report Celeste filed in February. She mentioned the women in it, so I think they'll be calling you, too."

"And you wanted to break it to me gently."

"Something like that."

"Thanks for the consideration, Greg. You're very thoughtful."

It took him by surprise. Alex wasn't given to remarks like that.

"By the way," Alex said, "aren't we going to do some consulting about your Robbie Carlton?"

Greg hadn't thought to bring it up. "Well, sure, whenever you're ready. He's coming in for his second session tomorrow."

"Then let's talk Friday. Can we?"

Greg marked it down. "Friday afternoon I'll call you at home around two. Sound good?"

"I'll be here. I'm not leaving the house for at least another week."

"Oh, so you're not going to Josh's funeral Thursday?"

"I'm not up to it. It wouldn't be discreet, anyway. I wasn't invited and I don't think he ever told his wife he was seeing me."

That struck Greg as being strange indeed.

"I think," Alex continued, "that I'd like to put Joshua Ferguson as far behind me as possible."

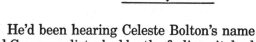

He'd been hearing Celeste Bolton's name too often lately, and Greg was disturbed by the feelings it dredged up. When he spoke with her last week he'd been too engrossed in Ferguson to feel more than a twinge of longing. No big deal—lots of men had occasional thoughts about old flames. But when she came up again—during a conversation with Mike—it went a bit deeper, from a twinge to an ache. Then, talking with Crawford just now, he'd almost stopped his friend mid-conversation to ask a hundred questions about the girl he'd once been so obsessed with.

Obsessed with, that was the key. Not in love with—certainly not in the way he loved Christine. The two were in totally and irreconcilably different categories. But the fact she was in any category at all was alarming.

He had no illusions about the sanctity of marriage. Never had he entertained serious thoughts about another woman; no one else's memory ever challenged his commitment to Christine.

But then, the competition in his memory banks was sparse. Plenty of girls wanted Greg as a teenager, but he wasn't easily won. He'd been infatuated twice in high school, obsessed briefly in college, and in love once and only with Christine. But, he admitted silently after hanging up with Alex, there was something unfinished between Dr. Bishop and Miss Bolton.

Mrs. Bolton, he corrected himself, *or Mrs. Something. Mrs., as in married like you are, jerk.*

He didn't like the conversation he was having with himself at all. He liked the feelings he was having even less.

Is that why he was afraid to call her? Ridiculous. They had business to discuss. She'd seen these women firsthand. Any information she had on them was useful, so didn't the situation warrant a phone call?

No, it doesn't. The police are taking care of it, he assured himself, *and they know better than you how to get the needed information from Celeste. As for these feelings, they're nothing more than the wounded vanity of a guy who got dumped and never dealt with it properly. It isn't the memory of Celeste that's causing the pain. It's the memory of rejection. Nothing to be concerned about.*

Then call her. Prove it. Get the facts, wish her well, and move on. And with that firmly in mind, he dialed.

"Dr. Crawford's office."

"Hello, Celeste? It's Greg Bishop."

"Oh, Greg, things have been crazy around this place. I'm so glad you called. You wouldn't believe how nice it can be to hear a friendly voice." He could tell—she almost sang that last sentence.

"Are things really going badly?" He slipped into his protective role without knowing it.

"Worse than ever. Dr. Alex is back home, did you know that? Anyway, I've had to tell all his patients he won't be working for at least another two weeks, and some of them are just freaking out! I try to refer them to another doctor, but they want him. And the press! Once they found out what happened here they've been hounding me for comments, interviews with Dr. Alex, all that stuff. This job has gotten so weird."

"We're in the same boat. Things have been crazy here, too. That's why I called."

"You're okay, aren't you?" Try as he might, he couldn't help comparing her voice to Christine's. Celeste's was soft and concerned; Christine's had taken on a sharp tone lately.

"I'm okay, but barely. Celeste, remember two women who applied for a job with Alex a while back? The interns?"

"The mannequins? I remember."

"Ha! You noticed that, too?"

"What do you mean? Did you meet them?"

He explained.

"Oh my, Gregory. How creepy."

"Nobody knows who they are. How much do you remember about them?"

"Let's see. They said they wanted to work for a Christian, which seemed strange to me because Dr. Alex doesn't advertise himself as a Christian psychologist. I gave them some employee applications and said I'd get back to them, but Dr. Alex wasn't interested. That's about it."

"Nothing else? You sure?"

"Well, that's all they told me. You want my impression of them?"

"Shoot."

"Mannequins, like I said. Everything they said was kinda stilted, like they were in a play or something. And they kept looking around the office."

"Oh?"

"Yeah, I had to answer the phone while they were filling out the forms when I noticed them looking the place over. I wasn't at all comfortable with them."

"You had the same experience I did," Greg observed.

"What do you think they're up to?"

"I'm not at liberty to say," he replied.

"Oh, you're being mysterious again! Come on, this involves me too! I'm the one who has to sit here and field all the calls. Come on, Gregory. Please?"

He told himself it was okay, drowning out common sense. "They stole a videotape from us. That's all I really know."

"Which tape?"

"Can't say. And I mean it. I really can't say any more."

"Men. You guys drive me crazy. Mitch hardly talks to me anymore, either. He thinks I'm too wrapped up in work, but who wouldn't be when things are this wild?"

"Christine says the same thing to me," he said eagerly. "She expects me to come home and forget what I've been facing all day, but nobody can do that."

"Exactly! And you and I shouldn't be expected to."

"Exactly."

The common bond was tangible to both of them. Worse than that, both of them *knew* it was tangible. Greg coughed.

"Well. Anyway, thanks. I just wanted to check it out with you. By the way, the police might call you. They know about this."

"Figures. Hey, Greg?"

He loved and hated the soft, breathy way she addressed him. "Yeah?"

"When you called last week?"

"Yeah?"

"I shouldn't have said what I did."

"What do you mean?" He knew exactly what she meant.

"When you said you were happy for me being married and I said 'Yeah, I'll bet.' I shouldn't have said that. I hope you didn't mind."

How to respond? Try innocence.

"Oh? Oh, I didn't mind, really. No, it was nothing. No problem at all."

"Hmm. Well, okay."

Blast it, this was getting clumsy! He heard another phone ring on her end.

"I better get that, Greg."

Thanks, Lord.

"Thanks, Lord," he said into the phone.

"What?"

"Uh, thanks. Thanks, Celeste."

"Call me, okay?"

"You bet."

"I mean it." She hung up.

See? No problem, he (nearly) assured himself. *You got what you needed.*

Which was?

Which was information, he answered himself firmly. *She doesn't know any more about the two women than you do. Your curiosity is satisfied. And,* he insisted, *you did the right thing in calling. And she didn't mean anything by that last remark. Don't flatter yourself. She's a Christian, you're a Christian, Mitch is most likely a Christian as well, and so is Christine, so God bless us, every one.*

...And lead us not into temptation.

"And good afternoon. This is Calvin Blanchard on 'Open Heart' coming to you weekdays at three on KLVE Orange County. I'll be here until five o'clock, talking with my guest and taking your calls, so I hope you'll stay with me. My guest today is Brad Chaffee, who most of you know as an expert in financial investment and real estate. His new book is out, and it's called *Sound*

Stewardship in Unsound Times. But before we get to that, let me share some thoughts of my own.

"I've gotten letters about the show I did last week with Pastor Ruben Anderson on gay rights. Now if you heard that show, you'll remember my asking the pastor if we couldn't learn to respect our opponents even as we disagreed with them. Evidently a few of you took issue with that, because it seemed I was defending the gay viewpoint. A couple of you even asked if I wasn't leaning toward the liberal end a bit. So let me clear up my position on the subject.

"I don't lean toward the liberal view on sexual mores. The Bible is clear on the matter, and I'm not about to step an inch outside the Scriptures. I'm also opposed to most of what the gay community wants. I'm outspokenly against, for example, AB101, the gay rights bill we were discussing last week. So rest assured, my position is solidly conservative and biblical.

"But does 'conservative and biblical' also mean 'unreasonable'? Does it mean we have to resort to exaggerations and half-truths to make our points? I don't think so. In fact, I think honest, polite dialogue is in the best conservative tradition. We sometimes forget that.

"Let me give an example from last week's show. Pastor Anderson stated that some gays were deliberately spreading AIDS. Now, it's one thing to say their behavior is immoral; it's something else to say they're deliberately killing people. They're not, believe me. Nobody wants AIDS, and nobody in his right mind, homosexual or not, would deliberately spread it.

"Other Christian speakers have said God hates abortionists, in spite of the Bible's teaching that He loves all people even when He hates what they do. And a few conservatives are suggesting the highest level of public education is run by communists, with no evidence to back their claims. When we make such huge, glaringly inaccurate statements, is it any wonder we've lost credibility with so many people? If we're willing to distort the truth just to win an argument, then we'd better ask ourselves what we're really trying to accomplish.

"To listen to some of us, you'd think our main goal was to defeat all our liberal foes and gain political power for Christians. Now, I'm all for political action, and I'd love to see our values promoted by the government. But that, in and of itself, should never be our primary goal. There are more important things than defeating the gay rights movement, or putting conservatives in office, or putting prayer back in the schools. As good as those things may be, they're secondary to preaching the gospel of Christ. After all, even if we could force people to conform to the Christian ethic, would that save their souls?

"I don't think I'm teetering toward liberalism when I suggest we keep our priorities straight. Let's present the gospel, the grace of God manifest in Christ, first. Then let's also fight for good values and resist the tide of ungodliness that's building up against us. And when we resist, let's do it honestly, fairly, and with an attitude of love and respect.

"That's something to think about."

Three more. Come on.
Six.
Two more. Pull. Don't think about it.
Seven.
Last rep. Do it. Pull harder. Scream. It's supposed to hurt. Scream again.
Eight!
He let his arms drop but held onto the barbell, then eased it onto the floor. He loved everything he felt just then: the shortened breath, bursting heart, flowing sweat, and scorched biceps. Long live the "pump," he mentally declared, God's gift of a natural high to anyone who'll push his body. The rush of blood and adrenaline outdid drugs a hundred to one. Greg was sure of that, though he'd never used drugs. Nothing could compete with the glow pulsing through him; the inner rewards for working out were magnificent.

The mirror on the wall of the gym displayed the outer rewards. He checked his arms in the reflection. They bulged, and veins strained against the skin. He glanced around self-consciously, then struck a quick Schwarzenegger pose. His biceps jumped to attention.

"I love it," he chanted. "I love it, I love it."

Did *she?* He sat on the bench behind him, grabbed his hand towel, and wiped his face. Christine used to comment on his physique regularly. When's the last time he got a compliment out of her? Last week? Maybe.

Oh, great, now we're keeping a compliment quota? Three "you're-a-gorgeous-hunk's" per day or Dr. Bishop's gonna pout?

No, but a little appreciation wouldn't hurt. And some respect for the situation he was in, less complaining about his work, and less wisecracking. That "love handle" business wasn't really funny. Or was it meant to be? He looked around again—anybody watching?—then pulled his shirt up and pinched his midsection.

Well okay, there's a little something there, but nothing more than those guys in the underwear ads have.

Listen to yourself!

He put the towel over his mouth to stifle a giggle. Underwear ads! What next? He ambled over to the preacher's bench for a set of curls. The weights were already loaded; he'd start with sixty pounds.

Christine is the best. You'll never find anyone as stable and dependable.

One.

And who else could put up with your nonsense? Your moods? The long hours you work and this mess you're in right now?

Two.

You've got it made. Thinking about an old flame—a flirty, shallow one, at that, remember?—is crazy when you've got the cream of the crop.

Three.

But what am I, a can of dog food?

Four.

She didn't do so bad, either. I've given her a decent enough life.

Five.

Better than decent. Why do I always put myself down? Because she wants me to?

Six.

She has a way of making me feel stupid. She can even make me feel like a burden sometimes.

Seven.

Is that how she keeps me in my place?

Eight.

Building me up a little more wouldn't hurt. If she did, maybe Celeste wouldn't be a problem.

Nine.

I just admitted she is *a problem.*

Ten. Stop.

Greg felt too dirty to notice the "pump" this time. He'd mentally betrayed Christine and it was devastating to admit it. He leaned his forehead into his palm and thought long and hard.

"Excuse me."

He hadn't noticed the guy standing behind him, waiting for the preacher's bench and looking perturbed. Greg was violating a cardinal rule of the gym: Never lounge on equipment.

"Excuse me," the man repeated, "but are you gonna do anything?"

Greg looked up. "Funny you should ask."

With only one client to see and light administrative work to do, there was enough free time for some long-overdue shopping. He wrapped things up at the office with a few calls and a counseling session, and by 2:00 he was whistling his way out the door.

"Aren't we chipper?" Nancy exclaimed.

"Aren't we, though?"

South Coast Plaza was ten minutes away plus a five-minute nuisance in the parking lot. He approached the task methodically, of course—the only way he could handle a trip to the mall. Christine could browse endlessly here without plan or purpose; he considered shopping the ultimate bore, something to be done as quickly and painlessly as possible. But today was different. He walked toward the buildings thinking it might even be fun.

Nordstrom's was the first stop, where he picked out a simple pair of bright-red earrings and a bracelet to match. Christine's taste wasn't expensive, thank God, but she was picky about colors, so Greg took no chances. Bright red was always safe; when she wore it, it sang.

The lingerie department at Bullocks was next. It usually intimidated him, but he waded into it like a good soldier and within minutes—without the aid of a saleswoman, an achievement to crow about—he nabbed a cream-colored lace nightgown and complimented the clerk on the pretty wrapping job as though he'd never seen gold ribbon. Next he headed to the Hallmark store. "When you care enough to send the very best," the sign on the window commended him. *I do,* he answered, proving it by purchasing a huge card with a poem to match his sentiments.

A salon on the first floor advertised men and women's cuts for $20. *Outrageous,* he thought, accustomed to $8 barber cuts, but he was looking shaggy. It took twenty-seven minutes—he counted the time to figure out what, per hour, these guys made. Then he paid and tipped, the stylist thanked him, and he weighed the chances of getting a refund if Christine didn't notice.

A dozen red roses from a florist finished off the shopping spree, and when he presented them, surprising Christine by getting home before five, she didn't know what to be more astonished at: the roses, the nightgown, the time, or the adolescent passion her husband was showering on her.

_____ THIRTEEN _____

Yelsom had another fifteen minutes to collect his thoughts before his flight touched down in Washington, D.C. Three hours in the air from Los Angeles to Dallas, a ninety-minute layover at the Dallas/Fort Worth Airport, and another three hours to D.C. and he still hadn't decided how to handle the interview with Melanie Stone.

"Relax and enjoy it," her producer had encouraged him over the phone. "Melanie is very supportive of gay rights, so you don't have to worry about hard questions."

As if he would. Yelsom operated outside the realm of worry, so that wasn't the problem. Puzzlement was. How, he wondered over his third Bloody Mary, should he come across? His usual rudeness wouldn't do, fellow BRAVO members had warned. He was going as an ambassador, not a terrorist. But thousands of conservatives and fundamentalists would be watching, and offending them was crucial to his plan. Yet if BRAVO, who saw this interview as a public relations ploy, was also offended by his behavior, he could lose clout with them.

He couldn't afford that.

He'd been leading the Orange County chapter for three months, having begun, with support from the founder of BRAVO himself, as soon as he'd returned to California. The prior leader had resigned under pressure to make way for Yelsom, and it was a bitter retirement that threatened to split the seven-month-old group right down the middle. Some BRAVO members felt New York had no right to send this usurper in to replace their man; others recognized that "their man" was not nearly influential or energetic enough to make BRAVO an effective force in a place as conservative as Orange County. So Yelsom had been welcomed, with reservations. He was just now gaining their confidence; this interview, and the Sacramento ones before it, were aimed toward that end. With the Ferguson funeral coming up Thursday, he needed the full cooperation of his troops.

Which brought up another complication. If Josh Ferguson had mailed the video to Greg Bishop, they probably knew each other. Greg might be at the funeral—an unpleasant thought. He'd keep his distance if he saw Greg; it was too early for them to settle things. Greg would see *him,* naturally. And hear him, too. But he wouldn't recognize him. Yelsom wouldn't allow that. Not yet.

"Ladies and gentlemen, our captain has turned on the 'Fasten Seat Belts' sign in preparation for our landing at Dulles International in Washington, D.C. Please be sure your seat belts are fastened and your seat backs and tray tables are returned to their upright and locked positions."

He leaned forward to do so when the perfect approach to the interview struck him: sinister chivalry. He would be polite, but with a cold edge of menace to keep the viewers on edge.

The flight attendant was moving down the aisle toward him, checking each passenger's seat belt. Yelsom decided to try his new role out on her. Of course, dressed in regular street clothes he wasn't nearly as imposing as he was in his "half-drag" outfit, but a good performer didn't rely on props.

"Sir, you need to buckle up, please."

He stared straight ahead for a moment as though deaf.

"Sir? Your seat belt. Please buckle it up."

Yelsom shifted in her direction, then arranged his face into a devilish glare and looked directly at her.

"Is my seat belt any concern of yours?"

The effect was unnerving.

"Sir," she stammered, then jerked back slightly when he raised his eyebrows and leered. Her composure returned. "Yes, it's my concern," she nodded firmly. "Please fasten your belt or I'll have to call the captain."

He kept his eyes fastened on hers while snapping his seat belt together with a violent flourish.

"Satisfied?"

She moved on, trembling slightly but visibly. *Bravo,* he commended himself. But an audience of one was never enough.

"Do you know how much I've missed you?" Greg murmured. Christine, nestled in his right shoulder, dozed lightly. Had he not wanted to enjoy the moment, he'd be doing the same. Instead he lay awake beside her, amazed to have considered another woman even for a moment.

The flowers brightened their dresser, the card and earrings haphazardly dropped beside them, and the nightgown had been admired, modeled, then discarded. But the feeling inspiring each gift remained and hovered.

She stirred. "What?"

He kissed her nose. "I said, do you know how much I've missed you?"

"I haven't gone anywhere."

"I have."

"Where?"

He shifted onto his right elbow to face her squarely. "Into my own little world, where else?"

"You've been preoccupied, that's all," she yawned, more fully awake now. "Anybody would, all things considered."

"But admit it. I haven't exactly considered you, have I?"

Christine never knew quite how to handle him when he was in his apologetic moods. Humor usually worked. "No, you've been abusive and cold. Buying me a nightgown and bringing me flowers—whoever heard of a man treating his wife that way? And those earrings! Honestly, Greg, how long do you think I'm going to put up with this?"

"Good try. Come on, I'm trying to be contrite."

"And you're trying too hard, so just stop it. Everything's fine." She stroked his hair, hoping to bring him out of his seriousness and back into his romantic mode, which was the one she liked best.

He kissed her hand when it reached his face. "I'm insecure."

"I'm Christine. How do you do?"

"No, I mean really insecure. I'm scared, actually."

She knew that. He wanted reassurance, so she prepared herself to give it and took on a practical tone. "What are you the most scared of?"

He sat up and stretched. "In order of importance? I'm scared of getting wrapped up in a police investigation on Ferguson more than anything else."

"What would happen if you did?"

"Depends. Like I said before, his wife could sue me. It's a long shot, because I'm sure she wants to lay this business to rest as soon as possible. But she could get awfully nasty with a psychologist who allowed vital information about her husband to get into the wrong hands."

"Does the law really hold you responsible for that?"

He shrugged. "Who knows? No," he reconsidered, "it's not likely. I'm supposed to take reasonable care that my client's privacy is protected. I think I'm covered on that base. If I'd left the tape in the waiting room it would be a different story, but the conference room is private. That girl had no business being in there."

"Okay, so what else are you afraid of?"

"Not knowing what it was Josh Ferguson wanted so badly to tell me."

"You'll know that when the tape's recovered."

"Fat chance of that."

"Then you were never meant to know it. That's called sovereignty."

He rolled his eyes.

"Well, doesn't God fit into this equation anywhere?" she demanded.

He conceded the point as inarguable, but reminded her that his reputation was still on the line.

"How do you figure?"

"Ferguson called me just before he killed himself, and I couldn't stop him."

He put up his hand when she started to argue.

"I know, I know, no one else could have stopped him, either. But it doesn't make me look like a hero, does it? People sometimes expect magic out of a psychologist, and I didn't deliver the goods."

"That alone isn't going to hurt your reputation."

"Maybe not that alone, but consider this: Not only did I *not* prevent a suicide, but when the suicide victim sent me an important item, I let that slip away, too. And it slipped away because I wasn't careful enough with two ladies who pulled the wool right over my eyes."

"Alex's office was broken into as well, you know, and they stole vital information from him. Is his reputation on the line, too?"

He hadn't thought of that. "No, I guess not. But he wasn't there when they stole the files. These girls stole something from the next room while I sat there interviewing them!" He didn't realize how bad it all sounded until he heard himself say it. "So. Dr. Bishop fumbles a suicide intervention, falls for a pitch from a couple of burglars, loses a valuable object and—oh, no!"

Christine sat up quickly. "What?"

"No, no, no." He slapped his forehead.

"Greg, *what?*"

"I just realized something. If I had just watched that tape all the way through the first time instead of freaking out like a scared rabbit, none of this would have happened."

"Because?"

"Because I'd have seen the whole thing last Wednesday, then locked it up somewhere. Then, when those women came in yesterday, there'd have been no tape in the conference room to steal."

Christine sighed. "Okay. So? You should have been able to predict the future?"

"I should have known how important that video was, and I should have watched it as soon as it arrived. For that matter," he went on, ignoring Christine's attempts to interject, "I should have recognized Ferguson's voice when he called, I should have tried harder to trace the call, and I should have been more protective of the property he sent me. Connect the dots and you've got a picture of a very sloppy psychologist."

"Okay, you win." She was exasperated. "You probably could have handled it better. You weren't perfect. So what are you going to do about it? Sit there and stew, as usual?"

He didn't know he'd irritated her that much. "Sorry. No, I'm not gonna stew. I'm just saying what it is I'm afraid of."

"And beating yourself up in the process."

"Okay." He grabbed her hand, hoping to change the mood. "I won't beat myself up. You do it. There! And there! And there, oh that was a good one!" he grunted, using her hand to punch himself in the stomach.

Christine pulled it away and crossed her arms. "I'll beat my husband up when I feel like it, and I don't feel like it right now."

"Oh, yes you do, and I'm gonna press charges and they'll make a Movie-of-the-Week about it and you *will* enjoy it!" His fingers found her ribs and dug in mercilessly.

Christine screamed and laughed. "Stop it! Right now! Ahhh!" She rolled onto her stomach, happy to see Greg show some humor and hoping it would last.

"Still," he moaned when he let her go, "it doesn't look good." She should have known better.

"Let's finish it," she said with a sigh. "What else is there to worry about?"

"Robbie."

"Oh, honey! I forgot to tell you. I picked up a couple of his CDs. I thought you'd like to listen to them."

He hadn't even thought of it. "Where's my head these days?"

"You'd have thought of it sooner or later. Anyway, want to listen to them?"

"In a bit. It should be interesting."

"You'll recognize some of these songs, I'm sure. Anyway, you were saying?"

"About Robbie. I don't know how to handle him. Alex is helping me out, but it feels funny taking on a problem I've never tried to solve before."

"He's got a few problems. Which one do you mean?"

"His sexual problem, mostly. How do you make a gay man into a straight man?"

"Maybe you can't."

"Maybe. But do I tell him that? 'Hey, Robbie, I'll give it a shot and we'll see, but if it fails, hey, you can always be a monk or something.' Is that good counseling?"

"You told him you didn't know how much you could help him in that area."

"I know, but it still sounds pretty lame. And what's he gonna do when BRAVO goes public with what they've got on him?"

"That's his decision. You're not there to make it for him."

"I've got a feeling he won't settle for that."

"He'll have to, won't he?"

"You're getting good at this. Now solve another problem."

"Yes?"

"What if I've dragged the whole church into this mess? What if the gays find out I had the tape—"

"They will, of course."

"Of course. Are they going to associate me with Josh Ferguson, or Alex Crawford? Are they going to start picketing us, too?"

"Oh, Gregory, come on. Why would they bother? And if they did, so what? It won't kill us."

"You should have seen them on the tape, barging into that Catholic church in New York. It's an ugly scene."

"Jesus was the center of a few ugly scenes, too. So was St. Paul."

"Babe?"

"Hmmm?"

"I love the company you're putting me in lately. Jerry Falwell, St. Paul, Jesus. My career's just skyrocketing."

"So's my appetite. Are we almost through with this talk? I haven't even started dinner." She looked at the clock.

"Let's fix it together. I've got one more thing I want to talk over with you, since you're on such a good advice-giving roll."

Christine rolled off the bed and pulled on her new nightgown. "I love this." She wrapped a bathrobe around her, then brushed her hair and flicked the bedroom light on. Greg put a pillow over his head.

"Come on, dinner's this way."

He adjusted to the light, found his own robe, and followed her to the kitchen.

She looked in the refrigerator and made a face. "It's too late to defrost anything, and you know what? There's nothing here to fix."

Greg tapped the wall phone. "Pizza!"

She disapproved.

"With mushrooms? Or pineapple? And a thick crust?" he grinned.

She relented. He phoned in the order and was told it would arrive in less than thirty minutes.

"We'll have a salad," Christine announced, pulling lettuce, tomatoes, and onions from the refrigerator. "That'll redeem the dinner a little." She washed lettuce while he chopped onions and cried.

The salad was done in five minutes. "Now," she said, wiping her hands and mixing the dressing in, "what's the last problem we've got to solve tonight?"

"Bennie Hudson."

She put the salad tongs down and wondered what to say.

He had referred to Bennie exactly two times since she'd met him. Once, when he told her the whole story through a wall of tears a week before they were married. And he only told her then because their premarital counselor (everyone married at Berean had to see one three times before Pastor Mike would perform the ceremony) had advised them to confess anything to each other that they still felt guilty about. In that case, the confession had done nothing to alleviate Greg's guilt, but it certainly had given the bride some insight into her groom-to-be.

The second time had been last Tuesday, when he'd phoned from the office in a panic.

"What about Bennie?"

"He's coming back. That's what Josh said, anyway. Remember? He interviewed him in New York, and Bennie mentioned me. That means he still thinks about it. About me, and that night. And he's coming back."

"What's this 'coming back' supposed to mean?"

Greg shook his head. "Back to California? Back to see me? I can't tell. But if he's turned into the kind of guy Ferguson says he has, then he's got some kind of vengeance on his mind. And somehow, I'm supposed to stop him."

"Are you afraid of him?" Christine asked.

"A little, I guess. 'We created monsters.' That's what Ferguson said. Sounds scary to me."

"All right, so he's coming back, and it sounds scary. Do you think he'll get in touch with you when he comes into town, or what?"

"He might be in town already. Josh made it sound that way. What do I say to him, babe? That's the question. What in the world am I going to say?"

"Besides 'I'm sorry,' what else can you say?"

"An explanation. He'll want me to explain why I did it, why they did it. And why I ran away and wouldn't lift a finger to help him. And, honey?"

She waited.

"After twenty-two years, I still don't have an answer."

Christine crossed the kitchen and clamped her arms around him, keeping them there until the doorbell rang.

Dinner was served.

After finishing off most of the pizza, they brought Diet Cokes and a blanket into the living room, sat on the carpet, and put three Robbie Carlton CDs into their player. Christine was careful to place them in chronological order ("You'll want to hear how his music has evolved over the past four years") beginning with his first recording in 1987, simply titled *Robbie Carlton.*

Greg checked the covers of each CD with some amusement. Robbie's producers were smart enough to feature his face on all of them, though each showed him in a different mood and pose. The 1987 debut cover displayed a serious Mr. Carlton, with a black blazer thrown over a white turtleneck, looking into the camera with resolve. The next cover showed Robbie the athlete, about to break the tape at the end of what appeared to be a marathon run. While other runners languished in sweat a few yards behind him, the immaculately groomed singer had nary a drop on his body, which was handsomely clad in running shorts and a tank top. *Finishing the Course* was the album's title, and Robbie was finishing his with every hair in place and every tooth showing. If the look wasn't authentic, it was at least marketable.

Greg was most interested in the third CD. Released in 1990, just one year earlier, its cover featured a thoughtful, tired-looking Robbie, leaning on both elbows over a counter with a pensive expression. *Still a Pilgrim,* it said. Since it was the most recent album, Greg was anxious to hear it. He supposed it would come the closest to reflecting Robbie's current frame of mind.

First, though, the songs of the debut album filled the room. They were beautifully arranged, semi-upbeat pop tunes, suitable for the thirty-something crowd. Greg was thoroughly impressed with his new client's blues stylings and resonant bass-baritone. His voice glided over and around the lyrics, sometimes playful, sometimes mournful. He seemed best suited to fast dance tracks and ballads; in the latter, he was superb. Under different circumstances, Greg thought, he might have become a crooner of the Sinatra variety. But the songs, lovely as they were, didn't entirely suit him. In 1987, Greg concluded, Robbie was still a young artist trying to find his niche.

In checking the credits on the first album, Greg noticed that none of the songs were written by Robbie himself. Ditto for *Finishing the Course,* the second album, which featured more rock-and-roll sounds than the first and was obviously attempting to draw a younger market. Greg did recognize some of these songs and liked them, but he preferred the first album.

On *Still a Pilgrim,* Robbie ventured to record some of his own material. The album featured five of his compositions; one of them was the title track. "You'll love this," Christine said when it came on.

A quiet piano began playing, lonely and soulful, and was met by a cello. Robbie's voice joined them:

> Your burden's polite, you bear it with grace,
> Acceptable stains aren't too hard to erase.
> And respectable pain brings no shame to your face
> Your struggles are well understood.
> You can name them and still be called good.
> I'd name mine if I felt that I could.
>
> But I'm still a pilgrim. We seek the same end,
> Different wounds, same Physician,
> Different trials, same Friend.
> If you saw the pit I've come from—
> Even worse, the sin I run from—
> Would you see I'm still a pilgrim?
> Different load, but still a pilgrim
> Same narrow road, a fellow pilgrim,
> Just like you.
>
> Some burdens are dark, not borne with finesse,
> Not polite, but unpleasant to name and confess
> Not respectable, no, and quite heavy, I guess,
> Just like mine—not the type that you'd know.
> Yours are normal; at least they seem so.
> That won't keep me from going on, though,
>
> 'Cause I'm still a pilgrim. We seek the same end,
> Different wounds, same Physician,
> Different trials, same Friend.
> If you saw the pit I've come from—
> Even worse, the sin I run from—
> Would you see I'm still a pilgrim?
> Different load, but still a pilgrim
> Same narrow road, a fellow pilgrim,
> Just like you.

Greg was overwhelmed. "Play that one again."

They listened to it three more times; by the fourth playing he'd committed most of it to memory.

Robbie had found his niche.

"That song," Christine observed, "says so much. I first heard it a couple months ago and almost cried. It could be written by anyone, you know? Anyone who has problems and is ashamed to say so."

"He came awfully close to tipping his hand when he wrote it, though, don't you think?"

"No, you just think that 'cause you know what he's going through. I don't think anyone else would guess. I didn't when I first heard it."

"Was it a hit?"

"It got some airplay, but it wasn't what you'd call a hit."

"It should have been." Greg looked again at the CD cover. "Remember what Carl said Friday night? 'If you had a problem like that I'd question whether or not you're a Christian.'"

"Maybe we should send him a copy of this. Robbie could autograph it."

"Yeah," Greg said, sarcastically. "'Dear Carl, thanks for nothing. Your questionably-a-Christian friend, Robbie.'"

He asked her to play "Still a Pilgrim" one more time.

"It should have been a hit," he repeated. "A major hit."

FOURTEEN

Yelsom strolled through the glass doors of the Phoenix Park Hotel in Washington, D.C., at 5:25, two-and-a-half hours before he was expected at the Washington Cable News Network studios and three hours before the 9:00 interview was scheduled. Time for dinner, a shower, and a change.

The ritual of checking in revived him considerably after the long flight. Something about being driven to the hotel where a room had been reserved and paid for by someone else—someone who felt he was important enough to have him flown across the country just to speak—put a spring in his step. Now he was approaching the desk as a "guest on the Melanie Stone Show," as someone special.

The reservations clerk knew his name—"Yes, we've been expecting you; was your flight okay?"—and a uniformed young buck swooped up his luggage without being asked. Two complimentary meal tickets for the hotel restaurant were waiting for him in an envelope, courtesy of the Melanie Stone Show, and his specific tastes were now being considered: "Smoking room, correct? What time should we have your cab ready? And would you like a wake-up call?"

It was elegant. More important, it was a place that made him feel *significant*. Significant as he signed his name; significant as he followed the porter into the elevator and up to his room, drawing a generous tip from his wallet; significant as he stepped into Room 621 and took in the furnishings, the decor, and the basket of fruit and cheese with his name on it. His old man, who had daily made him feel lower than dirt, had never been treated like this.

"Because he was never significant," Yelsom hissed once the door was closed.

It was his first television interview. Being asked for a few comments at the state capitol didn't really count; this was the first time he'd been given a chance to speak at length about himself and his cause. He'd settled on an approach and rehearsed his main points. Nothing to do now but enjoy it.

Dinner was next on the agenda. Power's Court, the more formal of the two restaurants housed at the Phoenix Park, offered a daily special in an atmosphere requiring "proper dress." So said the service guide next to the phone, and proper dress, he decided, would be a nice change. He unpacked his light gear to take out a pair of gray slacks and a navy blazer.

Power's Court served a reasonably good lamb and an extraordinary white wine, both of which he consumed in a mere fifteen minutes, then returned to his room. He liked, and could hold, large quantities of food and alcohol without noticeable effect. And he never stopped to think why.

The cab would be there at 7:55, the studio being only three blocks away. By 7:30 he'd shucked his proper attire and positioned himself in front of the makeup mirror. By 7:40, he was watching the news, lounging in his outfit, and killing time.

The desk clerk rang him at 7:54. Show time.

He strode down the hall a different man (some would say less of a man) than the one who'd checked in two hours earlier. This was the fun part. When the elevator doors opened to receive him, he hoped there'd be someone inside to shock, and he wasn't disappointed.

A lone, nervous businessman rode six floors with him, pretending his skin didn't crawl at the sight of his earringed, leather-and-makeup-adorned fellow passenger.

"My cab's ready?" he politely questioned the clerk who had no idea who he was.

"When were you expecting it, sir?"

"When you told me to, my dear. Room 621? Remember?"

"Oh!" She slapped on a frozen smile. "Yes. Your driver is right over there," she said, pointing at the couch next to the lobby doors.

The driver, who wasn't half the actor the desk clerk was, rose and gawked as he approached. "You goin' to CNN studios?" the man asked, and when Yelsom confirmed that he was Melanie Stone's guest, he said, "Figures. She has all kinds on."

He was delighted.

The drive took less than three minutes, and would have been unnecessary in the late spring or summer. But the March breezes were too chill to walk in, so Yelsom was doubly grateful for the lift. He got directions to the studio entrance from the driver, tipped him, kept the receipt for reimbursement, and jogged to the glass doorways where he was met by an efficient-looking production assistant carrying a clipboard.

He recognized her as the woman who'd spotted him in Sacramento and asked him to come on Melanie's show.

"I'm Brittany Carter; we met last week. Let's get out of this wind." With that she whisked him past the security guard, down and around an endless maze of hallways, and finally settled him into a cozy lounge. A tray with coffee, fruit, and biscuits waited for him beside a couch and footstool.

Brittany sat next to him on the couch. "I've been looking forward to this."

"Oh?" Yelsom asked, pouring himself a cup of coffee and offering her one as well.

"No thanks. Yeah, I was at the capitol covering some other business when I left for a lunch break and saw you on the steps being interviewed by OCN. We've been wanting to do a show on gay rights but hadn't located the sort of spokesman we were looking for. I saw you and knew I'd found my man."

"Not too many women say that when they meet me."

She laughed, then surveyed him thoughtfully. "You know, you're much more humorous than you appear. Nicer, too."

"Don't tell. Image counts."

"Your secret's safe."

"Actually," he continued, draining the remains of his cup and filling it again, "I can be nice, funny, threatening, or obscene. I've got attitudes for all occasions."

"And which attitude does this occasion warrant?"

"Wicked, my dear." He raised both hands and curled his fingers into talons, adopting the sinister tone he'd rehearsed on the plane. "Dirty, mean, and wicked." He stared into her eyes as her smile faded. When she looked nervously away, he felt vindicated.

Brittany checked her clipboard. "Tina will do your makeup in a minute," she said while looking the schedule over, then did a double take. "Oh, that should be interesting. Anyway, she'll do whatever she can to make you look good—"

"I'm so relieved." He injected more amiability into his manner. *Save the mean routine for airtime,* he told himself.

"—then she'll take you into the studio to meet Melanie. The first half hour it will just be you and Melanie, then you'll take calls from the viewers. Remember, this airs nationwide, so people should be calling in from across the country. Are you ready for that?"

"No problem."

"Melanie will start by asking you about your organization, a little about yourself, and what your goals are. That should take up the first thirty minutes. Have you done television before?"

"Only the Sacramento interviews."

"Well, remember to keep your answers brief. You'll be surprised how quickly an hour can fly when you're on the air. Ah, here's Tina."

The makeup assistant, a stout, no-nonsense-looking Hispanic woman in her mid-forties, stepped in from the hall behind Yelsom. "We're ready when you are," she told Brittany.

"Tina, this is Yelsom."

He stood up to face her. She put her hands on her hips and looked him over as though he were a messy room she was assigned to clean.

"We doin' a Spielberg movie or somethin'?"

"Just dab some powder on to keep his face from shining, then bring him over to Studio C."

Yelsom bowed slightly. "Once you get to know me, Tina, I'm sure we'll be friends."

"Now I have somethin' to live for. This way, gorgeous."

Studio C was cavernous, dark, and cold. Footsteps and voices echoed from every direction as sound engineers and cameramen exchanged signals and instructions. The walls, painted dark gray, were invisible in the dimness, giving the overall feeling of being outdoors on a starless night.

In the middle of the studio sat an executive chair behind a desk with two high-backed chairs facing it, a large potted palm, and a backdrop mural showing the Washington, D.C. skyline with "The Melanie Stone Show" displayed at the top. Three cameras and a teleprompter hovered around the desk.

The air buzzed with prebroadcast excitement. Yelsom had never felt it before, but it seemed natural and familiar to him, somehow.

The sound of high heels tapping on the concrete floor and echoing throughout the studio announced the hostess. The cameramen and crew turned in the direction of the sound, as did Yelsom.

Melanie Stone entered the set and headed straight toward him, ignoring two crewmen who tried to get her attention for a last-minute question. She was shorter than he expected, but her bearing was confident and alert.

She shook his hand briskly. "I'm Melanie. I hope your trip was comfortable."

"Very nice," he answered, taking in and admiring her appearance. A smart-looking woman in her late thirties, she wore a gray suit and black jewelry and was, as befitted the CNN image, immaculately groomed and very attractive. He was impressed, which was unusual.

"Did Brittany go over the format with you?"

"Basically."

"Step over here, would you?" She took his arm and walked him over to the chairs on the set, then gestured for him to sit down.

A young man appeared out of nowhere and clipped a lapel microphone onto his jacket.

Melanie remained standing. "I want you to know we don't allow any gay-bashing on this program," she stated in a low voice, "and I think what you're doing has merit. But I'll need to ask questions—"

Another man put a clipboard in front of Yelsom's face, asking him to sign a form in triplicate releasing CNN and Melanie Stone to use the content of the show in any way they chose.

"Questions," she continued evenly, "our viewers themselves would ask if they were here. So, if anything I ask sounds critical, please don't take it personally."

"Got it."

"We'll screen the calls. If anyone gets nasty, they'll be cut off, don't worry."

"I appreciate that."

"Just be yourself," she smiled. "That's why we asked you on. I want people to understand what the civil rights battle for gays is all about."

Her use of the term "civil rights" in reference to him and, by extension, BRAVO, surprised Yelsom.

Melanie winked. "So relax and let's try to enjoy this." With that she turned to the crewmembers who'd been standing behind her throughout the entire conversation, politely waiting for her attention.

"Two minutes," Brittany called out from across the room. Yelsom's pulse quickened.

Someone asked if he needed a glass of water. He did.

He shut both eyes and focused inward. A minute passed before he opened them again—in his new role. The change was, at first, perceptible only to Yelsom.

A glass of water was placed on the desk in front of him. Melanie sat on the other side of it and adjusted her microphone and smiled at him.

"Five, four, three, two—"

Upbeat music filled the room, a prerecorded voice announced Melanie Stone Live, she faced the teleprompter and began.

"Good evening. I'm Melanie Stone. Thank you for joining us."

Yelsom followed the teleprompter as she read from it.

"The long-overdue debate on homosexuality is engaging all factions of American culture, challenging and redefining our notions of what is normal, what is moral, and what is tolerable. Tonight we'll look at one aspect of the debate, the question of civil rights. Should homosexuality be afforded the same civil protection as race and gender, and, if so, how should that protection be secured? Some say gays are already too aggressive; others, including my guest tonight, say they need to fight harder. We'll welcome your thoughts on the matter when we open the phone lines, but first let me welcome our guest. His name is," she paused, "Yelsom. That's the name you go by, just Yelsom? Nothing else?"

"Yelsom will do," he said coldly; she noticed the change, faltered, then recovered.

"Why don't you use your real name?"

"When I moved to New York I left that name in California. I left that person there, too."

"But don't you live in California now?"

"Temporarily. To take care of some unfinished business. And to fight for Assembly Bill 101."

"The bill that would prohibit discrimination based on sexual orientation, correct?"

"Correct."

"We'll get to that in a moment, but first let's talk about you, and your organization. What exactly does the name 'Yelsom' imply?"

"That I'm noisy." He smiled sarcastically. "Or so my parents said."

"Ah." She had adjusted her tone, from businesslike to sympathetic, until the two of them were complementary—he, the infuriated activist; she, the concerned listener.

"And you represent"—she checked her notes—"BRAVO, which is an activist organization located—"

"A *terrorist* organization," he cut in.

She was mildly irritated, obviously wanting to put a good face on gay rights and just as obviously aware that Yelsom's attitude wasn't helping.

"*Terrorist?* Isn't that a bit strong?"

"The key word today is *terrorism*," he lectured. "Lesbians and gays have finally learned that they're going to be hated no matter what. So we may as well take the gloves off and fight for ourselves, because nobody's going to fight for us."

"All right, then. Tell us about BRAVO. It's a national group?"

"Our headquarters are in New York City; that's where we take most of our directions from. But we've got chapters across the country."

"And the name BRAVO means—what?"

"Bent on Removing All Vestiges of Oppression, and our prime target is the church."

"How does that tie in with Assembly Bill 101 in California?"

"The main opposition to civil rights for gays comes from the church. They're the ones who'll fight the hardest against AB101, so we have to weaken them now, before they pressure Governor Wilson into vetoing this bill."

"Aren't other gay groups doing the same thing?"

"Not really. Most of them fight for increased AIDS research, or against defamation. Of course, they fight the church as well, but that's not their main focus. Gays needed a group that would spend its energies combating the damage fundamentalists are doing to our cause."

"That's where BRAVO comes in?"

"Right. BRAVO was founded three years ago by a wealthy gay man who'd lost his lover to AIDS. Now, this man's lover was from a so-called Christian home, and hadn't spoken to his parents for years. But when he died, his family barged in and took over the funeral arrangements."

"Was that legal?"

He sneered at her. "They were the *natural* family. Their legal rights superseded his. This poor man had no say whatever in his own lover's funeral!"

"Terrible."

"It gets worse. They didn't invite him to the service, though he came anyway. And when he did, he had to sit and listen to a preacher explain that the wages of sin was death, and this man, his lover, had paid the ultimate wage for his sins. He stood up and screamed, 'My lover was no more a sinner than the rest of you!' They, of course, ejected him from the funeral."

"Are stories like that common?"

"Too common. That," Yelsom stressed, "is why we're so mad. And that's why BRAVO was formed."

"Out of anger toward Christians?"

"Bent on Removing All Vestiges of Oppression, remember? And the last vestiges of oppression come from the church. Therefore," he paused, "the church needs to be removed."

Melanie's mouth fell open.

"Come again?"

"You heard me." His eyes twinkled.

"I'm sure you're not suggesting—"

"Well," he said coyly, "let's just say the church's *influence* needs to be removed."

"Why?"

"Every other organization is open to new discoveries and to change. Law, medicine, psychiatry, education—you can reason with leaders in those fields. But the church, by and large, holds to ancient dogma straight out of the Dark Ages. They can't be reasoned with, so they have to be stopped. That's our motto, by the way—expose the church, scare the church, stop the church."

"And how do you propose to do that?"

"Expose them, first of all. We expose their bigotry and, whenever possible, we expose the closet cases among them."

"In case our listeners don't know, by 'closet case' you mean a homosexual who pretends to be a heterosexual?"

"Exactly. We help people like that to stop pretending."

"Now, that," Melanie interjected, "is the most controversial aspect of your group, isn't it?"

"And the most effective. If we can expose gays who are hiding in the church, then we can discredit the church. How, after all, can they go on preaching against something so many are guilty of doing themselves?"

"Your motto also says *scare* and *stop* the church. How is that done?"

"By guerrilla tactics, intimidation, protesting in front of their churches, disrupting their church services, you name it. We want them to know that when they preach against us, they'll have the devil to pay. Literally."

"Is that really an effective way of winning people over?"

That was Yelsom's cue to get nasty.

"If you're asking me to apologize, Melanie, you can forget it!" he lashed out. "If the church wants to go on preaching hatred against us, it can accept the consequences. The blacks weren't always nice during the sixties, were they? A war is a war."

She was stung by the remark and the attitude behind it. "And with that," she replied, "we'll take a break and return for your phone calls."

The music played while she unclipped her microphone. "You might consider toning it down a bit, Yelsom," she advised. "You sound like you're trying to be offensive."

He received it as a compliment.

Greg and Christine were none too happy to hear the phone ring.

"Are we here?" she asked.

Greg rubbed his eyes. "I'm not." They'd been dozing on the living room carpet listening to music. "Let the machine get it."

Even as he spoke, Pastor Mike's voice called him from the machine in the bedroom.

"Greg, are you there? It's Mike. Pick up."

Christine was exasperated. "No church business tonight!" she yelled at Greg when he leaped up to catch the phone.

"Greg, if you're not there, I wanted to tell you there's something on CNN you should see. Maybe I'll tape it—"

"Hey, Mike," Greg cut in. "What's up?"

"A guy from that BRAVO group is on Melanie Stone's show. You need to see this."

Greg looked over his shoulder at Christine in the living room, reclined on the floor and waiting. She wouldn't be thrilled.

"Okay, I'll check it out."

"It's back on now. Gotta go. I'll see you tomorrow."

Greg walked back into the room. "Honey, we really need to watch this." He explained; she refused.

"But you go ahead," she offered. "I want to keep my mind off this stuff for a while."

"Are you mad?"

"Sorta." She got up. "But I know you should watch it. Go ahead. I'm just not up to it."

She went into the bedroom with a book and closed the door. Greg switched the television on.

The first call came from Minneapolis.

"I'm a lesbian, and to tell you the truth, sir, I think your methods are all wrong."

"Then you're irrelevant, my dear." Arrogance was one of Yelsom's favorite approaches. "And you should be ashamed."

"You're the one who should be ashamed, sir, because people listening to you right now are thinking that all gays and lesbians are as hateful and dangerous as you are, and that just stirs up more prejudice against all of us."

"Are you saying," Melanie asked the caller, "that not all of you in the gay community agree with my guest? Or with BRAVO?"

"Absolutely not! I think what these groups are doing is actually setting the gay rights movement back. I wouldn't dream of disrupting someone else's church service just because they didn't agree with me."

"Then sit there and be Little Miss Passive," Yelsom mocked, "while the rest of us fight your battle for you."

"Thank you for the call," Melanie said. "Let's go to Bob in Atlanta. Hello, Bob, you're on the air."

"Melanie? Hi. I just want to tell your guest I think he's awesome, I'm proud to be gay and proud of him and his group, and I want to know if they plan on opening a chapter in Atlanta."

"Contact our offices in New York, Bob." Yelsom gave out the number. "And maybe you're the one who'll need to start it. Okay?"

"Let's go to Martha in Chicago. Hello, Martha," Melanie said. "You're on the air."

"I have something to say to your guest."

"Go ahead, please."

"How dare you," the caller demanded, "compare the black struggle to what you're doing!"

"I assume you're African-American?" Melanie asked politely.

"I am, and I want to know how on earth you can compare homosexuals to blacks?"

"Gay, straight, black, white," Yelsom chanted. "Same struggle, same fight."

"It isn't the same and you know it! You people weren't brought over here in chains, you weren't bought and sold, you've always had the vote—"

"We've been in invisible chains of ignorance that are just as strong as the ones your people were kept in!" Yelsom said forcefully.

"My forefathers would have gladly exchanged their visible chains for the invisible ones you're complaining about, fool!" the woman retorted. The anger in her voice was equal to that in Yelsom's. "Homosexuals haven't fought poverty like we have—"

"Now she brings up a good point, Yelsom," Melanie interrupted again. "Studies have shown the gay community averages a higher yearly income than the heterosexual community at large."

"That's right!" the woman went on. "And besides all that, we were born black! We're a race, not a lifestyle. How *dare* you use us to advance yourselves!"

"Nobody's using you, ma'am. But prejudice is prejudice, any way you look at it," Yelsom said, "and you should be grateful that gays are fighting to end bigotry of all kinds."

"Well, I think you need a history lesson on what black people really went through and are still going through, because I take it as a slap in the face when you compare yourselves to us. That's all I have to say."

"Thank you for the call. Now let's go to California, to a caller who doesn't want to be identified. Hello, you're on the air."

"It won't work, Yelsom."

The man's voice was confident and low.

Yelsom froze. "Pardon?"

"I said, it won't work."

"What won't work, sir?" Melanie tried to hurry the call along.

"Your plan. I should know."

"Because?" Yelsom asked.

"Because I'm one of your intended victims."

That voice is familiar, Greg thought. He'd heard it before, somewhere...somewhere recently...and then he had it.

"Honey!" Greg yelled. "Come quick! Now! Hurry!"

Melanie looked puzzled. Yelsom, wondering what approach to take, said nothing.

"Do you think telling everyone I'm a homosexual will make homosexuality normal?" the caller asked softly.

"It will help," Yelsom replied. "The more people see how many of us there are, the less likely they'll be to think we're abnormal."

"Ah," the man considered. "And how many people cheat on their wives?"

Yelsom missed the question; his mind was racing. *California. Intended victim.* It clicked. *Robbie Carlton. Stick to the plan,* he thought. *We gave the guy a deadline; I won't out him before then.*

"Do you want to take that question?" Melanie asked Yelsom.

"Huh? Sorry, what was the question?"

"How many people," the man repeated, "cheat on their wives?"

"Not having a wife, thank God, I wouldn't know." Yelsom's sarcasm had returned.

"You could find out. Then you could expose of all them, too. Would that make adultery normal?"

"I've no idea," Yelsom answered. "What's your point?"

"Some of us get angry, too. We hit people sometimes. If you

bring all the 'hitters' out of the closet, will that make violence normal, too?"

"Sir," Melanie said, "you do need to get to the point."

"I'm not proud of being gay, that's the point. I don't even call myself *gay;* I think that's a stupid word for homosexuality. I don't find it to be *gay* at all. So, you might force me to admit I'm homosexual, but there's one thing you'll never do."

Yelsom liked this man's spunk. If he was going to have enemies, he preferred they be the kind to give him a good fight. "What, pray tell, is that?"

"You'll never force me to call it *gay.* And you'll never force me to call it *good.*"

"And you say you're one of BRAVO's intended victims?" Melanie asked.

"Yes, ma'am. One who's going to fight back."

A challenge. Yelsom loved it.

"Well," he smiled, "I look forward to it." He pointed at the camera and winked. "Until then."

Christine liked it. Greg didn't.

"But honey," she said, "what Robbie said was wonderful! Aren't you proud of the way he stood up to that guy?" She pointed at the television; the show was over and the credits were rolling while Yelsom and Melanie sat talking on the set.

"I don't want him standing up to anybody!" Greg fumed. "Not yet, anyway. His career's still on the line, you know. What if somebody recognized his voice?"

"That's doubtful. Anyway, it was his choice—"

"He's got enough to worry about without taking chances. He needs time to think it over before he exposes himself. What he did just now was impulsive."

"Brave."

"Impulsive. Typical musician; emotion before rational process."

Christine hooted.

"Well," he admitted finally, "Robbie *did* sound pretty sure of himself. And he made some good points. I'm anxious to hear what he'll have to say tomorrow."

"Tomorrow?"

"Tomorrow is his first real counseling session."

"Are you ready?"

He watched the screen going black. Yelsom's white hair was the last part of the picture to fade.

"Nope."

FIFTEEN

And Samuel said unto the people, Fear not: ye have done all this wickedness: yet turn not aside from following the LORD."

It was Christine's turn to read, and Greg's to sip coffee while listening. The sleep hadn't left her voice; he still glowed from his morning jog.

They were almost batting a thousand, missing only two days of devotions since they'd recommitted to daily Bible reading and prayer. They congratulated themselves on that—"almost one whole week of faithfulness!"—then lamented their age and zeal, which were increasing and decreasing, respectively.

"And turn ye not aside: for then should ye go after vain things which cannot profit nor deliver..."

Their intention six years ago had been to make it a 365-day-per-year routine; their record so far hovered around three-and-a-half months.

"We read the Bible the way some people diet," Greg commented in the middle of her sentence. "A few chapters this week, none next week."

"At least we're reading it," Christine shushed him. "For the LORD will not forsake his people for his great name's sake..."

After they were done, Greg jumped off the bed and showered while she scrambled eggs. He heard the phone ring just as he was drying off.

Christine appeared in the doorway, her face white.

"A man's on the phone for you. He won't say who. His voice is weird. I think it's him."

He was at the bedroom phone before she'd finished.

"Dr. Bishop speaking."

"Seen any good movies lately?"

The voice was breathy, carried a now-familiar Bronx accent, and, yes, it was weird.

"Not lately." He tried to sound unruffled. Christine stood in front of him with a hand to her mouth. "Why?"

"That's not what *I* heard, Dr. Bishop. *Dr.* Greg Bishop! Who'd have thought it?"

"Can I ask who this is?"

"Don't you remember?"

Water and sweat were both dripping off him. Christine brought him another towel and listened. "I think," he said carefully, "I might have seen you on television last night."

"We met before that."

"I think so," Greg agreed; he'd wait for the caller to identify himself. Other than that, he had no strategy in mind. "Are you calling about the tape?"

"Don't you remember?" the man asked again. "Don't you remember me from the tape?"

"I don't, ah, think so." He didn't recall anyone with a Bronx accent on the tape. And if this was who he thought it was, he certainly would have remembered seeing him.

"I was the guy at the end."

"The end? I didn't see the end."

"Pity," the caller said with interest. "How much *did* you get to see?"

Greg had no time to think of any tactic but honesty. "Not much. I was interrupted when that professor was explaining the goals of the gay community or something like that."

"Interrupted. Too bad."

"By a friend of yours, perhaps?"

"I won't tell. *I'd* never betray a friend."

"Well, since I missed the best part of the movie, how about telling me how it ended? Educate me."

"You just educated *me*, Greg. Thanks."

But the man didn't hang up. Greg and Christine held their breath; he decided to ask.

"Bennie," he whispered. "Bennie, is it you?"

Silence. Then soft laughter. Then the dial tone.

Greg took Christine by her shoulders. "Sit down here," he commanded, practically shoving her onto the bed. "Don't move."

He stormed through every room of the house, wrapped in his towel, and slammed windows, double-checked the locks on the front and back doors, and fumed at the hole in the backyard gate he'd been meaning to fix.

He stomped back into the living room with his head down. Christine met him and he screamed when he bumped into her with a wild look that scared her more than the phone call.

"I said don't move!"

Christine recoiled.

He covered his eyes for a moment, envisioning the white-haired figure he saw last night extolling the virtues of terrorism to Melanie Stone.

The thought sobered him. He uncovered his face and held Christine. "I'm sorry. I'm panicking."

She took charge; somebody had to stay calm.

"So, what do we do now?" she asked.

He quieted himself. "Let's start with security systems."

Within ten minutes, he'd gotten the names of the nearest home security dealers from directory assistance. None were open yet; he tried them all, then kept the numbers to use again when he got to the office after 9:00.

"We should have gotten one installed years ago."

He wondered out loud if they'd been wise not to purchase a gun.

"Gregory," Christine sighed, "we don't need one." She was forcefully opposed to guns in the house; they'd argued over it for years and, so far, she'd won.

"Will you still say that if he comes knocking at the door while I'm gone?"

The idea was terrifying, but she warded it off with a wisecrack.

"If he shows up here, I'll give him some make-over tips."

He ignored or didn't hear her, and a bit of the wildness returned. "You won't answer the phone," he ordered. "Let the machine get it, and be sure to record any message he leaves. Don't answer the door. What are you doing today? Anybody comes around you dial 911. If it turns out to be a false alarm, who cares? Are you working? I don't think I should go in. I'll call Mike. I'm staying home today."

She put her hand over his mouth to stop him.

"I'm shopping today, then finishing up the brochures for Servico. I'll be here when you get home."

He mumbled; she held her hand in place.

"I never answer the phone anyway, you know that. I always let the machine get it. Nobody's coming over, but if they do, *they'll* need 911, not me, because I'm not in the mood for company."

She took her hand down. He started to speak; she put it to his mouth again.

"You, meanwhile, will call the police. Now. Talk to the same detective or sergeant you spoke with before. Explain everything. Then go. I'm busy, you're late for work, and we've got a house payment to make. We can't afford your hysteria."

He muttered indignantly under her hand.

"Yes, dear," she replied. "Hysteria. Yours."

It was 10:25 A.M., D.C. time. Yelsom's plane didn't leave until 12:03. He dialed long distance, anxious to pass on the good news.

"We can relax. Greg Bishop hasn't seen the tape."

"You're sure?"

"He told me so. I'm sure it was true; he sounded too scared to be pulling anything over on me."

"Did you identify yourself?"

"Not yet. But soon. Anyway, just wanted you to know we're in the clear."

"That *is* good news. By the way, you looked terrific last night."

"You liked it?"

"Loved it."

He hung up and cracked his knuckles, feeling frisky.

And I try, and I try.

He sprang joyously in front of the dresser mirror.

And I try.

Room 621 was twice the size of his apartment. More dancing space.

And I try!

The crowd in his mind was bigger than ever, their roar deafening.

I can't get no!

No, no, no!

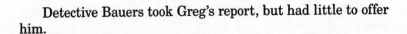

Detective Bauers took Greg's report, but had little to offer him.

"Look, getting a phone call from this guy doesn't mean much unless he threatened you or your wife."

"He didn't," Greg said dourly into the phone.

"Is your phone number listed?"

"Yes."

"So you're not even sure who it was."

"I'm sure, but I can't prove it, if that's what you mean."

"And the name of the man you *think* called you is Bennie Hudson, and the last time you saw him was in 1969, correct?"

"Correct."

"In Long Beach?"

"That's right."

"I've got it down. We'll contact you if anything turns up. Meanwhile, let us know if he calls again."

"Thanks. Good-bye."

Greg could practically see the man filing the report in the very-minor-things-to-get-to-when-I-can stack.

Well, why not? A stolen videotape didn't qualify as anything beyond petty theft, even if it was connected to the break-in at Dr. Crawford's office. The two crimes combined weren't earth-shattering.

Unless you were Greg Bishop.

He dialed the first home security company on his list and started pricing systems.

Thirty minutes later, he forced himself to attend to the administrative work Wednesday mornings were reserved for: case notes, MMPI scores, supervision reports on his two interns, and transcripts for court cases.

He went through the motions efficiently. Every half hour he called Christine.

Noontime crept up on him and he buzzed Mike to see if he was available for lunch.

"If we can take separate cars, sure. I'm going home early today. Meet me at the counter of Coco's at 12:30, Greg; we'll never get a table there in the middle of the lunch rush."

Greg was there at 12:20 and found two seats at the counter.

Conversations around him seemed to stop when he was seated. Or did they? He looked to both sides of the counter. Some of the patrons looked back at him blankly.

So what? People look at each other all the time. Calm yourself; you're not important enough for anyone to plot against.

"Oh, yes I am," he mumbled as he scanned the menu. "To some people I definitely am."

"Talkin' to yourself, doc?" A hand slapped his back; he flew off the stool.

"Whoa!" Mike was stunned. "Easy." He peered at Greg curiously. "Sorry, but I was expected, wasn't I?"

Several customers *were* looking at him now, with good reason. Greg blushed and they both sat; Mike still watched him.

The noise around the counter resumed. "So what's going on, Greg?" The waitress rushed past them, asking something about drinks. They both ordered coffee then checked their menus and decided on their lunches.

"I got a phone call," Greg explained after the waitress returned with coffee and scribbled their orders down. "From our friend."

"The guy on Melanie Stone's show?"

"The same."

Mike shuddered. "We should call the police."

"Already did."

"And?"

Greg shrugged. "They'll get back if they hear anything."

"What did he say?"

"He asked me if I'd seen the tape. I said no, only parts of it. That made him happy, I think."

"So he was baiting you?"

"Apparently. Now he knows that I *don't* know whatever it is he doesn't *want* me to know."

Mike nodded. "Anything else?"

"I asked him if he was Bennie."

"And?"

"He just laughed and hung up."

Mike sipped some coffee, then turned on his stool toward Greg. "Face it, from what he said last night, he's getting ready for some kind of showdown."

"Check."

"But if his main concern was guarding whatever info was on the tape, and if he knows he's succeeded in doing that, then there's a good chance he won't be hassling you anymore."

"But remember what he said last night? 'I'm in California to settle unfinished business.'"

"And to fight for AB101, Greg. That's got to be more important to him than you are."

"But Josh Ferguson said 'our monsters are coming back.' That sounds like a personal vendetta to me."

"Try to think like *he* does, Greg." Lunch arrived; they said a quick grace and Mike continued.

"If you were promoting a social cause, like he is, would you spend valuable time tracking down somebody that did you wrong over twenty years ago?"

"I wouldn't. But would he?"

"I doubt it." Mike chewed his food. "He seemed too smart for pettiness." He looked away when he said it. Greg noticed.

"Do you really believe that, Mike? Or are you trying to calm me down?"

Mike thought it over between chews. "A little of both."

Greg slammed his fork down. "Then level with me! If you were in my position, what would you do? No evasions, please."

Mike's eyes met his. "I'd be on my knees daily and earnestly."

"And?"

"I'd buy a gun."

At 1:45, Greg phoned Christine again, who informed him for the third time that she was fine, the house was secure, and no one was bothering her except her husband.

He quoted her the lowest price available for an alarm system. She approved and asked for the company's number so she could have the man come out to the house.

"No, I'll call them, babe. I just wanted to run the price by you."

"You haven't got time. Robbie's coming in at 2:00, isn't he?"

Robbie. Good grief! He gave her the number and said he'd see her at 6:00.

Nancy buzzed when he hung up. "Your client is here."

He panicked briefly; how could he concentrate on a client in the middle of all this? Christine, Bennie, tapes, the police. And Mike.

I'd get a gun.

He shivered.

A gun. Phone calls. Soft laughter coming through the receiver—

Everybody get in line, he ordered his thoughts. *On the double. Single file. Focus.*

Greg arranged the papers on his desk and straightened his tie, having no idea which of Robbie's problems to discuss first.

The simplest course came to him as he directed his new client into his office.

"Of all the problems you're dealing with," he asked as Robbie sat down, "which one do you want us to tackle first?"

Robbie was dressed more casually today: jeans, sweatshirt, and tennis shoes. Even in sloppy clothes, though, he resembled a model more than a singer. He smiled thinly at Greg's question.

"They're all so juicy, I can't decide. You pick."

"Uh-uh. Rule number one: You tell me what's foremost on your mind each session. Counseling isn't about me dispensing wisdom while you listen. It's about us working on your problems together. And you're the one who knows which problem is most important to you."

Robbie caught the sternness in Greg's tone. "What happened to the gentle shrink I met last week?"

"He's hiding behind today's special: Therapist à la No Nonsense. We've got no time for anything else," Greg explained a bit more gently. "By the way, I watched the Melanie Stone Show last night."

Robbie searched Greg's face for approval. "What did you think?"

"I think you were taking a big chance. But what you had to say was fantastic."

"You liked it?" he asked eagerly.

"I didn't say I liked it," Greg cautioned. "It scared me. Someone might have recognized your voice."

"Slim chance."

"Probably. I'm overly worried about you. But I loved what you said to that jerk."

Robbie beamed. "Thanks."

"Okay. So. About those problems?"

"Right. Well, I'm being blackmailed," Robbie said, putting his hand out and extending a different finger for each problem. "And I've got until April nineteenth to tell the world I'm gay or let the gays do it for me. Those two problems are enough to keep us busy, don't you think?"

"Are they the most important ones?"

Robbie considered. "A dear friend of mine just killed himself. And I'm gay, but I don't want to be."

"That's four big ones. Pick the winner."

"Blackmail."

"Good choice."

Robbie closed his eyes. "Any way you look at it, there's gonna be a scandal. That's how this all started, you know. With scandal."

"Scandal?"

"Remember the PTL controversy?"

"Who doesn't?"

"Josh did a big report on televangelists after that. While everyone else was digging up dirt on the Bakkers, he thought it was time the public heard about some of these other characters. So he did a special on televangelists. Maybe you remember that show?"

Greg remembered it well. It had aired in May of 1987. "Tonight on 'Limelight,' a special report: Freely You Have Deceived, Now Freely Live: Josh Ferguson Looks at the Lifestyles of the Blessed and Famous."

The ratings that night were understandably huge.

"Anyway," he went on, "I was just getting my start back then with Brian Decker. Remember him?"

Greg couldn't hide his surprise. "The evangelist from Ohio with the white suits?"

They'd been his trademark: white suits, gold bracelets, and a huge wooden cross hanging down the front. During Brian Decker's miracle crusades, hundreds of quaking men and women fell backward under his touch, reporting incredible (and unverifiable) healings. His television shows featured relentless appeals for money, to which people responded by the thousands. But others, Greg included, viewed Decker as little more than a religious carnival barker.

Robbie was mixed up with that guy? He read Greg's thoughts.

"It was my first exposure to that sort of thing," he explained. "At first, I thought I was lucky to work for him."

"How'd you come to work for him?"

"Brian heard me sing at a wedding back in '85 and asked me to join his crusades as a featured soloist. So I traveled with him for a couple of years, and was a regular on his TV shows. It really was a good break, and it gave me exposure."

"The right kind, I hope." Decker was one of Ferguson's victims on that notorious report. He and his miracle crusades had gone into obscurity shortly thereafter.

"In a funny way, yes, it was the right kind. See, that's how Josh discovered me."

"Discovered you?"

"When Josh was putting his report on televangelists together, he asked Brian for an interview, and for permission to tape one of the crusades. Well, Brian thought that was the cat's meow. He was so flattered to think Josh Ferguson would be interested in him that he gave Josh permission not only to tape the services, but to interview any of the crusade staff."

"Didn't he know Ferguson was doing an exposé?"

Robbie laughed. "You didn't know Brian. The only thing he loved more than his clothes was attention. I don't think he ever considered what Josh could really do to him."

"So Josh interviewed you?"

"Uh-huh, after a service in Chicago. I'd gotten a standing ovation that night, so of course that got his attention. He asked me some hard questions about Brian and the crusade, obviously fishing for dirt. I didn't have any to give him, though, because I never knew what was going on behind the scenes. I was just the soloist, you know," he added defensively.

"But Josh and I really hit it off," he continued. "Everyone else was afraid of him, and I guess he could be a pretty tough interrogator. But he warmed up to me right away. Then after the interview, he turned off his tape recorder, looked me in the eye, and said, 'What's a nice guy like you doing with a prima dona like Decker?' I was shocked. I told him I was happy there. 'No you aren't,' he said, 'not for long, anyway.' I had no idea he was about to ruin Brian's ministry."

He noticed Greg wasn't taking notes. "Are you getting all this down?"

"I'll remember it, believe me."

"Anyway, when Josh's exposé was aired, Brian's ministry went down the tubes. And we all went with him."

"Why's that?"

"We were all guilty by association. You see, Brian lived like a king, but nobody knew it. He'd beg for money as though the ministry was about to go broke, then spend most of the donations on himself. Discreetly, of course. We all thought the offerings went back into the ministry. But people assumed if Brian was a phony, then we were all phonies, too."

His face clouded.

"It wasn't fair! Most of us worked hard and never wanted to con anybody. We were so naive. Our salaries were about the same as minimum wage, but we were glad to be serving God, so we didn't care. Brian always said, 'We should be willing to live on dirt for the work of the ministry.'"

He said the last sentence in a fairly good imitation of the flamboyant evangelist.

"So, when Josh did his hatchet job on Brian, nobody was more shocked than me." He smiled with irony. "Can you imagine how I felt when I watched the show and saw the million-dollar house Brian owned? He told us he lived in a condo in Akron!"

"You must have been devastated."

"So were his followers. Donations stopped coming in, crowds at the crusades dropped to nearly half the regular size, and suddenly Brian was a leper. Four months later, he filed for bankruptcy."

"And you were left out in the cold."

"Only for a while. I got a call from Josh that September, asking for another interview. You'd think I'd have been leery, but I knew he wouldn't hurt me. Don't ask me how. Anyway, he featured me on a 'Limelight' story about up-and-coming gospel musicians, a very positive one, and that shot my career into orbit. Within a month, I had my first contract."

"And that started your friendship with Ferguson?"

Robbie grinned. "After my first concert in Florida, I got a letter of congratulations from Josh, saying, 'I made you, I can break you, and I like Italian food. So when are you buying me dinner?' We kept in touch regularly after that."

"You got to know him pretty well?"

Robbie's chest heaved as went from pleasant memories to painful ones.

"Josh was a very sad man. He'd been raised a Christian, but he was backslidden. I think something happened at his dad's church that turned him off. Maybe that's why he was so brutal about exposing people."

"Maybe." Greg saw no reason to comment on the information Ferguson had left him on tape.

"But he was foursquare behind my work. He even told me once that he prayed for me daily. Then one night, we were having a late dinner and the talk turned heavy. You know about that already."

"The night he told you the way he felt about you?"

"Right." Robbie thought of something. "By the way, his funeral is tomorrow. I'm singing at it."

"Oh?"

"Alma asked me to."

"I'll see you there."

"You'll be there?"

"Mrs. Ferguson asked me to come. I've never met her, so it was a surprise to me, too."

"Does she know Josh called you?"

"I don't know. It's puzzling."

"Yeah. The whole thing's puzzling."

Greg kept a small clock on his desk, turned strategically so it could be seen from any part of the room. He glanced at it; Robbie noticed.

"Did I get us off the subject?"

"Not at all," Greg said, embarrassed to have been caught looking at the clock. He prided himself on his ability to keep track of the time and to stifle a yawn, both without his clients noticing. But this client was too observant.

"So," Robbie continued, "it all began with a scandal. And now it ends with one."

"But *does* it end, Robbie?" Greg asked, getting back to the original subject of blackmail. "Have you decided this is the end of your career?"

"That decision is probably going to be made for me."

Greg understood. He agreed, too, but didn't want to say so. Instead he asked, "So, how exactly do you plan to handle this?"

"I've given it lots of thought. Lots of prayer, too. And it seems to me I owe it to my fans—does that sound arrogant, calling them my *fans?*"

"They buy your records and pay to see you in concert. No, I'd say they're your fans."

"Yeah. Anyway, I owe it to them to be honest. And I can't let those people, that BRAVO group, do my talking for me. So I'm going to make a public announcement, then retire."

"You're sure?"

"Positive."

"How?"

"How what?"

"How are you going to announce it? What will you say?"

Robbie's chin rested in his hand while he mulled it over, and Greg guessed the answer before his client gave it.

"I haven't got the slightest idea."

SIXTEEN

*C*alvin had never so keenly felt the need to confide in someone, nor had he ever been so convinced that confiding in anyone was out of the question. He'd barged into a mess of his own choosing; company would be nice, but it was a luxury he could ill afford.

He put his fork down and looked around him. The Baker's Square restaurant had a light evening crowd, partly composed of the regulars with whom he had a nodding acquaintance. Quiet Wednesday-night dinners here were part of the routine his life revolved around, and he'd liked it that way. No surprises, little excitement. Calvin Blanchard's lifestyle was a study in comfortable predictability.

His habits were a case in point: breakfast at 7:00; whatever independent production work was available from 8:00 to noon; preparation for the radio show at 1:00; broadcasting from 3:00 to 5:00; dinner; the evening news, and bed. Some radio personalities juggled speaking engagements, debates, and endorsements, but Calvin was rarely asked to address groups more colorful than junior high service clubs and an occasional women's luncheon.

He returned to his broiled chicken. *You are,* he thought, *a nice man getting involved in not-so-nice adventures.*

A smirk curled on his lips while he chewed.

He'd always been nice. A nice student whose citizenship marks never dropped below an A, a nice obedient son, a nice coworker, production assistant, or backup man. A nice confidant, too. Good listener, easy to get along with. No rough edges, always reliable, never one to rock the boat and never, of course, one to make enemies.

"*Nice* is a four-letter word."

He said it out loud. One of the regulars at the counter heard and cocked her head in his direction. He smiled at her and waved.

Calvin Blanchard was changing.

Crucial events have that effect on people, who later refer to their lives in terms of *before* and *after*. Before *I got married I was* this *type of person,* they say. *Or* after *such and such an event, I became more like* this *and less like* that. Events can be crucibles—life-changing points by which people mark their epiphanies.

Josh Ferguson's suicide was Calvin's epiphany, the event by which he would forever divide his *before* and *after.*

He finished his chicken, ordered coffee, and leaned back in his padded seat. This was his favorite booth, nestled in a corner of the dining room where he could quietly eat, observe the other customers, and think. *That's the story of my life,* he noted. *Sitting quietly in a corner, observing and reflecting. But not for long.*

When he'd heard about Ferguson's suicide on the morning news, he'd doubled over and screamed. Screaming was not his style, but scream he did, loud and violently, and on later reflection he knew the scream had been for more than his friend's death. It was the pent-up response to years of suspecting Josh's private torments. He'd experienced them himself; it wasn't difficult spotting them in another man.

The coffee arrived. Calvin sipped, then turned on himself bitterly.

If you experienced them too, big shot, couldn't you at least have told Josh there was hope?

Nice Calvin Blanchard, ever the diplomat, broke in.

Of course not! Josh never asked for help from you; you sensed he needed it, that's all. You sensed it when he brought Robbie Carlton on location shoots and couldn't keep his eyes off the guy, and you sensed it when his wife visited the studio and Josh related to her as though she was an unpleasant necessity. You sensed it when he talked with you about the report he was doing on homosexuals and the subject made him nervous and excited. Confronting him with what you sensed would have been way out of line.

But how many times had he stifled one simple sentence which might have made all the difference:

Josh, I think I know what you're going through because I've been through it myself and there is a way out.

No way. Not the old, unobtrusive Calvin. But the new one, blossoming even as the bitter thoughts flooded him, would not be so passive this time. He would find out what drove his friend over the edge. And maybe even do something about it.

But what, Calvin? Do what?

He sipped more coffee.

Formulate some questions, that's what. And get answers.

The BRAVO meeting had answered question number one. Why did Josh do it? Because he was about to be exposed as a homosexual. Even now, that was enough to drive some people to suicide.

Yes. But—

"More coffee?"

He looked up at the waiter. "Just a warm-up, thanks."

But was exposure that awful? So awful Josh would rather die than go through it? Couldn't he have retired? Even if his wife had divorced him, would that have been the end of the world?

Maybe. Probably. Who knows?

Scratch question number one. Move on.

He touched the coffee cup and decided to let it cool.

Question number two: What was BRAVO up to that had so intrigued Josh?

Expose them or stop them, the girl at the meeting had said.

So their plan was to expose more people. That could get nasty. But Josh never shied away from "nasty"; he made a living confronting it. And he never hid his work from other people. During preproduction, in fact, he was prone to show a work in process to his assistants for feedback.

So why did he suddenly forbid anyone else to view the taped interviews he'd done? What was he hiding?

Answer to question number two: He was hiding more than BRAVO's "exposure" plan. There was more to that group than "outing," and Josh knew it. But he didn't want anyone else to.

Sorry, Josh, I'm crashing the party.

He'd find out by attending more meetings. No one would know he was a local Christian broadcaster.

Keep telling yourself that, fool, Nice Calvin mocked. *But you are a Christian broadcaster and there are thousands of ways they could find out. What if one of them listens to your show and recognizes your voice? What if one of them sees you at church? What if you start a Gateway ministry, idiot, and one of them decides to join it, for whatever reason? Think!*

True. But he'd only go to a few more meetings. The odds were slim—present, but slim—that he and other BRAVO members would cross paths outside the meetings. He'd be careful.

He'd also get to know their leader, who definitely would *not* come to a Gateway support group meeting or to Calvin's church, although the thought of him showing up was amusing. He pictured Yelsom, black leather and all, prancing down the aisle on Sunday morning at the Mesa Baptist Church, asking for a visitor's card and directions to the new members' class.

Delightful.

No, Yelsom wouldn't bother with that. Their brief encounter had been enough to convince Calvin that BRAVO's leader confined himself to hardball, not pranks.

The encounter also convinced him that Yelsom was an egomaniac who might just fall for Calvin's hero-worship act. His nervousness in the parking lot had served him well, actually. Yelsom responded to it. He liked compliant followers. Fine. *Compliant* was a role Calvin had perfected.

His coffee had cooled. He gulped down half the cup.

To answer question number two, he'd follow Yelsom like a puppy dog, gain his trust if possible, and (cross your fingers and pray, kid) get the man to confide in him.

Impossible!

No. Well, maybe. But egomaniacs, even smart ones, could be duped. Stoke their pride and get them talking. Tell them you're on their side, you want to help, you'll be their right-hand man. Run errands for them. It worked, sometimes.

And sometime, if you're very good at this game (he was— didn't everyone assume he was nice and harmless?), he'll invite you to his home.

Where some real answers might be found.

He'd give himself two months to charm Yelsom into delegating some responsibility to him. BRAVO must have hundreds of odd jobs to attend to. Running a terrorist group can be such a headache, and good help is hard to find.

Spoken like a true smart aleck, Cal! All right!

Nice Calvin had his bags packed and was on his way out. New Calvin had work to do. He squared his shoulders and quietly, as always, adopted a new attitude.

For you, Josh, he whispered, then drained his cup. *We should have talked. I shouldn't have hid in the corner.*

He set the cup down and stared at the loose grounds on the bottom.

Forgive me.

Meanwhile, there was Pastor Cox to talk to about starting a Gateway ministry at the church, then Josh Ferguson's funeral to attend. And good people to work with and serve.

Which brought him to question number three: Why did bad people—people like Yelsom, for instance—have to exist?

So good people can become better people by resisting them?

The waiter appeared with the coffeepot and started to pour. Calvin waved it away; the waiter reached into his apron for the check.

"Will that be all, then?"

Calvin never ordered dessert, which was exactly why he picked up the pie list and looked for something wicked.

"A slice of the Chocolate Wipeout."

The waiter scribbled and started to leave.

"And I guess I will have some more coffee."

The man stopped, poured, then turned away.

"Hmmm."

"Yes?"

"Put some ice cream on the pie, would you?"

"Anything else?"

"Can you heat it up?"

"It's not a good idea."

"Great. Heat it up."

Greg slammed the car door shut before he noticed his keys were still dangling from the ignition.

"Blast it!"

He went to the front door and rang the bell.

"Oh, dear," Christine called out girlishly from the living room. "Someone's at the door. I mustn't panic!"

"Funny girl. Come on, open up."

"A deep-voiced man on the porch. Horrors! Are you armed, or just selling Avon?"

"I locked my keys in the car."

"That's an old line. Psychotics use it all the time. I'm calling 911."

"It's cold out here."

"My husband ordered me—ordered, do you hear?—not to open the door to anyone."

"I'm getting mad."

"Threats! I'm definitely calling 911. Oh, 911! 911! Yoo-hoo!"

"Chris-TEEN!"

She opened the door a crack and peeked through. "Darling, is it you?"

He glared. She put a hand melodramatically to her forehead. "I thought you'd never come." She flopped into his arms. "Hold me!"

"I need your keys. I locked mine in the car."

Christine fluttered her eyelids. "Thank heavens my competent man is home."

They had dinner in front of the television, laughing at Tracy and Hepburn in *Adam's Rib* while avoiding serious topics.

When it was over, Christine asked if he'd called the police.

"Yeah, but there's nothing they can do."

"At least they know he called."

"Assuming it was him. Any other calls today?"

She shook her head.

"How about the alarm system?"

"They're coming next Tuesday. How's Robbie?"

She never asked about clients. "He's fine," Greg said, evenly. "Good."

"I talked with Mike. He thinks we should get a gun."

"Okay."

Greg looked at her. "Just 'okay'? That's it?"

"That's it. Let's get one."

She sounded calm. He knew she wasn't, and loved her for faking it. "Good. I'll shop around. Are we ready for bed?"

"It's only 8:30!"

"Ferguson's funeral is tomorrow, and I'm beat." He stood up. "How about it?"

"Do you mind if I read in bed for a while?"

"No problem. I'll just nod off."

"But what if I need protection?"

He bristled. "Keep talking like that and you will."

Christine propped herself up against two pillows and thumbed through a magazine while Greg snuggled against her. He kissed her cheek, rolled over into a ball with his back toward her, and drifted off to the sounds of magazine pages turning and crickets chirping.

The chirping swelled and deepened into waves. Wind blew, traffic sounded in the distance, and the sand beneath his feet crunched lightly.

He was running away from the waves toward the wooden stairs on the cliffs. They were miles away, and since he was running in slow motion, it took forever to reach them.

Young voices heckled him from the beach, but he ignored them.

He finally reached the stairs and was sprinting up the steps two at a time, trying to keep a quick pace, but he was carrying Bennie on his back and he was so heavy!

"You'll have to get off!" Greg yelled over his shoulder. "I can't take you much farther!"

The wind howled, so Bennie couldn't hear him. His arms were locked around Greg's neck as he held on.

"Come and get it, Bishop!" Rick Mosley's voice boomed from the beach. "He's waiting for you!"

Greg stopped, caught his breath, then turned around. "No, he's not! He's up here with me. And I know him. He's an old friend of mine!" As he said it, he felt Bennie's fingers tighten around his neck.

He started to choke, then looked over his shoulder to tell Bennie to loosen his grip, only to find Bennie had been replaced and he was now carrying Mosley.

Their faces were inches apart. Greg screamed. Mosley howled in triumph.

"Me first!"

His eyes were wild and cruel, and the stench of his breath in Greg's face was revolting. Greg tried to throw him off, but the strong hands clamped even tighter around his throat.

"When I get inspired I just can't stop!" Mosley cackled.

Greg started to faint when he heard Bennie calling from the top of the stairs.

"I'm up here, Greg. You did it. I'm safe!"

Bennie started to disappear from view.

"Wait!" Greg called out. "Wait, Bennie! I need to tell you something!"

"Gotta go. Thanks for the lift."

"Please!" Greg clambered up the few remaining steps. "I've been wanting to tell you something. Please stay!"

Mosley, still hanging from Greg's back, whispered into his left ear. "Want me to get him back? I know how. I know how to bait him."

Greg tried one last time to throw him off, failed, then resigned himself to carrying Mosley, even though he hated him.

He reached the top of the stairs. No Bennie. Instead he saw Lisa and Roxanne approach him with employee applications in their hands. They smiled at him knowingly.

"Thanks for seeing us, Dr. Bishop. This isn't a bad time, is it?"

"Yes, it's a bad time," he whimpered. "It's a horrible time."

He staggered off the stairs onto the sidewalk and almost ran over the camera crew that was waiting for him. Josh Ferguson's voice reached his ears.

"*It's a horrible time,*' Dr. Bishop says. But just how horrible is it? That's the question we'll pursue on tonight's edition of 'Limelight.'"

Floodlights stabbed Greg's eyes, a microphone was thrust in his face, and Josh Ferguson stepped forward.

"Dr. Bishop, your failures are legendary. You failed to stand up for your friend, you failed to keep me from killing myself, you failed to protect the tape I sent you, and you locked your keys in the car. But tonight, you did manage to rescue Bennie. Is this the beginning of success?"

Mosley hopped off his back and grabbed the microphone.

"Don't count on it, Ferguson. Bishop's a loser. He dropped out of the fraternity."

Bennie reappeared at Ferguson's side. "And I pitied him," he said. "I really pitied him."

Greg pushed Ferguson aside and reached for Bennie's arm. "Bennie. I've got to tell you something."

"Too late for that, doctor," Ferguson interrupted. Bennie moved away and sat on a bench. Greg started toward him, but Mosley grabbed him and jerked him back.

"Forget it," Mosley sneered. "You can't help guys like that."

"He's right," Bennie yelled. "I am what I am and you can't help me!"

Ferguson's camera moved in for a close-up of Greg's face.

"Bennie, please," he begged. "Just listen to me."

"You can't help Robbie, either!" Bennie jeered.

The wind howled, the waves crashed, and it was freezing cold.

"You're just a liar who wants to make a quick buck!" Bennie's hair sprouted out, long and white, and his eyes were suddenly ringed with black mascara. *"Just a liar who wants to make a quick buck!"*

His fist sprang out and punched Greg's face.

"One!" the camera crew shouted in unison. "Two! Three! Four!"

Bennie laughed softly and Greg knew his old friend had run out of pity.

Christine found him at 3:00 A.M. sitting at the kitchen table. "Honey?"

Alma Ferguson's card announcing Josh's funeral was on the table in front of him. He pointed at it.

"I don't think I should go to this."

"Okay, don't go."

"But I think I have to." He was trembling.

"Gregory," she pleaded, "come back to bed. Come on."

He put out both arms and wrapped himself around her.

"My failures," he said. "My failures are legendary."

SEVENTEEN

Be specific, Calvin reminded himself. *Make your points as though you were presenting a legal case.*

He steered his Camry left on Fairview, heading from Santa Ana to Costa Mesa, then rolled his window down to let a blast of March air slap him awake. Too many cups of coffee last night, combined with a sugar high from the Chocolate Wipeout and the swarm of ideas buzzing in his head, had kept him up until all hours. He was drowsy, and that wouldn't do. Not this morning.

The air on his face revived him a little. Warner Avenue was coming up; in another ten minutes he'd reach the church. Then he'd be put to the test.

A legal case, that's it. Ladies and gentlemen of the jury, I offer Exhibit A: the hundreds, perhaps thousands, of women and men seated in our churches who fight a personal battle against their own homosexuality. They need our help.

Good point. There's a need in the church, and Jesus never ignored the needs of the people around him.

But prove it, Calvin. He could almost hear Pastor Cox say it. *Prove there's a need.*

No problem, sir. Just let me poll the congregation next Sunday.

Excuse me, folks, but would all of you out there who are secretly homosexual just raise your hand so we can get a count?

He braked for the light at Sunflower and Harbor and decided to skip Exhibit A.

Or, better yet, he could make himself Exhibit A rather than some unknown quantity of people. The masses of silent strugglers weren't meeting with Pastor Cox this morning, but he was. His own background could put a face on the issue which the pastor could identify.

I know what it's like, Reverend Cox, because I've been there, and I can tell you it's rough. Please help the others in our church who've got it rough like I did. Please help me help them. "Please, let's start a ministry here."

Paularino Street was coming up. Two more blocks, a right turn, and the Mesa Baptist Church of Costa Mesa would be there waiting. His heart thudded and he noticed, in spite of the morning chill, a sweat breaking out across his back.

He hadn't been this nervous when he'd crashed the BRAVO meeting. *This is sad,* he moaned as he reached the building. *I'm more frightened to talk honestly to my own pastor than I was to lie to a gay activist.*

The parking lot was nearly empty since it was Thursday morning, so he nestled his car in the spot nearest the main sanctuary. He still had seven minutes to kill before meeting Pastor Cox, and he preferred to spend them alone, collecting his thoughts.

He rolled up his window and breathed deeply. "Be specific," he repeated aloud. "And fair."

Especially fair. After all, there were hundreds of issues vying for the church's attention. Was Pastor Cox supposed to address all of them?

He fingered the Gateway manual and remembered the first time he'd seen one. It was in the spring of 1981 in San Francisco, while walking into a roomful of people who called themselves "ex-gays." He'd been skeptical and hopeful all at once. He stayed with the program for a year, attending support groups and availing himself of the personal counselors who volunteered for Gateway. It was life-changing; he'd never have made it alone.

He'd tell Pastor Cox about it and *make* him see how important it was.

He'd left his watch at home, so he clicked the radio to the news station for the time. 10:55. Five more minutes.

Another viewpoint intruded: Even if it was important, homosexuality wasn't the only problem in the world. Poverty, racism, AIDS, hunger, abortion, evangelism—weren't these enough to keep the church busy until the millennium? What right did he have insisting his ministry proposal was vital to Mesa Baptist, just because it had once been vital to him?

The answer eluded him until he stepped out of the car, walked through the glass doors of the church office, and told Pastor Cox's secretary he was here for an appointment. It came to him even as he spoke to her.

If he had a calling to do this work, he'd find a place and time to do it. If not here, somewhere else; if not now, then sometime.

His job was to knock on whatever doors were available; God's job was to open the right one.

The thought relieved him considerably.

Pastor Cox's pleasant secretary said he was running a few minutes late, so would Calvin please have a seat? She complimented him on his radio show then offered him juice or coffee; he declined and eased into one of the three blue couches in the waiting area. The room had a soothing feel: blue-gray carpet with matching sofas, oak tables, and silk plants. A modern orchestral arrangement of hymns lulled him while he browsed through the April edition of *Christianity Today*.

"Calvin, good to see you!" Pastor Cox announced, bounding from his office to shake hands. He was a tall man in his mid-fifties who kept himself in excellent shape. Regular cycling and tennis kept a spring in his walk and a tan on his face, and his manner—brisk and energetic—inspired respect.

"Thanks for seeing me," Calvin smiled. He stood and sucked his stomach in—a habitual response to Pastor Cox's trim, middle-aged physique which shamed Calvin's thirty-two-year-old paunch. "I know you're busy."

"No more than you, I guess." He gestured at his office. "Come on in. Your show's doing well, isn't it? I catch it whenever I can."

They sat on opposite sides of a huge oak desk cluttered with folders, memos, and framed photographs of the Cox children.

"I'm keeping up with it," Calvin shrugged, "and the sponsors haven't complained, so I guess I'm doing something right."

The pastor asked him about broadcasting and some of the guests he'd interviewed, showing a genuine interest. They joked about the media and the difficulty of pleasing station managers and listeners.

"But," he finally said, "you didn't come here to talk about broadcasting."

"No," Calvin began, "I have something to ask you."

The pastor assumed a neutral expression.

"Something that's hard to talk about, because it means telling you some unpleasant things about me."

The expression didn't change, but Calvin sensed the man's apprehension.

"Nothing's wrong," he stressed. "I'm not in trouble or anything like that. But there's something in my background I've never told you about. I've never told anyone about it, for that matter."

His pastor's eyebrows lifted slightly.

He reached for the manual he'd brought into the office with him. "Have you ever heard of Gateway Ministries?"

"Let me see that. Hmmm. No. Why?"

"Well, Gateway helps local churches set up ministries for people who've come out of the gay lifestyle."

Cox's face remained infuriatingly unreadable.

"Or people who've never been in the gay lifestyle but are tempted to go into it."

"Hmmm."

"And the reason I'm here is because I'd like to start one in the church."

"Umm-hmm."

"Because . . . I was helped by one of these ministries myself."

Saying it was like leaping off a high dive and waiting to hit the pool. And he saw nothing in his pastor's face to let him know if the water was deep or shallow.

A smile finally appeared. "Calvin," the man said softly, "that's great." The smile broadened; Calvin returned it. "It's great. I'd never have guessed."

"I suppose that's good."

"Do you know how rare your testimony is?"

"Not as rare as you might think."

"Ah." The smile faded. "And that's why you want to do this."

"Partially. I want to do it because it helped me, sure. But I also want to do it because there's hardly any help available for people who were in my shoes."

"True."

"And because I'm afraid."

Pastor Cox waited.

"The churches in Orange County are going to feel a lot of heat from the gays. And soon."

"What sort of heat?"

"Full-scale war."

If the pastor thought this was nonsense he certainly hid it well.

"What makes you say that?"

"One of their leaders was on CNN last night, talking about it. He said the gays are ready to do battle with us."

"Exactly who are these gays you're talking about?" Cox asked doubtfully. "Every homosexual in the county?"

"No, no. The radical ones. They've aimed their sights at the churches, and they've got a plan. A lot of people are going to be hurt. Some of them might be in our own congregation."

"How?"

Calvin knew this part would be tricky. "Do you know what a closet homosexual is?"

"I read the papers."

"Right. Well, plenty of closet homosexuals go to church. This group called BRAVO has a list of some of them and they're going to make that list public. Can you imagine the fallout?"

"I'd rather not."

"The victims will need us."

"Do some of the people on this list belong to our church?"

"No," Calvin admitted, remembering the names Yelsom had recited during the BRAVO meeting. "But plenty of Christians from this area *are* on the list. We could provide support for them, which they'll probably not find in their own churches."

"You're assuming that."

"With good reason."

Pastor Cox's expression had long since gone from neutral to perturbed. He looked closely at Calvin.

"How do you know who is or isn't on this list?"

Calvin's heart sank. They held a quiet staring match while he searched for, and couldn't find, an intelligent lie.

"I can't say," he finally confessed. "I'm sorry."

That didn't go over well; Pastor Cox pressed him.

"What have you gotten yourself into?"

"It's confidential."

"Do you have contacts with these people?"

"I can't say."

"Were you involved with them?"

"Not really."

"Then how do you know who's on their list?"

"I don't remember."

"This isn't a Watergate hearing, blast it!" Pastor Cox exploded.

Calvin knew the chance for a Gateway ministry was lost.

The pastor took his glasses off to rub his eyes. "Calvin," he sighed, "why can't you trust me?"

Time for the truth, Calvin decided. He met his pastor's gaze and held it. "Because," he said slowly, "I'm onto something which may be dangerous to me or anyone I talk to about it. I don't want to see anyone else get hurt."

"Anyone else," the man repeated. "Who's been hurt so far?"

"I can't say. Please understand."

Pastor Cox finished with his eyes, moved his hand to his forehead and massaged his temples, then put his glasses back on and shook his head.

"You've all but admitted some kind of inside knowledge about a plot the gays are cooking up against the church, but you can't tell me anything about it."

"Right."

"But you're involved in it, somehow."

"Right."

"And you expect me to let you start a ministry in my church?"

"Not anymore." Calvin got up abruptly, cursing himself for another missed opportunity. "I'm sorry I wasted your time. And I'm sorry for being so mysterious. I'm sure it was irritating."

Pastor Cox was off his seat and blocking the doorway before Calvin could reach it. "We're not finished."

Calvin was mildly shocked. The pastor laid a fatherly hand on his shoulder.

"You came to ask me about starting a ministry. I can't let you be the one to lead it. Let's be honest. Whatever it is you're doing could make you a serious liability to the church."

He didn't take it as an insult; it was quite true and he knew it.

"I'm open to the idea of a Gateway ministry, but not now. I know my congregation pretty well, and frankly, they're not ready for this kind of thing."

Calvin wasn't surprised.

"But let's keep it in prayer, okay?"

Calvin nodded.

"And I want to keep you in prayer. Starting now. Do you mind?"

Pastor Cox led Calvin back to the seats they'd occupied. With bowed head, he prayed earnestly for Calvin's protection, for guidance, for wisdom to know if he was in danger, and for the kingdom to somehow be advanced through his efforts. Together they prayed for the church, the county, the gays, and the terrible chasm, widening even as they prayed, between the homosexual and Christian communities.

Calvin was blinking tears when they finished.

"I wish I could tell you everything," he sniffed.

"Anytime you're ready. What you said meant a lot to me."

"It was true, you know. There's trouble coming."

"Not that. What you said about yourself. You trusted me enough to say it; that meant a lot to me."

Calvin put out his hand. The pastor ignored it and gave him a long hug.

"We'll talk again."

EIGHTEEN

*T*he drive from Garden Grove to Orange took fifteen minutes. Greg turned off the 22 freeway onto Tustin Avenue and headed south for Fairhaven Street, then west on Fairhaven toward Waverly Chapel at the Fairhaven Mortuary. He left the radio off; golden oldies weren't appropriate today.

Fairhaven turned from a residential street into a tunnel running between rows of orange trees, and the change was lovely. Greg drove slowly, enjoying the view and nearly missing the entrance to the funeral home.

Two brick columns framed a wrought-iron gate with a gold sign in the middle announcing "Fairhaven Mortuary." The gate was opened partway in the middle.

He drove through into a circular courtyard, beyond which a tiny road led into acres of gravesites and family crypts. The Fairhaven offices were to the left of the courtyard; on the right sat a replica of a Scottish cathedral with stone walls, oval stained-glass windows, and massive iron doors. A marble plaque on the south wall welcomed visitors to Waverly Chapel.

Two small parking lots, located at the front and right of the building, accommodated chapel visitors. The front lot was nearly full; while maneuvering into it, Greg noticed a row of cars parked in the right-hand lot. People were seated in each car, waiting. They ignored Greg's curious looks.

He found a space in front and glanced again at the visitors in the parked cars. Their clothes were dark but too casual for a funeral: dark T-shirts, blouses, and jackets. None of them moved or spoke.

Greg walked toward the chapel entrance, where an usher handed small programs to the women and men, mostly middle-aged, professional-looking people, who'd come to pay their respects. He joined them, admiring the wood paneling and wire meshed grate separating the foyer from the main chapel.

The seating area was small, made up of twenty wooden pews surrounded by European stained-glass windows depicting various biblical scenes. A larger one in the back featured a huge display of the Second Coming, replete with saints and avenging angels. Greg's footsteps echoed solemnly as he followed a second usher to the third pew from the front on the right.

An appropriately hushed mood prevailed. Conversation between the attendants, none of whom Greg recognized, was muted, and an organ played soft Brahms melodies from the left of the altar. Greg glanced at the program then examined his surroundings. In spite of the occasion, the beauty of the room delighted him and he promised himself to bring Christine here under happier circumstances.

The narrow seating area opened up to a vast central space where Ferguson's casket, closed and decked with wreaths, sat in the middle. Brass candelabra, lit and glowing, stood on either side of the casket, and a black-and-white photograph of the deceased smiled at the congregation from a wooden stand in front.

Beyond the central space, an elevated platform supported a podium, altar, and singer's lectern. An immense, thick Persian carpet covered most of the platform; antique lamps illuminated the altar. Beyond the lectern, Greg spotted the corner of the organ and guessed that Robbie was seated next to it, waiting to sing one last number for his benefactor.

Greg's eyes lifted to the ceiling, high and vaulted, then fell on the front row of pews. There, three rows ahead of him, sat a tiny white-haired woman with her head down and the arm of a friend or relative wrapped loosely across her shoulders. He guessed, correctly, that he was watching Josh Ferguson's widow.

He unfolded the program and read it again, rose to allow an elderly couple to find their seats next to him, then sat watching Mrs. Ferguson and wondering what passed through her mind just now.

A stirring from the back made him look up, then left. Several people were murmuring and turning their heads toward the foyer, much as wedding guests do when the bride enters. Greg followed their eyes to the back of the chapel and saw not a bride, but, for all intents and purposes, a monarch.

She was tall, silver-haired, alone, and very much in command of herself and everything around her. Even the usher, who'd walked ahead of the other guests while seating them, opted to stay a cautious three feet behind this one. Greg guessed her to be in her early fifties; he also assumed she'd always been, as she was now, extraordinarily beautiful. High cheekbones and upswept hair framed her milky complexion, and her clear, blue-gray eyes appraised the room with cold certainty. Her contours were lean and strong, draped in an ash-gray silk suit with matching purse and shoes. A string of pearls completed the ensemble.

The woman was in no hurry. She stood in the foyer entrance, scanning each pew as though looking for someone. The usher timidly whispered a question to her; she shook her head and continued to look the chapel over. Finally she spotted the widow in the front row who, Greg noticed, kept her head down in spite of the stir. She then nodded at the usher, pointed to the left of the chapel opposite Mrs. Ferguson, and indicated where she wished to be seated. He nodded, gestured toward the chosen pew, and walked behind as she started toward it.

Her long strides, purposeful and graceful, reminded Greg less of walking than prowling. A panther, he thought: sleek, elegant, predatory. How many men had desired and feared her over the years?

The admiring glances she evoked from the male attendants, contrasting with the glares the female ones shot at her, put the question to rest.

A trail of whispers followed her to her seat. Greg tried, but failed, to catch what people were saying, though the gist of it was clear. She was well known... and controversial.

She reached the pew directly across from Greg and seated herself gracefully. The whispers died; her demeanor suggested she'd noticed them but was above responding. Instead, she sat, upright and immovable, staring at Josh Ferguson's picture.

Alma Ferguson hadn't moved. The man next to her watched her closely, saying nothing, and Greg detected a new stiffness in her shoulders, as if she knew who this strange woman was and where she sat. And, if she could help it, she would not acknowledge her presence.

The organ music faded and, without introduction or announcement, Robbie Carlton appeared on the platform and faced the congregation.

Taped orchestra music filled the chapel and Robbie began singing the Bill Gaither standard "Because He Lives." He was dressed in a double-breasted, dark-brown suit and looked, as always, impeccable. His powerful baritone carried the song with no need for a microphone, and Greg, proud and protective, wanted to nudge the couple on his right and say, "I know that guy." He tried to catch Robbie's eye, then thought better of it. No need to distract the man.

The song ended with a powerful chorus, then Robbie disappeared to the left again, replaced by an elderly minister who crossed the platform and walked slowly to the podium.

He cleared his throat, checked the notes he'd placed in front of him, and began.

"Beloved, we're here to celebrate a great life, and a great man. Most of us will depart this world without leaving a lasting, permanent legacy. Most of our words will be remembered by a precious few, and our wisdom, no matter how great, will be passed on to a limited number of family and friends. But that cannot be said of Joshua Ferguson, who leaves a vacancy that breaks our hearts but bequeaths upon all of us the inspiration of a lifetime of remarkable, lasting achievements."

He left more than that, Greg reflected, *and he needn't have. I'd have settled for the inspiration; he could have kept the tape.*

"Joshua Ferguson should be remembered first and foremost for this: He loved truth. He loved seeking the truth, he loved passing it on to the rest of us, and yes, he loved exposing evasions and lies when they threatened to cloud the truth. By all accounts, he loved—"

"Young men in their early twenties, preferably blond and athletic-looking!"

The shout crashed across the chapel and boomed off the four walls. Women screamed, the minister dropped his notes in astonishment, and Greg bolted out of his seat and whirled around. He saw the avenging angel on the stained-glass window in the back, then the wire-meshed grating in the foyer, then a man in black.

Yelsom.

"Let's talk about the *real* Josh Ferguson, shall we, dearly beloved?"

He carried a five-foot-high sign with printing on it, displaying it in front of him as he stormed down the aisle toward the terrified minister.

"I'm carrying a blown-up photograph of notes from his therapy sessions with Dr. Alex Crawford!"

An usher lunged toward him and Yelsom used the sign to fend him away.

"Back off!"

He continued toward the front, with twelve BRAVO members rampaging behind him, blowing whistles and shouting obscene warnings into bullhorns. Several of the women covered their ears.

"Lies and evasions, reverend? I'll give you lies and evasions! Look at *this!*"

He thrust the sign into various faces at random, snarling and threatening whenever a hand reached out to stop him.

"Here's proof that Mr. Limelight wanted to avoid the limelight himself!"

Key phrases from Dr. Crawford's notes were underlined on the sign: "Patient admits illicit contact with young men in anonymous encounters.... Patient fears contracting AIDS.... Patient seems racked with guilt over his marriage...."

Greg, like the others, was shocked motionless by the pandemonium. Yelsom reached the casket just as the side doors of the chapel slammed open, allowing more BRAVO terrorists, all in black like their leader, to swoop in with whistles and shouts. They were of both sexes, all ages and sizes, but their faces were uniformly contorted and furious.

"Will somebody call the police?" the minister shouted.

A line of BRAVO members linked arms in front of the casket, blocking the entire altar area.

"We've planned a memorial service of our own!" one of them, a stocky young man wearing a motorcyle cap, yelled. He grabbed a candle off the candelabra and blew it out.

"*There!* In memory of the thousands of gay men who've died of AIDS because of the hypocrisy of people like Josh Ferguson."

"Hiya, reverend! You'll share the stage for a moment, won't you?" Yelsom stomped up to the reverend and grabbed the microphone from his shaking hand.

"Please, somebody! Call the police!" the man begged, backing away from Yelsom and looking for escape.

"And *there!*" Another candle was blown out. "In memory of the gays and lesbians who've died in the closet because hypocrites like Josh Ferguson refused to come out and show the world who they really were!"

Alma Ferguson dropped to her knees, moaning and crushing her white hair with her frail hands.

Whistles blew, voices bellowed out *Bravo!* and hands clapped.

"And *there!*" The young man extinguished another candle. "In memory of the thousands of gays and lesbians who've yet to die because of the hypocrisy of people like Josh Ferguson!"

Yelsom stood behind the podium and clutched the microphone in one hand while brandishing his sign in the other. He looked out over the chaos gleefully. "Josh Ferguson's legacy, dearly beloved, is an empty closet!" He threw the microphone at the casket; it bounced off with a reverberating whine. "Come *out,* Josh! Come *out!* No? Then we'll *bring* you out!"

He started toward the casket and several men from the congregation, Greg included, were jolted into action. They flew out of their pews toward Yelsom, but were blocked by the BRAVO contingent, whose human chain held fast.

Yelsom banged on the coffin and began to shake it, and the triumphal shouting from BRAVO's ranks became all the louder. The wails of protest from Josh Ferguson's friends intensified in response, and Alma Ferguson's screams, long and agonizing, could be heard above it all. And every scream was her husband's name.

Yelsom stopped his banging to make one more pronouncement.

"This message is brought to you courtesy of the Orange County chapter of BRAVO! Welcome to the apocalypse!"

Robbie leaped off the platform and grabbed Yelsom by the neck, who sent him flying backward with a punch to the jaw.

Greg saw and yelled for Robbie, who couldn't hear him.

The clash between the men from the congregation and the intruders continued, as the men clawed and pushed at the demonstrators. Shirts were ripped, faces were bloodied, and bodies flailed on the ground. Greg, being the youngest, made the most headway, throwing his full body weight into two men and breaking through the line. He fell facedown on the other side, in front of the casket, and looked up to see BRAVO's leader staring at him in surprise.

Another man grabbed Greg's waist from behind; he threw his elbows into the man's chest, knocked him back, and scrambled toward Yelsom.

"Police!" somebody shouted.

Yelsom backed away from Greg, then gave him an elaborate bow before flying off the platform and out the side exit.

Seven policemen entered the chapel from the foyer at the same moment, and the rioters shot out the side doors as quickly as they'd burst through them. The sounds of cars screeching away from the parking lot, then being stopped by the police, could be heard from outside. Greg found Robbie lying next to the organ, dazed and reeling from Yelsom's blow. His jaw was swelling; Greg applied his handkerchief to it.

The screams died, more police arrived, the minister huddled in a corner, and three men helped Alma Ferguson to her feet.

It was over in less than five minutes.

Greg cradled Robbie's head and surveyed the chapel. A pile of injured men were disentangling themselves from each other while their distraught wives fussed over them. Moans and weeping could be heard throughout the room. Police questioned the minister and several of the guests; handcuffs clinked over the wrists of BRAVO members who hadn't escaped in time, and voices informed them of their rights in monotonous tones. Yelsom wasn't among them.

"Greg?"

He looked down at Robbie.

"Easy, Robbie."

"Greg?"

"I'm here."

"I'm gonna fight them."

"Shh. It's okay now."

Robbie sat up quickly. "No it isn't." He handed the handkerchief back to Greg.

"Are you all right?"

Robbie stroked his jaw. "I should be proud. That was my first fight."

"Congratulations." He pulled Robbie to his feet. "Steady, now. Can you walk?"

"Sure."

"Better put some cold water on that jaw."

"Right." He headed for the restroom. "I'll be right back. Wait for me, okay?"

"I'll be here." Greg stared at Josh Ferguson's casket, scratched and covered with crushed flowers and candle wax. His photo lay on the carpet next to a snuffed candle; a footprint was smeared across his chin.

A small hand with long fingernails dug lightly into Greg's shoulder.

"Dr. Bishop?" a tiny woman's voice asked.

He turned to see Alma Ferguson, tear-stained and exhausted.

"Mrs. Ferguson, I'm so sorry." He took her hand and held it. "I don't know what to say."

She looked at him, trembled, then removed her hand to reach into her purse and give him a card.

"My phone number. Please call. We need to talk."

"Whenever you'd like." Two men stood behind her; Greg recognized one as the man who'd sat in the pew with her. They looked at him suspiciously.

"Soon. As soon as you can, please."

"Tomorrow," he promised. "First thing in the morning."

She turned away without answering, and the men escorted her out of the chapel.

They passed the silver-haired lady on their way. Of all the guests who'd endured the attack, she was the least ruffled. She nodded at Mrs. Ferguson, who ignored her, then strode out the side exit.

Guests were clustering in small groups to comfort each other. Several planned to accompany Josh's casket to the gravesite.

Robbie returned, holding a wet paper towel to his face.

"If they'd do that to him when he's dead, think what they'll do to me while I'm alive."

Greg had been trying not to think of it. He looked toward the parking lot, where police were still making arrests. "I have never in my life seen anything like this."

A policeman approached them and asked if he might question Robbie. "I'll see you next week, Greg," he said, following the officer to a pew.

The service was over, but the final duties weren't. Greg stood alone at the altar and watched six of the deceased's friends clean the flowers off the coffin and position it, the funeral director hovering over them with advice and directions.

They struggled, got their grips, then lifted Josh Ferguson up and away. His photo remained on the floor, smiling at them.

The aisles cleared. The pallbearers moved slowly away.

NINETEEN

I lost three pounds," she announced.

"I'm really proud of her," he nodded. "Not because the weight matters—"

"Oh, yes it does! Come on, we said we'd be more honest."

"Okay. It does matter, but you're taking care of yourself. That's what really matters."

"And I'm not hungry! The meals are fine, and you get three snacks on this plan. I just have to get used to smaller portions—"

"She's taking better care of herself," he said to Greg.

"He *knows* that. Can I finish?"

He patted her knee; they giggled in unison.

"I'm getting used to smaller portions," she went on, "and I feel more energy already! It affects everything."

"Her temper's *much* better."

"So's *his!*" she whispered confidentially to Greg, pointing at her husband.

More giggles.

Greg had been analyzing the funeral all night; he hadn't stopped.

Why? Why pull a stunt so appalling it could only disgust the general public? Could gay rights be furthered by conduct like that?

"—so I decided to leave it alone. It's *her* body. And you were right about my remarks aggravating the problem. So I'm just shutting my mouth from now on."

"So am I, and I'm losing weight!"

Bennie had a chance to duke it out with me. Didn't he want to take care of unfinished business? But when he saw me—

"The real benefit is honesty. Instead of stuffing my feelings I'm letting them out when they come. Like you said, that's why I ate. I was stuffing my anger at him. But now that he's listening to me I can just tell him how I feel and I'm satisfied."

"I'm trying to listen without judging her, Greg."

—he jumped away as though he was afraid of me, which was ridiculous, considering the way he was acting.

"That's all I needed," she told her husband.

Maybe he didn't know me.

"You're really helping us."

The police were coming; that's why he dashed out. He'll call again.

"—where we go from here?"

It wasn't a church service, and Ferguson wasn't known as a religious man, so why expose him? Wasn't the plan to expose the church; stop the church? That's what he said on CNN. But this was a funeral!

"And we're open to whatever ideas you have."

If they keep this up, nobody's going to believe them when they say gays need the civil protection of AB101. People will think the rest of us need protection from the gays.

"So—what do you think?"

He'd kept his eyes on both of them, nodding and grunting his approval while his thoughts played hooky at Waverly Chapel. The question caught him up short.

You're on, idiot. What do you think?

"I think," he replied, "hmmm." He kept a thoughtful pose while diving into his bag of catch-all phrases.

"You think *hmmm?* That's helpful."

"Honey, let the man think."

Greg stared meaningfully at them.

"I think you're accepting responsibility for your own actions, and that's a surefire sign of growth."

They both glowed. "Exactly!" she declared. "That's what I've been trying to say, but I couldn't find the words."

Whew!

"But what now?" the husband asked again. Figures; husbands were usually the ones wanting to know exactly where their counseling was taking them.

"How's your communication?" Greg fished.

They both looked puzzled.

"Well, like we said," the husband answered, "it's been better since our last session."

Last session, last session. What did I tell them?

"You remember?"

Communication exercises!

"Communication exercises," Greg said firmly. "I suggested you start working on them again, so I guess you gave it a whirl this week?"

"Twice. We went through the workbook Saturday and Tuesday nights," he said proudly. "The chapter on active listening."

"Good. Tell me about it."

"We needed a refresher course," she replied, "so we took turns letting each other say whatever was on our minds without the other one interrupting—"

Maybe they're doing the good cop/bad cop routine. They come on mean and heavy at first to scare you, then try a softer approach to negotiate with you after they've worn you down.

"—and I couldn't *believe* how patient he was!"

But attacking people doesn't wear them down. It just makes them mad. Doesn't it?

"—makes you less defensive, doesn't it?" the man asked his wife.

"Sure it does," she told him.

"Sure it does," Greg agreed, coming back to where he belonged. He fixed his eyes on them, determined to pay attention for the rest of the session.

It ended well. He complimented them on their progress; they expressed gratitude.

"Tell me, Greg," she asked when they rose to leave, "isn't it hard to sit there all day listening to people's problems?"

"Actually, no."

"I can't imagine how you keep track of it all."

He shrugged. "I do my best."

They left the waiting room pleased; he remained, ashamed. Letting his mind wander during a session was loathsome. Clients paid good money for counseling, trusting him to listen, analyze, and advise. He was in bad form this morning.

"Sometimes you'll reach the end of a session thinking you've been useless," Dr. Crawford once said. "Your thoughts will have strayed and your insights will seem trite, yet the patient will thank you profusely as though you've been brilliant. Remember, patients do most of the work in counseling; you just facilitate the process. Sometimes they'll seem to get better with no help from you at all!"

This was one of those sometimes.

Greg went back to his office to do what he'd been wanting to since arriving at 9:00. He drew Alma Ferguson's card out of his wallet and dialed.

A recorder answered the second ring. Greg jumped when he heard the voice.

"You've reached 546-7908," the voice of Josh Ferguson said. "We're not able to come to the phone, but at the sound of the tone, please leave your name, number, and the best time to reach you, and we'll return your call as soon as possible."

"I doubt that," Greg mumbled.

The machine beeped and Greg began speaking.

"Mrs. Ferguson, this is Greg Bishop. I'm calling at ten-o-five and I'll be at my office for another—"

"Dr. Bishop?" Alma Ferguson broke in.

"Mrs. Ferguson. How are you?"

"I'm screening calls. Reporters have been phoning day and night." Her thin voice was hoarse; he could only imagine the sort of night she'd had.

"I'm sorry to hear it."

"When can we meet?"

He flipped the appointment book open. "Let me see."

"Today?" she asked hopefully.

Greg was surprised; didn't she want some time alone? Today was booked solid, anyway.

"I'm sorry, I've got clients coming in all day. I have Monday morning open; would that do?"

"Yes, and any time."

"How about eleven?"

"Fine. Could you possibly come out here? I know you're a busy man, but it's hard for me to get out."

He'd figured on that. "No problem. Can you give me directions?"

"Do you know how to get to the Orange Hills?"

He did. She gave him the address, and he recognized the street as being one of the more exclusive ones in the neighborhood.

"I appreciate your taking the time out for me," she said after giving directions and repeating the address.

"Not at all. I'll look forward to seeing you."

"I noticed you came to the service alone yesterday. Are you married, Dr. Bishop?"

"Yes." Why did that matter?

"Please bring your wife along. If she'd like to come, that is."

That threw him. "Oh! Well, sure. I'll check with her. She works too, so she may not be able to take time off."

"If it's convenient, I'd like to meet her."

"Thank you. If she can, I'm sure she'd like that. She would have come yesterday, but I didn't know whether to bring her," he said, awkwardly.

"My oversight. I'll see you Monday, then?"

"At eleven. I'll call if Christine's coming."

"There's no need to. I'll just expect her. No harm done if she can't make it."

They said their good-byes, Greg offering his condolences and Mrs. Ferguson thanking him again.

He hung up nervously; the thought of Christine coming was unsettling.

"Dr. Crawford called to confirm a telephone appointment this afternoon," Nancy said over the intercom.

"Ah! What time?"

"He said that you said you'd call his home at two o'clock."

He looked at the appointment book; a two o'clock session was already scheduled.

"Can you call Brad Welstein and ask him to come in at one instead of two?" He gave her the number. "Then call Dr. Crawford and tell him two o'clock is fine."

Yelsom had watched the Thursday evening news at four, five, and six o'clock, then tuned in for the ten and eleven o'clock editions as well. While watching one station, he videotaped another to get all the stations' perspectives.

Friday he did the same with the morning news broadcasts, and of course he scoured both the *Los Angeles Times* and the *Orange County Register* for their coverage of the event.

Every commentator condemned BRAVO's disruption of the funeral as ruthless, unwarranted, despicable.

The *Times* editorial exceeded all others in eloquence, branding the action as:

—an unprecedented display of barbarous facism
which insults the nobility of the gay rights movement
and besmirches the humanity of all involved.

He immediately cut the column out and framed it.

Thirteen arrests had been made; no one was detained for
long. And a slap on the wrist was surely the most they could
expect.

He was giddy. He took a bow. This was big time.

Greg's 10:00 client canceled, leaving him two hours for a
workout and lunch. His 12:00 client showed, as did Brad Welstein at 1:00, and Greg struggled to keep his mind on his clients
and away from yesterday's chaos. He was reasonably successful.

At 1:50 he said goodbye to Brad, found a legal pad for note-
taking, propped his feet on the desk, and called Dr. Crawford.

For the second time, the doctor's response—an unenthusias-
tic "Hello, Gregory"—left Greg feeling unsettled.

"Is this still a good time for you, Alex?"

"Certainly."

"You've heard about the funeral, I'm sure."

"Of course."

Greg's brow furrowed. *Of course? Nothing else to say about
the desecration of a former client?*

"You'll forgive me, Gregory," he continued, "but it's hard to
talk about Mr. Ferguson just now."

"Of course." Greg's manner was becoming stiff and professional—a reflex to Crawford's. Neither spoke for a few seconds,
then Crawford broke the silence.

"I have to take care of myself."

Greg sensed undercurrents of meaning in the remark.

"Well, then," he said brightly, to diffuse the tension, "can we
talk about Robbie? He came in this week."

"And how did he seem to you?"

Crawford had adopted what Greg called his Perry Mason
tone: persistent, incisive, methodical.

"He seemed aware of the severity of his situation without
being overwhelmed by it. That's what most of the session was

about. His first priority is deciding what to do with his career once word gets out about his homosexuality."

"That's a routine decision-making process; I can hardly help you with that aspect of treatment."

"True, but once the immediate crisis is over, he'll want to address the sexual problem."

"Yes."

"So. Where do I start?"

"Start with the manuscript I'm sending you."

"You wrote a book?"

"An unpublished one; I started it years ago but I've decided not to release it. It's on the treatment of homosexuality."

"Why not publish it?"

"I'm not up to the trouble."

What a change a heart attack can make, Greg considered.

"Thanks," he said aloud. "I'll look forward to reading it. Meanwhile, do you have any pointers?"

"I've jotted down some main ideas for you, Gregory. Stick to these and you should be fine."

Greg readied his pen.

"Don't let your patient become obsessive about his sexual feelings."

"Obsessive?"

"Some patients come into therapy believing the only problem they have is the presenting problem—same-sex attractions, in this case—when, in fact, their perception of the problem may be a problem in and of itself."

Greg put his pen down, thoroughly lost.

"Come again?"

"I'll bet Robbie's desperate to rid himself of his feelings for men."

"Of course! Why shouldn't he be?"

"Because his anxiety about homosexuality may be blocking his ability to cope with it. Try to get him to see himself as *more* than a homosexual. Broaden his perspective."

"Broaden his perspective," Greg repeated while writing.

"While you're at it, determine why he's upset over his sexuality. He may be in treatment for all the wrong reasons."

"Which are?"

"Fear of society, pressure from parents, a desire to be like everyone else."

"And what are the right reasons for seeking treatment?"

"Basically, sexual issues are ethical issues. When a patient says, 'I want to change because I don't feel comfortable as a homosexual,' or 'I want to change because my belief system forbids this practice,' then I know the patient's motivations are sound."

"I'm pretty sure Robbie's are sound."

"No doubt, but check anyway."

"And then?"

"Obviously, encourage him to resist homosexual attractions, whether in behavior or inner fantasy. Remind him that every time he reinforces those feelings, he makes more work for himself."

"As with any other sin," Greg said. "The more you indulge it, the harder it is to overcome."

"You're talking like a fundamentalist rather than a psychologist."

"Can't help it. I'm both."

"Help him understand his cycles. When is he most inclined to have these attractions? When he's anxious? Insecure? Overwhelmed? Help him identify his cycles and learn to endure them without resorting to sexual thoughts for escape."

"That's good advice for anyone."

"Now you're getting it. He'll become stronger in the process. And here's perhaps the most crucial part: Help him understand the emotional needs he's trying to fulfill through men, and help him find legitimate, nonsexual ways to fulfill them."

"That's a mouthful."

"An effective mouthful. Nothing's worked better with my patients than this approach."

Greg had filled three pages of notes by now. "This is good. Very practical."

"You'll find more in my book, but those are the main points I've come to adhere to in therapy. Use them and you should do well."

"But what," Greg asked, "can Robbie realistically expect? If he follows these principles, what's going to happen?"

"He'll get stronger in general, which is always a desirable result. And his homosexuality will either dissipate or he'll be better equipped to cope with it. Either result is also desirable."

"I know the one he'd prefer."

"Help him accept the possibility of the other. For some men, homosexuality is a transitory problem. For others, it's a life condition they'll always have to cope with, to some degree."

"That sounds bleak, especially for a Christian."

"Ah, the fundamentalist is back!"

"He never left."

"But, Gregory, don't all Christians spend their lives coping with one sin or another?"

"Yes, but that's no justification for giving in to sin!"

"Who's talking about giving in? I'm talking about homosexual *temptations*, not homosexual *behavior*. And even though I'm not the avid Bible reader you are, I know the Scripture teaches us to resist temptation without guaranteeing that temptation will disappear entirely. Good counseling does the same. It teaches the patient to reduce his problems as much as possible, and cope with the problems that remain."

Half an hour had already passed and Greg had more information than he'd be able to digest before Robbie's next session.

"You've dumped a lot on me, Alex. When can we talk again?"

"I've been meaning to discuss that with you, Gregory."

Greg perked up at the change in Alex's voice.

"I'd prefer," Alex began hesitantly, "we discontinue discussion of Robbie's case."

"But—"

"I know I said I'd help, and I hope I have helped a bit."

"Oh, Alex!" Greg reassured him. "You've done more than a bit! No, if you'd rather not supervise this, I understand. I'm just grateful for all you've given me so far."

"I hope my other patients will feel the same way."

"You mean—"

"I'm retiring."

Greg should have been happy; Alex had weathered a fine career and deserved to rest.

Then why did he feel so uneasy?

"That's, uh, great! Great, Alex! What are your plans?"

After a long pause, the doctor replied.

"They're indefinite right now."

Clearly he didn't want to elaborate; Greg took the hint.

"I'm happy for you. It's just unexpected. Say! Can Christine and I take you to dinner? To celebrate?"

Greg heard a gasp, then a sniffle. Was Alex crying?

"Not just yet," he finally answered. "But," he whispered, "thank you so much for asking."

"Alex, I'm going to let you go. Thanks again. I'll call next week, okay?"

"Do that. God bless you, Gregory."

He started to say, "You too, Alex," but the doctor hung up before he could.

TWENTY

And good afternoon! This is Calvin Blanchard with 'Open Heart' on KLVE, coming to you weekdays from three to five with in-studio guests and taking your calls, perspectives, and comments. But first, it's my turn to share some perspectives of my own.

"By now you've probably heard about the hoodlums who desecrated Josh Ferguson's funeral service yesterday in Orange. But in case you don't read the papers or haven't been within ear-shot of a radio or television today, let me fill you in.

"Midway through Mr. Ferguson's service, an army of gay activists calling themselves BRAVO stormed into the Waverly Chapel and took over, shouting and blowing whistles and terrorizing the people who'd come to pay tribute to Joshua. They pillaged the chapel and mocked Ferguson's memory with accusations. Mrs. Ferguson is reported to have fainted, probably to BRAVO's delight. By the time the police arrived, the last rites of Josh Ferguson had been reduced to shambles.

"And what crime had he committed to earn this treatment? According to BRAVO, he was a homosexual. Yes, the word is out. Someone we all knew and who many of us respected is now rumored to have been gay.

"'Wait!' you say. 'If he was gay, why would other homosexuals do something so horrible to one of their own?' Ah, but you see, Josh wasn't proud to be gay. According to BRAVO, he kept it a secret and even tried to overcome it. And to people like BRAVO, that was unforgivable.

"Several questions are raised by this incident, the first being, Where were the police? According to news reports, they'd been warned about the incident in advance...."

By yours truly.

"The Orange police department says it patrolled the area in response to the warning but, since they saw no sign of disturbance, didn't bother to assign officers to the funeral. They did come, eventually, but by then it was too late.

"Other questions remain to be answered: Was Josh Ferguson really gay, or was this an assumption on BRAVO's part? If he was, how did they find out? And why are they using such cruel, barbaric methods on innocent people? No doubt, we'll be speculating on these questions for years, but here's one I'd like you to speculate on now. Has your opinion of Josh Ferguson changed since you learned of his alleged sexual preference?

"If so, consider this: Spencer Tracy and Katherine Hepburn, two of our most beloved screen personalities, had an adulterous relationship for years. In case you've forgotten, God's not fond of *that* sin, either. You probably knew that, but do you watch their movies anyway? How about Tchaikovsky? I'll bet you've heard *he* was gay, but do you switch the dial when the *1812 Overture* comes on the radio? Not if you've got any taste in music! The point is, you probably appreciate the contributions these people have made, while disapproving, and rightfully so, of certain aspects of their conduct.

"Can you extend Joshua Ferguson the same favor? Without justifying his alleged homosexuality, can you retain your respect for his achievements and see the many other good qualities that existed in the man? If you can't, you're playing right into BRAVO's hands. Here's why.

"Their leader appeared on Melanie Stone's television show last week. You might have seen it. He declared openly that BRAVO plans to expose other so-called closet cases. Why? Because, in his words, *'If we can expose gays who are hiding in the church, then the church will reject them.'*"

"Did you hear that? They're counting on us to reject homosexuals who might be in our churches. So, if we reject them, offering no grace or help in overcoming their problems, we're doing just what the radical gays are counting on us to do. Have you already rejected Josh Ferguson in your mind, now that you've heard he was gay? Then you, in a small way, are already an ally to BRAVO.

"That's something to think about, anyway."

Christine readily accepted Alma Ferguson's invitation; Greg, dubious at first, decided her presence would help.

During the two morning sessions Greg's mind was elsewhere, anticipating what his conversation with Alma Ferguson
would be like. He planned on volunteering nothing about the
tape or Josh's phone call. It would be an unnecessary burden for
her to carry.

Hopefully, she wouldn't ask any difficult questions. He still
didn't know how to answer if she did.

He'd thought of it all morning when he should have been
thinking of the clients sitting in front of him.

"If I'm not careful," he told Christine while turning onto
Chapman Avenue, "they'll find another couch to sit on. Clients
have a way of knowing when the counselor isn't paying attention."

Christine had brought a handful of roses from their garden;
she kept them in her lap while finding a station on the radio.

They drove onto Chapman Avenue and headed east for the
Orange Hills. Christine held the written directions while navi-
gating, though she didn't need them. She'd grown up less than
three miles from their destination.

"Which street do we turn on?" Greg asked.

"Jamboree. It won't come up for another few miles." She
found a jazz station and adjusted the volume.

"Do you realize, babe, we're meeting a woman who's involved
in a major news story? I'll bet everyone wants an interview with
Alma Ferguson, especially since the funeral. It's still in the
news. And she invited *us* to talk with her."

He waited for some acknowledgment.

"So don't you feel important?"

Christine sighed.

"Just a little?"

"Yes," she conceded, "this is an adventure."

"The genuine article."

They reached Jamboree and headed south into a vast ex-
panse of hills and housing developments. Christine flicked off
the radio and recalled riding horseback through the area they
were turning into. "There was nothing here but hills and trails. I
hate to see them building it all up!"

"Now, what street are we looking for?" Greg asked after
turning right, left, and right again. "I'm lost."

"Rocking Horse Lane is near the top. I'll tell you when we're
getting close."

Each street they turned onto revealed larger, more stylish residences. Two-story tract housing gave way to sprawling Mediterranean-style homes. These, in turn, faded next to the custom-designed structures looming on the side of the hill the car was now scaling.

"Right at the next stop," Christine instructed. "Then right again. The next street should be Rocking Horse Lane."

Greg steered accordingly, and they found themselves gaping at the landscapes of the estates greeting them. They rounded one last corner, spotted Rocking Horse Lane, cruised while checking addresses, then braked in front of their destination.

Four-zero-seven Rocking Horse Lane was protected by a thin, five-foot-high fence, meeting at a small gate and enclosing an acre and a half of understated elegance. The lawn beyond the security gate rolled serenely to meet a brown, Tudor-style mansion. Two floor-to-ceiling windows balanced each other to complement the carved-oak doors stretching seven feet over the porch. A cobblestone driveway divided the impossibly green lawn, bordered with low-slung, manicured shrubs. Spires and angles on the roof jutted into the clear March sky.

"Wow," was the most intelligent comment they could finally muster.

They parked in front the entrance, stepped up to the porch, and rang the bell.

Westminster chimes sang. Footsteps answered them.

The doors opened and a man with a military bearing stood looking at them. He appeared to be in his sixties.

Greg recognized him as the one who'd sat with Alma at the funeral.

"Dr. Bishop?" he asked politely. "And Mrs. Bishop? I'm Leonard Henderson, Alma's brother. Come in, please."

He ushered them into a tiled entryway opening onto a formal living room with more high windows. A glimpse of a tennis court could be seen.

"I'm glad you could come." His manner was grave and firm, much as it had been on Thursday. "Did you have any trouble finding us?"

Greg began some small talk about their drive as Alma Ferguson stepped in from the living room. Away from the distraction of the funeral proceedings, Greg got his first good look at her. Dressed in a woolen skirt and white blouse, she appeared less fragile than during their first encounter. She was small and well-groomed, a gracious lady with the air of one who'd lived a privileged life. Grief was still etched on her face, but a gentle warmth showed through it.

Greg smiled and greeted her, but it was Christine she went to.

"I'm so glad you came," she told Christine earnestly, clasping Christine's hand in both of her own. "Thank you."

"Mrs. Ferguson," Greg interjected, "this is my wife, Christine."

"Thank you for inviting me." Christine extended the roses. "These are from our yard."

"Aren't they lovely! Oh, you're sweet to bring them. Leonard, can you find a vase for these?"

He stepped forward.

"And put them in the living room, would you?"

He nodded and bowed slightly.

"This is Colonel Henderson, my brother."

"We've met." Greg nodded at the colonel as he took the roses from his sister.

"And thank you, Dr. Bishop, for coming," she said, turning to Greg.

"Greg. I'm Greg, please."

"And I'm Alma."

She led them into a large sitting room to the right of the entryway.

The front lawn looked doubly majestic from inside the house, framed in the picture windows at the far end of the long room. Built-in bookcases supported volumes and framed photographs, and in a brick fireplace, the room's focal point, a quiet flame crackled. Two long blue couches formed an *L* over the cream-colored carpet, offset with antique tables. A tray with two urns, chocolate wafers, cups, and sweetener with cream was waiting on the long coffee table in front of the couches.

"It's hardly cold enough for a fire, I know, but it cheers the room, don't you think?" Mrs. Ferguson asked Christine as she gestured for them to seat themselves.

"If I had a fireplace like that," Christine answered, "I'd have logs burning in the summer."

Mrs. Ferguson smoothed her skirt. "Tea or coffee, Christine?"

"Coffee, please."

"Greg?"

"The same."

She poured, offered the wafers, which Greg and Christine accepted, then sat back and appraised her guests.

"Thank you for bringing Christine, Greg. I've got strong feelings about wives staying involved in their husbands' affairs."

The remark sounded strange to Greg, who couldn't think of a response.

"We're both so sorry about Mr. Ferguson," Christine said. "That sounds so empty, I know, but we're really so sorry."

Alma waved the condolence away. "I've had more sympathy than you can imagine, Christine." She glanced out the window at a car that had slowed in front of the house. "And more curiosity than I can tolerate!" She stared at the car until it drove on, then turned back to the Bishops.

"But thank you," she answered Christine.

She sipped her tea, set it back on the table, then looked at Greg.

"I want to talk to you about your involvement with Joshua. And I need some honest answers from you."

"It's minimal, Alma. I never really met him."

"Not as minimal as you may think." She looked over her shoulder toward the living room and raised her voice.

"Leonard? Can you bring those papers, please?"

Colonel Henderson appeared with two manila files in hand. She took them and thanked him while Greg and Christine's curiosity rose.

"Do you need anything else?" her brother asked.

"No. Thank you, Leonard."

He left quietly.

"He's been good to me, these past few days," she whispered, opening one of the files and looking for something. "He came right over from Newport Beach as soon as he heard the news. He's been staying with me since then, handling all the details. Here." She pulled out a thin paper and handed it across the coffee table to Greg. "Tell me if you've seen this before."

A quick glance told him he had. It was the faxed note from BRAVO.

Alma Ferguson paid close attention to his response; he decided to respect her request for honesty.

"I've seen it."

"Thank you. I knew you had."

Greg knew he'd just been tested and passed.

"It came over Josh's fax machine March 11," she said, "the day before he died. He didn't know I'd seen it."

She pulled out another paper and gave it to Greg. "He put *that* note into an envelope with *this* one and taped it to his dashboard that night."

Greg took it while Christine kept her eyes discreetly averted; Alma noticed.

"You can read it as well, Christine."

Greg unfolded the note while Christine read over his shoulder.

> Alma:
>
> Now you know. I won't blame you for hating me. Don't try to understand. I don't believe you ever could.
>
> Josh

He looked up from the note.

"You'd be doing me a great favor by telling me everything you know about this, Greg."

He stared mutely at her.

"I know he sent you a message by tape. He set up a video camera in his den. I listened outside the door. I heard all of it."

Greg closed his eyes, grimacing inwardly.

"I heard him rhapsodizing about *her*," Alma added.

She picked something else out of the file. A wallet.

"They found this on him. And in it"—she pulled out a snapshot—"*this.*"

Greg knew what it was before she handed it to him, but accepted it anyway.

The girl from Kentucky.

"Did you see her at the funeral?"

Clear, cold, blue-gray eyes. Perfect features. Dark hair turned silver over the decades.

Of course. It had to be.

"Alexandra Chappel," Mrs. Ferguson said bitterly. "Do you know who she is?"

The name was vaguely familiar to Greg. "I've heard of her somewhere."

"She's one of the better-known Republican women in the country."

"Alexandra Chappel!" Christine exclaimed, remembering. "You know, Greg. She's a lobbyist. She did fund-raising for the Reagan campaign in '84. I think she's been involved in a lot of conservative causes, too, hasn't she?" she asked Alma.

"Causes are her specialty, Christine," Mrs. Ferguson answered. "Antifeminist causes, antigay causes, antinuclear disarmament, anti-immigration. She aspires to be Phyllis Schlafly, but believe me, she's no Phyllis Schlafly."

"Oh?"

"She'll never have Mrs. Schlafly's class."

Her voice carried waves of contempt.

"She was married to Senator Chappel from Georgia, but she'd gotten her hooks into politics long before that. When he died, she moved to California to make a name for herself, which she's done."

"I've definitely heard of her," Christine said. "She's a very public figure, come to think of it."

"She is," Alma conceded, "a terrific speaker and fund-raiser. A born leader. But people in the know are very leery of her. She passes herself off as a traditional conservative woman, but scratch the surface and you'll find a sick extremist."

"What was her connection to Mr. Ferguson?" Christine asked innocently.

"I believe she killed him."

Even Greg hadn't expected that. He and Christine stared. Alma Ferguson looked at them steadily and nodded.

Greg swallowed. "Why do you believe that?"

"She was blackmailing him."

The photo, suicide note, and message from BRAVO were laid out on the coffee table. Greg looked at them. They *did* spell blackmail, but not from Alexandra Chappel.

"This note's from BRAVO," he began.

"BRAVO," Alma interrupted, "knew about him because Alexandra conveyed the information to them."

Greg was unconvinced. "Oh, no, that can't be right. A conservative lobbyist wouldn't acquaint herself with people like BRAVO. And she certainly wouldn't convey information to them!"

"She's a viper, Greg," Alma retorted. "Nothing is beneath her. If Joshua were alive he'd tell you the same."

"But they found out about your husband by breaking into Dr. Crawford's office and stealing his records!"

"And how did they know the records were there, if she hadn't told them?"

"I think," Greg said, "they broke into Dr. Crawford's office to get any records they could. They didn't know Mr. Ferguson was one of his patients."

"They knew," Mrs. Ferguson said with confidence. "And they knew because of her."

Greg tried to grasp the notion of Alexandra Chappel leaking information to activist gays. It didn't make sense.

Alma poured herself more tea. Without asking, she refilled Greg's and Christine's cups with coffee, sipped from her own, then regarded Greg purposefully.

"Let's exchange stories, Greg. Tell me what you know about my husband and I'll tell you what I know about Mrs. Chappel."

He considered.

"I can explain how you got involved in all this," she offered. "You want to know, don't you? I'm sure Christine does."

Christine nodded.

"Then, please. Let's talk."

He decided the request was fair; the exchange of information was enticing as well. As concisely as he could, he walked her through the night of March 12, when he'd received her husband's call. Then he described key subsequent events: the package, Robbie's first visit (he skipped the details of their conversation; that was privileged material), and the portion of the tape he'd viewed so far. He wasn't ready or willing to let her know the tape had been stolen, and he hoped against hope she'd not ask where it was now.

His explanation seemed to satisfy her. "What you've told me so far," she affirmed, "matches all that I know. Now, let me fill you in."

She folded her hands and began.

"Joshua never got over what happened between him and Mrs. Chappel when they were teenagers."

"Their relationship?"

"The way it ended. The bare facts of the story he told you were true, but when I heard him telling it I nearly laughed out

loud. Joshua never felt the sort of passion he described to you for
anyone. But he saw their fling through rose-colored glasses. To
him, she was a sainted martyr, and he was the cad who betrayed
her. It wasn't love, Greg, it was guilt."

Or, Greg thought, *it* was *love and* you'd *prefer to call it guilt*.
She read his doubts.

"I'm not kidding myself about that, Greg," she asserted. "I'd
prefer to believe it was another woman I'd been competing with
all these years. I'd have known how to fight that."

Greg smiled. This woman was sheltered, but not naive.

"Josh was twenty-three when we met, and I was thirty-one.
I'm sure you noticed the age difference between us."

Greg had, but wasn't about to admit it. "No, not really."

"Bless you for pretending. Anyway, Joshua told me early in
our courtship about the girl he'd never forgotten."

She smiled ruefully at Christine. "Wasn't I a fool to marry
someone who thought he carried the torch for someone else?"

"I wouldn't have," Christine said candidly, "but that doesn't
make you a fool."

She continued. "He was drawn to strong women. I'm strong
in my own right, though in a different way than Alexandra. A
motherly way, I guess, which is what he wanted. I supported
Joshua in the early days when he was struggling to make his
mark. He appreciated that. And when he proposed, I knew that,
although our relationship lacked a certain passion most young
couples enjoy, he was going places. And I loved him."

She broke off and looked pleadingly at them both.

"No matter what I say about Joshua, you'll know I loved him,
won't you?"

They assured her they would.

"If he had problems with men back in those days, I certainly
didn't notice. Maybe that thing was always there. Maybe he just
pushed it down."

Greg had heard homosexuality called many things before,
but not "that thing."

"The early days were good. He wasn't romantic, but he was
considerate and a good provider. Successful, too; you know that.
Problems didn't come between us until both our children were
grown."

Alma pointed at two framed photos on the bookcase. "Katherine. She's twenty-three and married, and John, twenty-five. He's in law school."

She gazed at the pictures; all three did, and Christine felt a sudden longing for children. They were clearly Alma's main source of comfort now; who would *she* have, if Greg died?

"Joshua was on the road quite a bit, as you can imagine. But when he was home he was a family man, always spending time with the kids and puttering around the house. And then, a few years ago, his career lost its excitement. He got restless, maybe because there weren't any real challenges left."

Greg remembered the awards on Ferguson's wall.

"He became distant. Even when he was here, he *wasn't* here. Does that make sense?"

It was a common complaint wives made about their husbands. Greg heard it frequently; he told her so.

"He started drinking. Heavily. He'd leave the house at odd hours to go for drives. He said he needed to unwind. He'd be gone three, four hours at a time with no explanation. When I'd ask for one, he'd resent it. Finally, he shut me out. I'd nag and threaten, but he simply wouldn't let me in on whatever it was he was going through! Finally, I stopped asking. I'm strong, but not very aggressive, Christine. I hope you'll do better."

Christine smiled.

"The late-night drives became routine. But I never got used to the smell of cigarette smoke on him when he'd come home. Joshua never smoked. Or the occasional matchbooks I'd find with phone numbers written on them. All the classic signs of an affair, right? I think he was finally giving in to his problem because there was nothing left to distract him from it."

Her fists clenched again.

"Not even me. I was never enough."

Greg felt he had to say something.

"Alma, from what I know of homosexuality, no woman could have been enough."

"Then what about *marriage*, Greg?" she flared. "Thirty-two years together wasn't enough? What about his family? Thirty-two years of building a home wasn't enough to persuade him not to throw it all away for a bunch of men he didn't even know?"

Nobody could have answered that.

Alma leaned back wearily. "I finally confronted him. He swore to me, very sincerely, that he'd never been with another woman."

She let out a cold laugh.

"He was telling the truth!"

Greg and Christine watched helplessly.

"Can anybody tell me how I could have known?" Her shoulders quivered; she looked disgusted, either with Josh or herself. "Greg! Are there symptoms wives should beware of to let them know their husbands prefer men?"

"None that I know of."

"But if their man seems infatuated with a good-looking young gospel singer, most women would suspect."

She eyed Greg carefully as she said it. He shifted on the couch, wet his lips, and made a decision.

"There was nothing sexual between your husband and Robbie Carlton. I know that for a fact."

"Oh, don't give me that!" she exclaimed. "There *was* something. Maybe not on Robbie's end, but certainly on Joshua's."

"But nothing—how can I put it? Nothing *happened*. It wasn't that way," Greg said.

"Is that supposed to comfort me? My husband loved another man; that's too much for any woman to deal with!"

Greg nodded quietly.

"But thank you for the reassurance. I always wondered," she said feebly. "Robbie's not to blame."

"No."

"Josh was thinking of him till the end. I heard him say so."

"On the tape?"

"Yes. I'd have known anyway. He perked up whenever Robbie was around."

It occurred to Greg that she was grieving not only the loss of her husband, but years of unreturned love.

Alma sipped more tea and stared into the cup.

"I finally caught on last April."

"How?"

She looked up at Greg, then out the window, remembering.

"He shot back to life when he began production on that report. I hadn't seen him so excited about anything in years! It was to be his swan song, did you know that?"

"No."

She nodded. "His last project before retiring. Journalism lost its charm for him years ago. He only kept it up to put the kids through college, I suppose. But this was different."

Christine, who'd said little up to this point, entered the conversation.

"What was different?"

"His enthusiasm. The report was a challenge, because none of the studios wanted him to do it. They're terrified of offending the gays. They knew there'd be trouble if they did a story on them. Unless it was a positive one, of course, and Joshua's reports seldom were."

Just ask Brian Decker, Greg thought, remembering Robbie's account of his time with the televangelist.

"How," Greg asked, "did Josh go about doing these reports?"

She thought for a moment.

"Well, they began with a concept: What subject did he want to investigate, who could he interview to cover all sides, and why is the subject important to the general public?"

"What made him decide on gay rights?" Christine asked.

"I still don't know." She frowned. "The timeliness of it, perhaps? His own secret? Who knows?"

There's more awful truth to find out, Ferguson had said. Key points from their only conversation stood out sharply to Greg.

"Then the interviews began. He always," Alma explained, "contacted his subjects by region. The East Coast was his first region to cover. He contacted dozens of people, who gave him names and phone numbers of other dozens of people, and finally narrowed them down to the choicest interview subjects. He researched all of them, then flew back East to talk with them on-camera. That's how he got your name."

"From Bennie."

She nodded. "Joshua was very moved by Bennie's story. He told me all about it, apparently—"

She stopped.

"Apparently?"

"This is difficult."

"It's all right, Alma," Christine spoke up. "We know Bennie told Mr. Ferguson about that fight on the beach."

"It wasn't a fight," Greg said miserably.

"Anyway," she continued, "when Josh asked Bennie what made him a gay activist, he said that night was a turning point. He named you, said he thought you were a psychologist in southern California. He even said, off the record, that he planned on coming out here to see you."

Greg held his breath.

"For a—'confrontation,' I think that's what he told Josh."

She noticed Christine had gone pale and leaned forward.

"Christine, honey, *please* don't be afraid!" She put out her hand and touched Christine's lightly. "People threatened Joshua all the time; it used to terrify me! But nothing ever came of it."

"Promise?" Christine asked, shakily.

"Why, has anything happened?"

Greg's eyes shot a strong message to his wife's: *I don't want her to know he's already here.*

"Is he in town?" Mrs. Ferguson asked anxiously.

The question relieved Greg. *Good. She doesn't even know it was Bennie who spearheaded Thursday's horror show.*

"He hasn't confronted me," Greg hedged, "but we're ready if he does."

Alma bought it.

"Did you actually see the taped interview Josh did with Bennie?" he asked.

She shook her head.

That explains why she didn't recognize him. Now change the subject.

"Okay, so after the East Coast interviews, then what?"

"Then he listed the people in California he wanted to talk with, got background information on them, and went to work. That's when I learned about Joshua's problem."

Greg cleared his throat and poured himself more coffee.

"How?"

"In late May, I believe, he interviewed Dr. Crawford and told me about the work the doctor did with homosexuals. Shortly after that, he decided to get professional counseling for himself. For drinking and depression; that's what he told me. He said his psychologist's name was Dr. Navarro."

She shrugged.

"He'd never wanted to see a counselor before, but who was I to argue? And it did help. He cut his drinking down to almost nothing. More than that, the late-night drives were over. He stayed home. We started communicating again. I felt closer to him, and he seemed more peaceful."

Alma had been smiling; her face clouded suddenly.

"But in January he came home from one of his counseling sessions in such a state! Very agitated. I asked why and suddenly I was again on the outside looking in. No answers, no explanations. He took off again one night without telling me why. 'We're back to square one,' I told myself. Only this time, I refused to be shut out!"

Her eyes flashed.

"Not after having a taste of a decent marriage again! I did something I'd never done in all our years together."

She looked at them defiantly.

"I spied on him. I went through the records in his den and started checking receipts, appointment books, or anything else that could explain his sudden change. I found my first surprise in his checkbook register."

"Which was?"

"Monthly payments made out to Dr. Alex Crawford."

"None to Dr. Navarro?"

"If there ever *was* a Dr. Navarro, Joshua never wrote a check to him! I wouldn't have thought anything of his seeing Dr. Crawford if he hadn't lied to me about it. But two and two is four. I couldn't deny the obvious."

She looked back at her children's pictures, then at Christine. "He fathered my children. Could I turn my back on him?"

Christine shook her head.

"It was clear he'd gone to Dr. Crawford for the kind of help the man specialized in. And the doctor *did* help him. Whatever or whomever he'd been involved with, it was over. At least for a while. But the secrecy started again. Then I found his appointment book and got a second surprise."

She pointed at Alexandra Chappel's photo.

"On Wednesday, February 20, he blocked off 6:00 to 9:30 P.M. for her."

Christine reacted visibly. "Was her name in his appointment book?"

"Just the last name. 'Chappel,' written across the time slots, and a phone number."

Greg was confused. "When was the last time he'd seen her?"

"Not since he was a boy, as far as I knew! I was amazed. I still didn't confront him. How could I admit I'd been snooping? That was beneath me."

She laughed ironically.

"The things we do for pride! Then I thought maybe it was another Chappel. So I called the number. A woman answered. I asked for Alexandra. 'This is she,' the woman said. I hung up."

"Oh, Alma," Christine commiserated.

"First, I was hit with the fact he was gay. Then I learned he'd been successfully treated. But for what? To have an affair with an old flame? After the hell I'd gone through with him? No, no."

"But you still didn't tell him what you'd found out?"

"I couldn't. I never knew how to get through to Joshua when he closed me out. I felt helpless."

For the first time, Greg and Christine saw Alma Ferguson's tears flow.

"Don't *ever* shut her out!" She said it to Greg a little wildly, pointing at Christine. "That's why I wanted her here today. A wife should never be left out of her husband's affairs!"

The word *affairs* was ill-advised, he thought.

"Everyone was shut out of Joshua's life after that," she sniffed. "Even his associates. And suddenly," she observed, "he wouldn't let anyone work on the report with him. He turned downright nasty when people pressed him to see how it was coming along."

"You have no idea why?"

"None! I went back to snooping through his desk, but nothing turned up. But in late February, I heard him on the phone, late at night, talking to someone. I picked up the bedroom extension and listened in. *She* was on the other end, saying something like, 'I'm not going to let you throw it all away!' And he was saying 'It's over. End it now.' She threatened him. I distinctly remember her saying, 'I'll drag your name through the mud,' and he said, 'I'd rather die than let you manipulate me like you do everyone else.'"

"He was trying to end the affair?" Christine offered. "And she was going to blackmail him for that?"

"Not all scorned women are as patient as I was, Christine."

"So it was retaliation?" Greg asked.

"Nobody says no to Alexandra Chappel. He started an affair with her, then was foolish enough to tell her he'd been seeing Dr. Crawford, then tried to break it off. You know the rest."

Not entirely, Greg disagreed silently.

"He went into deep depression after that. I was scared. He'd been taking sleeping pills. I checked the medicine cabinet and noticed he had two full bottles of Phynothal."

She pressed her forehead.

"And I had the most horrible feeling! I didn't care anymore about what he'd done; I just wanted him back!"

She whimpered lightly, pressed her hand to her mouth, and fought more tears.

"Then the fax came." She pointed at it. "And I lost him for good."

Her breathing came hard.

"I heard him in the den, slamming drawers and cursing. Then he came downstairs and grabbed a video camera, went back to the den and locked himself inside. I crept up the stairs and listened, heard some shuffling, then came right up to the door and put my ear to it. I heard him say, "Hello, Dr. Bishop." I recognized your name and knew whatever he was taping was for you."

She was looking up the stairs beyond the entryway as she spoke.

"I heard him telling you about Alexandra, and his father, and the pastor. I was terrified. I knocked on the door, but he yelled at me to go away. At a time like this, he wanted me to go away!"

Her voice turned brutal.

"And I stood on those stairs and realized he'd been telling me that all his life! 'Go away, Alma, I've got work to do! Go away, I want to be with Robbie! Go away, I've got a date with other men, or Alexandra Chappel; anyone but you! Go away!'"

Now Christine was crying; Mrs. Ferguson didn't notice.

"So, I finally gave him what he wanted. I went away. I walked downstairs, sat on this couch, took off my wedding ring, and consigned him, from the bottom of my heart, to the devil."

Her face was grim and determined.

"He went to the studio for something, then returned. I ignored him. Twice I caught him looking at me but I pretended he didn't exist. That evening he dressed and told me he was going for a drive. I didn't answer. I didn't even look at him. Then he stood behind me and said something."

She closed her eyes.

"'Can I have a kiss?' Just like a little boy. 'Can I have a kiss, Alma?'"

She opened her eyes.

"I said, 'Why bother? I'll still be here for you to ignore when you get back.'"

The room chilled.

"That's how we said good-bye."

She looked at her left hand.

"I still haven't put his ring back on."

Christine moved off the couch and sat next to Alma. Their shoulders lightly touched. Mrs. Ferguson looked at her.

"He killed himself three blocks away from here. He didn't want me to discover his body. Wasn't that considerate? But didn't he know I'd be the one who'd have to drive to the morgue and look in a huge drawer and tell a stranger, 'Yes, that's my husband'?"

The words hung in the air; nobody spoke.

Then Christine stroked Mrs. Ferguson's shoulder, drew her into her arms, and held the woman while she sobbed.

Greg watched his wife, in awe.

Mrs. Ferguson composed herself and sat meekly on the couch.

"I'll answer for that," Alma husked.

"For what?" Christine asked.

"For letting him go like that. Do you know when I realized how much I still loved him?"

"When?"

"At the funeral, when they screamed those horrible things about him. I couldn't have cared less about me or the others there; I just wanted them to leave Joshua alone."

Alma smoothed her hair.

"I honestly think," she reflected, "that I could have killed every one of them."

After more silence, Mrs. Ferguson seemed to remember herself. "Look at me!" She touched her face, then looked at Christine. "I hope I didn't ruin your blouse."

She excused herself to use the washroom.

"Are you going to tell her about the tape?" Christine whispered as soon as Alma was gone.

"No need. Unless she asks point-blank, why lay that on her?"

"Because she might have a clue where it's gone!"

"She doesn't even know who it was that led the BRAVO troops at the funeral. No, she wouldn't have any clues."

"Shouldn't she know anyway?"

"Not until we're sure what they're going to—"

"Do we need more coffee?" Alma, composed and touched up, reappeared.

"No," Greg said, "and I'm sorry, Alma, but I'll have to get back to my office."

"A question before you go." She returned to her spot next to Christine. "Have you any idea why that woman came to the funeral?"

"None." He was happy to answer at least one question without evasions. "I didn't even know who she was."

"She might have come to gloat," Christine thought aloud.

Greg shot her an exasperated look; Alma wagged a finger at him.

"No, no, Greg, she's probably right." Then, to Christine, "You've got her pegged."

"From what you've said, she sounds like the type."

"But then"—her jaw quivered; she put up both hands—"no! I'm all right, really. But why did *they* come? Those people had nothing to gain by attacking a man who'd passed on!"

"I can't answer that one, either," Greg admitted.

Alma was crestfallen.

Greg rose. "I didn't answer the two most important questions you had for me. If you were a client, I'd give you a refund."

"You *can* answer this one." Alma stood to look squarely at Greg. "I heard Joshua tell you to stop them."

"Yes."

"Will you?"

"Somebody will."

There was little left to say. Greg thanked Mrs. Ferguson for her time and honesty, relieved he hadn't been asked whatever became of the tape. Christine got Mrs. Ferguson to promise a dinner date soon, and Alma tried to express her gratitude to them both.

The visit ended with mutual thanks and a promise to talk soon.

Christine hugged Alma, Greg kissed her cheek and was starting to escort Christine from the entryway onto the porch when Alma snatched his arm and planted it across Christine's shoulders.

"Keep her close, Greg."

TWENTY-ONE

*D*ebriefing was fun.

Anyone who was so inclined had a chance at the podium to share her or his perspective on the event, and few who'd actually been there passed up the chance. That, of course, stretched the meeting far past the appointed closing time, but who cared?

So intense was the mood of the speakers, so celebratory and triumphal, that for the first time a sense of elitism pervaded the group. Those Who Were There held a status Those Who Weren't sensed and envied, yet even Those Who Were There were divided, through speeches and comparisons, into select classes: Those Who Broke Something held special merit; Those Who Scuffled with the Old Men ranked a notch higher. He Who Snuffed the Candles enjoyed distinction; Those Who Were Arrested were war heroes.

Sainthood was reserved for and conferred upon Yelsom, who oversaw the proceedings from his throne next to the podium.

"I was scared," the man taking his turn admitted, "and I almost chickened out on the way into the chapel."

Boos flew up from the crowd; smaller than the last meeting, but twice as energized.

"But I made it, and I'm proud!"

Applause.

"Once Yelsom stepped in with his excuse-me-I-hope-I'm-not-disturbing-anything approach—"

Everyone howled while Yelsom shrugged modestly.

"—I felt a rush go through me, and let me tell you, I finally knew what the freedom fighters in the sixties felt like."

Cheers.

"Because I was fighting for my own and I'll *never* stop!"

He stepped down to more applause and BRAVO chants.

The parade to the front continued. Speaker after speaker regaled the group with different experiences, each noticeably more striking than the last. The next speaker recounted the terrified faces she'd thrust her finger into, the next assured them some gentleman's Brooks Brothers suit was no longer good for anything but dusting the furniture. Another swore he'd drawn blood; another boasted he'd been pummeled in the line of duty and still had the bruise to prove it.

The testimonials reached their hysterical peak when a young woman described hearing God's voice just before marching through the side chapel doors.

"She told me She'd subdue our enemies at our feet, and She did!"

On that note of edification, Yelsom rose and took charge.

"How sweet it is!" he shouted, his arms upraised.

They agreed loudly, for about three minutes.

When the shouting died, he bestowed special honor on those who'd been arrested, reminding them that civil disobedience was in the finest American tradition, making them more traditional than their so-called traditionalist enemies.

Calvin watched from the seventh row, where he'd found a seat next to two friendly women whom he'd struck up a conversation with before the meeting, breaking his own rule not to socialize.

He'd been standing against the back wall before the meeting began.

"Looking for a place?" the taller one had called out to him, smiling and pointing to the empty chair next to her.

He'd nodded and feigned gratitude; he'd rather have stayed in the back.

"I'm Roxanne," she said after he'd settled into the seat. "And this is Lisa."

He shook their hands. "Jeremy Rolfing."

They warmed to him immediately; he liked them in spite of himself.

Now, watching the meeting from an observer's vantage, he sensed a change in BRAVO. Fewer in attendance, for one thing. Something more, though.

Tension.

The vocal participants were wilder than before, reminding him of wild dogs having tasted blood and salivating for more. They were enjoying themselves hugely.

Others who had not gone, listening to their comrades retelling the stories about an event *they'd* missed, seemed slightly resentful, miffed at the insinuation they'd been somehow less committed by declining to show up.

Still others were downright uneasy. Commentators, civic leaders, and citizens of all walks had been saying for days that BRAVO was a disgrace, a blemish on Orange County's image. And they were not entirely happy to be grouped with a blemish. Their expressions showed hesitation to applaud the tactics employed at the funeral, even as their hands and mouths openly applauded it. Some grimaced while Yelsom bragged about charging Ferguson's casket. Calvin was insightful enough to recognize their uncertainty; things were, perhaps, going too far for them.

Interesting.

"So, the next event will take place in *their* territory," Yelsom was concluding. "No meetings until April 18."

"Any wake-up calls sent out in the meantime?" someone asked.

"Not yet. We'll let people consider Ferguson's fate for a while and wonder if something similar is waiting for them."

"Carlton's wondering, you can be sure!" another man yelled out.

"We gave him plenty to consider," Yelsom agreed. "And anyone stupid enough to challenge us on national television like he did deserves the best pageantry we can provide!"

Sickened, but aware of his surroundings, Calvin clapped and joined the BRAVO chant. From the corner of his eye, he watched Roxanne; she was, he felt, less than enthusiastic.

Yelsom raised both hands. "Until Thursday the eighteenth."

Meeting adjourned.

Calvin stood with Lisa and Roxanne.

"So!" Roxanne said. "I've never seen you around. Are you from this area?"

He'd rehearsed his story; this was his first recitation. He informed her he lived in Fountain Valley, had only recently come out, and was a full-time student at Cal State Fullerton. He'd come into an inheritance which allowed him to study broadcast journalism full-time; that detail gave him a way to discuss his studies intelligently. Lisa and Roxanne were interested. Then the conversation turned to sports (all three loved hockey and were glad Anaheim was considering a home team), movies (they liked old, serious films and lamented the trends toward violence;

he was a Meryl Streep devotee), and country music. Only his identity was false; his enjoyment of these two women was no act.

Thus, he didn't see Yelsom make his way toward him and tap his shoulder. He turned and gasped.

"Still wanna get more involved?" the New York voice demanded.

"Sure! Hi, Yelsom, how ya doin'? Yeah, sure."

"Hi, girls," Yelsom nodded. They smiled thinly; "girls" was a patronizing way to be addressed.

"I've forgotten your name," he said to Calvin.

So had Calvin.

"Jeremy," Roxanne said to Yelsom.

"Jeremy. Right."

Calvin seized the chance.

"I really do want to get involved. Why, is there anything you could use some help with?" He asked it directly into the eyes he was growing to hate.

"There is. How about a drink? We'll talk."

"Okay."

"All of us." He nodded to Lisa and Roxanne. "Okay?"

Lisa looked at Roxanne; Roxanne approved. "Sure. Let's go."

Yelsom started to leave. "The Shaft. About half an hour; sound good?"

"We'll see you there," Lisa answered, then turned to Calvin. "That's a man's bar, but we like it anyway."

"It's Yelsom's hangout, isn't it?" Calvin asked.

"I take it you don't go there."

"I don't go to bars much."

"Good for you," Roxanne nodded; Lisa agreed.

"There's more to life than bars," she said. "You wanna ride with us?"

"I'd better take my car, in case it gets late. Where's The Shaft?"

They gave him directions; he promised to meet them there.

It should have taken twenty minutes at the most; an hour had passed before Jeremy/Calvin stepped cautiously into his first gay bar.

The drive gave him time to talk himself out of it and head the other direction toward home. Nice Calvin nearly persuaded his renegade Other into being sensible; New Calvin sneered at sensibility and reminded himself that nothing he'd been doing lately qualified as sensible.

And, he insisted, *you'll never get next to Yelsom without playing the part all the way.*

The Shaft wasn't hard to find; walking into it was another matter.

Calvin parked two blocks down from the wooden sign identifying the place, which sat between a darkened travel agency and a laundromat. He'd barely covered the first block when the questions hit him.

Will you drink beer or Coke?

Coke. I'll say I don't drink—any crime in that?

Won't your nervousness show?

I'll pretend it's Yelsom making me nervous; he likes that.

What will you do if you see someone you know in there?

Don't even think about it.

He was about to cross the street onto the second block when his unruly legs refused and turned him left instead, around the corner and down the street away from the bar.

Halfway down that street he pivoted and turned in the direction he'd come from, hoping no one was watching and certain everyone was.

Back to the corner then left toward The Shaft. One more block to go.

The water's cold, so just jump in. Don't try to get used to it first. Just jump.

He did. Right past The Shaft and into the laundromat next to it. A Hispanic man was pulling his clothes from the dryer. Calvin blinked at him, then leaned against the wall and casually asked if he knew where the change machine was.

The man pointed at the machine Calvin was leaning against.

"Thanks. *Gracias.*" He inserted a dollar, which the machine refused. He pulled another from his wallet, pushed it in and scooped out four quarters.

"Good night," he told the man.

"Uh-huh."

He walked slowly out the door. The man watched him.

He watched the man.

"Good night!"

"Uh-huh."

He was halfway to his car again before he caught himself, spun around, and headed for The Shaft.

And past The Shaft again, then past the open door of the laundromat, where the Hispanic man folded T-shirts and shook his head at crazy gringos.

Down another block to a liquor store, where he loitered over a *Time* magazine and looked for anything he could find an excuse to buy.

He hadn't had bubble gum in years. He bought three pieces.

Back to The Shaft, blowing bubbles as he passed the laundromat while refusing to look at his friend, but imagining the man's expression.

Down another block.

Stop.

Either do it now, this instant, or call it off. All of it.

He didn't care who watched as he stood on the sidewalk, considering.

Josh Ferguson's dead. His funeral was trashed. You want answers.

Back to The Shaft and straight to the front door.

Dance music spilled onto the sidewalk. The windows were painted over; no way to see what he was walking into.

The third movement of a Roman orgy in D minor. Are you coming?

He put out a hand to pull the door open, then held it there.

"Why don't you just go in and get it over with?"

The customer from the laundromat stood on the sidewalk, laundry bag in hand.

"Thanks. I will."

The man said something in Spanish and walked away.

Calvin let his fingers grip around the knob and pull.

The music hit him first, then the cigarette smoke. The lights were low, but every part of the room could be seen clearly.

He first noticed the mirrored wall behind the bar, from which patrons could see themselves and each other. Posters of singers and models were haphazardly taped to the mirror; various beer and wine displays hung from the ceiling.

He'd jumped in; now he'd take a minute to acclimate himself.

Seven customers sat at the counter with their backs to him, tended to by a muscular, thirtyish man in a tight blue T-shirt. He looked up from the ashtray he was wiping and greeted Calvin with a nod; three men at the bar turned around, glanced at him, then looked back at their drinks. Stools were set along the wall to his right; seven men loitered around them, holding beer bottles and laughing. Snatches of conversation reached him.

To his left, a pool table sat under a suspended light. Three men flanked it; one was breaking. Balls tumbled into pockets; the sound carried.

Beyond the pool table another seating area waited; he couldn't see who was or wasn't using it. He noticed a crunch under his feet and was surprised to see sawdust thrown over the floor.

Calvin tried to look as though he were trying to find someone, then reminded himself that's just what he *was* doing. But he was also trying to take in every detail of the place.

It was, he decided, pretty tame; not at all what he'd expected. But then, having never been to a bar of any kind in his life, he had nothing to compare it to.

He studied the customers. No familiar faces, thank God. Not an unusual-looking group, either. A couple of the guys sported cowboy hats and boots; most were in typical casual garb. After the BRAVO meeting, they looked blessedly normal.

I'd have expected Yelsom to hang out someplace wilder than this. I'm glad for my sake he doesn't.

He heard his alias called out, turned left, and saw Lisa coming to him from the seating area behind the pool table. He smiled; she reached him and punched his shoulder.

"We thought you stood us up on our first date!" She took his hand. "Come on. Yelsom's waiting for us."

She guided him between customers, past the pool players, and into a corner where Yelsom and Roxanne sipped their beers.

Yelsom patted the chair next to him. Calvin took it; Yelsom slammed a bottle into his hand.

"I ordered you a Bud."

He stammered. "Ah, I don't drink."

"No problem; I'll keep it."

Yelsom grabbed it back; three empty bottles sat in front of him and he seemed inclined to add a few more. "If you want something else from the bar, you'll have to get it yourself."

Away from his flock he seemed slightly more human; more normal. The arrogance was still there, but the intensity wasn't.

Of course, his appearance was intense enough, but the other patrons weren't put off by it. Calvin wondered why, then realized he, too, was doing fewer double takes in Yelsom's presence.

"What's the name of your friend?"

Calvin missed the question; the uninterrupted *thump-thump* from the jukebox took some getting used to.

"Your friend who comes here," Yelsom repeated. "What's his name?"

"Wayne." *Glad I reviewed my script!* "He's not here."

"And you said he's been coming to meetings?"

"Only once. It was too much for him, but he knew I'd want to come. That's when he told me about it. And you."

He endowed *And you* with enough admiration to gag himself.

Yelsom tipped his chair back, emptied his bottle, and looked cockily at his admirer. "Tell me about yourself."

Calvin related the same story he'd given Roxanne and Lisa; Yelsom approved.

"You just came out?"

"Uh-huh."

"And already you're committed to activism?"

"Totally."

Roxanne slapped his back. "Nice to see, huh, Yelsom? Usually they play the bar scene for a few years before they get serious about anything."

Yelsom looked him up and down superciliously, then winked at the women.

"He'll do."

"For what?"

"For me."

Calvin froze; the women stared.

Yelsom exploded, slamming his bottle on the table.

"No, idiots! Not that. I need an assistant."

The news was a minor relief.

"What kind?"

"An available one with half a brain that's willing to work." He snapped at a passing waiter for another round. "Hey! Bring a Coke for Junior."

Calvin/Jeremy had been rechristened; henceforth, Yelsom would refer to him as Junior—a term, Lisa and Roxanne noted, far less flattering than *girls*.

Calvin noted it, too, but didn't care; it was dawning on him. *Yelsom's assistant. With access to Yelsom himself.*

Thank You, Lord, if indeed You're in the business of arranging things even in a gay bar. Thank You. Protect me, please.

The drinks arrived; Yelsom paid with a flourish.

He raised his beer. "To BRAVO!"

None dared to disagree; even customers out of Yelsom's vision lifted their glasses.

"What sort of help," Calvin asked over his Coke glass, "will you need?"

"Odd jobs. Give me your phone number; when something comes up, I'll be in touch."

"That's it? Just wait to hear from you?"

Yelsom turned his eyes on Junior; Junior was immediately sorry to have asked.

"You want the job?"

It was no job, but yes, he wanted it. He nodded meekly.

"Then I'll be in touch."

The four of them—Christian broadcaster disguised as gay activist, activist lesbians formerly disguised as Christian counselors, and activist leader with an undisclosed agenda, each of them unaware of the others' secrets—toasted again to BRAVO and to new ventures.

Yelsom left early; Lisa challenged Calvin to a game of pool.

"I don't play," he declined.

"Never! No brother of mine is going to be a non-pool player!"

Brother? He liked the word, and the feeling behind it. There were no sisters in his home, and these two were downright fun.

Lisa strode to the pool table; he followed obediently.

Brother? Where are you, Calvin?

She chalked her cue and racked the balls.

His hatred for everything BRAVO represented couldn't have been stronger, but tenderness and genuine affection were growing for these two.

"Take a cue; here's how to chalk it."

He chalked a stick automatically.

How could such enjoyable people be connected to such blatant evil?

"I'll break. Here's the best angle to shoot from."

But he'd been just as deceived himself, years ago. What right did he have to judge them?

"Try not to hit the center ball head-on."
But what they were doing had to be stopped. And exposed.
"Your turn. Hey! Jeremy?"
What right did he have to like them?

TWENTY-TWO

Greg had five counseling sessions with Robbie before April 19, the date of the Irvine concert and the deadline set by BRAVO. He conducted them looking for what Dr. Crawford called the "mutual benefit."

"When the psychologist/patient relationship truly works," the doctor had lectured, "both parties will get something out of it. Certainly, the emphasis must always be on the patient's well-being. But the psychologist will also grow from the experience, learning something new about himself, or about people in general. That's the mutual benefit inherent in good counseling."

The psychologist did grow from the experience; the first benefit he derived from it was a bigger chest. Meeting with Robbie reminded him of his forty-one years and the downhill slide his body would take without regular exercise.

Greg's attitude toward his other clients needed work, too. Their problems still affected him, and he dutifully listened, empathized with, and advised them as best he could. But his professional interest, normally spread out over his entire clientele, became more and more focused on Robbie Carlton.

It's understandable, he assured himself. *This case involves death, sexual problems, public figures, and a personal challenge. How could it not affect me?*

Greg began the treatment, as he always did, by reviewing the client's family history. Robbie's father, an engineer whose view of his son's artistry was less than positive, was a sore spot.

"He tolerated my music lessons," Robbie complained during their third session, "but he approved more of my brother, the athlete."

"How did you know that?"

"He bragged about Bob's football-playing all the time, but he hardly ever told his friends that his other boy was a singer."

"Did you ever talk to him about that?"

"Just once. I asked him why he never came to my recitals, but never missed any of Bob's games. That irritated him. He said he was paying for my lessons; wasn't that enough? He told me I was too sensitive, but if I really wanted him to come hear me sing, he'd do it. I declined. I didn't want any favors from him."

"And that made you angry?"

"It made me want some attention from him! I tried being a jock, but that didn't work. I got good grades, but that didn't impress him, either. I felt like there wasn't any way to please Dad, so I wrote him off. By the time I was fifteen, it was like he didn't exist anymore."

"Then it stopped bothering you?"

"I pretended it did. Mom liked my music, though. She's the one who got me started at church, singing solos and stuff like that. That's the only place I really felt appreciated. People at church thought I was special, which felt good. Is that wrong?"

"Hardly. Why shouldn't it feel good when people appreciate your gifts?"

"But sometimes that's the only time I feel good. I don't relate to people that well. Men, especially. When they talk about sports and all the guy stuff, I feel left out. But when I'm singing and people are applauding, I feel respected and completely in control. It's like a drug."

"But you can't always be onstage. How do you get this 'drug' when you're not singing?"

"By doing extravagant things," Robbie admitted thoughtfully. "Like buying meals or expensive gifts. Or doing things that are so theatrical they get everyone's attention."

"That can be dangerous."

"I know. I tend to get too dramatic sometimes."

Through all the discussion, one singular issue was often brought up but never resolved: what to do about BRAVO. April 19 was fast approaching with no answer in sight.

"I'll retire," Robbie would decide one moment, only to recant minutes later with, "But why should I let them do this to me? I said I'd fight, and I will! Let them tell everyone I'm gay! I can always deny it, can't I?"

Greg would listen without comment.

"Or I could announce it myself and take a leave of absence for a year until it all dies down. Right?"

"Possibly."

"No," he conceded moments later, "it would never die down. Even if I kept recording, nobody would buy my records. I'd always be known as the fag who sings gospel. I heard a great joke yesterday. You know what a fag is?"

Greg shrugged.

"A homosexual gentleman who just left the room."

Robbie laughed.

Greg didn't join him.

The question of his career and BRAVO's exposure still hung heavily in the air.

And while Greg and Robbie struggled with the intricacies of a therapeutic relationship, Calvin and Yelsom formed their own dark bond.

It centered around chores. Shortly after agreeing to be Yelsom's right-hand man, Calvin received a call from his new superior.

"What're you up to, Junior?"

The call came at 7:15 A.M. three days after their conversation at The Shaft.

"Just waking up," Calvin murmured. Did this guy have no consideration whatever?

"I call at odd hours. Get used to it."

Good morning to you too, Calvin thought, but answered, "No problem. What's up?"

"I need you to run some errands. Got something to write with?"

And so began the routine of Yelsom calling at a whim, dispensing a list of chores needing immediate attention. Calvin agreed to keep his days relatively free until 3:00, when (he told Yelsom) he had to be at school. He ran errands for the leader of Orange County's gay terrorist group for half a day, then sat behind the microphone of Orange County's Christian radio station during the second half.

The chores tended to be menial, tedious, and assigned with no explanation.

Some were self-explanatory, though. Calvin's first job was to place a new order for the black T-shirts favored by BRAVO members, pick them up, pay the bill, and distribute them at the next meeting. Bullhorns, too, needed to be purchased for future demonstrations, as did whistles and materials for signs and posters. This was, Calvin assumed, grist for the BRAVO mill. But other assignments he received were harder to comprehend.

A quantity of black felt pens was ordered, purchased, then mysteriously no longer needed once Calvin delivered them to Yelsom at The Shaft.

"Take them back," was Yelsom's abrupt response. "We don't need them anymore. Be sure to get a full refund."

On another occasion, Yelsom informed him that a dozen DC comic books were suddenly crucial to the future of gay rights. Calvin found the desired comics—"Be sure at least seven of them are Superman; you can pick out the rest yourself"—and delivered them to Yelsom, who rewarded his right-hand man with a contemptuous "Good, Junior."

Calvin never saw the comics again and could only conclude that his unbalanced superior liked Superman.

Similar ridiculous assignments included a trip to the drugstore for hairpins, the purchase of three Marie Osmond cassette tapes, and the distribution of discount coupons for Kentucky Fried Chicken to the startled Jehovah's Witnesses who stood on the corner of Chapman and Grand, distributing their own materials.

Each assignment was carried out obediently, without question or comment. Yelsom was pleased, and Calvin finally realized he was being tested. If he would follow these silly instructions to the letter, he could be trusted to carry out more important duties. That, at least, is what he hoped Yelsom was thinking. Time proved him right.

Every "chore" Calvin performed convinced Yelsom he'd found a veritable slave who'd be useful for future conquests; every time Calvin charmed Yelsom with his subservient "Sure, I'll do that!" Calvin realized how easily this egomaniac could be duped into trusting him.

He gradually put that trust to the test by posing innocent questions.

"Isn't it hard," he asked once at The Shaft, "for you to come all the way from LA to meet me here?"

"I live in Santa Ana. What made you think I live in LA?" Yelsom responded.

"Oh! Someone said you have a big house in west LA."

"Shows what they know. My apartment's no bigger than a bread box."

He tried similar fishing tactics on the subject of Josh Ferguson.

"Too bad Josh Ferguson didn't just come out and admit he was gay," Calvin mused over his Coke while they sat at the bar on one occasion. "It would've been great to have him on our side."

Yelsom was noncommittal.

"He sure knew how to rip the masks off people," he went on. "His reports were killers!"

"He wasn't so smart," Yelsom grunted.

"I sure wouldn't want him doing a story on me! Would you?"

Yelsom set down his beer and stared at Calvin.

"What do you mean?"

"Wouldn't it be weird if he had done a story on you? Or on people like us?"

Yelsom's eyes narrowed. "People like us?"

"Gays," Calvin ventured, knowing he'd hit a nerve. "Politically active gays, you know?"

"No, I don't know."

"Well," Calvin said innocently, "he did stories on every other group. Why not us? It'd have been an interesting report, don't you think?"

Yelsom's eyes bored into him. He faltered; had he gone too far?

"I've always wanted to see more coverage of groups like ours," Calvin said quickly, "and of people like you. I'm studying journalism, remember? I know how important coverage is for a movement, and you're just the kind of guy people need to see more of. You were so awesome on the Melanie Stone Show. What was it like, being on TV?"

Yelsom's eyes softened as he launched into a recounting of his triumph on live television, and Calvin breathed a silent sigh of relief as he pretended to listen raptly.

Other tidbits of information were gleaned during his fishing expeditions: He learned Yelsom was from Long Beach, had a terrible relationship with his father, was supported with funds drawn from a trust fund on the East Coast, and had become an activist after some fateful event in 1969.

He loved the Rolling Stones, and was prone to hum one of their songs whenever the mood struck.

"Because I love the message behind it," he once explained. "Satisfaction is impossible to come by."

So was true love, according to Yelsom, which was why he never went out on dates.

"I live like a monk. I don't have time for a lover. Who needs one, anyway? I've got my work."

He also learned Yelsom never entertained at home. No one even knew where his apartment was. Calvin was determined to change that.

His first thought was to trace Yelsom's license plate through the Department of Motor Vehicles, but try as he could, he never got to see his car. At their first meeting he'd tried, but was too far away; the plates were obscured in the dark. And during their daytime meetings, Yelsom always arrived at the bar long before he did, making it impossible to know which car he'd come in. He couldn't ask exactly where Yelsom lived or what car he drove without arousing suspicion, so he determined to find another way to locate the apartment.

The opportunity came the second week of April when, on a Tuesday afternoon, Yelsom ordered Calvin to meet him at The Shaft for a round of drinks with some friends.

As usual, the reason for the request was unclear. As BRAVO's leader, Yelsom had to schmooze, as he called it, with any number of people in the community. But Calvin's presence hardly seemed necessary. When he arrived, Yelsom introduced him as his assistant but barely addressed him throughout the afternoon's conversation, except when drink refills were needed. He sat quietly at the table with Yelsom and three other men while they discussed local politics and gossiped.

"Junior," Yelsom snapped after the third round was finished, "grab us some more brew. And a Coke for yourself."

Calvin ordered and paid for the drinks, returned to the table balancing them on each arm, leaned over the table to set them down, and proceeded to slosh beer across Yelsom's denim jacket.

"Terrific!" Drinking hardly improved Yelsom's attitude. "Look at my jacket!"

Calvin flinched, grabbed a napkin and started wiping. Yelsom shoved him away.

"That won't do any good!" he growled, whipping off the jacket. "Here." He threw it at Calvin. "Take this next door to the laundromat and wash it. Go ahead! Just machine-wash and dry it. Don't come back till it's done!"

The others were embarrassed and obviously sorry for Calvin, but they said nothing. Knowing Yelsom, they knew better.

Calvin was flustered and angry. Was there no end to this man's attitude? He clutched the jacket and nearly shot back a reply when he felt something hard and sharp in the left inside pocket.

Keys.

"I'm very sorry, Yelsom," he said, politely. "I'll have this back as soon as it's clean."

"Then get out of here and do it!"

Calvin needed no encouragement to hurry. He strode out of The Shaft into the laundromat, yanked Yelsom's keys out of the jacket, threw it in a machine, and stood in the doorway, thinking.

He looked up and down Seventeenth Street. Small businesses lined both sides. A tire store. Pharmacy. Liquor stores. Wasn't there a hardware store up the street?

He stepped to the curb and strained his eyes.

The sign was three blocks west.

Hardware. Locks and keys.

He started for his car, then hesitated. What if Yelsom came looking for him and found him gone?

No, no. He was too wrapped up in drinking and bragging. No time to think about unimportant things like Junior.

He ran for the car.

Eleven minutes later he was back with a new set of keys. Yelsom's jacket was in the rinse cycle.

He sat down and looked at his purchase.

Seven keys. Two for a car, the rest could be for anything. But one, at least, had to be an apartment key.

The machine buzzed. Calvin took the jacket out and threw it in the dryer.

Fifteen minutes later he presented it, dried and fluffed, to its owner, who received it grandly.

The others at the table had clearly become intoxicated while trying to keep up with Yelsom. They smiled weakly. Calvin stood with his hands in his pockets.

"Grab yourself another Coke. Oh, wait! I'll buy."

Calvin fingered the keys in his left pocket while he waited and smiled.

TWENTY-THREE

On April 17, Greg received four complimentary tickets in the mail for Robbie's April 19 concert at the Irvine Meadows Amphitheater.

A note was enclosed with the tickets.

> Greetings! I'm sorry, but I'll have to cancel our appointment Wednesday. Rehearsals are grueling and I really can't get away for our session. I'm doing fine, though.
>
> Bring your wife and a couple of friends.
>
> Please come, Greg. I need you to be there. I've got a plan.
>
> Sincerely,
>
> Robbie

He telephoned Robbie immediately and wasn't surprised to reach an answering machine.

"This is Greg, Robbie," he said after the beep. "I got the tickets, which I appreciate, and of course I'll come. But I'd really like to talk to you before the concert. You mentioned a plan in your note. I'm concerned. Please call and tell me about it when you get a chance, okay? Thanks."

He hung up, perturbed.

"Please, Robbie," he said aloud. "Don't do anything rash. Don't get flamboyant or theatrical. There's too much to lose!"

He buzzed Pastor Mike.

"Wanna see my new client in concert on Friday?"

"Love to! Can we get tickets this late?"

"I've already got them. He mailed me a set."

"Taking perks, are we, doctor?"

"If your conscience bothers you, you don't have to come."

"Why should my conscience bother me? It's your sin. I'm just coming along for the ride."

"How about dinner before my sin?"

They made plans to meet at an Irvine seafood restaurant with their wives two hours before the concert.

Robbie's cancellation left Greg with a free hour. He spent it brooding uneasily.

He never got the return phone call he was hoping for.

"The T-shirts are here!"

Everyone stampeded to the back of the basement where Calvin stood, holding a box.

"Easy, folks!" he shouted while they mobbed him. "One at a time!"

"And remember," Yelsom shouted over the din, "these are just for the people who don't already have one."

A groan rose up from the group.

"Come on, now! Supplies are limited. Don't line up for a T-shirt if you've already got one."

Calvin called out sizes, hands shot up from the group, and he tossed out shirts one by one. His manner was remarkably changed since his first meeting; word had gotten around about his close association with Yelsom, making him something of an authority figure. He threw shirts and barked out "medium" and "large" with the relaxed air of a man in charge who enjoyed his position.

He *did* enjoy it somewhat, and it gave him a vantage point from which to study the members of BRAVO. They were, he decided, not as strange as they appeared. Their behavior as a group was deplorable; individually, apart from the activist rhetoric and noise, they seemed more like average gay men and women.

Or so he assumed. Never having been an active part of the gay community, he was in no position to compare gay activists with their moderate gay counterparts. He'd never been inside a gay bar in all the years he privately struggled with his sexuality, nor had he ever engaged in a homosexual relationship. So the irony of his frequenting The Shaft and BRAVO meetings at this time of his life was not lost on him.

"Three more mediums!" he called out. "Any takers?"

The one quality these people share, he thought as he threw the last of the shirts out, *is rage. In every other respect they seem average; it's rage that sets them apart.*

Lisa and Roxanne were good examples. After their pool game in March, they'd invited Calvin to their apartment for coffee. He accepted, seeing it as a chance to get to know them and, possibly, learn more about Yelsom. That proved to be a dead end; like most BRAVO members, they knew little or nothing about his background.

"He likes it that way," Roxanne had commented. "He thinks being mysterious makes him impressive."

"It doesn't impress me," Lisa added.

"He's good at what he does, don't get me wrong," Roxanne explained. "But sometimes he's so—oh, how can I put it? He's so—"

"Male," Lisa said. They'd all laughed.

The conversation had turned to the women's involvement in BRAVO, and Calvin caught his first glimpse of the pain underlying gay rage.

Lisa was sexually abused by her stepfather; the violations spanned her first fifteen years.

"We prayed over meals every night. He asked God to bless the food; I asked God to kill him. I guess God listened to him instead of me, 'cause the food was fine, and he's still alive."

"A fact we're less than happy about," Roxanne interjected.

"We're both members of the same Baptist church in Pasadena," Roxanne said.

"We *were* members," Lisa corrected her.

"I met Lisa through the high school group," Roxanne continued. "We got to be close friends before either of us admitted to being lesbian. Then someone spread rumors about us.

"I was never molested or abused," Roxanne told Calvin. "But I've heard so many stories like Lisa's."

"What caused you to join BRAVO?" he asked them.

"Anger," they answered in unison.

"And a lot of our anger," Lisa went on, "is with the church. So many so-called Christians are stone-blind, Jeremy. They condemn women like us without having the slightest idea what we've been through."

Calvin knew better; plenty of churches offered compassion to victims of all sorts, but he was in no position now to argue.

"That's why we joined BRAVO. It's the only group going nose-to-nose with the right-wingers."

The memory forced him to look at BRAVO in a different, though not favorable, light.

"Sorry, that's the lot of 'em!" he announced as he threw out the last shirts.

Yelsom called the meeting back to order; several members had put on their new T-shirts already.

"Looks good, people!"

Everyone clapped, and those with BRAVO shirts puffed out their chests.

"But we're not wearing them tomorrow."

They answered with a disappointed "Ahhh!"

"No, no!" Yelsom raised his hands. "We need the surprise element tomorrow night."

He paused to let everyone quiet down.

"I want everyone to dress straight for the concert."

"That's against my religion," a woman yelled out.

"Yeah, and it's downright unnatural!" a man answered.

"But needful," Yelsom replied. "We want to catch Carlton off guard. I've got a whole section reserved for us at the amphitheater, and I don't want us drawing attention to ourselves until the moment's right. Got it?"

They nodded.

"Junior will hand you a ticket as you leave tonight. Show up at the theater in groups of two or three, four at the most. Don't let on that we're all together."

"If we're dressed straight, why would that matter?" Lisa asked. "Lots of big groups go to concerts together."

"We're taking no chances. Carlton knows something's in the works; he might have alerted the security staff."

"Does he know we're outing him tomorrow night?" another woman asked.

"Who knows? Like I said, we'll take no chances."

Calvin had been walking down the aisles, passing out small Styrofoam packets as he went.

"You'll notice Junior's handing out a little something to you. I call it the "first stone" package. We're gonna cast the first stone when I give the signal."

The packets were in the shape of a small rock; nestled in each was a crumpled sheet of paper.

"Each 'first stone' has a paper in it. Go ahead, check it out."

They examined their "stones" and found the paper stuffed inside. It read:

> This is to inform you that, according to files obtained from Dr. Alex Crawford, Robbie Carlton is gay and admitted as much to Joshua Ferguson. This information is documented in Mr. Ferguson's file. Mr. Carlton has been keeping this information from you; we thought it was time you knew the truth.
>
> More will follow.
>
> Revealingly yours,
>
> BRAVO

"Bring these with you tomorrow," Yelsom instructed. "We'll be throwing them into the audience when I give the signal. But first, we'll practice a little cheerleading." He clapped his hands sharply. "Come on, everybody. Stand up!"

Calvin rose as uncertainly as the rest of them; Yelsom hadn't told him about this.

"The concert starts at 7:30. At 8:30 on the dot, we all stand. If he's in the middle of a song at 8:30, we'll wait till it's finished. Keep your eyes on me; I'll signal you. Then we'll go into our pep drill. Now repeat after me:

> Two, four six, eight,
> How come you pretend you're straight?"

Everyone but Calvin laughed and howled.

"Come on, come *on! Everybody!*"

BRAVO repeated the lusty cheer.

"Again!" Yelsom shouted.

They yelled it in unison three more times, until Yelsom approved.

The yelling stopped abruptly; the echo was chilling.

"Yes!" he roared. "That's our first cheer. We'll shout it directly at Carlton, then turn around and face the audience and give 'em this one:

Hey, hey,
Ho, ho!
Homophobia's got to go!
Ho, ho,
Hey, hey!
Guess what? Robbie Carlton's gay!"

They already knew the first part; it was a chant commonly heard at gay demonstrations. The second half they learned, and loved, immediately.

"Again!"

They repeated it.

Yelsom swooped his arms and struck his fist into the air. *"Yes, and again!"*

Again, louder and clearer. The air was electric.

"Again!"

Three more repetitions, each growing in volume and passion. Calvin mouthed the words weakly. The ground swell of rage made him dizzy.

"Now put 'em all together!" Yelsom ranted.

The horrible recital thundered while Yelsom conducted. His arms waved and his eyes flashed; sweat flew off his face and streaked his black makeup, matting and tangling his shock of white hair. No one but Calvin seemed put off by the ghastly display.

On the contrary, his newfound comrades were part of it. At Yelsom's direction they shrieked the first chant facing forward, then pivoted and threw the second chant to the back wall—rehearsing for the moment they'd face the audience—then whirled again toward their leader, who led them through five more rounds.

What began as a precision drill had become a frenzy, and Calvin understood once and for all the power of collective wrath. Each shout was an exercise in triumph, a howled protest of the years of rejection and injustice this sect's members were certain they'd endured. Some had been beaten by gay-hating thugs, others had been called names and rejected by friends and loved ones. Others were simply convinced that to be a homosexual was to be a martyr. All but one shared a tenet of faith learned in the catechism of gay protest: They were victims who'd had enough. Retaliation was their goal; words were their weapons.

> Hey, hey,
> Ho, ho!
> Homophobia's got to go!

A command, no longer a chant. A patriotic affirmation binding them as one.

> Ho, ho,
> Hey, hey!
> Guess what? Robbie Carlton's gay!

Had they chosen obscenities or real rocks with which to attack Robbie, the effect wouldn't have been so unnerving. But this method—prankish, even childish—was all the more chilling for its simplicity. They would shed no blood, these terrorists; they'd take no captives and throw no bombs. They'd just be a bit rude and interrupt a gentle concert by spouting words that would shipwreck a man's future.

And, Calvin realized, this was only a rehearsal!

He glanced sideways at Lisa and Roxanne, hoping to see less enthusiasm on their parts—but no. They joined in as passionately as the rest.

Calvin forced himself to go through the motions without thinking about the words he was shouting or the man they'd be shouted at.

Finally, Yelsom crossed his arms in front of him then threw them apart.

"CUT!"

In the silence that followed they looked at each other, men

and women with sweat-streaked faces and sore throats, exhilarated.

Yelsom stood erect and still.

"When we're finished, we'll throw these"—he held a Styrofoam clump in his hand—"into the crowd. By then, I'm sure, the security guards will have moved in on us."

"Will we be arrested?" someone asked.

"Does it matter?" Yelsom challenged.

Silence was the only answer.

"So," Yelsom continued, "remember. At 8:30, you watch me for your cue, then stand and deliver! Everyone ready? Good. Let's call it a night."

People began saying their good nights to each other while Calvin prepared to make his excuses to Yelsom for not coming to the concert. He'd been putting it off, knowing he, of all people, would be expected to participate. But that was out of the question. Should someone at the concert recognize him as Calvin Blanchard, it would surely blow his cover. How could he participate in BRAVO's demonstration? He'd formulated an excuse to get out of it and was mentally polishing it when Yelsom approached.

"Junior!"

"What a meeting, Yelsom!" Calvin enthused.

Yelsom was lightly dabbing his forehead with his bandanna. "I hope," he said, "you won't be too disappointed, but I can't let you come tomorrow night."

Calvin was speechless. "What—why can't I come?"

"Because I need you to go underground." Yelsom looked Calvin up and down, then nodded. "You've pretty well proven yourself. Now it's time for you to really go to work."

Calvin feigned disappointment. "Wow, I was looking forward to it," he said in a crestfallen voice. "My first time out, you know?"

"Sorry."

Calvin wasn't, but Yelsom couldn't know that.

"But," Yelsom explained, "I need you to go start hanging out with some of these church people, and if they see you with BRAVO, they'll never let you anywhere near. Got it?"

"But exactly what do you want me to do?" he asked.

"I want you to get inside information on somebody." Yelsom handed him a piece of paper with a name and phone number on it.

Calvin glanced at the name; it didn't ring a bell.

"What kind of information do you need?"

"I'll let you know after the concert. Just be sure to stay home tomorrow night." Yelsom turned to leave. "I'll call you."

Calvin stuffed the paper in his shirt pocket.

"Good night, Yelsom," he said to the man's back.

People were already lined up at the back waiting for their tickets. Calvin moved toward them, wondering who Dr. Greg Bishop was and what Yelsom wanted to know about him.

TWENTY-FOUR

If thou, LORD, shouldest mark iniquities, O Lord, who shall stand?"

Calvin paused to let the listeners reflect.

"Psalm 130, verse 3. Interesting question, don't you think? If God took a tally of our sins and printed it in the *Los Angeles Times*, would we buy extra copies for our friends?"

He was treading dangerous ground. This afternoon he was putting out a plea for compassion; tonight Robbie Carlton was going to be shamed under a spotlight. Would anyone suspect he was preparing them?

"I want to talk about unity today. About closing ranks and getting behind each other...."

But his committment was to *do* something, not to play it safe. Risks were part and parcel of the bargain.

"Remember Corrie Ten Boom, the Holocaust survivor? I once heard her say that the Christian church was the only army she knew of that shoots its own wounded...."

So, without question, something had to be done for Robbie Carlton.

"We all carry wounds of some sort, right? I doubt that our leaders are any exception. In fact, if you look at men like King David, Abraham, or Jacob—all of them leaders of some kind—you'll see some very imperfect saints!"

Warning him was top priority; he'd done what he could with less than twenty-four hours' notice. Immediately after the meeting he'd spent the night tracking every lead he knew to get in touch with Hal Babcock, Carlton's manager. His connections paid off; at 9:00 this morning he'd phoned Babcock and left word—anonymously—that BRAVO would be at the concert, ready to strike at 8:30 on the dot. The confused manager promised to relay the message. The rest was in God's hands.

"Do we allow imperfections in our leaders today?"

The only other action he could take was to try to make a statement without giving himself away.

"Don't answer too quickly. I've had pastors on this show who complained to me, off the air, that their congregations would lynch them if they knew how human they really were. And I've interviewed evangelists who've confided in me that their greatest fear was falling off the pedestal the public had erected for them...."

Maybe this commentary would soften some hearts toward last year's Grammy award winner, who was about to slip from a lofty pedestal, indeed.

"We expect our leaders to maintain high standards, of course, and let's not excuse them if they don't! But can't we give them the right to struggle with their humanity, like the rest of us?"

Thank God he didn't have to be there tonight! Watching BRAVO rehearse their ambush was painful enough. But the news about Robbie Carlton would rip through the community like a cyclone. Calvin had already begun writing the commentary he'd make on it during Monday's broadcast.

"Take your pastor, for example. You want the best from him, right? Good sermons, godly counsel, strong leadership. That's a fair expectation, but it creates a bit of pressure, don't you think? What if the pressure affects his home life? Can he and his wife see a marriage counselor without fearing someone will spot them in the waiting room and begin the gossip?"

Monday's commentary would be in defense of Robbie. Nothing, so far, could be done about Josh. Getting Yelsom's keys was a good start, but getting his address would be trickier. Getting into his apartment would be miraculous.

"If a pastor can't admit his marriage has problems, should we be surprised if he winds up divorced? Or what if he gets depressed or burned out? Does he have to hide that, too? If so, isn't a nervous breakdown waiting for him down the road?"

Even if he got into Yelsom's apartment it didn't guarantee he'd find the reason for Josh's despair, though somehow he sensed he would.

"What if—God forbid—but what if your pastor had carnal temptations? You know, the kind *you* have, but pretend not to.

"Oops! Anyone offended? Come on, folks. You and I have a hundred wayward desires a day, and having 'Rev.' in front of your name won't change that. Do you pray for your pastor's integrity? For his ability to resist temptation and stand firm? Do you pray for his peace of mind, for harmony in his family, and for his emotional and spiritual needs to be met while you expect him to meet yours? If not, why not?"

God must have guided him so far. The alternative was unthinkable.

"If we want solid leadership, let's commit ourselves to two simple excercises. First, daily prayer for our leaders. How can we expect them to give us what we need without it? Second, let's extend grace. Grace enough to anticipate their humanity and, when it shows, to reassure them of our support. I'll bet we'd see a whole new face on Christian leadership if we did those two things."

And backing out wasn't an option. Not anymore.

"That's something to think about."

The JW Seagrill on Von Karman Drive was packed. Greg and Christine were scrunched together in a tiny wooden booth opposite Pastor Mike and his wife, Adelle, all of them maneuvering elbows and wrists while spooning Boston clam chowder which, they agreed, was worth the discomfort.

The soup was finished and cleared by 5:30; dinner would take at least another twenty minutes to arrive. The waiter apologized. Mike and Greg passed the time chomping on breadsticks and arguing.

"Once you think you can keep people from making stupid decisions, you're doomed," Mike lectured. Rock music blared from the lounge; he raised his voice to be heard over it. "I learned a long time ago to let the sheep learn from their mistakes instead of trying to prevent them from making any."

"But you warn them!" Greg countered. "That's part of your job. Good grief, Mike, you warn me left and right."

"For all the good it does."

"And you expect me to at least check with you before I do something stupid."

"You don't have enough checks."

"I just wish he'd have told me about his plan," Greg said evenly. "That's common courtesy."

"Maybe he thought you'd try to talk him out of it," Christine observed.

"He knows better than that. I'd respect his decision; I just wish I knew what it was."

"What difference would it make?" Mike asked.

"It would keep me from worrying!"

"You'd worry anyway, honey," Christine answered. "I've never seen you so wrapped up in a client."

They'd gone through the breadsticks; Adelle signaled the waiter for more. She was a short, feisty woman with angular features and a quick wit to match her husband's. She and Christine had dressed up for the concert—she in a brown suede suit, Christine in a burgundy jumper. Their outfits were light; the spring air was agreeable that night.

"Speaking of explanations," Adelle went on, "have you heard anything more about the tape those women stole from the office?"

"Not a word. It's still floating around out there somewhere."

"In the wrong hands," Mike added.

"But did Mike tell you we got a call about it from an old friend?" Christine asked. She shuddered with the memory. Adelle nodded and sympathized.

"That must have scared the daylights out of you."

"It's not that," Christine answered. "It's just that there's too much suspense these days. Too many mysteries. Josh Ferguson, this Yelsom guy, the tape...Robbie, too."

"Did you ever get that alarm system put in?" Mike asked Greg.

He nodded. "And a gun."

Adelle's eyes widened. "Is that necessary?"

"Yes," Greg said, just as his wife said "no."

"But," Christine continued, "I think Greg feels better having one."

"Darned tootin'."

Their dinners arrived. Greg picked at scallops and listened while the other three lightened the conversation with talk about Robbie's music and the direction the gospel music industry was taking.

At 6:15, his beeper went off. He whipped it from his belt and checked the number. It was unfamiliar, but he guessed who it was.

"Excuse me."

A busboy directed him to the phone, where he punched the number and waited.

Robbie's voice answered, distant and muffled, barely audible with instruments tuning and voices yelling in the background.

"Robbie?"

"Greg! I'm backstage. I couldn't return your call. Sorry."

"What's going on?" Greg shouted into the receiver.

"I'm getting ready," Robbie shouted back.

"Are you all right?"

"Fine! I just wanted to tell you I feel at peace."

Greg stuffed the phone against his ear. "I can barely hear you!"

"I said I'm fine! They're gonna jump me at 8:30, but it'll be okay."

"*Jump* you?"

"The gays. BRAVO. They're gonna jump up at 8:30 and start screaming at me. I've been warned."

"Did you tell security?"

"Nah. I don't wanna."

Greg panicked. "Robbie, listen to me! You saw what these people are like! You don't want that. Tell the security guards to keep an eye out for them—"

"You don't understand! I'm gonna steal their thunder."

"Steal their—Robbie, what are you talking about?"

"I just wanted you to know I'm okay. Come backstage afterward. You'll be there, won't you?"

"Yes, but you've got to—"

"I gotta go! Greg, just pray for me. I know this is the way to handle it."

"*What* is the way to handle it?"

"Gotta go. Come backstage. Greg?"

"I'm here."

"You're fantastic. You've already done me so much good. I don't know how I'd have made it this far without you."

"Then tell me—"

"I'll see you after the concert. No, really, I've gotta go. 'Bye!"

Greg heard a click, then slammed the phone into its cradle, livid. What on earth was this kid up to?

He stomped back to the table. Christine, Adelle, and Mike looked at him expectantly.

"Robbie?" Christine finally asked.

He plopped into the booth and nodded.

"And?"

"How should I know? I'm only his counselor."

They ordered dessert and ate in silence.

The Irvine Meadows Amphitheater sits off the San Diego freeway, next to what used to be the Lion Country Safari—a live animal park complete with giraffes, lions, and rhinos. The theater itself rests a mile inland from the freeway; only the parking area and the marquees are visible to motorists.

"April 19. Live in Concert. Robbie Carlton," it announced. Driving past the sign to the parking lot, Greg was confronted for the first time with his client's enormous popularity.

Over ten thousand people had turned out to see Robbie. The first lot was full; Greg had to drive (with Christine beside him and the Cains in the back) to the second lot, pay $3.50, and walk over a mile to see the man who confided in him weekly.

"I don't make him go to this much trouble when he comes to see me," he nudged Christine, walking the path toward the amphitheater.

The walk from the lot to the theater took fifteen minutes, most of it uphill. Greg checked the people jostling on both sides of him, wondering and guessing. Christine took his arm.

"Looking for BRAVO?"

"Yeah." Greg glanced around at the crowd. "No black outfits. Everyone looks normal."

A teenage girl with green-streaked hair parted to one side passed them arm-in-arm with her boyfriend.

"Relatively normal," he reconsidered.

They reached the entrance, showed their tickets, and were directed to seats in Section B. Twenty rows from the stage, they found their places. Christine and Adelle went from there to the restroom; Mike went for drinks while Greg scanned the outdoor theater.

Behind him, the seating area sloped upward sharply, backed by trees and the Irvine Hills. The combined seats formed a massive shell flaring up from the stage, over which a forty-foot gray backdrop was topped with colored lights and a banner welcoming concertgoers to the Third Annual Orange County Pro-Life Benefit. The entire upstage area was lined with orchestra seats and instruments; stage right housed the band section, and a raised platform was set up stage left with three microphone stands for Robbie's backup singers.

All this, Greg thought, momentarily forgetting the threat of BRAVO, *for Robbie. All the people, footlights, stagehands, ushers, programs, and excitement—for him. And I know more about him than anyone else.*

"They're not back yet, huh?" Mike asked, making his way toward him with a cardboard carrier full of Cokes.

"I'm sure there's a line." Greg took two cups from Mike and set them under his seat while Mike eased into his own.

"So what do you think will happen?"

Greg looked around. "I can't tell. He said they'd jump him, or scream at him."

Someone called Mike's name; he waved to a couple seated four rows to his left. "Shouldn't he have a bodyguard?"

Greg waved to the couple as well. "He doesn't want any help. Don't ask me why." He took a Coke from under his seat and sipped it, spilling some in his lap. Mike watched him.

"You're nervous."

"You're not?"

"I'm praying. We both should."

Their wives returned and settled in.

The orchestra filed onstage from both sides, tuning and shuffling music sheets. It was 6:55; the seats were nearly full.

Greg craned his neck every direction, checking for black T-shirts or leather jackets. He saw several; none of them were worn by people resembling the BRAVO gang.

"Where *are* they?" he asked out loud. Christine squeezed his knee.

At 6:56, the crowd starting clapping and stomping in unison.

Greg shook his head, confused. Christine patted his hand. Mike and Adelle sat quietly, heads slightly bowed.

At 6:58, the lights dimmed and cheers went up from all sections.

The band members jumped onstage from the wings and positioned themselves. Greg's pulse raced.

◆

Thirty-seven inconspicuously dressed men and women filled the back row of Section F. They had something in their pockets.

"Here we go," Yelsom muttered.

The band struck up a hard-driving theme; speakers blared it out over thousands of shouting fans. Whistles and stomps flew up, and the clapping now punctuated the backbeat of the hard-rock score.

A cool splash of blue light fell stage left, where two women and a man—Robbie's backup singers—appeared, swaying and welcoming a fresh round of applause. The music went up a key, the tempo quickened, and the brass section from the orchestra joined in.

"Ladies and gentlemen," a clear, amplified voice rang from all directions, bouncing off the hills and across the amphitheater, "Orange County for Life welcomes you to its third annual concert. And Orange County welcomes the 1990 Grammy-award-winning Gospel Artist of the Year, MR. ROBBIE CARLTON!"

A thin spotlight pierced center stage, then widened to engulf Robbie, who seemingly had stepped out of nowhere to be embraced by a roar of screams and a musical tidal wave. Band, orchestra, and singers united in the introduction to his first song, while ten-thousand-plus concertgoers rose as one to welcome the singer.

He stood center stage and bowed deeply; the cheering escalated and he shrugged, wide-eyed, putting on an exaggerated aw-shucks-it's-just-me look. It was a boyish, charming entrance, and it worked. The cheering reached a crescendo, the band vamped, and Robbie strode downstage, bowed again, grinned, waved, nodded, and pointed, each move accented by screams and whistles from the audience. A barely contained pandemonium washed over the theater; no one was more caught up in it than Greg, who cheered, in spite of himself, like a dazzled adolescent.

The roar hadn't begun to fade when Robbie broke into "Finishing the Race," an appropriately hard-driving, upbeat song from his second album. The crowd stayed on its feet, clapping in time, jumping and dancing in place, and Greg marveled at his client's ability to work an audience.

Dressed in denim pants and an untucked flannel shirt rolled at the sleeves, Robbie exuded godly joy and California cool. He ripped a microphone from a stand center stage and stalked the platform, punching the lyrics and strutting back and forth. Between verses he crouched and beat time with his fist while the band played, then sprang up, leaping with arms outstretched to the crowd's delight, paced, and sang again.

Greg, proud and protective, smiled broadly.

Good looks and superb showmanship were part of the package, he thought, but there was more to Robbie Carlton than glitz.

There was integrity.

I've kept that promise. I've been tempted, but I've never actually done it.

There was vulnerability and power.

But when I'm singing and people are applauding I feel respected, and completely in control.

He'd displayed plenty of vulnerability in counseling; until tonight Greg only imagined Robbie's power. But seeing was believing; his control over the thousands was tangible, mesmerizing. No wonder he'd called it a drug.

And there was a peculiar slant toward brash action.

I'm gonna steal their thunder.

How?

Everyone finally sat down and the mood settled.

Robbie finished his second number, spoke briefly about the honor of representing Orange County for Life, bantered lightly with some kids in the front row, then struck up a ballad.

Greg's mind and eyes wandered. Thirty minutes since the concert began, and still no sign of BRAVO. If they were planning to barge in as they'd done at Waverly Chapel, they'd get no further than the gates.

They're not that dumb, he thought, *so they must be in the crowd already, waiting.*

He looked again at Robbie, so vibrant and beloved, thought of Yelsom's assault on Ferguson's casket, and realized how deeply and unreservedly he was coming to hate the gay rights movement and everyone connected with it.

More ballads, anthems, rearranged hymns, and original compositions. Kind words for the pro-life movement; admonishments to Christians not to shun their civic responsibilities.

Greg looked for, but couldn't spot, fear in Robbie's eyes or voice.

Forty-five minutes later, he introduced a children's song he'd written for his fourth album, and invited all the kids in the audience to come onstage to join him in the chorus. A swarm of youngsters descended on him, and proceeded to paw and cling to the delighted performer.

Greg watched him pick up a seven-year-old towheaded boy with utmost tenderness and nudged Christine.

"I want one of those."

"Hmmm?"

He pointed at the child.

They'd spoken about it before, but never decided on the right time.

The song ended and the children dispersed, leaving Robbie at center stage, alone. The lights dimmed and the mood quieted.

It was 8:26. Robbie surveyed the crowd.

"I wrote this song," he began, "a few years back when I felt I was the only one in the world who had problems."

Piano and cello began to play softly.

"Maybe you can relate to it."

Greg recognized the orchestral introduction.

"It means more today than when I first wrote it. Listen."

Greg checked his watch.

Robbie sang quietly, looking into as many of his fans' eyes as he could, singing directly to them.

> Some burdens are dark, not borne with finesse,
> Not polite, but unpleasant to name and confess.
> Not respectable, no, and quite heavy, I guess,
> Just like mine—not the type that you'd know.

The crowd's respectful, sympathetic mood matched that of the song.

> Yours are normal; at least they seem so.
> That won't keep me from going on, though,
> 'Cause I'm still a pilgrim.
> We seek the same end...

Except for a stirring in the back row of Section F, the audience was reverent and attentive.

Mike and Adelle sensed the time without looking at their watches.

Greg's eyes shifted from one side of the theater to another. 8:29.

Yelsom lifted up one finger which only his associates noticed. He cocked it; when it dropped, that was their signal.

> Different wounds, same Physician,
> Different trials, same Friend.
> If you saw the pit I've come from—
> Even worse, the sin I run from—
> Would you see I'm still a pilgrim?

"Hold it, please."

Half the orchestra kept playing; the other instruments halted unevenly. Musicians, stagehands, and singers stared at Robbie, wondering.

His back was to the audience; he addressed the stage.

"Hold everything, please. Stop the music. Now."

The others heard; the amphitheater was silent.

He turned toward the disoriented crowd.

"It's 8:30, ladies and gentlemen. Has anyone got a message for me?"

The back row of Section F, like the rest of those in attendance, was thoroughly startled. Yelsom's finger trembled. He kept it up, glanced sideways and frowned, shaking his head.

"Come on, now, don't be shy! Doesn't somebody have a message for me?"

The question hung over the audience, reverberated, and died unanswered.

Robbie Carlton stood downstage and eyed his listeners closely.

"Last chance."

Heads turned. Whispers darted from all sides, but nobody spoke aloud.

Yelsom stared at the stage; his followers looked to him for a cue. He didn't give it.

Finally a timid, hesitant voice floated down from the top section.

"We love you, Robbie."

Scattered applause started up, increased in strength, and became a tension-breaking affirmation.

Robbie, unmoved, nodded slightly.

"I believe you. Now I'm going to put that love to the test."

Greg covered his face with both hands. Christine poked him.

"I can't watch," he whispered hoarsely.

Robbie moved closer downstage, toward the audience.

"We're celebrating life tonight. Aren't we?"

Someone cheered, "Amen!"

"Yes. Life which begins in the womb and cries out for protection."

No one disagreed.

"And which, after entering this world, may not have such an easy time. We love the unborn, but is our love extended to them after they're born, years later perhaps, when they've picked up some bruises from life *outside* the womb?"

The question was met with more puzzled silence.

"I'm one of those lives."

Greg understood the plan now.

"Can any of you guess why I wrote that song?"

Silence.

"It's my autobiography. I have a problem most of you probably can't understand."

Ten thousand minds began speculating fiercely.

"But some of you can."

Yelsom, finally catching on, began to laugh; quietly, at first, then audibly. Someone two rows behind shushed him.

"Nice move, Carlton," he said aloud, then to his group: "Forget it. Game called on account of rain."

"You remember the tragedy of Josh Ferguson, the reporter?" Robbie asked. "His suicide, and that horrible attack on his funeral? And the revelation that he was homosexual?"

Embarassed silence thickened the air at the word *homosexual*.

"I knew Josh Ferguson."

Murmurs started up again.

"And I loved him."

Silence. A long one, this time.

"As a friend," Robbie added.

Sighs were exhaled, row by row.

"But I have," he continued mercilessly, "the same problem he did."

Greg would have paid dearly to know the thoughts of the legions of Robbie Carlton fans seated around him.

"And the same people who attacked him are now attacking me. They're here tonight, in fact."

Heads flew back and forth in all directions. Murmurs and gasps followed.

"Oh, yes! They're shy. Darned if I know why, but they're here." He waved both arms. "Hello, BRAVO! What, no whistles and bullhorns tonight? Have you become a noninstrumentalist gay terrorist group or something?"

A few people laughed nervously.

"They're here," Robbie repeated softly, "because they planned to scream my problem at all of you tonight. But since I have the microphone and my voice is nicely warmed up, let me spare them the trouble."

He cleared his throat, shuffled, looked at his feet, then back at his audience.

"I've had feelings all my life. Unnatural feelings. I didn't ask for them, but here they are. And I've done my best not to give in to them."

No one made a sound.

"I'm still doing my best. I've lived as godly a life as I know how. You expect that of me, and I haven't betrayed your trust. But I've always felt this problem should be kept private. Sadly, there are people who think otherwise. They wrote me this note."

He pulled BRAVO's warning from his shirt pocket and read it to them.

Greg sensed the crowd's mood evolve from shock to sympathy, then from sympathy to rage as they listened to BRAVO's ugly threat.

"They say I've got until tonight to come out of the closet," he announced, lifting the note over his head. "So be it! I'm out."

He crushed the note into his fist loudly.

"But not like they want me to be!"

He threw the paper down dramatically, rejecting its threat and philosophy.

"Gay isn't good, folks. Don't let anyone tell you it is. It's a *problem*, not a civil right. And by the grace of God, here's one kid who's going to move heaven and earth to overcome it!"

Pastor Michael Cain was the first to stand. Greg, Christine, Adelle, and ten thousand cheering, weeping Christians joined him, and the Irvine Meadows Amphitheater shook under the weight of a riotous show of support for Robbie Carlton and all he stood for.

The people seated in the back of Section F resembled late-comers who'd just realized they'd walked into the wrong movie house.

Never, before or since, had Robbie Carlton received such an ovation. When it abated, he pointed directly in front of him toward Greg.

"Spotlight on Section B, please?"

Greg and his party were blinded by white.

"I want to publicly thank the man who's had a hand in my healing so far."

Greg paled.

Dear God, no! Come on, Robbie! No theatrics! Haven't we had enough for one night?

"And I want to recommend him to anyone you know who might have a problem similar to mine. He's the kind of counselor who restores my faith in the mental health profession."

I'm gonna be sick right here and that will be my contribution to this historic event, Greg groaned to himself.

"I don't know what direction my life will take after tonight, but I'm sure of two things: God will be with me every step of the way, and so will Dr. Greg Bishop!"

Another roar went up. Faces turned to him, Christine looked on helplessly, Robbie smiled like a child hoping Dad was pleased, and Greg wondered, as he grinned and waved weakly, if the lobotomy he planned to give Robbie would affect his singing voice.

___ TWENTY-FIVE ___

Words like *gay, terrorism,* and *outing* were fast becoming regular items in the daily news.

Josh Ferguson's suicide and postmortem exposure were still hot topics; Robbie Carlton's public admission fanned the existing flames and added a new dimension to the public debate over homosexuality. Opportunists on both sides of the issue engaged in mutual accusations and wild prophecies.

"Typical of the gays to make life miserable for innocent people," one person wrote in a letter to the *Los Angeles Times*. "Considering the way they flaunt their perversion and attack everything normal, is it any wonder God sent the AIDS crisis?"

Gay extremists were no less restrained.

"So justice is served," an editorial in the *Vine* boasted, "when the blood of closet cases is spilled in the public square. They exist to be hunted, and *kudos* to those who track them down. Bravo, BRAVO! Do it again; we like it!"

The mainstream press was initially eager for comments from the principals, especially Carlton himself and the psychologist named Bishop who'd been drafted into the fracas. But comments were slow in coming. Both Robbie and Greg (at Greg's advice) refused interviews until the matter had been discussed between them. Which, of course, slowed down the media speculation not one whit.

"Dr. Gregory Bishop was named Friday night," the *Los Angeles Times* informed its readers, "as a psychologist who 'cures' homosexuals. Sources say his treament includes aversion therapy, a form of shock treatment designed to negate homosexual impulses."

The sources in question remained anonymous.

Christine laughed uproariously. Her husband didn't.

"You'd better start making big bucks off your graphic art, lady!" he warned. "More stories like this and my credibility won't be worth dirt!"

Robbie's own celebrity status rose, though for reasons he'd never planned. A well-known gospel singer admitting to homosexual yearnings was unheard of; both the religious and secular communities weren't sure how to respond. Nor did they know what to make of his endorsement of Greg at the concert.

Greg himself had a few questions on that score. Torn between concern and fury, he, with Christine, Mike, and Adelle, had spent hours with Robbie in his dressing room after his "coming out."

"Was it in your best interest to drag me into it?" Greg asked after ascertaining his client's state, which was exhilarated, scared, and relieved.

"It was spur-of-the-moment," Robbie admitted, wiping his forehead with the towel he kept around his neck. "But I'm sure other people need your help, Greg. As long as I was publicizing my problem, why not publicize the solution?"

"I'm not the solution!" The prospect of such a reputation terrorized him—*Dr. Greg Bishop, the Solution: All Your Homosexual Worries Are Over!*

"I thought you'd be pleased."

"I just wish we'd talked it over first."

Robbie had seemed mildly hurt by Greg's disapproval; Christine, Mike, and Adelle looked at Greg reproachfully.

"I'm just saying," he went on more gently, "that when you came out of the closet you brought me with you!"

Indeed. The name "Dr. Bishop" was thrown around casually as speculations grew about his connection to the gay issue. And hovering over it all was the status of Assembly Bill 101, soon headed for more discussion, and discussed heatedly among gays, politicians, and conservatives.

Ferguson, homosexuality, Carlton, suicide, gay rights, and Dr. Greg Bishop were firmly fixed in the limelight.

The board of elders called a special session Monday evening to discuss the recent startling events surrounding Greg Bishop and, by extension, Berean Community Church. The church's governing board had mixed feelings about the controversy engulfing them, as did their pastor and clinical director. But Greg and Mike, after much discussion over the weekend, decided to bring something redemptive out of this chaos by attempting to form a ministry to people like Robbie.

"Like it or not," Pastor Mike reminded the board, "the county is watching us. Greg's been avoiding the press since Friday night, but we promised to give them a statement after meeting with all of you."

The twelve elders were in attendance; Nancy took notes and Greg, who had no vote in the matter but was necessary to the meeting, fielded questions from the board.

"As I see it," he explained, "we need to clarify exactly what we're doing in the counseling center."

"Because?" Kevin Henderson, one of the twelve, asked.

"Because already there's speculation that we're doing some exotic form of therapy to cure homosexuals. Somebody even suggested we're doing shock treatment! Can you imagine? So, we'd better explain exactly what we offer at Berean Counseling."

"And," Mike cut in, "now's a good time to consider something that's been on my heart. None of the churches in Orange County offer help to people like Robbie Carlton. I'd like us to give it a shot."

Ruben Anderson was ready.

"All of the churches in the county offer help to people like him, Mike. They preach the gospel and teach the Word. Are you saying that's not enough?"

"Hold your horses, Ruben. Please. Let Greg finish, then we'll discuss your concerns. Greg?"

"Whether or not we start a ministry to homosexuals is one issue," Greg continued. "Clearing up what we already do is another. I've got to make a statement, soon, describing the counseling I'm doing with Robbie."

"So what's stopping you?" Ruben asked.

"We've gotten calls—how many, Nancy?"

"At least twenty."

"Calls from people in Robbie's position who've been fighting homosexuality all their lives and had no idea help was available!"

"Lots of calls came from parents, too," Nancy added. "They want to know what to do about their gay sons or daughters."

"Which means plenty of other people could use our help."

Ruben groaned; a few of the other elders joined him.

Greg ignored them. "And Robbie gave us an advertisement Friday, in front of thousands. So the question is, do we announce publicly that, yes, we *do* have an outreach to homosexuals, or do we keep it quiet? And if we keep it quiet, what should I tell the press tomorrow? Believe me, they'll ask."

"Have you already decided how to explain the work you're doing with Carlton?" another asked.

"I think I've got that down. I'll explain it in the most basic terms possible."

"But we still have to decide whether to start a group for others," Mike said, "so Greg will know what to tell the press when they ask."

Randy Sayer, one of Berean's long-standing leaders, regarded Greg curiously. "Gregory, how do *you* feel about starting this type of ministry?"

"I'd propose a ministry for gays who want help. Gays who don't *want* to be gay."

The others, except for Ruben, concurred.

"What qualifies you, Greg, to do even that?" Ruben asked pointedly. "How much experience have you had working with, as you put it, gays who don't want to be gay?"

"Not much. I'd need help, for sure."

"And where would you get it?"

"I'm not sure," he admitted.

"But the work Greg's done with Robbie Carlton counts for something, doesn't it?" Mike argued.

"If we're talking about professional counseling, sure, Mike," Randy agreed. "But that's different than an organized outreach. I say we approach this carefully."

"Which is not," Ruben huffed, "the way it's been approached so far! What that boy pulled Friday night was as irresponsible and theatrical as anything I've ever seen!"

Greg didn't take kindly to anyone criticizing his clients, but he couldn't argue the point.

"He shouldn't have brought me into it," he agreed. "But that's a dead issue now."

"The *live* issue is," Mike persisted, "do we want to form a ministry, or not?"

"Spell out exactly," Randy answered, "what you have in mind."

Greg took over.

"I've learned a few things from Robbie in the short time we've worked together. One is that these people are scared. They think they're the only ones in the church struggling with this problem, so I'd propose a weekly meeting for them, led by me or someone else we agree on, where they can get some support and encouragement."

"Why," Ruben demanded, "isn't the church's support enough?"

"Why isn't it enough for alcoholics, or people recovering from divorce, or single parents? We have special groups for all of them, don't we? I've never heard you criticize those groups, Ruben."

"Because none of those groups are a threat," Anderson replied darkly.

The elders reacted in consternation.

"Yes, a threat!" he repeated. "Imagine a roomful of homosexuals getting together weekly in the church. What if they get involved with each other? What if they bring AIDS into the church?"

"That's a possibility, Ruben," Mike acknowledged. "Should we run scared?"

"No, we should walk wisely. Why sacrifice the comfort of the entire congregation for the needs of a few?"

"Is comfort what we're all about?" Mike pressed. "Because I don't see much comfort in Christ's ministry. Or Paul's, for that matter. Seems to me he had riots following him wherever he went!"

"And," Greg added, "I think you're jumping the gun, Ruben. I'm not suggesting we go out and preach at gay bars. I'm saying let's offer help to the ones who want it. That shouldn't start a riot."

Ruben was dubious, but he backed down.

"It seems to me you need a clearer plan," Randy advised. "I'd support a ministry like the one you've got in mind, but I need to know exactly what you'll do in these meetings."

"I haven't worked it all out yet."

"I'd be more enthusiastic once I saw the blueprints."

"How about this, then?" Mike offered. "Let's authorize Greg to announce we're working on an outreach to gays and we'll be voting to approve it next month. Will that be enough time, Greg?"

"Should be. What do I tell people who call us in the mean-time?"

"Tell them we hope to have a program ready in a month."

"Then I move," Randy said, "that we commission Greg to develop a program and submit it for our approval in May, and that he advise the media accordingly."

Mike seconded the motion, which passed eleven to one.

Ruben scowled. "We could be loosing the devil himself on our congregation."

Yelsom rarely summoned him at night, which only added to the intrigue Calvin was feeling. He stepped into The Shaft, ordered a Bud and a Coke, found his normal spot behind the pool table, and waited.

They hadn't spoken since the concert, but no one was better acquainted with the details than Calvin. His commentary that afternoon had been on Robbie, naturally, and the phone-in response was overwhelmingly in his favor. Some callers had questioned the wisdom of such a showy disclosure, but all expressed support for the singer.

He was anxious to hear Yelsom's version. No acting up, no exposure? After all that rehearsal? Why?

And Greg Bishop! *There* was a whole new mystery! Robbie had referred to him, the media were now hounding and commenting on him, and Yelsom wanted Calvin to get the dope on him. What dope? Fascinating.

"When am I gonna reform your nondrinking habits, Junior?"

Calvin had hunched over his Coke and hadn't heard Yelsom coming to the table.

"You'd prefer me alert, I'm sure," he said politely, drawing out a chair for Yelsom.

"Hear about the concert?" Yelsom wanted to plunge right in tonight; no small talk.

"Every detail."

"Talk with anyone from the group?"

"No, but you obviously didn't do anything there. Why?"

Yelsom gulped, belched, and wiped his mouth. "No fear factor."

"Fear factor?"

"You've gotta learn the number-one rule of activism," he replied. "The fear factor. Without fear, there's no power."

Even as the man said the words, Calvin felt his anxiety rise. Yelsom stared harder at him.

"Feel your heartbeat go up?"

Calvin did, and hated himself for it.

Yelsom laughed and resumed his normal expression. "That's the idea! Listen, it works." He slapped Calvin's back.

"But what do you mean," Calvin asked, his heart resuming a more normal pace, "about the concert?"

"Carlton took the wind out of our sails," Yelsom said matter-of-factly. "He outed himself and got their sympathy. He even exposed *us*, not vice versa. So the shock value was gone. Everyone knew we were there and what we'd planned. If we'd have gone ahead after that, it would have just looked silly."

Calvin nodded. *This guy can be very astute at times,* he admitted to himself.

"Always remember," Yelsom lectured, "our goal is to instill fear. Anything done apart from that is a waste of time."

"Got it."

"Now. About Greg Bishop."

"Who is he?"

Yelsom's eyes twinkled. "Someone important. I gave you his name and number?"

"Right."

"We knew he was Carlton's doctor, but we didn't expect Carlton to advertise for him. This is perfect! Now everyone's gonna think Bishop is the healer of homosexuals!"

Calvin chilled. Memories of protests against Gateway Ministries flooded him. He pushed them back.

"So here's the plan. You, poor little Jeremy, are now a distressed gay man who wants to be cured. And you're the one who'll give us every detail of what that quack does behind closed doors. He's the new Alex Crawford."

Another memory rose—BRAVO members rejoicing over Crawford's heart attack.

"East Coast called me today."

East Coast. The vague reference to the BRAVO leaders in New York from whom Yelsom took instructions.

"They say we should proceed with the list now and focus on outing and attacking AB101. Those are our priorities, in that order."

Calvin found his voice. "So what exactly do you want me to do?"

"Just go for counseling. You're stable enough; it won't mess up your head. Record every session, then give me the tapes. We'll use every ridiculous thing Bishop says against him, and he'll never know how we did it. Later on, too, I'll want you to get into his records. But for now, just start seeing him. You still got the number?"

"Sure."

Yelsom rose. "Then make an appointment tomorrow. I'm going for more beer."

Tuesday morning, Greg walked into the waiting room of the counseling center to meet two television cameras and six reporters. Both local papers—the *LA Times* and the *Orange County Register*—were represented, as was the Orange County News Network (one of the television cameras), the *Orange County Vine* ("The Only Gay Voice Behind the Orange Curtain" its banner proclaimed), and Channel Seven News, the second camera. One man representing the local Christian radio station had come as well. Greg was pleasantly surprised that all the networks hadn't turned out. His dealings with the media had been minimal; he liked it that way.

"Can't I go get my teeth drilled instead?" he'd asked Mike when the pastor insisted some sort of statement from Greg was required.

Robbie was already seated, talking quietly with reporters, off the record, and sipping the coffee Nancy had provided for the event.

He and Greg greeted each other quietly.

"You okay?" Greg whispered as they took their seats on the couch.

"Fine. This should boost CD sales all over the place!"

Greg was mortified; Robbie slapped his knee and laughed.

Both men had typewritten statements. Greg began the conference.

"Mr. Carlton and I will both read from prepared statements. Mr. Carlton has chosen not to take questions, but I'll take fifteen minutes to answer your questions, then we'll be finished. Robbie?"

Robbie checked his notes, looked at them, and smiled.

"I have been a Christian musician for five years now, and have tried to maintain the standards expected of a man in my position. Through circumstances beyond my control, however, records were illegally obtained from the late Joshua Ferguson's therapy notes which indicated I was homosexually oriented. Let me stress that I do not engage in homosexual activity, nor do I celebrate the gay lifestyle. Indeed, I do not refer to myself as gay, as I feel that to be a social and political term not applicable to me."

The reporter from the *Vine* raised his hand.

"Please wait until I'm finished," Robbie said firmly. "As he said, Dr. Bishop will answer your questions."

The reporter frowned.

"Members of the group BRAVO had threatened to publicly disclose this information about me if I did not disclose it myself. I chose the latter, seeing it as the more dignified option. I have been in treatment with Dr. Gregory Bishop since early March and have been pleased with the results so far, though our therapeutic relationship has obviously been a brief one.

"On April 19, I disclosed the issue publicly to my supporters, and I hope they, and Christians around the country, will remember me in prayer. Dr. Bishop was unaware of my plan to disclose this, as he was unaware of my intention to publicly endorse him at the concert. Indeed, that action has become, I think, a bone of contention between us."

He looked playfully at Greg.

"Right?"

"The whole skeleton, not just a bone," Greg growled.

"My future plans," Robbie read from his paper, "are uncertain. I am under contract to finish one more recording, the release date of which has been postponed one year. I will not be touring meanwhile, as I wish to use this time for personal growth and finding a new sense of direction."

He put the paper down.

"Thank you."

Greg took over; Robbie remained in his seat.

"My name is Dr. Gregory Bishop, and I serve as the clinical director of Berean Counseling Center. As I consider it unethical to use a client to promote myself or my work, I will not discuss Mr. Carlton or any aspect of his treatment, other than to confirm the facts he's already stated. I do wish to clarify my stand as a therapist and a Christian on the homosexual issue, and explain what I do and do *not* believe and practice."

"That was a mouthful," Robbie observed in a stage whisper.

"I do not attempt to cure homosexuals, as one report has implied. Apart from Mr. Carlton I've not treated homosexuality. I do believe that homosexuals who are dissatisfied with their sexuality should be given an opportunity to modify their behavior. Those who are satisfied with their orientation, of course, should be allowed to live their lives as they see fit. But as a Christian, I believe there is, for those who choose it, a better way than the homosexual option. To that end, we will be forming a program for those who struggle with homosexuality, as we feel it is not enough for the church to condemn a sin. We must also assist those who want to abandon the sin we're condemning."

He looked up from his paper to see five disapproving faces and one inquisitive one. The room felt cold.

"Any questions?"

The reporter from the *Vine* shot up his hand.

"Dr. Bishop, your statement contained a great deal of rhetoric about behavior modification. Could you be a bit more plain in explaining *exactly* how you cure homosexuality?"

Greg expected the question; the tone rankled him, nonetheless.

"I *treat* homosexuality," he emphasized, "I don't cure it. As for the specifics of treatment, I do not discuss that publicly."

Three reporters groaned indignantly.

"You said," the man from the *Vine* pressed, "you were here to explain to us what you do and don't do. You've explained what you don't do, but that's all you've explained."

Greg drew a deep breath. "That's because I've only treated one person with this problem so far, and to explain my treatment with him would be tantamount to discussing him, which I refuse to do."

The representative from the Christian radio show nodded sympathetically; the others looked almost scornful.

"What do you say," the *Vine's* reporter asked, "to those who are offended at your insinuation that their sexual orientation is a problem?"

"I don't want to offend anyone. I'm only offering the Christian viewpoint."

"A viewpoint many lesbians and gays find destructive."

"Can anyone discuss this issue without offending someone?" Greg demanded. He wasn't used to the hot seat; his voice was strained.

The *Times* had the next question.

"Where do you stand on gay rights?" the woman posed.

"Gays should have the same rights we all have," Greg said confidently. Nobody, he was sure, would take issue with that.

Wrong.

"Then you're saying they should be allowed to marry?"

"Well, no—"

"And be protected from discrimination in housing and employment?"

"That depends on what you mean by—"

"And file joint tax returns and receive insurance benefits?"

"No!"

"Then you *don't* believe they should have the same rights you have?"

His head swam; he tried to recover. "I'm saying you have to draw the line somewhere. I certainly don't want these people discriminated against—"

"Then you support Assembly Bill 101?"

"No, I just don't want people *unfairly* discriminated against. AB101 sounds like it would—"

"Is there such a thing as *fair* discrimination?"

"We *all* discriminate in some ways!"

"Then you feel," the woman concluded while writing, "gays and lesbians should *not* have the same rights you have."

Greg, throwing his hands up, was tied in knots.

"Oh, knock it off!!"

Robbie's harsh shout shocked everyone.

"Why not just say it, Greg? We have a standard in this country—which most people still adhere to, by the way—which promotes heterosexual marriage as the norm. Homosexuals should *not* be mistreated, but if you're saying we should grant them official sanction for something most of us still believe is immoral, you're asking too much!"

Reporters scribbled furiously; Greg's eyes widened. Was there no end to this kid's surprises?

"So, Mr. Carlton, you're against Assembly Bill 101?"

"Definitely."

"And you, Mr. Bishop?"

"I didn't come to talk politics," he said, miserably. "But since you ask, yes, I'm against it."

"Because?" the *Register's* representative asked.

"I'm sorry, but we're out of time. Thank you very much for coming."

They knew he meant it. They also knew, as he did, that they'd successfully flushed out the kind of remarks that made good press.

Robbie went for more coffee, reminding Greg he'd see him tomorrow for their session. Greg sat on the couch quietly as the press filed out. One stayed behind—a friendly looking young man with a slight paunch.

"Dr. Bishop, my name is Calvin Blanchard. I host 'Open Heart' on KLVE. Could I make an appointment to speak with you?"

TWENTY-SIX

One!

Thirty days to come up with a plan. Not too hard; Crawford's book gave him some helpful insights. Putting them in a group format wouldn't be tough.

Two!

But would the plan satisfy the press? No matter how he put it, they'd take issue with the idea.

Two hundred and sixty-five pounds was close to the maximum weight he could bench press; he was already straining.

Three!

Who cares about the press?

Four!

That woman from the *Times* couldn't wait to report that Greg thought gays shouldn't have the same rights he did. Other reporters suggested he was part of the latest wave in gay-bashing, a fundamentalist whose agenda included punitive measures enacted against homosexuals. Now he didn't care if he never gave another interview.

Five! Whew!

Three clients today; two after Robbie. And Mr. Blanchard from KLVE was coming in at 1:00. It was 11:30; light administrative chores at the Center left plenty of time for a good workout.

Six!

His chest was on fire; his shoulders screamed.

Sev—sev—ugggh!

"Come on!"

Someone had seen he was stuck and was offering a spot, lifting the barbell lightly.

Seven!

"Keep going, bro. Come on."

He smelled workout sweat and saw a blue tank and large deltoids. The voice wasn't familiar.

Eh—eh—

"Up!" Another light lift.

Eight!

"One more. Come on."

NAEEE—NINE!

"That was too easy. One more."

T—ta—teh—oohhh!

"I'm not gonna help on this one!"

ARGGGH!

"Come on! How ya' gonna straighten those homos out if you're not big and strong?"

The barbell flew up, courtesy of Greg's sudden shock. The stranger caught it and laughed.

"*That* got ya' goin'!"

Greg sat upright on the bench, whirled toward the man, and appraised him speechlessly.

Greg's age, younger perhaps. Athletic, blue-collar looking. Short-cropped black hair, dark complexion, firm chin, laughing eyes.

Laughing face. His expression invited a guessing game.

"Do I know you?" Greg panted.

The man folded his arms and grinned without answering.

Greg stared. "From church?"

The stranger shook his head.

"We've met?"

"Aw, *buddy!* My feelings are hurt. I recognized *you* without too much trouble. Though you have been in the papers lately; that made it easier."

The face *was* familiar.

"Need a hint?"

Greg nodded.

The man put an arm around Greg's shoulder and led him away from the bench press. "The last time I saw you, you were heading for the hills."

They stopped in an empty corner of the gym. Greg wiped his forehead and looked in the mirrored wall at both their reflections. "I still don't follow you."

"We had our own form of treatment for queers back then."

"We?"

"You didn't approve."

It hit him in a rush. *Queer bait is a guy who baits queers—* Greg, stunned, kept his eyes on the mirror and saw two college students, dumb and brash, willing to do anything to get into the Argonauts until that night. One ran; the other—

Me first.

He searched the dark, sweaty face.

"Rick?"

Mosley laughed.

"Rick Mosley?"

Rick punched his shoulder; Greg staggered backward, smiling and huffing. "You! You? What are you doing here?"

"I live here."

"In the gym?" Greg asked, wiping his face again.

"Practically. Come on, I'll buy you a juice."

They sauntered over to the juice bar, where the gym manager greeted Mosley by name. Rick, in turn, introduced him to Greg.

"I've been reading about you, Greg," the manager—Tom Wooding—said, pumping Greg's arm. "Very interesting stuff."

Greg thanked him and turned to Rick, who'd ordered two protein shakes with orange juice.

They looked at each other with the faltering, excited energy of old friends wanting to catch up and having no idea where to start.

"I've never seen you here," Greg began.

"I'm here most mornings, probably before you arrive."

"Definitely. I only work out at odd hours; usually late morning or early afternoon."

"But I saw your name on the sign-in sheet when I checked in today, and I thought, *nah, couldn't be.* But when I saw you barely able to handle a simple bench press, I said, 'It's gotta be Bishop!' "

It felt fun, juvenile, brotherly. Truthfully, though, Greg wasn't sure whether he was glad to see Mosley or not. Their last meeting had in fact been that terrible night, and Rick's behavior had been monstrous. His remarks about "queers" just now showed some of the same colors.

The shakes arrived. Greg sipped.

"What are you doing now, Rick? You live in Orange County?"

"Fullerton. I work for Western Life; you heard of them?"

Greg shook his head.

"Medical insurance. I'm a claims manager. And you? The paper said you're a religious psychologist or something?"

"Just a psychologist. Well, religious, too. It's hard to explain."

"I heard you turned into a Jesus freak way back when."

The term wasn't said viciously; Greg chalked it up to Rick's limited vocabulary.

"I'm a Christian, yeah."

"Isn't everybody?"

Greg hated questions like that; they were setups for arguments going nowhere. "Well, I'm a Christian of the fundamentalist variety, if that helps explain it."

Rick looked blank. "Whatever."

"Are you married, Rick?"

"Divorced. Remember Jeanine Shaw?"

"That's right! You were going together back then."

Rick swallowed some juice. "Terrific girlfriend, terrible wife. How about you?"

"Married. Very happily."

"Do I know her?"

"Nope."

"Kids?"

"Soon, I hope."

Something in the way Rick was looking at him—the manager, too, who Greg suddenly realized had been listening to everything—was unsettling.

Rick watched while Greg watched him, then looked at Tom Wooding, who nodded and turned back to Greg.

"We know what you're up against, Greg."

Greg stared at them both; Tom nodded.

"And there's lots of people around here who are sympathetic."

"I'm completely confused."

"Hardly anybody," Tom said, "has the guts to speak out against the gays. That's why I appreciate what I've been reading about you."

Greg was about to protest that the press made him out to be much more extreme than he was.

"It did my heart good," Rick nodded, "to hear a religious leader tell it like it is. So many of you guys—sorry, no offense—but so many of you guys are turning all touchy-feely and don't take a stand on anything!"

"Well," Greg stammered, "I'm not—I'm not all that right-wing, you know?"

"That's not what I hear," Tom smiled.

Mosley smiled and scooted his stool closer to Greg. Tom, from his stool, leaned closer, too.

"You're already a bit of a hero in some circles."

The news didn't bode well.

"What makes me a hero? And to whom?"

Someone stepped up to the juice bar; Tom lowered his voice even more.

"You'll slam 'em right back into their closets!"

Greg reared back. "You guys have got me wrong. I subscribe to the old 'hate the sin, love the sinner' saying. Got it?"

Tom and Rick had listened to this with ever-broadening smiles.

"That's it exactly!" Tom grinned. "Perfect!"

Greg's confusion was stronger than ever. Rick looked at the juice bar, made sure he wasn't being heard, then continued.

"There are a bunch of us forming a citizens' group in Orange County. We're concerned about what we're seeing. You know, the Josh Ferguson thing, the radicals, the gay rights bills—"

"We want," Tom added, "to form a united front against them."

"How about coming to a meeting, just to check us out?"

Rick looked at him intently.

"Please?" Tom asked.

"For an old buddy?" Rick added.

What could it hurt? "No strings, right?" Greg asked.

"None. Just show up."

Tom handed him a card with directions to a home in Newport Beach. Tuesday, 7:00 P.M. was written on the back. Greg accepted it, then checked his watch.

"I've gotta get back to work."

Mosley asked if he could use a workout partner; that suited Greg fine, as he'd wanted to increase his workout anyway. They agreed to begin meeting Mondays, Wednesdays, and Fridays at 6:00 A.M. for some intense weight lifting. Tom and Greg shook hands, Mosley ordered another juice, and Greg went to the showers.

The card Tom gave him was still in his hand. He looked at the front of it.

No address was shown. Just a phone number and a name: "Citizens United."

Greg would remember that Wednesday as a day for making new friends and abhorrent discoveries. His encounter with Tom and Rick at the gym was ominous, though he agreed there was nothing wrong with at least meeting these concerned citizens they'd spoken about.

But his meeting with Calvin Blanchard went beyond ominous. Their conversation was frightening, but educational and, ultimately, hopeful.

"You're kidding."

He said it so many times that Mr. Blanchard, exasperated, reminded him there was nothing funny about his situation.

"I haven't confided in anyone so far. Please believe I'm not kidding."

"Tell me again."

Again, Calvin began at the beginning: his history with Ferguson, his infiltration of BRAVO, his assignment to pose as a client, his self-appointed mission to find out about BRAVO, and what Josh had discovered about them to make his report such a closely kept secret. Again, he related the background of "Unforgiven Sins"; again, he reiterated his desire to start a Gateway ministry, and how ironic it was Greg had announced a similar desire to the press.

"All our purposes seem to be converging," he said. "You want to start a ministry; so do I. Yelsom wants me to infiltrate your organization; I'm already infiltrating his. You're helping Robbie Carlton; I'm trying to make sense of what happened to Josh."

"And I," Greg realized aloud, "know a bit about the tape you're looking for."

"*No!*"

"I've seen it."

"When?"

"Last month. Some of it, anyway. Then it was stolen."

It was Greg's turn to explain; Calvin, afterward, had another bomb to drop.

"I know those girls!"

"The ones who stole the tape?"

"The very same."

"And you know Yelsom well?"

"Somewhat."

"Has he told you he knows me?"

"Never!"

"His real name," Greg explained, "is Bennie Hudson. And he has a personal grudge against me."

He explained why. Calvin listened carefully, understanding a bit more about Yelsom's rage, then told Greg about his own background.

And so it went—each man revealing secrets useful to the other.

"So now what?" Greg asked when they'd covered every pertinent detail they could remember.

Calvin thought, then spoke carefully.

"Yelsom wants me to be your client. You want the tape back. The girls, I think, gave it to Yelsom. And I have the keys to his apartment."

"Can you get in?"

"I have to find it first."

"It'll answer both our questions."

"Eventually. Meanwhile, you and I need to work together," Calvin suggested.

"Obviously."

"Yelsom wants information from me. You and I will decide in advance what that information will be."

"Then he'll only know what we want him to know," Greg observed.

"I'll get the tape, by hook or crook."

"And you'll keep me posted about their plans?"

"As much as I know. Yelsom doesn't tell me much until the last minute. He says it prevents leaks."

"So! How are we gonna set you up as my client?"

They both thought for a moment.

"Maybe," Calvin ventured, "I don't have to be your client."

"Isn't that the plan?"

"Yes, but I've got a better idea."

———◆———

After seeing Mosley, Tom, and Calvin, a session with Robbie seemed blessedly normal.

"You handle the press well, my friend," Greg complimented him when he sat down.

Robbie was relaxed and enthused. "Did you see what the *Register* said about me?"

"'A zealous convert to fundamentalist thinking who hopes other gays will follow his example,'" Greg quoted. "Are you sure you want to be known that way?"

"Do I have a choice? They'll say whatever they want to say."

"Perhaps."

"Besides," Robbie said, "what have I got to lose now?"

Greg conceded the point, and the session began. The focus of it was on Robbie's need for approval.

"I felt you were mad at me last Friday."

"Not mad. Concerned."

"Because I dragged you into this?"

Greg was uncomfortable, knowing he'd have to be honest about this.

"Partially. I still wish you'd checked with me first."

"I thought you'd be proud."

Powerful stage presence or not, Robbie needed lots of reassurance offstage. Greg tried to provide it without overdoing it.

"I am, Robbie. Very proud. And let me say plainly, I was impressed watching you onstage, even before you blew BRAVO's cover. I was proud to know you. But why," he asked, getting to the real point, "is that so important?"

Robbie's father, as usual, came up. Crawford's book explained the connection many theorists felt lay between male homosexuality and a father's love or the lack of it. Greg wasn't convinced all homosexuals were the product of bad parenting, but in Robbie's case, the theory of a search for male affirmation, sprung out of some break in the father/son bond, proved true.

"That," Greg commented, "could explain why Josh Ferguson was such a powerful influence in your life. You'd finally found the perfect dad."

"It *seemed* that way," Robbie said sadly. "Then he left."

"As though he abandoned you."

"You see it that way?"

"I'm wondering if *you* do. A loved one's suicide is often seen as an abandonment."

Robbie punched a pillow on the couch. "Couldn't he have at least talked to me? Why didn't he trust me?"

"Who says he didn't? Try, Robbie, not to read too much into his decision. You'll never know for sure if you're right."

"Maybe." He sighed. "So tell me. If I work through all this mess, will I ever be able to love a woman? In the normal way?"

"Let's work on you learning to love men first," Greg answered firmly. "In the normal way."

Yelsom loved the plan.

"Bishop's that stupid?"

"He must be!" Calvin beamed. "After talking to him for ten minutes, he said I didn't need counseling, but would I consider helping lead this group he's forming!"

"Wonderful. Perfect!"

Yelsom's pleasure was scarcely contained. Calvin felt closer than ever to his goal—surely, the man would trust him now!

"So I'll be in on all the planning details," he said. "I'll be able to get any records we need."

"We'll need a lot. If closet gays start going to him for counseling, you'll be in a position to add their names to the list."

"The list?"

"The one we got from Ferguson's office."

"Right."

"So, Jeremy!"

He wasn't calling him Junior; that must be significant, Calvin thought.

"You have to steer clear of any public work BRAVO does. Come to the meetings, but that's it. Nobody can know you're with us. From here on, you're a spy."

As if he didn't know.

Unlike Yelsom, Christine was *not* thrilled with the idea.

"This confirms everything I was afraid of!" she snapped when Greg got home that night and told her about Calvin. "You said you wouldn't get involved in gay rights battles, and now you're up to your neck in them!"

Greg argued, persuasively, his innocence in the matter. He had not, after all, gone looking for any of this—a point he'd reminded her of countless times the past two months. And he wouldn't, he assured her, get involved in politics.

"Let's commit ourselves to two things, okay?" he asked over dinner. "I'll keep you up on everything I'm doing. When you're uncomfortable with something I'm involved in—"

"I'm uncomfortable with *everything* you're involved with!"

"I can't help that. But I'll try to stay away from controversy, I promise."

"Fat chance."

"But I'll try!" His patience ebbed again. Did she think he wanted to be hooked into all this?

She nodded dejectedly.

"And," he said, tracing her cheek with one finger, "I want us to keep our home a safe place. No undue talking about work, okay? I mean it. I want to forget all that when I come home."

She turned her head away from his touch. "How am I supposed to forget it? Just turn it off?"

He dropped his hand. "I guess not," he said coldly. "Let's watch TV."

"Fine."

The tension didn't ease for the rest of the evening. They watched television in silence, without laughter or affection. Greg, having given up on laughter for the night, gave affection one more try when they got into bed.

Christine, unresponsive and distracted, stared at the ceiling.

Greg rolled over on his side wordlessly. *This routine*, he thought, *is getting old.*

But if his marital problems were getting old, his work-related problems were taking new turns with amazing speed. Calvin warned him about the next development, which would again bring Greg face-to-face with BRAVO, this time on his own turf. And the event Calvin warned him about underscored Pastor Ruben's prediction at the board meeting, convincing Greg, and many others, that the devil himself had indeed been loosed on the Berean Community Church.

TWENTY-SEVEN

*T*he first sign of trouble could be seen from the street in front of the church. When Greg and Christine turned the corner by the parking lot, they spotted signs hoisted in front of the sanctuary. Greg accelerated; upon entering the lot the messages on the signs, and their carriers, became clearer.

"Jesus would throw these hypocrites out with a whip" was the first saying Greg deciphered. Others, obscene and blasphemous, were unrepeatable. Still others made the point of the demonstration clearer:

"Once queer, always queer!"

"Leopards don't change their spots; gays don't change either!"

"Love thy neighbor, Dr. Bishop!"

Greg whipped into a parking slot, jumped out of the car, and ran, dragging Christine by the hand, toward the church.

An arc of demonstrators had surrounded the front entrance, their backs to the door, and were screaming and chanting at the crowd gathered for the 10:30 service. The 9:00 service had ended, but the worshipers, blocked inside by the protesters, were unable to leave through the glass doors. They huddled in the foyer, instead, peering out fearfully. Those who'd come to attend the next service stood a respectful distance from the picketers on the lawn outside the church, repelled by the sight and noise in front of them.

Young couples clutched their children close; an elderly woman wept quietly. Some of the younger men, trying to reason with the protesters, were rebuffed with curses and shaking fists. One woman, seven months pregnant, was spat on.

BRAVO had come to visit.

"Calvin said they'd stay on the sidewalk!" Greg exclaimed.

"Apparently they forgot their manners," Christine answered.

"They've been here for half an hour," a Sunday school teacher on the lawn told Greg when he asked what had happened. "At first, it looked like they were gathering peacefully, then they just swooped in on the doors. Nobody can get in or out!"

Chants and shouts assaulted the crowd:

Stop the violence, stop the hate!

Sexist, racist, antigay,

Born-again bigots,

Go away!

They were a sorry lot, these violent bigots of Berean Community Church, and were no credit to the labels being slapped on them. Some knelt and prayed, others waited quietly for the police. No one lifted a hand against the protesters; no one shouted back at the human blockade.

But what an assortment of humans it was! The women, infuriated and agitated figures in black and denim, wore their hatred plainly. They screamed and seethed demoniacally; nobody of either sex with half a brain would have crossed them. But it was the men who truly sickened the bystanders.

Those not dressed in the standard BRAVO attire—black T-shirt, jeans, and bandannas—chose to dress instead in women's clothes. Not just *any* kind of women's clothes, though. Had this been a masquerade ball, the costume of choice would appear to have been that of a psychotic prostitute.

One wore purple fishnet stockings and heels, a tight red leather miniskirt, a leotard top, and a slash of lipstick to complement his mustache and beard. Another sported a nun's habit with a swastika patch sewn onto the sleeve; another preferred evening wear, flouncing about in a gold lamé gown slit up both sides and low-cut, exposing a hairy back and chest. Earrings and cheap, garish jewelry were standard wear; posing in a horrid burlesque of everything feminine was the standard behavior. The men minced then bellowed, showed their legs like harlots then spouted the language of whoremongers. The spectacle could have been funny under other circumstances; instead, laced as it was with threats and catcalls, and seething in front of a church in the Sunday morning light, it was hideous.

Greg looked for Yelsom, who was nowhere to be seen.

Pastor Ruben walked in front of the rioters and yelled, "The police have been called! You *will* be arrested for trespassing if you don't move to the sidewalk, now!"

They shouted him down before he could finish the sentence. He tried again, was drowned out again, then threw both hands up, disgusted. After turning on his heel, he saw Greg and marched up to him.

"Thanks, Greg." He saluted him sarcastically. "Thanks a lot."

One of the protesters heard Ruben call Greg by name.

"Dr. Bishop!" she yelled to her friends, pointing at him. "That's Dr. Bishop!"

His name was a battle cry; BRAVO turned their collective fury on him and, to his horror, Christine.

What they shouted was hard to ascertain, as they overrode each other with insults and threats hurled at the Bishops.

"You stupid quack!"

"Our rights aren't as important as yours? You pitiful excuse of a Christian!"

"Queers don't need to change—*you* need to change!"

"Hey, Mrs. Bishop! Let me know when you crave a *real* man!"

A heavy-set woman in denim had shouted it while posturing lewdly at Christine; without knowing what he was doing, Greg leaped toward the demonstrators. Ruben caught the end of his jacket and yanked him back; three other men stood in front of him.

"Easy," they said, pushing him back on the lawn. "Don't give them what they want."

Christine broke down; Greg strained against the men and screamed at BRAVO, who howled in delight.

A small crowd gathered around the Bishops protectively.

Police sirens wailed over the din, and six officers appeared, clearing the area and arresting protesters who'd refused to move.

Another handful of officers stayed in front of the church, giving the all-clear signal to the ushers, who released the parishioners who'd cowered in the lobby.

"Animals!" Greg repeated over and over. He hugged Christine with his right arm and clenched his left fist.

He saw Pastor Ruben's son, one of those trapped inside, run toward his dad. Ruben picked him up and pointed at one of the last protesters, the man in fishnets, being led away.

"Look closely, David," Ruben said. "That's what a homosexual is. That's the way they behave. Never forget."

Greg turned to Christine.

"You want to go home?"

She'd collected herself. "And why should we?" she asked firmly. "We came to worship. They can't stop us. Can they?"

Greg didn't answer.

Pastor Mike, visibly shaken by the scene, conducted the worship service gently, stopping at least twice to pray that the women and men who'd come in hatred would have seen the love of Christ in this place. Several in the congregation said "amen"; Greg wasn't one of them. Nor, he noticed, were several of the other men.

The singing was weak. No one felt buoyant, and the sermon was utterly forgettable.

Pastor Mike led the congregation in confessional prayer for the communion service, and the ushers gathered in front to take the elements.

A hymn and a prayer of consecration followed.

"We remember our own sins even as we recoil at the sins of others, Lord," Mike prayed, "and as we take Your body and blood, we ask forgiveness for ourselves."

"You need it!"

Mike was pelted with an object that splattered red down the front of his suit before he could open his eyes to see where the shout came from.

Greg knew the voice.

"While you're at it, consecrate these!"

Yelsom and three other men, having sneaked in during prayer, flew down the aisles and hurled condoms filled, like water balloons, with blood. They hit the communion table and two ushers; the others jumped out of the way.

"For Dr. Bishop from us! For every gay he kills with his so-called treatment, their blood will be on your altar!"

They were gone before anyone could reach them.

Half the congregation had shot to their feet; the others crouched in the pews. Everyone froze—Mike, dripping red with the communion cup still clutched in his shaking hand, the ushers, ashen and confused, and the members of Berean, a congregation under siege.

They looked to Mike, then Greg, then back at Mike.

Slowly he lowered the cup, not bothering to wipe the blood from his face and clothes, and signaled to Greg.

"Gregory, come up here. Bring Christine."

Greg took Christine's hand and started forward in a daze.

Mike gathered them both in a bear hug, then turned them to face the congregation.

"No backing down." He said it to the Bishops, pointing his finger at both. Then, to the congregation:

"We have a choice—fight or flight. I know what mine will be. Those who want to join me, stand now and extend your hands toward Dr. and Mrs. Bishop."

Nobody stayed in their seats.

"And pray for them. And for our church. Not that we'll be spared any further trouble, but that we'll never let trouble entice us to fear. Or to hate."

So they prayed, long and hard. Greg kept his eyes open, watching his family offer their hands and hearts, then looked at his wife.

Christine's head was bowed slightly. There were no tears.

Blood from Pastor Mike's suit had smeared her blouse.

Greg stumbled out of bed at 5:15, ran a cold shower, kissed his sleeping wife, and drove to the gym.

One!

"Come on, Bishop, biceps don't grow without a little help!"

His first Monday 6:00 A.M. workout with Rick Mosley was a killer.

Two!

"Push, push! No cheating!"

Three!

"You're slowing down. Come on!"

Four! Barely.

"You've got six more. What's the matter?"

The barbell curled halfway up, faltered, then shook.

"*Come on!*"

Greg grunted, squeezed, and trembled.

"I'm not gonna help ya! Come on!"

He tried again; his arms failed. The barbell fell back. He lifted it again; again it stuck midway.

"Imagine," Mosely whispered in his ears, "that the barbell's got twenty of those BRAVO fags on it and you're slamming them into the ceiling!"

Five! Six! Seven!

"Go for it!"

Eight! Nine! Ten!

"That's enough."

Eleven!

"Bishop! Hey!"

Twelve! Thirteen! Fourteen!

Exhaustion and stress made his workweek drag at a snail's pace.

Calvin called first thing Monday morning.

"Greg, I'm so sorry!"

"Why didn't you warn me?"

"I did! At least about everything I *thought* they were going to do. Yelsom said he'd keep everyone on the sidewalk. You were prepared for that, weren't you?"

"Sure. But not for the blockade."

"Yelsom changes plans sometimes without even telling me!" Calvin complained.

"Well, try to get him to confide in you a little more, Calvin. That bit with the condoms was disgusting!"

"Everything they do is disgusting. Promise me something, Greg."

"Yeah?"

"Promise you'll never be like them. No matter how mad they make you, don't ever be like them."

"I could never be that weird. Or scary."

"That's the plan, Greg. They're trying to scare you and everybody else to death!"

He wasn't scared. But if distracting him was part of the plan, it succeeded handsomely. Sessions with clients, even Robbie, barely held his attention. Most of his clients seemed not to notice; Robbie, on two occasions, stopped in the middle of the hour and asked Greg if he was still there.

Not a good sign.

Meetings with Pastor Mike centered on security plans for future protests and ways to minimize the tension growing in the congregation. So far, they were solidly behind Greg and the plans, referred to by Mike after his prayer for Greg and Christine, to start a ministry to gays. But some were afraid to come to church.

"Because of me," Greg lamented.

"Because of *them!*" Mike countered. "And we're not gonna let them drive us away."

"It's me they want to drive out."

"Greg, don't."

"I'm a Jonah. I brought the storm."

"Hey!" Mike snapped. "Who am I talking to? Greg Bishop, my friend whom I admire?" He glared. "No, not today. I'm talking to Dr. Wimp. I want my friend back."

Greg slumped in his chair like a chastened boy.

"I don't see your wife backing down, or Robbie. You could use a little of their *chutzpah!*"

"I hate these people."

Mike buttonholed him. "You want them to win?"

Greg shook his head feebly.

"They want you to hate them. Can't you see that? Then you'll become what they are, no better than any of 'em! And you'll become what they say you are—a mean, hateful bigot!"

They can't win, Ferguson had warned, *unless we become what they want us to become!*

As the summer months progressed, Greg could barely remember what life had been like before he'd first heard those words. His counsel became listless and routine, his marriage—already under noticeable strain—was eroding. Fights with Christine became a weekly event; the church's prayers notwithstanding, they weren't holding up well as a couple.

"We're miles away from each other," Christine noted one Sunday on the way home from church. "Miles and miles."

"We need to pick up our devotions again," Greg answered. They'd dropped them weeks ago and, with them, much of their communication.

"We need more than that," Christine returned. "We need to get away."

"Things are too hectic right now."

Christine just sighed.

Life was eroding for others in Orange County, too, as retaliation from BRAVO extended not only to the Berean Community Church, but to a long and distinguished list of enemies.

"Now we begin in earnest!" Yelsom roared to his followers, three weeks after the Berean protest. "Ferguson and Carlton were dress rehearsals. Now it's show time!"

And the show had a long run. From July to September, notes were sent to all the members on Ferguson's list, many of whom had driven from Orange County to see the doctor. Yelsom, ever secretive, wrote the notes himself and informed no one, including Calvin, who was being outed in a given week. And so, Calvin was unable to warn Greg, as if warning could have prevented the actions. He and Greg could only meet weekly and pray for whomever was next on the hit list.

Slowly, one by one, prominent Orange County figures decided it was best—their duty, in fact—to come out of the closet. Anaheim was shocked when one of its school board members announced her lesbianism; three Corona del Mar socialites, married men, no less, publicized their gay proclivities and newfound zeal for gay rights. Never mind the families that were shattered and the question marks slashed across their careers. They were, they insisted, moved by conviction and a passion for honesty. A schoolteacher, an assemblyman, and two policemen were next. By September, "coming out" announcements were almost passé.

Not all were smooth; one ended in suicide.

"But," Yelsom challenged BRAVO during a late-July meeting, "how do you make omelettes without cracking eggs?"

"You stole that from Jack Nicholson!" someone shot back.

"And he," Yelsom asserted, "stole his best devil roles from me!"

BRAVO responded enthusiastically to the outings and their effects on the public. As public attention drifted from Ferguson and Carlton to BRAVO's activities and the fate of Assembly Bill 101 (about which Governor Wilson was now waffling), their actions were all the more significant.

"Keep 'em coming!" Yelsom would scream after each public revelation. "The people fear us, the press quotes us, and the more openly gay people there are, the more pressure Governor Wilson will feel!"

Churches, too, felt BRAVO's wrath. The scene at Berean was repeated at various places of worship on at least two Sundays a month. These actions Calvin could warn Greg about, as all BRAVO members were informed about them in advance, and Greg in turn warned the pastors of the churches about to be hit.

The BRAVO plan, unveiled by Yelsom in August, included threatening any church daring to preach against homosexuality. Orange County pastors were deluged with notes warning them to expect a demonstration if they said anything negative about gays. That, predictably, inspired a wave of sermons against homosexuality, which inspired a wave of protests. Churches became accustomed to riotous activity on their sidewalks; each one, forewarned by Greg who'd been forewarned by Calvin, would inform the police before each demonstration that their assistance was needed. The police ensured boundary violations didn't occur, BRAVO's tantrums were confined to the sidewalks, and Christians throughout Orange County made their way to church past signs, screams, and men in fishnets.

A strong and growing antigay sentiment festered; pastors encouraged their people to love without compromise; people throughout the county wondered quietly how long they could go on turning the other cheek and, for that matter, how many cheeks they were required to turn.

That was a matter of no small concern to Greg and Calvin, who began meeting weekly to discuss their newly formed Gateway ministry. As the months passed, they prayed not only for God to stop the radicals from harming the churches, but also for the Christians to learn to forgive the radicals. That prayer was commonly heard at the Gateway meetings, which were begun in July and held at the Berean Counseling Center.

Calvin's pastor gave his blessing, though the ministry was on Berean grounds, so long as it was overseen by Greg, not Calvin.

"I'm still worried about you," Pastor Cox noted when he signed the papers. "Don't get in too deep, Calvin."

The next hurdle to jump had been the approval of the Berean board of elders, who reviewed the program Greg promised to draw up, voted their approval (again, eleven to one), and agreed that Mike should announce the plans to the church the following Sunday.

And so the second Sunday morning in August, Mike announced, to applause and cheers, the formation of the Berean Community Counseling Center's Gateway ministry.

Seven people showed up for the group meeting that week; within a month, twenty were regularly attending the two-hour sessions of prayer, mutual accountability, and education on human sexuality from a biblical perspective, taught by Greg.

Robbie Carlton, thrilled at the prospect, attended the first session and never missed a meeting thereafter. His counseling progressed; he reported a lessening of homosexual desire, and relief at finally having the problem out in the open.

Did he miss performing? Greg asked.

"Not too much. I'm making friends; that helps."

"You didn't have friends before?"

"Not as equals. I was always the star. I'm one of the guys now. I love it!"

And Greg, distracted and upset by the whirl of tension he lived in, nonetheless grew to love Robbie as he'd loved no client since beginning his practice.

He said as much during a rare phone conversation with Dr. Crawford.

"That stands to reason, Gregory. He's—what did Joshua call him? He's your second chance."

That was the last time Greg ever heard Dr. Crawford mention Joshua's name. Retirement suited him, he told Greg.

"I don't envy what you're going through with the gays," he said. "I remember how they can fill your head up with all sorts of worries."

"Tell me about it."

"But your calling is to be a healer for those who want it. Try not to let yourself get off-track fighting the ones who don't."

"Did you, Alex?"

"Miserably. I honestly think that's what landed me in the hospital. Be forewarned, Greg. Life's too short."

Calvin, meanwhile, reported faithfully to Yelsom about the Gateway group's activities.

At first he was sure he'd have to lie, as he didn't want any information leaked to BRAVO that would hurt the ministry. But the ministry activities were so reasonable, so absent of fanaticism under Greg's direction, so low-key—in fact, so bland—that Calvin could safely relay them to his leader without fear of consequence.

"What about records?" Yelsom asked.

"We don't keep any," Calvin answered truthfully.

"Names?"

"The group meetings are on a first-name basis only," he lied.

"Try to get names, anyway. Every one of those people is good outing material."

Calvin promised to provide names. He and Greg made a few up, he relayed them to Yelsom, and was content no harm could be done.

Still, his heart was set on gaining entrance to Yelsom's home. The tape, always in the back of his mind, *must* be there.

And Yelsom, frustrated at the lack of good dirt he was getting on Greg Bishop and his group, turned his attention from discrediting Greg to terrorizing churches and keeping BRAVO's spirits up.

The summer ended with an increase in BRAVO terrorism, a strong bond developing between Greg and Robbie and Greg and Calvin, a weakened bond between Greg and Christine, a one-sided bond between Calvin and Yelsom, and the fate of Assembly Bill 101 more questionable than ever. On September 13, it was voted in by the California Assembly and sent to Governor Pete Wilson's desk for approval or veto.

TWENTY-EIGHT

*Y*ou're late!"

Greg found Rick already working out at the triceps machine.

"Sorry. Marriage duties, you know."

"Must be nice."

They went through a grueling tricep and deltoid workout, showered, wrapped towels around themselves, and headed for the sauna.

"There's enough time today," Greg commented. "Usually I can't."

His body welcomed the dry heat; he groaned luxuriously.

"You don't relax much, do you?" Rick asked. Both were seated on wooden benches facing each other.

"Not these days."

He was growing to like Mosley, somewhat. Rick was a typical good old boy, much of which was fine with Greg. But occasional comments he made recalled his college-days attitude. Just when Greg would be enjoying his company, he'd blurt out a racial slur about the Hispanic man they saw working out every morning, or he'd crack a blatantly sexist joke about the women in the aerobics room. Greg decided he could only take the man in small doses. Best to keep him as a workout partner, not a friend. Three days a week was enough.

"I hear you're number one on the gays' hate list!"

"Am I?" Greg asked, offhandedly.

"Aren't you?"

"Yeah," Greg yawned. "At least that's what my sources tell me."

Just last week Calvin had congratulated him on becoming, according to the *Vine*, one of Orange County's distinguished homophobes.

Mosley laughed upon hearing it. "Oh, that's great! I'd be proud."

Greg didn't comment.

"Hey," Rick asked, "I've always wanted to ask you something."

"Hmmm?"

"Did you really know that guy?"

"What guy?"

"The fag on the beach. The one we—you know."

That caught Greg's attention. "What made you bring that up?"

"I dunno. I've always wondered. He said your name, but you said you'd never met him. Remember?"

Greg took a deep breath. This was bound to come up sometime. He looked squarely at Mosley.

"That fag, as you call him, was my friend. And he was a good guy until you all ruined whatever chance he had at a normal life. Now he's a—"

"Yeah?"

"Who knows what he is? But whatever it is, it's pretty sad."

To Greg's surprise, Mosley listened carefully.

"You're probably right," he said, to Greg's even greater surprise. "I can't stand fags, but that was a rotten thing to do to anyone."

They sat in silence.

"How do you know what he's become?" Mosley asked.

"I'm not sure."

"You mean you don't want to talk about it."

"Right."

"Fair enough."

More silence.

"Greg?"

"Yeah?"

"You're doin' a great job."

Greg shook his head.

"No, really! I think it's great you're helping these guys. My group could sure use some help, too."

Citizens United. Greg had forgotten his promise to visit one of their meetings.

"What kind of help?"

"They're good people, but they're basically a bunch of rednecks."

Figures, Greg thought.

"They're mad about this whole gay thing, but they want to do something constructive about it instead of just talking about how horrible it is. Problem is, nobody's taking the helm, you know?"

Greg grunted.

"Nobody there is articulate like you are. They don't have good leadership, so nobody takes them seriously."

"Mosley," Greg began.

"I know! I just wish you'd come by sometime, that's all."

"When there's time."

"When would that be?"

"Don't ask me."

After his first session, Nancy told him an Alexandra Chappel was holding for him.

"Put her through."

A rich, deep female voice came on.

"Dr. Bishop? We haven't met, but I'm Mrs. Chappel. I was an old friend of Joshua Ferguson's?"

So I heard.

"Yes, Mrs. Chappel. What can I do for you?"

"Quite a bit, actually. I've been following your career with real interest."

"You're in good company, ma'am."

"And I appreciate the work you're doing with the gays."

Something about the way she said *the gays* made it sound as though she was referring to the Crippled Children's Society.

"Thank you."

"If I may ask, are you supported by any organization?"

The question was odd and very forward.

"Well, my clients pay a fee for my services. The counseling center is nonprofit, so the fees are minimal, but they keep us going."

"Do you take donations?"

"Certainly. And gladly," he laughed.

"I'd like to make one. I'd also like to speak with you about your work."

She's a viper! He could practically hear Alma's contempt.

But she's a viper with answers. She knew something. It's worth a shot.

"I'd like that, Mrs. Chappel. But I must confess I'm curious. What is it about my work you'd like to discuss?"

"Expanding it. There's such a need, don't you think? Perhaps I could help."

Sorry, Alma, it's too good to pass up.

"I'd like to hear your ideas, Mrs. Chappel. Maybe we could meet next week?"

"What are your weekend plans?"

Greg balked.

"Oh, I know it's short notice, but I like to get right into things."

"Well, I'm not sure—I'd have to check with my wife."

"Bring her! How about dinner this Sunday night? My treat, of course."

Greg laughed. "You *do* move quickly, ma'am!"

"It's the best way to move, I find. Dinner at 7:30? Five Crowns Restaurant?"

That alone was enough to entice a yes; his budget hardly afforded him trips to restaurants like that.

"I'll double-check with Christine, but I'm sure that will be fine."

He took her number, just in case.

"I've heard so much about you, Dr. Bishop. I'm looking forward to seeing if it's all true."

"I hope you're not disappointed, Mrs. Chappel. I'll look forward to seeing you."

"Yes. And, doctor?"

"Yes?"

"My name is Alexandra."

"Ooh, lovely!" Christine gushed. "Sunday dinner with the local dragon lady from the KKK."

"Josh said it was just her parents who belonged to the Klan."

"Oh, that's right. She's above white sheets and such. She prefers married men and blackmail. We'll have so much to talk about!"

"She wants to make a donation."

"Ha!"

"And she's followed my career. She said so. I think it would be interesting to at least see what she's up to."

They'd settled onto the couch. Greg had just come home from work. Dinner could wait; the whole weekend was free.

"I don't trust her," Christine said.

"You think I do?"

"You better not. She may have put Josh Ferguson in his grave!"

"According to Alma," Greg reminded her, "whose judgment isn't exactly impartial."

That point made, they agreed on Sunday dinner. They also agreed to walk carefully around Alexandra Chappel, limit their association with her to just one night, and reveal nothing they'd been told about her.

They fixed a pepper steak together and ate it leisurely in front of the television.

"Why," Christine asked during a commercial, "haven't we followed up on having Alma Ferguson over?"

"We haven't followed up on much lately."

"Well, I want to call her."

"Don't tell her we're meeting the Lady Chappel!"

"Never! But I've been thinking a lot about Alma lately. I wonder why she hasn't called."

"Find out. I'd like to know what she thinks about the news that's hit the stands these past months."

Christine turned the volume back up.

"No more talk about work," she announced.

The evening news announced a poll taken of California citizens regarding Assembly Bill 101. A bare majority disapproved of homosexuality being given civil protection.

Another meeting was scheduled for Sunday night.

Yelsom's turning into a slave driver, Calvin thought. His

latest "chore" had been a run for gasoline cans, with no explanation about their intended use. He'd just returned from The Shaft, where he dropped them off with his drunken, surly leader. He turned on the news and heard the latest about AB101.

Yelsom wouldn't be pleased.

Or maybe he would. He thrived on new injustices to rail about and seemed almost bored with the antics he'd been staging in front of churches. The list, too, was used up, but he spoke of the next phase excitedly, without giving a clue as to what it would be.

The thought grew, connecting itself somehow with AB101, and Calvin felt drawn to prayer.

The drive from Garden Grove to Corona del Mar, where the Five Crowns Restaurant served its elite clientéle, couldn't have been more pleasant. Greg and Christine chose surface streets over the freeway, taking Jamboree through the Orange Hills and across Irvine to the Pacific Coast Highway to enjoy a view of the beach and the September sunset. Praise music ("No oldies, Greg, I want something edifying") played softly and enticed them to sing along; the Sunday outing had become a worship service by the time they reached the Five Crowns.

"Valet parking, of course," Greg grumbled.

"Who cares? It's all we'll have to pay for tonight."

"Unless she doesn't like us."

They stepped out of the car, opened by two valets, and strolled up to the restaurant. Its English style—stone walls overrun with ivy, iron grates, truly beautiful oak panels—reminded Greg of Waverly Chapel.

"How appropriate," he remarked, opening the door for his wife.

Alexandra Chappel greeted them imperiously in the foyer. She might as well have been welcoming them into her own home; Greg noted again the sense of ownership she displayed wherever she went.

Taller than he'd remembered, and resplendent in a burnt-orange wool suit and (again) pearls, she addressed Greg in the same familiar tone she'd used over the telephone.

"Dr. Bishop, hello. And Christine? I'm Alexandra. Greg, she's so cute. Oh, that's a darling blouse! Our table's not ready. Let's have a drink in here, shall we?"

The "darling blouse" bit was delivered offhandedly and didn't go over well with Christine; Greg felt her stiffen. They exchanged looks as they followed her into the lounge.

The lounge could have been its own restaurant: Its tables were certainly large enough, and the atmosphere was that of a proper dining room, not a bar.

They seated themselves and a waiter appeared immediately. He went straight to Alexandra.

"Will you be having drinks before dinner?" he asked her. Greg felt utterly passed over; wasn't he the man at the table? He detected a suppressed smirk on his wife's face.

"Christine?" Alexandra asked. "What will you have?"

"Perrier," she told the waiter.

"She'll have a Perrier," Alexandra repeated, as though Christine hadn't said it clearly enough. "And you, Greg?"

"You first, please, Alexandra."

The waiter looked nervous.

"Ah! A glass of Chablis, I think."

"Perrier for me, too," Greg ordered.

"I forget sometimes when a gentleman's around," Alexandra said, folding her hands on the table, "that I'm supposed to order first. I'm too used to being on my own."

And being in charge, Greg mused.

"Christine," she went on, "Greg told you, didn't he, that I've been interested in his work?"

"He did. I think he's flattered."

"And you, dear?"

"I'm curious."

"Oh, I like that."

Drinks were served. Alexandra toasted.

"To ventures."

Greg and Christine raised their glasses and their eyebrows.

"My late husband used to toast to ventures incessantly. He was a senator. Raymond Chappel from Georgia; maybe you have heard of him?"

"I'm embarassed to say I haven't."

"Don't be, Greg. Why should you know of him? He died quite a while ago. But I was always interested in his work."

"Are you involved in politics, Mrs. Chappel?" Christine asked, knowing full well she was and assuming, rightfully, that she expected Christine to be thoroughly aware of her illustrious career.

"Very much, yes, Christine."

"Christine" sat much better with her than "dear" had.

"I've chaired several social committees."

"Recently?"

"Not recently, no. I do more independent work, now, sponsoring different groups and fund-raising events."

"What sort of events?" Greg asked.

"All kinds. The kinds you'd appreciate, I think."

She sipped her wine; Christine nudged Greg's foot under the table.

"And what kind," Greg asked over his Perrier, "would that be?"

"I think our table's ready." She rose from her chair. "Yes? Let's eat."

Robbie clicked the microphone into the stand, switched the tape on, and listened to the introduction.

He loved rehearsing alone.

Orchestral music filled the church; his voice, lightly amplified, joined in.

He didn't miss singing for big crowds. Too much had happened lately for him to even think of returning to theaters and concert halls. But he did miss singing at church.

His old church—*old* to him was anything predating April 19, when his life had so radically changed—used to be delighted to have him sing. But things had changed.

He'd anticipated that.

"Sure," his pastor had said after his announcement, "we'll support you in this. But keep a low profile for a while, okay? People here are going to be a little leery of you. Give us time. We're not used to this sort of thing."

That's when he'd decided he was in the wrong church. Pastor Cain had been incredibly warm that night, coming into the dressing room with Greg and offering his best wishes and prayers.

And Greg went to this church as well; wasn't that enough to recommend it?

They'd asked him to sing at next Sunday's service, his first public singing since April. He was as nervous as he'd been the first time he sang in church as a boy, wanting so much to please and finding it so hard to believe he could.

He'd asked Pastor Mike if he might have some time to rehearse in the church. Sunday evening, Mike said. After the service. Just stick around; I'll leave you a key to lock up with.

Service ended at 8:00; it was 9:15 now. Just Robbie, God, and the music.

Like it was in the beginning.

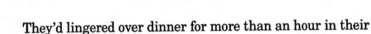

They'd lingered over dinner for more than an hour in their high-backed velvet chairs, dining in a manner Greg could easily become accustomed to.

He'd ordered a twenty-dollar lobster tail as casually as if he had it weekly, ignoring Christine's glances. She tried the prime rib; Alexandra ordered duck, with a tone of voice suggesting anything less would have besmirched her reputation as a lady and a fund-raiser.

Conversation had zigzagged from religion (Alexandra had no particular profession of faith and seemed quite content to keep it that way) to modern feminism, which she attacked like a zealot. Christine shared some of her college experiences with women's-libbers and, to Alexandra's delight, did mock imitations of the more dour feminists she'd known. Greg introduced the topic of health and fitness; Alexandra complimented them both on the shape they kept themselves in and lamented her generation's lack of interest in fitness. Throughout the meal, Greg measured his wife's response to Mrs. Chappel. It was still chilly, with just a touch of admiration.

At 9:00 the waiter, having cleared their places, presented them with the dessert tray.

"Oh, now, you must!" Alexandra exclaimed when they hesitated. She recited the pastries and puddings she'd tried at the Five Crowns, and insisted no meal there was complete without them. Greg and Christine relented, conceding to tarts and cheescake, and coffee was served while they waited for the goods.

"Now," Alexandra said while stirring her cup, "let me get to the heart of things."

Greg and Christine waited attentively.

"Is anybody standing up to the gays?"

The blunt question caught them off guard.

"In what way?" Greg asked.

"In any way! We're all of the same mind on the gay issue; I know that. Is anyone really taking a stand for our viewpoint?"

Greg thought it over. "Well, sure, some are."

"A handful of clerical windbags and televangelists, if that's what you mean!" Alexandra snapped. "How intelligent do they sound when they speak on the issue?"

Christine looked at Greg; he frowned. "That isn't fair. There are some very good spokesmen out there who don't get a chance these days."

"Like you."

She said it so simply he thought he'd misheard.

"Like you," she nodded. "You've got it all. You're handsome—forgive me, Christine, but he is—and articulate. And you're moderate; I like that. You present a very favorable impression, but you need exposure. So does your work, naturally. That's why I asked for this meeting."

I thought it was dinner, not a meeting, he thought warily.

"Have you ever thought of doing more public speaking?"

"Not really. Why?"

"Because people need to hear from you. There's no solid leadership on the antigay side."

Hadn't he just heard this speech, but from someone less cultured and infinitely less intelligent?

Dessert arrived; Greg and Christine picked at theirs.

"You help the gays who want to change; that's fine," Alexandra continued. "But you also have been fighting the rest of them. You're the kind of man people would rally around. You could lead some very important battles that are coming up."

Greg started to protest his utter disinterest in any more battles; Christine cut him off before he had the chance.

"We don't want any more fighting, Alexandra. We're here to help people, not do battle with them."

"And exactly what have you been doing, dear? Hasn't it been both?"

"Only when we've had to," Greg answered.

"You'll *always* have to. They've marked you, Greg. You'll not get off the hook. They threw blood at your pastor because of you; have you forgotten? As long as you run that group out at the church, you'll be their sworn enemy."

"All the more reason not to agitate them," Christine returned.

"Your very presence is an agitation to them, can't you see?"

He looked at his coffee.

"I could sponsor you. I could get you speaking engagements across the country."

"What would I speak about?"

"How to organize resistance to the gays and help the ones who want our help. Speaking," she said pointedly, "can become a very lucrative career."

"I have clients. I can't leave them."

"We could work around your schedule. And I'd see you were compensated well for your time."

Christine had listened without comment. She looked at Greg uncertainly; he smiled at her.

"No." He patted her hand, then looked at Alexandra. "I'm really appreciative, Alexandra. Don't think I'm not. But Christine and I have had it rough these past few months. Frankly, it's been a strain on our marriage. So I need to slow down."

Alexandra looked at both of them with an inscrutable face, then smiled tightly.

"I appreciate that. Maybe you'll just keep what I said in mind? And I still want to make a donation to your work."

She reached into her purse and took out a scented envelope. "I hope this helps."

Greg pocketed the envelope without looking inside. "I'm sure it will. Thank you. Thanks even more for your confidence." He squeezed Christine's hand again. "I guess we're just not ready for any more excitement."

Alexandra didn't answer, but looked steadily at Greg and Christine's joined hands.

Meetings had dwindled over the summer, even though activites had been at an all-time high. Calvin knew why; it was becoming routine.

Even Yelsom had lost some of his zip. Watching him tonight while he explained the new phase, Calvin noticed less dazzle. BRAVO's leader was more prone to lecture, rather than excite, these days. And tonight, the lecture was boring.

No cheers, no wild plans. The list was old business, having been discarded weeks ago. Church protests had been done and redone; people still came, but excitement ran low. Phase two, whatever it was, had better be good, Calvin thought, or BRAVO itself would soon become a tired cliché.

"A turning point in Nazi Germany's development," Yelsom explained, "was the 'Night of the Broken Glass.' Anyone remember studying that?"

A few heads nodded.

"It marked the beginning of a real move to unite—"

"Wilson vetoed!"

Roxanne and Lisa, late for the meeting, barged in and shouted it.

"What?" Yelsom was astonished. Everyone perked up.

"He vetoed AB101! They say he got phone calls from fundamentalists all over the state telling him to. They say he caved in. He said AB101 would hurt small businesses."

Groans rose up from every part of the room, then cursing, then protests.

"Wait!" Yelsom took control. "Are you sure?"

"It's on the news right now! People are in the streets everywhere! West Hollywood, Sacramento, everywhere!"

Calvin felt the old spirit in the room: hostility, discontent, outrage. And fury, growing and consuming.

People stood and threw up their hands. Curses and threats echoed off the walls, men and women hugged and consoled, then slammed chairs and stamped, cursing the governor's name.

Vetoed? After all his promises, all his talk about his support for gays and lesbians?

The hot blood stirred; Yelsom wouldn't let it rest—not if he was half the activist he claimed to be!

"Hear me!"

They all stopped and looked up at the stage.

"They're on the streets in West Hollywood and Sacramento. What are we doing here?"

The roar was evidence enough that BRAVO was readier than ever.

"Where do we belong?"

All of them had different ideas and shouted them at once.

"No!" Yelsom thundered. "Who called him? *Who called Pete Wilson and told him to can our rights?*"

All of them seethed, remembering their common enemy.

"Then we need to call them!"

A battle cry erupted.

"Berean Community Church! Come on! Come on!"

Robbie's voice was tired. *He* wasn't; singing always energized rather than drained his body. But when the voice was gone, the rehearsal was over. He sat on the platform and looked over the empty pews, the organ, and the six stained-glass windows flanking both sides of the church.

Sitting alone here at night was wonderfully peaceful and mysterious. He flicked the microphone off, enjoying the silence and appreciating the sanctuary. Here he'd found another home, an understanding pastor, an astute counselor. His career had, perhaps, dive-bombed, but he was content. He'd sung prerecorded pieces; now he felt moved to praise spontaneously.

Wait. The lights. Wouldn't it be nice to pray and worship in the dark?

He walked the length of the room, found the main switches, and flicked them off. Then he found his way back to the platform in front, sat down, and prayed aloud.

Robbie offered thanks. Then requests. Then praise, soft at first, then stronger, less inhibited. His voice found its strength again, lifted in a private song, tailor-made just for Him.

So, at first, the footsteps and whispering outside didn't come to his attention. But the clang of something—a can of some sort—did.

He froze.

More footsteps, hurrying along both sides of the building. Cans rattling, sounding like—spray paint?

Aerosol hissing, more footsteps, muffled laughter.

Kids, he thought. Neighborhood kids painting graffiti on the church.

He rose from the platform and started for the door, then stopped cold when he heard more voices.

Deep-voiced men; adults, not kids, swearing urgently. And something else. A sloshing sound.

The footsteps were receding now, quieter, distant.

Then silence.

He stared out over the blackness of the sanctuary, straining his ears.

Nothing.

Then the corner of his left eye caught something dancing outside the window on his left.

He turned. It was gone. Then back again; a bright flicker of orange light.

Then another, sharper and higher, to his right.

Then the first three windows from the back glowed.

Something crackled over his head.

Robbie jumped off the platform, landed with his full weight on his ankle, twisted it, and fell forward, crashing his head into the arm of the wooden pew in front of him.

He lost consciousness in an instant.

The flames shot across the ceiling, and the curtains became torches, and the smoke filled his lungs, and the fire finally claimed the young man sprawled across the carpet. But he felt nothing.

Greg's beeper went off while he and Christine were still in the car, halfway home, comparing notes on Alexandra Chappel. He hit the display button, she jotted the number down, and he turned it off. Plenty of time to call when they got home.

Thirty seconds later it went off again. Same number; again, he flicked it off.

Then again, in less than thirty seconds.

"Somebody's persistent," Christine said.

"What's the number?"

She read it aloud.

"Calvin," he said. "And he's persistent for a reason."

He pulled over at the next gas station and dialed the number.

"Hello?" Calvin sounded desperate.

"Calvin, it's Greg."

"Greg, hurry! They're heading for the church!"

"Who?"

"Yelsom. BRAVO. All of them. I called the police as soon as I could, but I had to wait till everyone was cleared out of here!"

"What's the plan?"

"I couldn't tell. But they're furious. Wilson vetoed AB101, did you hear?"

"No. Why?"

"Everybody's rioting. I'll drive over to the church now. I'm not supposed to show up at protests, but I can drive by without being noticed. Greg! Hurry! They're really worked up this time."

Greg jumped in the car and floored the pedal. It took thirteen minutes to get there.

It took less than that to see the result of BRAVO's wrath. The flames had been put out, but smoke still hung over Berean Community Church and into the streets. Fire trucks and police cars were parked near the entrance; an ambulance sat at the curb.

People from neighboring homes clustered near the parking lot; Calvin was among them, shouting and waving at Greg as he drove up and parked. He ran to the car.

"They torched it, Greg!"

Greg flew out and ran toward the church. A policeman blocked him just as he reached the entrance.

"I work here!" Greg yelled. Calvin and Christine caught up with him.

"You've got to stand back," the officer said. Two paramedics emerged from the foyer carrying a stretcher.

"Was someone in there?" Greg screamed. "At this hour?"

The man nodded just as Greg caught sight of Robbie's car—the Jeep he'd driven to all his sessions—parked near the front.

The paramedics were on the lawn now, twelve yards away. A blanket covered the person they carried.

From head to foot.

Christine put both hands to her mouth.

Greg moved toward the lawn. The officer grabbed his shoulder.

"I might know that person," Greg heard himself say, even as he refused to believe it.

The policeman let him go.

He moved to the two men carrying something. Somebody.

He pointed at the stretcher. The paramedics asked him something. He nodded. They pulled the blanket back.

Christine saw her husband stagger, pivot, clutch his stomach, and double over. She ran to him; Calvin followed.

The paramedics carried the stretcher away. Christine huddled over Greg, who fell to both knees and stared at the wall next to the glass doors.

Someone had left a spray-painted message on the doors:

The first stone has been cast.
BRAVO

Even as he took in the words, Greg felt himself change. Something—compassion, or restraint, or both—was leaving him, and he knew he was not, nor would be for some time, the same man who had driven up to this scene.

Calvin and Christine approached him hesitantly.

"Honey?"

"Greg?"

He ignored his wife and pointed at Calvin.

"Don't say it. Don't even think it."

His tone was menacing; they both froze.

"Don't be like them?" Greg whispered hoarsely. "Is that what you're going to say?"

Two policemen walked toward them.

Greg stepped forward and took Calvin's face in his hands. "I *will* be like them!"

An officer tapped Greg's shoulder. "Let's calm down, okay?"

"I will be *more* than like them!"

Greg's squeeze tightened.

"Sir? Let go of the man. Did you hear me?" asked the officer.

"I WILL BE THEM!"

TWENTY-NINE

*I*t was the worst of times: bitter, devastating, unforgettable. Blood had been spilt, gauntlets thrown down, communities divided. Newspaper accounts of the events underscored the divisions.

Los Angeles Times
Monday, September 30, 1991
Page A-1

Governor Vetoes Gay Rights Bill

SACRAMENTO—In a gesture angering gays and disappointing gay rights advocates throughout California, Governor Pete Wilson vetoed Assembly Bill 101, which would have granted sexual orientation the same protection now afforded race and gender in housing and employment. Citing the burden it would place upon small businesses, Governor Wilson, who had in the past indicated support for AB101, expressed his continued concern for the rights of lesbians and gays throughout the state, but claimed he could not sign the bill into law in its present form.

Spontaneous demonstrations broke out in cities throughout California upon announcement of the governor's veto, most notably in San Francisco, Los Angeles, and Orange County, where the burning of a Newport Beach church building has claimed the life of renowned gospel singer Robbie Carlton.

The Orange County Register
Monday, September 30, 1991
Page A-1

Gospel Singer Killed in Protest Arson

NEWPORT BEACH—In what police are calling an act of arson protesting Governor Wilson's unexpected veto of AB101, gospel artist Robbie Carlton was found dead last night inside Berean Community Church, which had been set ablaze at approximately 11:30 P.M. According to paramedics the cause of death was smoke inhalation. Carlton, a Grammy-award-winning singer whose recent disclosure and disavowal of homosexuality ignited controversy among gays and fundamentalists alike, was apparently rehearsing alone in the Newport Beach church when the fire was set. There are no indications the arsonists involved knew of Carlton's presence in the building, and no suspects have been identified.

An anonymous phone call to the Newport Beach police department at 10:40 P.M. warned of a potential incident at Berean Community Church. According to department spokesman Officer Wesley Lane, a caller informed police that protesters would be gathering at the church site, but officers dispatched to the area saw no sign of a demonstration. "The other demonstrations were intentionally visible, which is what our officers looked for when patrolling," Lane said. "Whoever started this fire was working in a more clandestine manner, and there were several other visible, immediate disruptions throughout the area needing our attention."

While scattered incidents of arson and vandalism by gay protesters have been reported statewide in response to the veto, last night's death marks the first casualty in any of the demonstrations by gays and gay sympathizers.

"We are shocked and saddened beyond belief by this tragedy," Rev. Michael Cain, pastor of Berean Community Church, told the *Times*. "Mr. Carlton had taken a strong, sincere stand against homosexuality, but he meant no harm to gays. For him to have become a victim of this sort of thing is unthinkable."

Gay leaders across the county were quick to distance themselves from the incident and to condemn its perpetrators. "We abhor violence in any form," said Jean McClellan, director of Orange County's Lesbian and Gay Caucus. "It is unfair and inaccurate to assume the arsonists responsible for Mr. Carlton's death were representative of the lesbian and gay community at large, if indeed they were connected to our community in any way."

"We're not about violence," added Christopher Garvey of the Gay Men's Health Center. "We're incredibly angry and betrayed by our governor's actions, and our demonstrations are meant to convey that. But you simply don't find gay people out there killing in the name of equality. That's not us."

Police investigators speculate that radical fringe groups may have been responsible for the incident, but they have no leads at this time.

Gays were outraged over AB101; Christians were outraged over gay rage and its frightening consequences, and the indignation among church members which had festered during months of harassment from BRAVO found its voice the following Sunday in a multitude of sermons.

"The anarchy of Sodom was resurrected September 30," one pastor noted. "Homosexuals of *that* city, who'd come to rape Lot's visitors, were possessed with the same bestial nature displayed by Robbie Carlton's murderers."

"What did we expect?" another posed. "Militant homosexuals have harassed us, intimidated us, stepped on us with impunity. Should we be surprised at their willingness to kill?"

Some exhorted their flock to fight any further advancements of the gay rights movement through political action. If this was how homosexuals behaved when their so-called rights were denied, they posed, what merciless control might they exert if they were granted state approval? Other pastors enjoined their people to prayer; still others cited September 30 as yet another apocalyptic sign. In even the most heated sermons, retaliation was discouraged. But a course of action in lieu of retaliation was seldom proposed.

One exception was Berean Community Church, whose leaders, headed by Pastor Mike, granted one press conference on Tuesday, October 1.

Standing on the church steps with his board of elders and looking utterly exhausted, Pastor Mike called for countywide prayer. "Christians and conservatives," he said, "ought not to use Carlton's death as an occasion to hate." Quoting the Sermon on the Mount, he beseeched peacemakers to work for healing among the community, and promised Berean would rebuild, and that services would continue in the building while it was under repair.

"We're shattered, not destroyed," he announced. "Their hatred is strong stuff, God knows, and we could become bitter over this, even violent. But Christ gives a love you can draw from when you've got none of your own left. I hope people will keep that in mind."

His sermon that week, preached three times in a packed, charred sanctuary, was titled "Ashes to Gold."

But some in the county were beyond the reach of his words or sentiments. Most of them were young, disinterested in church, and impatient with polite discussion. They loathed gays and resented the social climate which made it unfashionable to say so. Faggots, they assured each other, were a bunch of pushy freaks that ought to be shipped off or gassed. Had they been religious, they'd have invoked the judgment of God against sodomites but would have little use for ramblings about mercy and compassion. September 30 had been the last straw; something had to be done, and now.

It began mid-October.

A middle-aged Laguna Beach man was found howling in the alley behind a gay bar, his knees shattered with a tire iron.

Two lesbians were pelted with bricks from a passing car in front of a feminist bookstore in Santa Ana.

A teenager leaving the Gay Community Center in Garden Grove was pulled from the sidewalk into a van, where his abductors shaved his head, scorched his cheeks with cigarette butts, then threw him from the vehicle while it sped away.

"You're lucky we didn't burn *you* to death!" they shouted.

He landed headfirst on the sidewalk.

The victims told police their attackers had worn ski masks, and that they were male, young, and very strong. With each attack, fear grew among the gays. And anger seethed.

Gay bars in every city posted warnings, encouraging patrons to walk the streets in groups. Self-defense classes were offered at the Lesbian and Gay Community Service Center, and by November canisters of mace had become standard accessories among the bar patrons of Laguna and Newport Beach.

Religious conservatives, now being vilified as the Religious Right, were blamed by gays for the attacks. Sermonizing against homosexuality, they said, inspired people to attack homosexuals. Never mind that no studies or proof of any kind supported such allegations; the Christians were the most logical, obvious target, and they would henceforth be known among committed gay activists as The Enemy. But they shared the title with another group—one with whom they were the most unlikely of bedfellows: BRAVO.

"Thanks a lot, BRAVO," had become a standard, sarcastic response among gays whenever an assault was reported. Though no evidence had emerged against them, locals were certain the group was responsible for the attack on Berean Community Church. And since BRAVO was blamed for the attack, they were partially responsible, in the eyes of the gay community, for the antigay backlash pouring out of churches and, indirectly, into the streets. So resentment seethed against BRAVO and the Religious Right in equal portions.

BRAVO was, of course, far from guiltless. Sixteen members had participated in the arson; all of them, fearing criminal charges, kept quiet. In the wake of that night's rioting, which had occurred statewide, investigative efforts to locate witnesses were frustrated. Only one person had volunteered information, but he'd done so anonymously, in a letter, tipping police off that BRAVO set the blaze. It was scant evidence and of little use.

But their guilt was assumed. Who else would have gone so far? Once celebrated as warriors for the cause, they were now outcasts, condemned by gay leaders as harmful and misguided. The injustice of Wilson's veto was eclipsed, they said, by BRAVO's rash act. BRAVO, in turn, denied responsibility for Carlton's death.

That was half-true. None, including Yelsom, knew Robbie was inside the church when they started the blaze. They had seen his Jeep in the parking lot, but made nothing of it since the building was dark. They had only meant to teach the fundamentalists a lesson. Because Greg Bishop had replaced Alex Crawford as the most visible purveyor of antigay propaganda, and since Berean was Greg's place of business and worship, the church—guilty of supporting a homophobe—was the most logical target in the county.

The BRAVO ranks thinned quickly. Only eleven attended the November 4 meeting, their first since the fire. The diminished size was demoralizing, but a new problem was evident as well: The members were divided in their opinion of Yelsom.

Arguments flared in the basement before he arrived for the meeting.

"I joined to fight the church, not kill it!" Roxanne declared. "Yelsom has gone over the edge."

"Then we went with him," another woman replied. "We were there, too."

"But not to hurt anybody!"

"He didn't know that guy was in there any more than we did."

"I don't know," Lisa said. "I wouldn't put anything past him."

She, Roxanne, Calvin, and three others whispered in a tight circle near the back wall. Other members held counsel in similar groups, huddling together against the fall chill which the basement walls were no protection from.

The BRAVO family was split into nervous schisms. Nobody knew whom to trust.

"How does everyone else feel?" Calvin asked, glancing about the room.

"I dunno," Lisa answered. "Everyone's scared of saying the wrong thing."

"And," the first woman added, "everyone's scared of leaks."

"Has anyone talked to the police?"

Nobody knew.

"Somebody'll leak," Calvin nodded.

"Whoever does will be turning himself in, too," Lisa warned.

So they were stuck with each other, they decided, for better or worse.

Yelsom burst into the room and sensed the uncertainty.

"Courage, people!" he shouted while striding to the podium. "Grab a seat; let's go! What, are we gonna faint over our first casualty?"

Men and women found their chairs and looked at him curiously. In contrast to their hesitant manner, he was frisky and energized. Relaxed, too, which made no sense at all.

"Ready? Good. New rules, okay? Listen up."

He took an index card from his jacket, looked it over, then began.

"First, no talking about September 30. Not in the meetings, not among yourselves. The subject is closed."

Everyone understood and nodded. The less said, the safer for all.

"But suppose," Roxanne asked with a raised hand, "not that I'm saying anyone *would,* but just suppose someone slips at a future meeting and says something, uh, *irresponsible* in front of people who *weren't* there?"

"Not to worry," Yelsom said evenly. "Meetings are closed from now on."

A muted "What?" could be heard from the group.

"No more announcements in the *Vine,* no more new members. We're it. Plan on being here the first Monday of each month from now on, same time. No need for us to even talk between meetings."

Again, no one argued.

"We've got more plans to cover," he continued.

"More? Half the community hates us now, Yelsom!" It was Lisa, usually the quiet one, who stood and challenged him. "They blame us every time someone gets beat up! I say we lay low until things die down."

Yelsom pointed a long finger at her. "And I say backing down is the same as admitting guilt." His eyes swept over the others. "We move ahead or we call it quits. So decide now, all of you."

Lisa sat back down, slowly.

"Forward or nowhere!" He studied them; no one moved.

"Your faces say *maybe.* I don't like *maybe! Maybe* is for people who can't commit. FORWARD OR NOWHERE!"

He barked the last phrase at high volume. Everyone flinched; his scowl brimmed with contempt, making them all (except Calvin) momentarily ashamed of their doubts.

"Did you think," he snapped, "it would be a lark? That we'd make a little noise, vent some steam, then go have brunch? This is *WAR!*"

He slammed the podium.

"Bloody, gruesome, mean, butchering *war!* You ever hear of a war called off because"—he adopted a high, effeminate voice—"oh dear, someone got hurt, goodness gracious!"

He glared, then stepped toward them menacingly.

"Lisa! Don't look down; look at *me!*"

She looked at him sullenly.

"Worried about the community hating you, huh? Did you join BRAVO to be Miss Gay Orange County? *Did* you? You want popularity, go back to Daddy and be a homecoming princess!"

No worse insult could have been hurled at her; Roxanne put a protective arm around Lisa and started to protest.

"*What,* Roxanne? Gonna be the white knight protecting your lady? Do her a *real* favor and tell her to toughen up!"

"Wanna leave?" Roxanne murmured. Lisa shook her head. *"Jeremy!"*

Calvin's head snapped up.

"You look pale! Things gettin' too heavy, Junior?"

Calvin met the man's eyes, determined not to so much as blink.

"They're heavier than I thought they'd be, yes," he answered.

"Little boy lost," Yelsom sang mockingly. "Maybe you're not half of what I thought you were."

Calvin comforted himself with the accuracy of the statement.

"The rest of you, listen up!"

The others were relieved not to have been singled out.

"Warriors aren't honored until after the battle, so if we're not popular now, who cares? The gay community will thank us later. The public...well, since when were we popular with them?"

BRAVO considered; some nodded.

"We're *queers*, remember? Since when have queers been popular? Or have you forgotten?"

They hadn't.

"So!" His tone lowered. "We move on."

To everyone's surprise, Calvin stood. Even Yelsom was taken aback.

"But Yelsom, we never joined to hurt anyone. Some of us—" he glanced at Lisa and Roxanne, who nodded at him—"some of us need to know that nobody else will get hurt. If we move forward, can you promise that?"

Yelsom stared; Calvin stared back, and the two held their positions while the rest held their breath.

Yelsom finally sighed. "No one gets hurt."

The others exhaled loudly.

"That was never the plan, anyway. Besides," he added, "we can't afford it."

Calvin sat down.

"Forward, then. Yes?"

They looked at him.

"*Yes?*"

They nodded.

"Forward," the remaining BRAVO members said, almost in unison.

"Humiliation was phase one. We outed them; we humiliated them. Intimidation was phase two, and we haven't done half-bad on that score, have we?"

No response.

"Well, we haven't. But there's one phase left to complete."

THIRTY

On November 4, a despondent Christine penned a note to her mother.

Hello, Mom.

    I've just hung up after talking with you. I'm sorry I was so abrupt, but Greg was within earshot and I really couldn't say all I wanted to.

    I'm plunked down on my side of the couch writing while Greg's curled up on his side, zoning out on TV. He's a sight these days. He's let himself go completely. He doesn't shave anymore or even trim his beard. He shuffles around in his bathrobe all day—doesn't even let me wash it!—and mutters a few sentences every hour or so. Not to me, mind you. He hasn't got much to say to me, so he talks to himself. Or to someone, I guess.

    I know Greg's depressed, and I know how horrible this has all been for him. Did I tell you he's on a four-month sabbatical from counseling? Pastor Mike and the board were so worried about him they made him take the time off with pay. They'd have been even more worried if I'd told them everything Greg said to Calvin and the police that night. I honestly think he had a nervous breakdown when he saw Robbie's body.

    At first I was glad the board gave him a sabbatical. He needs time to recover from all this. Besides, he was so agitated he wouldn't have been any good as a counselor. For the first week he was nonstop rage, cursing gays and Bennie (that's his old friend who's the gay activist now) and pounding the walls. Literally! I tried so hard to stay out of his way, I was walking on eggshells around here. Anything I said would just set him off again.

That lasted right up until Robbie's funeral a week later. Greg could barely speak to anyone at the service. Most of us there, about a hundred or so, cried buckets, but not Greg. He withdrew into some private spot I still haven't been able to penetrate. That's when things really deteriorated.

He calmed down, then went to the other extreme. Started sleeping late, which he never does, and got into the habit of watching TV, eating junk food, and ignoring the rest of the world. He barely speaks to me, but it's not out of rudeness. He just doesn't have anything to say, and I've run out of ideas. The worst part is, I don't know what he wants from me. If I leave him alone I feel like I'm abandoning him, but if I sit with him he doesn't even acknowledge me, so I feel like I'm crowding him! And nothing I say seems to be right. On Pastor Mike's advice, I'm sitting tight and riding it out. I'm glad I've got a few design jobs to distract me, because looking at him in this condition all day would be too much.

Calvin, the man who's gone underground with the gay group, came by last week to talk, but Greg wasn't too interested in going on with their plans. He still wants that videotape, though, and told Calvin if he ever finds it, Greg wants to be the first one to know. Pastor Mike has come by a couple of times, too, just to check up on us. Greg doesn't want us to go to church for a while, which I kind of understand, although the fellowship could do us some good. And Mike (God bless him!) is being supportive and gentle; he doesn't push Greg at all. He just wants him to get better.

But will he get better? There have only been a few times he has shown any signs of life, and that's what really scares me. Scares me bad.

So yes, Mom, I'm tense. Worse than that, I'm scared. You asked if there was anything you could do, remember? There is. Please bear with me. I think I'm going to be a little girl needing her mom for a while, you know? Because everyone feels sorry for Greg, losing his client and all, and I guess that's fair. He was so invested in Robbie. I think when Robbie died Greg felt he'd somehow failed again. But I don't think anyone realizes what it's like being Mrs. Bishop. Nobody feels sorry for me, so how 'bout it, Mom? Feel sorry for me, okay? Just a little?

And pray for us. Nobody prays like you do.

Love,
Christine

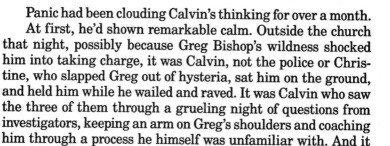

Panic had been clouding Calvin's thinking for over a month.

At first, he'd shown remarkable calm. Outside the church that night, possibly because Greg Bishop's wildness shocked him into taking charge, it was Calvin, not the police or Christine, who slapped Greg out of hysteria, sat him on the ground, and held him while he wailed and raved. It was Calvin who saw the three of them through a grueling night of questions from investigators, keeping an arm on Greg's shoulders and coaching him through a process he himself was unfamiliar with. And it was Calvin who drove the Bishops home, even walking Greg to the door and helping Christine put the shattered doctor to bed.

But whatever enabled him to play best man during his friend's crisis was gone by sunrise, when panic set in.

You're in bigger trouble than you ever bargained for.

Of all the jumbled thoughts assaulting him, that was the preeminent one. It became nonstop background music from that day on; it was playing even now as he drove.

He was headed for Lisa and Roxanne's apartment, where he had been invited for coffee after the BRAVO meeting to finish the conversation they had started earlier. Tonight was the first time they'd connected since... what could he call it? The Night Robbie Died? The Night I Had a Hand in Murder?

Calvin shivered at the thought, blocked it, and decided to refer to it, now and always, as That Night.

His first instinct that night had been to tell the police everything. He had almost, in fact, spilled the beans to the officers who were there, but somehow felt it better to wait.

You were scared, that's why you waited. You weren't sure if implicating BRAVO and Yelsom would implicate you as well. Saving your rear was uppermost, and helping Greg through that night doesn't change the fact.

Then he considered calling the police the next day. Surely he wouldn't incriminate himself by telling the truth, would he? After all, he had tried to stop it, tipping off both Greg and the police before the fire was set. And he couldn't have known what would happen. Yelsom never mentioned burning a church as part of the BRAVO agenda.

But he was part of BRAVO. And he was at the meeting that night.

His limited knowledge of the law left him prey to wild speculations. Who wouldn't believe he was an accomplice of sorts, even a coconspirator? What about the others? If questioned, wouldn't they point to Calvin as Yelsom's right-hand man? And would any investigator believe Yelsom's right-hand man really didn't know what Yelsom planned to do? Would Yelsom stand up for him? Hardly.

He remembered the bizarre Manson family trial in 1970. Only a few of Charles Manson's followers actually participated in or even knew of the murders, but all the "family members" were suspect, several were arrested, and all of them were permanently tainted.

I wasn't there, though. He repeated it again and again; it became a mantra of sorts. *I wasn't there. I didn't know. I didn't do it.*

But so what? Even if the law did excuse him, would the church? How many Christians would look kindly on what he'd done—running around playing Columbo, solving mysteries he had no business meddling with, rubbing elbows with gay radicals? If his secret got out, would he ever have credibility again in the Christian media, no matter how good his intentions were?

The goals that inspired him mere months ago—solving the Ferguson mystery, retrieving the stolen tape—were distant. So was the confidence he had recently acquired.

Most of his responsibilities with both BRAVO and Berean were lost, too, in that night's aftermath.

First came the call from Yelsom two days after the fire.

"Lay low and keep your mouth shut. You don't know anything; you weren't there. The less said, even between you and me, the better."

"Where *are* you?" Calvin had nearly screamed into the phone. "Why did you do it? I would've never helped you if I thought anything like this would happen!"

"Nobody knew this would happen." Calvin detected a slight crack in Yelsom's voice when he said it. "Sit tight. I'll call you."

Which Yelsom did three weeks later, only to tell Calvin about the meeting and have him call the other members. "I won't be needing anything else from you for a while," was the only explanation Yelsom gave. Typical.

Then the Gateway ministry at Berean closed down. At Pastor Ruben's insistence, the board of elders held a special meeting to reconsider the wisdom of hosting such a ministry under these volatile conditions. Calvin attended.

"If we'd have weighed the liabilities more responsibly, we would never have exposed our congregation to this danger!" Ruben told the board. "I was never comfortable with the idea in the first place." Hinting that his had been the only voice of reason, and declaring "I told you so" without telling them so, he moved to discontinue the group; the motion was seconded and passed unanimously.

Calvin had been too weakened by private conflicts to offer any kind of a challenge. Pastor Mike sadly accepted the board's decision.

Also discouraging was that communication with Greg Bishop had been minimal. After two visits to the Bishop home and seeing the condition Greg was in, Calvin knew he would be seeing less and less of the doctor. But after their last visit, Greg made him vow he wouldn't give up on finding the tape. Calvin promised.

Maybe that's why he attended tonight's meeting. Maybe that's why he'd already decided, panic notwithstanding, to continue the charade with Yelsom, the girls, BRAVO. *Maybe,* he thought, *some stubborn part of himself wasn't ready to write off the time and effort he'd invested into finding the tape.*

But it was the fire, not the tape, that kept him up nights. And it was fear that kept him sweating and praying. His work got sloppy, interviews became lifeless and dull, and most of his energy was spent as it was being spent now—behind the wheel on the way to Lisa and Roxanne's, pushing down the unruly questions haunting him at every turn.

Why haven't you reported this to the police?

He was afraid to; it was that simple.

You know who killed Robbie. Will you carry that to your grave?

Hardly; he would carry it another three months, max. If he hadn't found a way to retrieve the stolen tape by then, so be it. He would reveal everything he knew to the police, the press, everyone. But anonymously. There would be no more violence. Somehow he believed Yelsom's promise and Yelsom's insistence that he didn't know Robbie was in the church. Calvin recognized BRAVO's leader as a madman and a prima donna, but lacking the stuff deliberate killers are made of.

You're a Christian involved in lying, covering up manslaughter, stealing, and God knows what else. Justify that, please.

"I can't," he said aloud, driving into the guest parking lot in front of Lisa and Roxanne's building.

You're in bigger trouble than you ever bargained for.

He parked and waited for his heartbeat to slow down.

Just as BRAVO adjourned their meeting across town, Christine finished her letter, glanced sideways at her husband on the couch, and decided enough was enough.

She reached for the tea urn Mrs. Bishop had given them last Christmas and held it toward Greg. He had gained over ten pounds from an inactive month of junk food and television, and it showed plainly. His scraggly beard made his face seem bloated and added at least seven years to his appearance.

He was glued to the news.

"More tea?"

He scratched his chest, extended his cup toward her and nodded.

The news stories ended; a guest commentator lamented California's immigration problem.

Christine took her cup from the coffee table in front of them and considered her husband.

"Would you care for another cup, ma'am?" she asked herself aloud. Greg glanced sideways at her.

"Thank you, my dear," she answered, returning the cup. "I'd prefer the whole pitcher. Just crash it on the table, please."

She smiled at Greg. His left eyebrow arched.

"Christine?"

She kept her eyes on him, lifted the urn high as in a toast, then let it fall with a crash onto the coffee table.

Glass, tea, and chips of porcelain flew everywhere. Greg leapt off the couch.

"Christine!"

"He moves."

"What . . . ?"

"And speaks! To me, no less."

"Are you crazy?"

She crossed her legs.

"Abundantly."

He looked at the mess on the coffee table and shook his head. Christine smiled sweetly.

"I thought we needed a wake-up call."

"Well, lady, you sure gave us one!" He snapped the television off and sat back down. "What *is* this?"

A thin stream of tea ran from the table to the carpet. Christine sopped it up with a napkin, put the pieces of porcelain in a small pile on the table, then pointed at it.

"That's an unexpected mess." She nodded firmly at the little heap. "Unexpected messes happen sometimes. Think we can deal with it?"

Greg sat, hands in lap, without answering.

"Shall I start?" she asked, and he knew what was coming.

"I know I haven't been much company lately," he offered weakly.

"You haven't been *any* company lately."

He looked at her and, as if suddenly conscious of his appearance, pulled his robe around him and smoothed his hair. "No," he answered. "No, I guess not."

"Five words. Not bad." She half-smiled as she said it. He grunted a response, then started to pick up the broken cups from the table.

"No. Please?" She grabbed his wrist. "Later. We're on a roll. You just said five words to me. Let's keep going."

Greg couldn't resist when she teased, even now. He grinned, leaned back into the sofa, and plopped his legs atop the right corner of the coffee table—the only spot not covered with Christine's stunt. "You first," he said in a lighter voice than she'd heard in weeks.

He must have been ready for this, Christine thought. *Praise God!* She tucked her legs under her and moved closer to him. "I just wrote a whiny letter to my mother."

"About?"

"You." She patted his leg. "Us. Everything. I was writing because I was lonely, and it just struck me how absurd that is when you're sitting right next to me."

He looked thoughtful; not nearly as defensive as she had expected. "Babe," he said gently, "did you expect me to be Mr. Personality after all that's gone down?"

"You know I don't!" The question hurt; she stroked his shoulder. "Nobody would. Don't you think I know what you're feeling?"

Even as she asked she knew it was the wrong question. "No," he said with a level voice.

"Okay, right. Sorry. No, I don't know what you're feeling, but whatever it is, it must be awful."

"Then don't I get a break? Like a little time and space to get over it?"

"You've got both. And I don't begrudge it."

"Then what do you want?" It was a serious question, not a challenge.

Her hand had worked its way up to his hair; she found a loose strand and curled it with one finger thoughtfully.

"I want some definition. Take all the time you need to get over this; just don't leave me guessing. You don't want to talk? Say so. You want to be alone? Be my guest. But don't assume I know what you need."

He nodded, and she noticed his expression was less vacant, more tender. They looked at each other quietly. "Fair enough," he finally said, then took her hand from his hair and brushed it lightly against his lips.

"Well then," she said crisply, "since I've got you in a better mood, can I ask one more thing?"

"Uh-oh."

"It's not a big thing, really."

He looked back at her. She pointed at his face.

"Is that ever gonna go?"

He stroked his beard then puffed his chest out. "Why? Doesn't it remind you of the old Hercules movies? He had a full beard."

"Orson Welles didn't play Hercules," she said delicately.

He was off the couch in a flash. "That's it. It goes—now." He headed for the bathroom. "And this week I'm going back to the gym."

Christine took it as a good sign. The entire conversation, in fact, was a success. They were talking, even kidding, and he was coming alive. She followed him into the bathroom while he lathered up.

"I was kidding about the Orson Welles part, you know," she said loudly over the running water.

"Liar, liar, pants on fire."

"Half-kidding. You have put on a little weight, but you've got a long ways to go before you need to worry."

The steam filled the bathroom quickly; Christine wiped the mirror while Greg cut, stroked, and flicked clumps of hair off his razor.

"*Blast* it!"

"What?"

"Nicked myself."

She grabbed a towel to dab his face. He stopped her hand. "Don't mess up the towel. Toilet paper is fine." He kept his eyes on the mirror, reached for the end of the paper roll, and jerked too hard. The entire apparatus flew off the wall toward him, followed by a stream of yellow tissue. He roared, then stood dejected in the middle of the bathroom, toilet paper in hand.

Christine noticed a similarity between him and Charlie Brown trying to fly an uncooperative kite. She doubled over, giggling.

He glared at her, checked his reflection in the mirror, cracked a smile, and finally laughed with her.

"Greg," she gasped, "you're so funny! Everything's going to be all right as long as you're still funny."

———◆———

Yelsom sauntered into his apartment at 1:30 A.M. reeking of smoke and beer and feeling cockier than ever. He slammed the door shut, threw his jacket on the floor, and attempted a quick two-step into the kitchen, where he lost his balance immediately.

"Whoa, big guy." The room tilted. All this after only four beers? He put a hand out to the kitchen table and steadied himself.

No, five beers. Or an even six-pack?

"I'm entitled!" he snarled. He was beginning to understand the resentment the old man must have felt when Mom nagged him about *his* drinking. No wonder he hit her. What was the big deal about drinking, anyway?

He belched, forgot what he had come into the kitchen for, then retreated into the bedroom and flopped across the spread.

"Yup, a hand across the face is sometimes what the doctor ordered," he declared. "When people get outta line, ka-*pow!*"

Like those BRAVO wimps, for example—cowering in the basement like mice. Whining. Worrying. How typical.

Still flat on his back, Yelsom fished a cigarette out of his shirt pocket, found a lighter in his jeans, flicked, puffed, and sighed.

Just shows how weak and uncommitted those people are.

He heard their whisperings when he walked into the basement, concerned about the police and legal problems. Why did those dummies think BRAVO had a first-name-only policy at meetings? Why did they think he was known only as Yelsom? What did they think anonymity was all about, anyway?

The ash at the end of the cigarette grew, curled, and fell on his chest. He blew it off.

Okay, maybe it wasn't just that. They felt bad about Carlton. Well, so did he, but he would die before he'd admit it.

Except to himself. Carlton didn't deserve to die, and he was genuinely sorry about that. It wasn't his intention to hurt anyone. But the alarm system had to be turned off, he knew, or their fire would have been a waste of time. The lights were out and there was no sound. So how could he have known? But even Carlton's death served a purpose.

People would be angrier than ever.

Yelsom inhaled deeply and smiled.

Christians would be furious, and the community at large would be scared of gays. And, as he knew better than anyone, fear turns so easily, so quickly, into hatred.

Then the fun and games could begin.

The bedroom swayed gently. His eyelids fluttered, then he remembered his lit cigarette and, with effort, stamped it out in the ashtray next to the bed. No lights were on but the room wasn't quite dark; he'd left the kitchen light on.

Too bad. He rolled back to the middle of the bed. *Get it tomorrow.*

His thoughts returned to Carlton, but why? Because—

Slight nausea rumbled his stomach, but not enough to warrant a trip to the bathroom.

What was he just thinking about?

Carlton. Worth thinking about. Because of...

Greg Bishop.

Who must be so disappointed his case study got fried.

Sorry, Greg. But I was disappointed in you, too.

The room was in constant motion now, rocking Yelsom to sleep.

THIRTY-ONE

Greg and Rick Mosley trooped into the sauna, towels around their waists, and flopped onto the marble benches. They had the facility to themselves; few customers worked out at this hour of the morning.

True to his word, Greg had begun working out again with Mosley at 6:00 A.M. daily, and the effects were immediate.

"My triceps are coming back in," he noticed, flexing his left arm. He sat upright with his head back. Mosley lay flat on his back.

"See?"

Mosley opened one eye and grunted, unimpressed.

"You've let yourself turn into a Pillsbury doughboy this past month. It'll be some time before your arms are anything to write home about."

"Be sure to let me encourage you, too, next time you need it."

True, Greg's shape wasn't what it had been, but the pounds were melting and the body was definitely toning up, no matter what Mosley said. More important, pumping up was reviving Greg's spirits. A little, anyway.

He was still far from the congenial man Christine had married, but his depression had lifted and he was showing signs of renewal by puttering in the yard and reading books in lieu of watching television. However, there was still no socializing with mutual friends, and no attending church, much to Christine's disappointment. And still no lifting of his bitterness toward gays in general. But all in all, he was coming out of the fog.

"You don't know what you're doin' to me," he grumbled at his workout partner. "I've used up two tubes of deep-heating rub in less than a week."

It was two weeks now since his discussion with Christine and his first workout of the year with Rick, who was delighted to have him, as he said, "back in the fold."

"The soreness should go any day now. Just let your flabby old body get used to moving around again."

Greg leaned back against the wall, breathed in the steam, and sighed.

"So how are things with you and your lady?" asked Mosley.

Greg's eyes flew open. Mosley never asked about his personal life.

"Okay. Better. Why?"

"Just askin'."

He sighed again. "She's had it rough, being married to a psychologist who needs a psychologist."

Mosley chuckled. "I got a theory about you guys."

"Yes?"

"I think you all started studying psych because your own heads were screwed up. You kept taking classes, thinking you would figure yourselves out, which you never did. But by the time you realized it wasn't doing you any good, you'd racked up enough classes to get a degree, so you decided to become psychologists. Am I right?"

Greg's laugh boomed. "Well, you may have something there. I'll discuss it with my colleagues."

Mosley turned onto his side and leaned on one elbow, looking squarely at Greg. "Hey. Seriously, Greg."

Greg's eyes were closed now, his face turned upward while he inhaled deeply, letting the steam clear his sinuses. "Hmmm?"

"Where's your head these days?"

"Whoa. Now who's playing psychologist?"

"You're different, and it doesn't take a shrink to see it."

That struck Greg as a stupid remark.

"Rick. These past few months my church and I have been harassed beyond all limits by a bunch of freaks, I've had to take a stress leave, and you're saying I'm different?"

Mosley listened closely. "You're mad," he said softly, approvingly.

"Dogs go mad. I'm angry."

"Me, too. Hey, Greg, sorry to step on touchy territory, but just for the record? When I heard about that fire my fist went through the wall."

Greg was taken aback. They had never discussed it. It was tacitly understood, from the day two weeks ago when he called Mosley and asked if he'd like to resume their workouts, that the subject was off-limits. And here he was, bringing it up without permission.

"It's not an open subject," he said flatly.

"Because you're mad."

"What is this?" Greg was irritated now; it wasn't like Mosley to get in his face about anything.

Rick sat up. "Didn't you say I'm your motivator?"

"Come again?"

"When you called and said you needed to start working out again. *You're my motivator, Rick.* That's what you said, so here I am. Motivating you."

"Physically," Greg shot back, bringing his legs up to his knees. "Motivate me physically. Leave my head out of it."

"Not when your head is affecting us both. Hey, come on, don't I have any rights? I've known you since high school."

Greg laughed and hunched over, stretching his back. "What got you so touchy-feely, Rick?"

Mosley stood up and twisted his upper body back and forth. "I'm not being touchy-feely; I'm just looking out for my workout partner."

"You just worry about keeping up with me once I'm back in shape."

"That'll never happen. Not when your head is in the fog."

Mosley had stopped moving and spoken, his eyes fixed on Greg, just a little too seriously. Greg looked up.

"You're gonna start back to work in a few weeks, right?"

"Right."

"Counseling gays?"

Greg bristled at the word *gay*. "Some, maybe."

"But that won't ease it."

"Ease what?"

"The fire right *there*." Mosley stepped forward and jabbed his forefinger into Greg's chest.

"Hey!" Greg slapped his hand away.

Mosley nodded as if a point had been proven. "When I said *gay*, you reacted. When I hit on the subject you stiffen up. That's what has been eating you since your patient was killed, since they burned your church down. Admit it! It isn't stress or burn-out or anything wrong in your marriage. It's *them!*"

Careful. Something in Greg said it loud and clear. *This is the same guy who couldn't wait to beat up Bennie.*

It dawned on Greg for the first time that he and Mosley had become friends of sorts, even though it was Mosley who took such pleasure in the incident that had haunted Greg all his adult life.

But Mosley's observations were right on the mark, and something in this conversation made Greg feel a certain sympathy, even a camaraderie, that he had never felt with Mosley before.

Me first. Remember?

He looked at his workout partner, now a responsible adult in his thirties. Things change. He wasn't a schoolyard bully anymore—just a friend trying to help. The thought brought Greg's defenses down.

"Them. Lord, is it ever *them!*" he finally said, and Mosley laughed. "I never thought I could hate a whole class of people, but this last year has been one whale of a training session."

"I'll bet."

"And you know what?" Greg went on eagerly. "When I started counseling the ones who wanted help, the rest of them called me a homophobe. I wasn't one then, but after all the trash they've thrown at me, they've turned me into one!"

It felt good to say it out loud to someone who so obviously understood.

"Right on," cheered Mosley.

Greg had an ally; he could freely say the things he had to hide from Mike and Christine. He stretched his legs out and yawned, feeling understood. Mosley was grinning.

"Hey, know what G.A.Y.S. stands for?" Greg asked.

"What?"

"'Got AIDS yet, sucker?'"

"Pretty good, Bishop!"

The two traded "queer jokes," as they called them, for another half hour. Greg was delighted with Mosley's company, enjoying the freedom to say what he wanted without a *tsk tsk* from his wife. He was sick of polite company; sick of watching his every word and being so darned good for everyone else's sake. Sometimes, he thought, a man just needs to cut loose for a while. Mosley was, he decided, a man's man. Someone he could relax with. Maybe that's why he'd fallen apart lately. He couldn't relax when he was surrounded by a disapproving wife, a nosy pastor, and a bunch of people draining him every day with their problems.

He and Mosley may as well have been tipping beers in a pub for the way they were laughing and backslapping.

"So," Mosley said when they'd both run out of jokes. "You admit you're mad."

"Mad as they come," Greg conceded gladly.

"Can I make an observation, doctor?"

"Shoot."

"Counseling them won't make you any less mad at them."

"But I'm counseling the good ones!"

"That's the point. They're not the ones you're mad at. Don't you want to fight back?"

Greg knew, and didn't mind, that Mosley had been building up to something all along.

"Without getting arrested? Sure. Got any ideas?"

"Come on board. There's a meeting tonight in Huntington Beach."

Greg figured that was the pitch; Mosley had asked three times before if he would attend a Citizens United meeting, and each time Greg, weary of any kind of meeting, had found excuses not to come.

"Tonight?"

"Don't tell me you have plans. Not this time."

"No, not really. What's the agenda?"

"Plans for 1992. We need to set goals, Greg, and we need leadership. We still don't have an official spokesman."

"Who's been leading the group so far?"

"Tom is the president. You know Tom—the manager here. He keeps it going. But we don't have anyone like you: sharp, full of baloney and big words. We've got some good ideas for fighting the whole gay agenda, but we need a public face. Someone people can relate to and respect. You'd be perfect."

Greg wiped his forearm across his face and flung the sweat off his hand. "Where will I get the extra time?"

"We'll work with your schedule."

Greg considered, then something occurred to him. "Hey, Rick? You're so gung ho for me to do this, but what about the rest of them? What makes you think they'll want me?"

Mosley smiled confidently. "They know you. They'll go into a frenzy if you say you'll help out. Remember what Tom said? You're a hero to us."

He meant it. Greg loved the word *hero*. When was the last time he'd been a hero to anybody?

Careful, careful. Watch it. It was still there, but fading fast.

A chance to do something constructive with his anger. Isn't that what he always told his clients to do? Just one meeting—not a commitment, of course, just a visit—might be a nice break in the old routine.

Mosley was waiting.

"How do I get there?"

THIRTY-TWO

Christine was nervous about the whole idea, opting not to join Greg and reminding him he needed a minimal amount of stress in his life. He ought not, she insisted, take on any responsibilities.

"Duly noted," he said on his way out the door.

He forgot to kiss her when he left.

Citizens United met that night at Tom Wooding's condo on Pacific Coast Highway, overlooking the surf and surfers at Huntington Beach. The group, or at least the 24 who showed that night ("We've got over 50 members but they never come at the same time," Tom assured Greg) were generally under 40, somewhat upscale, mostly male, and very affable. They greeted Greg with grave respect—"You're the doctor who the gays were harassing, right? Gosh, you really went through it!"—and offered condolences and gratitude for the stand he'd taken publicly against the homosexuals. They remembered the press conference he gave with Robbie Carlton, the work he had started at Berean, and the horrible way those gays had harassed him and his wife that morning. He was somebody special here.

Tom called the meeting to order and, with no regard for traditional parliamentary procedures, proceeded to ask for any ideas on how Citizens United could address the homosexual problem.

Greg learned quickly that the group attracted a variety of ideologies. Several people identified themselves as evangelical Christians, although their language at times was far from orthodox. Other people had no obvious religious affiliation but were sympathetic to the Christian view, which, they said, was the correct view when it came to social issues.

One young man suggested glass jars to can the fruits in. Another thought a fumigation tent over a few of their bars might just do the trick. When the serious suggestions began, though, Greg could see he was among some politically savvy folks.

The traditional gay-bashing, they agreed, wouldn't work. And simply reading selected Bible texts at public meetings wouldn't suffice either.

"Pastors are doing that every Sunday," a woman reminded them, "and what good is it doing?"

"Well," Tom replied, "you'll notice the gays aren't harassing churches anymore."

"They're biding their time," the woman said. "It'll all start up again."

"We're missing the point!" a professional-looking man named Jason spoke up. "What we need is a concentrated effort to unite an opposition against homosexual indoctrination. That means opposing the promotion of homosexuality in public schools, opposing gay civil-rights bills like the one Wilson just killed, and opposing gay marriages, which, by the way, are on the horizon if we don't watch it."

"Hear, hear," Tom agreed.

Mosley raised his hand and was acknowledged. "But we'll need a public spokesman. Press conferences. A figurehead for people to unite around."

All eyes turned to Greg, and he knew instantly that they'd discussed this and decided beforehand that Greg Bishop was their choice, if only they could get him to say yes.

No one spoke, so Greg finally broke the ice. "What exactly would be required of this public spokesman?"

Tom jumped in. "That's easy. He—or you, Greg, if you take the role—would start by speaking at rallies, churches, anywhere we could book you. You'd see what kind of support you could drum up for an all-out effort to stop the gays in their tracks. That would be the beginning. Then we would develop our offensive into the schools and local government once we have enlisted our supporters."

Greg considered. "Yes, but we will need a more detailed strategy than that."

"So we'll work on one. First we get a leader, then we get the troops, then we work out the plan."

In two weeks, Greg thought, he'd be returning to a diet of counseling, writing reports, and coming home to television and Christine. Not a bad life; not exactly the stuff thrillers are made of, either. Here was something new—a chance to make his mark.

A chance to say no to them. And encourage other people to do the same.

Forget Ferguson. Forget the tape; you'll never find it. What good did that wild-goose chase do, anyway? Robbie's dead, the Gateway ministry is history, nothing worked out as planned.

So try a new plan.

He looked again at Citizens United and liked very much the way they looked back at him.

"When do I start?"

Applause broke out all over the room.

After the meeting, amidst welcomes and encouragement, Greg asked Tom about the differing backgrounds of the Citizens United members.

"Some religious types like yourself," Tom answered, scanning the room. "Some sinners like me. Why?"

"I'll need to get some kind of consensus on how we should present ourselves."

"We're all kinds. We've got some Mormons, Jehovah's Witnesses—"

"Jews?"

"None that I know of."

"No blacks either, I see," Greg noted. "At least not tonight."

"No."

"Too bad. People in the black and Jewish communities should know about us. I'll bet there's a lot of support we could drum up there."

Tom looked uncomfortable and mumbled something about not being ready.

"Ready for what?"

"You're our man!" an older fellow roared, barging between the two of them to pump Greg's hand and offer some fund-raising suggestions. Tom excused himself. Greg didn't get a chance to finish the conversation.

Christine wasn't pleased. She was so far from pleased with Greg's appointment, in fact, that she retired an hour before he did and was fast asleep before he came to bed.

Which was fine with him, because at 11:30 that night he received a phone call he knew Christine wouldn't approve of.

"Greg, it's perfect!" Alexandra Chappel gushed.

"Alexandra?" he shouted, then glanced toward the bedroom and lowered his voice. "What's perfect?"

"You and Citizens United. A perfect marriage."

"But how—"

"I've known the Wooding family for years," she cut in, "and you're in good hands, believe me. The group is young, but the right people belong to it. I was so disappointed in your refusing my offer last fall, but this is a better outcome than I'd have imagined! You'll enjoy working with Citizens United."

"Yeah, once we have our plans set. Of course, the time constraints will be a problem."

"What time constraints? I thought you were off work for a while."

He hadn't mentioned that to her. They hadn't spoken since that night at the Five Crowns. What on earth—?

"Well, I return in two weeks."

"Gregory, you'll never find time to work with Citizens United if you're working full-time at Berean as well, will you?"

"Well, no, it'll be tough. But I do have a wife to support."

"You're returning to work only for the money?"

The question sounded funny; why else did people work?

"Well, yes, and... well, I do enjoy it. It's my profession."

"Would you be willing to extend your sabbatical if you were financially supported while you promoted Citizens United?"

"I'd consider it," he said uncertainly.

"Consider it, please. I'll match whatever Berean pays you if you'll take at least another three months to get Citizens United off the ground."

Another three months. No regular hours. New challenges.

"Alexandra? Let's get together soon."

Tonight was a night for saying yes to new ventures, Greg thought to himself.

THIRTY-THREE

*N*ot everyone in Orange County, however, was pleased with Greg's newfound cause:

Berean Community Church
1703 Mesa Blvd.
Newport Beach, California 92643
Rev. Michael Cain, Senior Pastor

January 25, 1992

Gregory Bishop
12702 Black Spruce Ave.
Garden Grove, CA 92704

Dear Greg:

As per our telephone conversation, I have put before the board your request for an extension of two months on your sabbatical, provided Berean discontinues your salary for that period of time. The board has granted your request, but I'd be remiss if I didn't add some of my concerns at this point.

As you know, several people come to the Berean Counseling Center because of your gifts and good reputation in the community. I'm sure your clients, who have been led to believe you were returning in two more weeks, will be quite disappointed to learn of your extended absence. They may or may not even wish to continue their counseling under these conditions.

Furthermore, I'm concerned about your sudden interest in leading a political effort to withstand, as you said over the phone, the gay agenda. Greg, no one is more concerned about militant homosexuals than I am, and you know I have suffered, as well as you, at the hands of such people. So I applaud Christian involvement in the political process. But somehow, Greg, I find it hard to believe you are following God's calling in this matter.

Far be it for me to tell you God's will for your life. But let me ask this, in all sincerity: Are you getting involved with this group out of anger or out of conviction that God's hand is in it? Will you please ask yourself that and prayerfully consider the answer?

I will miss your presence at the church, and hope (no guilt trip intended) you'll discontinue your habit of neglecting Sunday worship. I'm always here, and hope you'll keep in touch.

Sincerely,

Mike

January 25, 1992

Dear Mom,

Thanks again for the crystal piece you got for my birthday. It's perfect! You should see it on the dining room table when it catches the light—very classy.

Greg bought me pearls, and they're gorgeous. I might be more excited about them, but they came instead of the birthday present I wanted from him most: to give up this crazy new group he's gotten himself involved with. After the first night he met with them, I knew I'd lost him.

Remember when he was zoned out on TV and ignoring the world? Don't laugh, but I'd give anything to get that Greg back! He came back to life all right, and walked right into Right-Wing Disneyland. We're talking ultraconservative now—not just moderate conservative, which is what we've always been. And he's taken to this group like a duck to water.

I thought after all we went through last fall, we were finally going back to a normal life. Ha!

I guess one reason I'm so jumpy about his new venture is he's being sponsored by Alexandra Chappel. Heard of her? Maybe not. Anyway, we met her for dinner last September. I was not impressed. She's too arrogant for words. She asked Greg all sorts of questions about his future as though he was applying for a job with her. And now, once he joins this right-wing group, she decides to supplement his income to keep him involved with them.

That's right. He's not returning to work for another two months. Instead, he's getting this organization off the ground. Their main goal, as I understand it, is to fight the gays, which is understandable considering what he's been through. But what's scary is that he's going to be their public spokesman, meaning he's the one the gays will protest and harass just like they did before. He plans to lead rallies for support, give press conferences, debate, whatever. What does he think took him to the brink of a nervous breakdown in the first place? When I asked him that, he told me this was his way of fighting back instead of being a victim of his own anger. Don't ask me what he means by that.

And that's not all. Greg has lost the gentleness he used to have. He's always had a little trouble with the ol' male ego, sure, but there's always been a kindness about him. When he started the counseling center he used to call it a ministry. But everything is business with this new group. All I hear him talk about is numbers and money, numbers and money. He's not what you'd call backslidden, but he sure isn't setting out to do this stuff for the kingdom. And that's what bugs me the most. I think, basically, Citizens United is a good thing. But I'm not sure if Greg and some of the other leaders are doing it for the right reasons. There is a hardness about these people, but Greg says I'm oversensitive, so who knows? I could be all wet.

Not Alexandra Chappel, though. She's spooky. She calls everybody "dear" and struts around in her Nieman Marcus suits and pearls and her perfect hair.

And if I didn't know better, I'd think she had designs
on Greg. At first he didn't like her either, but now he
thinks she's dynamite. She acts like she owns him
sometimes, and like I'm the outsider. But then again
she acts like she owns everybody. Yuck. I hate her
hair and everything it stands for. And I can't believe I
just said that.

Their first rally is this Saturday. I'm helping with
registration, but I hope my attitude doesn't put a
damper on things. We've reached an understanding
about it: I don't have to agree with what he's doing
just because he's my husband, and he doesn't have to
stop doing things I disagree with just because I'm his
wife. That's fair, don't you think?

So why am I so scared?

Love,

Christine

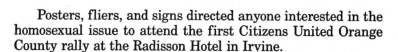

Posters, fliers, and signs directed anyone interested in the
homosexual issue to attend the first Citizens United Orange
County rally at the Radisson Hotel in Irvine.

"For citizens concerned about the wave of homosexual terrorism sweeping Orange County," the ads explained, "Citizens
United is an organization giving the silent majority an opportunity to speak and be heard in the public arena."

Dr. Gregory Bishop was billed as the speaker. Registration
was a mere $40 per person; the doors would open at 8:30 A.M., the
conference would begin at 9:30.

By 7:30 A.M., Greg and Christine, Mosley, Tom Wooding, and
a handful of Citizens United volunteers were at the Radisson
preparing one of the banquet rooms. The facility could hold 240
people; 51 had preregistered and it was anyone's guess how
many would register at the door.

"If we get 100 people we're doing well," Alexandra said, "for
our first effort."

Sixteen rows of padded chairs with an aisle down the center
were made available by the hotel, along with tables for the back,

front, and lobby areas. Greg and Mosley folded and stacked the programs Christine designed for the occasion; Christine busied herself with flower arrangements. Volunteers tidied the rows of chairs, repositioned display tables, and fetched water pitchers and coffeemakers under Alexandra's direction.

Christine and Alexandra treated each other with polite coolness. Christine's breezy, natural openness clashed with Alexandra's restrained socialite dignity. The tension between them was palpable, but both were too ladylike and self-contained to draw attention to it. Greg's admiration for Alexandra didn't thrill his wife; he sensed it, and kept his admiring remarks about Mrs. Chappel to a minimum when Christine was around.

Christine's job was to beautify the room; Alexandra's was to act as hostess, which she seemed born to do. When the first guests arrived for the 8:30 registration, she began a nonstop stream of flattery, patronizing, and gushing that, from Christine's perspective, threatened to drown every man, woman, and child in a sea of schmooze.

Greg started counting heads at 9:00; he was delighted to see over 100 people so far with a steady flow still coming. By 9:20, 247 people had arrived and registered. They added more chairs, against hotel and fire regulations, to accommodate the overflow. The guests found themselves packed in, which only added to the excitement. There was nothing, Greg noticed, as energizing as an overcrowded room full of expectant, like-minded people unified by mission and belief.

Pastors, businessmen, university students, housewives, parents with children in tow, some press reporters, and a few servicemen filled the seats, rubbed shoulders, adjusted legs, and made small talk in the conference room.

"We hit a nerve!" Greg whispered jubilantly to Christine as he passed her at the registration table. He was on his way to get more chairs; she was chatting with some people from Berean who had been interested in the Citizens United concept.

She didn't answer, but flashed a token smile.

At 9:29 Tom Wooding made his way from the back of the room, through the crowd, and up to the podium.

He wished the crowd an enthusiastic good morning and introduced himself, to much applause, as the president of Citizens United.

"Your presence here," he assured them, "is an encouragement to every Orange County resident who looks for a safe
environment and who wants an end to the craziness that threatens
our community."

More applause drowned out his last three words. The crowd
was clearly pumped.

Christine stayed at the registration table "to handle late-
comers," she told Greg when he suggested she find a seat inside.
But she didn't want to be inside. The table in the lobby was a
pleasant alternative.

Funny, she thought while listening to Tom's opening address.
She agreed with every word he was saying. And with the concept
of Citizens United. *So why*, she wondered again and again, *am I
so uncomfortable?*

Spirits were high in the banquet room. Pastor Gilbert LaRue
from Eastside Fellowship in Laguna offered a nondenomina-
tional invocation; an assemblyman and his wife were recognized
and welcomed by Tom.

Then the pitch began.

"Let me take a few moments, before introducing our speaker,
to tell you about Citizens United. We formed last spring when a
number of us started holding discussion groups in my home. At
that time, you'll remember, there was a sort of mass hysteria
about coming out of the closet, as the gays say."

Some titters and groans could be heard from the crowd.

"It seemed as though every time you picked up a paper you
read another gay sermon in the editorial section."

"Not just the editorial section!" a man from the front-left row
said loudly. The crowd murmured its agreement.

"And as the gays got bolder and bolder, we were hit with
their propaganda, their demonstrations, and their fear tactics.
All of us got tired of it, and some of us got mad."

More applause, loud and sustained.

"We saw our churches taken hostage. We saw gay tantrums
being thrown right and left. And finally, we saw murder."

The room chilled.

"Murder," Tom repeated. Standing against the back wall
waiting to be introduced, Greg wondered why they needed him.
Tom was a forceful, persuasive speaker.

Greg closed his eyes and breathed deeply. Tom would call
him up any minute.

"You have to come on strong," Alexandra had warned him earlier in private before the first arrivals. "Pull out all the stops when you're speaking. You're the new leader. Be bigger than life or nobody will follow you! Persuasion is showmanship, I don't care what anyone says! When you let yourself get comfortable with that you can do anything."

"And we knew that if we didn't do something quick there would be blood in the streets. So Citizens United has kicked off our 1992 effort to straighten out the gay nineties!"

Enthusiastic applause broke out row by row.

"Here to tell us how to do that," Tom said when the noise subsided, "is our speaker. Many of you have read about him in the paper and are familiar with his work. But for those of you who aren't, let me give you a bit of his background."

He checked a note card in front of him.

"Dr. Gregory Bishop is the clinical director of Berean Community Counseling Center. He's a licensed psychologist who pioneered, last spring, a program to help cure homosexuals."

Greg blushed. His work could hardly have been called a pioneer effort, but Tom made it sound so darned good he decided not to correct him.

"Remember Robbie Carlton? Oh yeah, we all do. Incredible, wasn't it? There was a young man brave enough to stand up to the gays right there in the amphitheater."

He didn't have much of a choice, Greg thought bitterly.

"And in front of thousands, he acknowledged our guest speaker as the one man responsible for his deliverance from homosexuality!"

More applause and admiring glances came toward Greg from people who turned in their seats to nod and smile at him. For a nonbeliever, Tom was using a good deal of Christian lingo, and exaggerating to boot. But never mind. Never mind that Robbie hadn't quite put it that way, and never mind that he'd decided not to pursue homosexuality long before he met Greg, who was hardly the one man responsible. Wooding was building him up superbly, and Greg began to see the wisdom of exaggeration in the service of a good cause.

"Robbie Carlton is dead. Dr. Bishop's work is not. Please welcome Dr. Gregory Bishop."

His feet were moving before he could even say, *You're on!* to himself. Greg strode between rows of cheering, applauding supporters like Moses through the Red Sea, looking manly and terrific. His chest bulged under his dark-brown suit, his arms swung freely, and his smile was huge and heroic, taking in everyone he passed and making them feel as though he smiled at them personally, not collectively.

Greg fairly leaped up to the podium, got a quick hug from Tom, adjusted the microphone, tried to look humble but not timid, gave an aw-shucks-it's-only-me grin, and held up his hands to quiet the applause.

"Thank you. Thanks so much, Tom. Thanks to all of you for coming."

He let the people settle, cough, and adjust their positions.

"This morning," he began, "I'm going to avoid talking about abstract issues. Instead, I want to tell you about people. Two people in particular. Both of them afflicted with homosexuality, both choosing different ways to deal with their affliction."

Greg had never spoken of it as an affliction before, but noticed the term sat well with the crowd.

"One has given himself over to hatred; the other showed courage. And from their lives, we can find answers to the question that brought us all here: What can we do about homosexuality?"

Energy swelled up from Greg's stomach and flowed through him, warm and electric. He stepped back from the podium and surveyed the room full of people who had come to hear him—*him!*—and sat respectfully taking in his every word. He was in perfect command of the crowd.

The moment that thought crossed his mind, his eyes fell on Alexandra Chappel standing in the back, watching him. Proudly. She nodded slightly when their eyes met, and a fresh surge of enthusiasm hit him. She knew he was coming into his power, and she celebrated it.

Christine was also somewhere in the back, but Greg didn't see her.

"The first man calls himself Yelsom."

Greg waited for the name to sink in. Some people in the audience recognized the name and reacted audibly.

"You may have seen him interviewed on television. He makes quite an impact, intentionally. Yelsom is a homosexual and he's angry, and he wants to make sure you know both of those facts. And he succeeds. Everything about him screams, "Danger! Angry homosexual approaching!"

They liked that one.

"He dresses the part," Greg went on. "He wears his hair a bit like Alice Cooper does, only our boy is a blond. Bleached blond, I should say. And heavy circles of mascara around the eyes, along with earrings, black leather, and lots of attitude."

He thought for a moment.

"I guess he hasn't figured out whether he wants to be an ugly woman or a freaky man."

They liked that one even better. Alexandra was right; this sort of power he could easily and willingly become accustomed to.

"But his presence is no joke. If you've seen him you know exactly what I'm saying. He exudes bitterness. And his goals?" Greg pulled an index card out of his shirt pocket. "Listen to what he has said on the record: 'The church's influence needs to be removed. They can't be reasoned with, so they have to be stopped. We want them to know that when they preach against us, they'll have the devil to pay. Literally.'"

Gasps and indignant remarks flew from every part of the room.

"That's right, folks. That's verbatim what he stated on TV. Gay rights? Not on your life. They're fighting for *gay supremacy!*"

The applause indicated he'd touched a nerve.

Alexandra had advised Greg to keep track of remarks that went over well with the crowd and recycle them.

Gay supremacy. That would make a good sound bite for future interviews.

"And how does Yelsom fight? Dirty, that's how. He leads his band to demonstrate, if you could call it that. Not the peaceful demonstrations of a Gandhi or a Martin Luther King, but wild, offensive types. The examples are right there in the open. You've seen them terrorize our churches, as Tom said earlier. You've heard what they planned to do to Robbie Carlton. And let's not forget Josh Ferguson's funeral, where they desecrated the service and nearly tore the deceased out of his coffin!"

Strong words, and they worked. People were thoroughly disgusted.

"In short, Yelsom is a man who has given himself over to evil. His actions and his presence are evil."

It no longer bothered him to talk about Yelsom this way. He'd chosen this fight, not Greg.

"He is evil."

A few "Amens" could be heard.

"But then, there's the other side of gay militancy. Take Robbie Carlton, for example."

If it was maudlin to use a former client for an illustration in a public lecture, it never occurred to Greg.

"Contrast the very appearance of a repentant homosexual to that of an unrepentant, hardened one. You've seen pictures of Robbie? Many of you have, I'm sure. Contrast his handsome face to Yelsom's scowl. Compare his grooming—impeccable, neat, respectful—to Yelsom's wild attire. And compare his attitude. Robbie had the decency not to throw his affliction in our face as Yelsom did. Rather, he had the courage to admit it gracefully when Yelsom and his cohorts tried to force him to. And he sought help for his problem. I know."

Discussing any aspect of his sessions with Robbie was a no-no. To even mention it was to step up to, if not cross, the line.

"I was there."

Greg trampled the line with nary a concern. It was, like many future compromises, for a good cause.

"And I wish you could have seen him! Pouring his heart out, grieving over these vile tendencies he wanted so much to tame, and wishing, praying, begging for some sort of deliverance. And patiently—oh, you wouldn't believe how patiently!—waiting for the day he could find the girl who would spark the natural instincts in him and, with her, build the family he knew was his natural destiny."

Greg had watched several television preachers, taken the best of their moves, and incorporated them into his presentation. Each sentence was punctuated by a step, a raised arm, an increase or decrease in volume. Stalking the front of the banquet room with a microphone in one hand and the other pointing and waving, he cut an impressive figure and won the crowd.

Women, and some men, were already crying.

"But that natural destiny was cut off one night," he solemnly declared, building up to the climax. "One brutal night, when gay rage flared all across our state because our governor had the good sense to say no to their silly claims of discrimination—"

Applause interrupted him. He didn't mind.

"—and they decided terrorizing innocent churchgoers wasn't enough to satisfy their blood lust. 'Tonight,' they conspired, 'we'll burn a church right down to the ground!'"

Sweat began to appear on Greg's forehead as he delivered the story.

"And inside that church, one precious young man sat in silence, practicing music, minding his own business, doing no harm. And in that sanctuary—a place you'd expect refuge—he met his death at the hands of the very people who make themselves out to be martyrs."

Everyone knew the story; hearing it retold with such gusto and style, though, inflamed them anew.

"Oh, we can't prove it was them. There weren't any witnesses or fingerprints. But the graffiti left on the church walls made it clear who destroyed the building . . . and the young man inside it, who dreamed of a wife and family."

Women now sobbed openly. The men who were dry-eyed (and many of them weren't) stared at Greg with muted, raw anger.

Now the pitch.

"So what do we do with the Robbies and the Yelsoms in our society?"

He let the question hang so everyone could envision their own solution. Then Greg offered his.

"We support the Robbies."

Again heads bobbed.

"And we establish organizations to help them become what they're meant to be. And we applaud their decision to leave that evil lifestyle behind!"

Strong applause.

"And what do we do with the Yelsoms?"

It didn't take much imagination to guess what some of the men in the group were thinking. Greg began his suggestion with a bit more moderation.

"We pity them, because they are pitiful people indeed. We watch them, because they are insidious. And we stop them."

Heads nodded, row by row.

"Because the Yelsoms in our society have to be stopped," he concluded firmly.

The applause indicated a point well taken.

"By a show of force equal to their own! No more can we afford to let them congregate in public without receiving a public rebuke! No more can we sit idly by while they terrorize us. They've been walking all over us, friends, because we've allowed it! But the question I must pose, and the question you must ask yourselves again and again for your sake and your children's sakes is this: Why do we allow it? Why?"

The nearly violent applause told Greg that collective anger had just been tapped into. Which was exactly what he, Alexandra, Mosley, and Tom were counting on.

"What can you do? Join us. Join us in a show of force to match theirs. Do you remember how Ronald Reagan gained the respect of our enemies? By making sure our enemies never had more weapons than we did. That's how you deal with communists, and that's how you deal with gays!"

Linking Reagan to his proposal was just the right touch.

"Our public rallies will need your support, and our demonstrations—which we'll stage whenever there's a gay event or a gay attack—will show Orange County that a grass-roots effort by concerned citizens like yourselves can squelch gay terrorism." Greg then wrapped up his speech, after noticing Mosley pointing at his watch, with a reminder that social action carries a price tag, pledge cards were available, and the best intentions would remain just that unless backed with capital.

All in all, Greg decided when he left the podium, a two-minute standing ovation wasn't bad for a first-timer.

By late afternoon the last of Greg's well-wishers had trailed out of the hotel. Greg, Alexandra, Mosley, Tom, and Christine stood in a tight circle by the registration tables, reviewing the pledge cards and mailing list sign-ups.

Greg still glowed from more back slaps, hand squeezes, and hugs than he'd ever thought a body could endure. "You're our man" must have been thrown at him 30 times today. It had an addictive ring to it, not unlike the applause punctuating his speech earlier. He was exhilarated and energized; last month's depression was already a dim memory.

"So now it finally begins," Mosley nudged Tom. They all were huddling like campers drawing warmth from a fire, shivering pleasantly.

Greg missed the meaning behind Mosley's remark, but Tom and Alexandra both indicated they caught it and agreed. Greg shrugged; Christine seemed lost in her own private concerns.

"But we've got to ride this momentum," Alexandra said sharply, pulling Tom, Greg, and Mosley to attention. She clearly had little patience with basking in the glory of the moment. "People have short memories when it comes to their commitments to a new venture." She eyed Greg knowingly. "You were awfully good, Gregory. Did you enjoy yourself?"

"Would you believe me if I tried to be humble and said no?"

"Never. That's why you need to go on the road. I've put together a three-month plan for exposure. Your exposure. Interviews, church meetings, maybe a little television. This issue is hot; there'll be plenty of media interest. Are you ready?"

His eyes said it all. Alexandra, Mosley, and Tom moved in closer to him.

As they did, perhaps without realizing it, they edged Christine out of the circle.

THIRTY-FOUR

After the first Citizens United rally, the media's interest was, as Alexandra predicted, aroused. Both the *Register* and the *Times* covered the event with a negative slant, quoting Greg's most controversial remarks and repeating them to gay leaders, then including *their* remarks in the article. Greg was startled, in spite of his earlier experiences, to see himself referred to as "an active crusader dedicated to the squelching of every gain made by the gay movement."

"Don't take it personally," Alexandra warned when he complained. "In fact, don't take it any way at all. Remember, when you stand against something you'll always be painted as the bad guy. Just like people for abortion are called 'pro-choice,' which sounds much more positive than the rest of us who are labeled 'anti-choice' or 'antiabortion.' But no matter. The more they write about you, the more it will draw people with our viewpoint out of the woodwork, so take heart. There is no such thing as bad publicity."

Which was good news indeed, for bad was the only sort of publicity Greg had over the next three months as he toured, lectured, debated, and preached. His name was soon associated with fanaticism, homophobia, extremism, and reactionary views—none of which detracted from the fact that he was a hit. People loved or hated him; there was no middle ground. Conservative Christians considered him, at least in the beginning, to be an answer to prayer. And producers of radio and television talk shows were soon made aware of him, thanks to Alexandra's connections, and were delighted to find guest material in such a colorful, controversial package.

He made his media debut by debating the pastor of a local gay church. Greg had been aware such churches existed but knew almost nothing about their beliefs, especially in the area of homosexuality. The notion of anyone trying to marry homosexuality and Christianity was beyond Greg; the Bible passages on the subject were so clear he didn't even bother to review them. He went into the debate hungry; he left it only half-full.

The gay pastor turned out to be verbally sophisticated, a master at twisting Scriptures and rationalizing. Greg responded by calmly pointing out the absurdity of the man's reasoning, and was confident, he said, in the listening audience's ability to discern the obvious from the outrageous.

Greg hadn't been as brutal as he would liked to have been. The gay pastor, smug and serene in his offbeat opinions, had pushed all Greg's buttons.

"Let it out next time," Alexandra chided him after the interview. "Play to the people who agree with you; don't worry about convincing the others. They won't be convinced anyway. Our side wants you to come on strong, like a prize fighter. Don't be such a gentleman next time."

He wasn't. His next opportunity was the Craig Sinclair Show, the nationally televised talk show with the second-highest ratings. The subject was whether or not gays and lesbians should be allowed to adopt children. The producers had heard of Greg; would he be interested in discussing his view on gay parenting with two other guests from the lesbian and gay community?

To Greg's delight, the other guests were confrontive. The show soon erupted, as Craig Sinclair's show was obligated to do, into a shouting match between the guests, the audience, and the host, who pretended to be distressed by the very chaos he had encouraged his guests to create before they went on the air.

During the course of the one-hour fracas, Greg was asked to present the biblical viewpoint of homosexuality. But remembering his last on-air encounter, he was determined to be the prophet, not the Bible scholar. So what if he went astray theologically and factually when he informed the studio audience that gays were naturally inclined to child molestation because of what the Bible calls their appetite for strange flesh. If he was crass when he suggested the danger of homosexuals satisfying their appetites on children they'd no doubt adopt for that purpose, and if he assured the viewers something had to stop sexual perversion from flourishing in America, which was why God was zapping gays with AIDS, and if he referred to the spirit of Sodom as being the demon possessing all homosexuals and inspiring unmentionable sadomasochistic practices, well, he told his conscience and his wife—the only two forces who seemed to find his performance that day abominable—it made for a memorable television appearance and a strong antigay statement. And what was more important than that?

Alexandra and Mosley called Greg at home after the show to commend him; Tom Wooding sent a note of congratulations, and donations for Citizens United, which was at Greg's insistence mentioned throughout the show, flowed.

New avenues of exposure for the controversial Dr. Bishop opened as each prior one closed. In April, one of the county's smaller towns considered an ordinance granting civil protections to homosexuals—protections much like those in the bill Wilson had vetoed.

Greg represented Citizens United at the city council meeting which was called to consider the ordinance. Several Citizens United members accompanied him. ("Just in case," one of them said.)

Greg spoke vehemently against the proposed ordinance, refining his flamboyant presentation into a clearer, more professional argument—"The granting of special protections to a special-interest group like gays sets a bad precedent when no need for such protections exists!"—and he scored big that night. His testimony swayed two council members, the ordinance was killed in the final vote, and after the meeting Greg found himself surrounded by gays who had testified at the same meeting.

The predictable curses and threats ensued, cut off abruptly by fellow Citizens United members, who positioned themselves between Greg and the gays, creating a formidable wall of muscle and attitude the gays wisely chose not to scale.

"We're on your side now," one of them said to Greg as the gays dispersed. "Stand tall."

Under the circumstances the advice was easily followed. But the next morning Greg was made aware of an unsettling trend.

Three gays had been randomly selected for beatings after the city council hearings. Violence against gays had abated in the past months; the series of assaults seemed to have peaked, then ebbed, around the New Year.

Greg might have dismissed the attacks as coincidence if a pattern hadn't soon emerged with frightening regularity: As he accepted more speaking engagements, he took more harassment from gays who'd come to heckle, confront, and intimidate him. And with each confrontation there was another random assault on a homosexual somewhere in the county. It was as though someone kept a grisly tally on Dr. Bishop and the gays, retaliating every time the gays attacked the doctor in any way.

"Why not accept it as a blessing?" Rick Mosley asked in all sincerity when Greg mentioned it to him at the gym.

"A *blessing?*" Greg nearly dropped the barbell he and Mosley were sharing. "People getting thrashed within an inch of life isn't a blessing. Even if it's *those* people."

"It's a war, my man. People get hurt. That's the price you pay for social order. Remember what they said about Nazi Germany?"

"Uh-uh."

"It was terrible, but at least when Hitler was in charge, the trains ran on time."

Greg Bishop was articulate and impressive in interviews; daunting before councils. But it was in church that he was at his colorful, passionate, electrifying best.

His media exposure drew him to the attention of pastors whose churches had been targeted by BRAVO the previous summer, and pastors concerned about the next wave of gay terrorism were the most eager to have Dr. Bishop fill the pulpit as a guest speaker. And from those pulpits he developed a potent, dramatic presentation: the life and death of Robbie Carlton and the mission of Citizens United.

Mosley or Tom would sometimes accompany Greg; otherwise, he would arrive at these engagements alone. After coming with him once and seeing a side of her husband she wished she hadn't, Christine refused to join him.

The presentation always began with an exhortation to love the sinner while hating his sin—a tired expression, to be sure, but still effective and not without merit. That having been said, he would launch into his tale.

"Tonight, let me tell you about the tragedy and triumph of a young man bound by homosexuality, then delivered and healed, only to be struck down by forces more hateful than you'd ever imagined could exist, even in this fallen world."

The story was essentially the same: Josh Ferguson was never mentioned since he was inconvenient to the story and because Greg wanted Ferguson out of his thoughts and life forever. He, his suicide, his videotape, and his final commission had long since been banished from Greg's interest. That battle had been lost; this one had the chance for a happier outcome.

Instead, Robbie (whom everyone knew, making the story all the more fascinating) was presented as a tormented young gospel artist with a dark secret and a broken heart. Depending on the mood of the audience, Robbie was presented as having been angry and bitter, or, at other times, remorseful and afraid. (Sometimes, having told the story so frequently, Greg changed the details to keep himself from getting bored.)

"He came to me desperate for help," Greg would explain, his face etched and haunted by the memory. "And so I began the toughest assignment of my professional career: the successful treatment of a homosexual."

Depending on the church Greg was addressing, the treatment varied. For the more conservative and sedate denominations, Greg described the traditional, twice-weekly psychoanalytical treatment he provided young Robbie. The Baptists, tending to be a bit more fundamental, were told about the discipleship-style, Bible-based counseling Greg specialized in and, of course, prescribed for Mr. Carlton. The Pentecostal congregations were thrilled to hear about the weekly exorcisms Greg performed on poor possessed Robbie.

The lurid climax of the story, too, was subject to embellishments. Sometimes Robbie's screams could be heard coming from the flames; at least twice Greg even allowed himself the luxury of rushing into the church only to be expelled by fire fighters who had to hold him down to keep him from rescuing Robbie. The horrifying ordeal of identifying his patient—one of the few details of the story he accurately related—never failed to inflame the congregation, ripening them for the final pitch.

Citizens United, of course, was the answer to the problem so vividly illustrated by Robbie Carlton's tragedy. Citizens United would fight the gays, uphold moral standards, educate the public about the homosexual issue, and stop the spread of perversion.

The response was always immediate. Sometimes altar calls would follow exhortations to stand firm with Dr. Bishop in his crusade; sometimes a demonstration of support for the doctor was virtually commanded by the pastors, one of whom (an unusual fellow so extreme few pastors seriously considered him a colleague) insisted that his lively congregation march that very evening to the local gay bar and, under Greg Bishop's leadership, stand at its door and cry, "Enough, enough, enough!" Their missionary efforts were rewarded with a confrontation between the unamused gay patrons and what the press later referred to as Dr. Bishop's zealots.

The police intervened, but not before fistfights broke out and injuries were sustained.

"Easy, Gregory," Alexandra warned afterward, deflating and chastening Greg. "You'll lose credibility with the public at large if you repeat a scene like that again. You can't afford to go too far. Not yet."

THIRTY-FIVE

*N*ot all the reports of Greg's efforts were favorable:

Orange County Register
Tuesday, April 12, 1992
Editorial Section

What Price Success?

At first glance the formation of Citizens United, the Huntington Beach-based group formed to address conservative concerns, seemed a reasonable, even commendable thing. After all, liberal groups have long been forging ties over social concerns such as homosexuality and abortion, so we welcomed, initially, the formation of one such conservative group as an answer to the sometimes virulent pro-gay rhetoric we've been subjected to.

But now we wonder. With each new interview or rally conducted by Citizens United's Dr. Greg Bishop, it appears that success—financial support, media interest, heightened exposure—may well be the ruin of yet another good effort.

We can only be intrigued, if not repelled, by Dr. Bishop's descent into the ludicrous. He began promoting reasonable ideas last January: a balanced viewpoint of sexuality in the schools, resistance to the sort of gay militancy we've grown weary of, alternative forms of counseling for gays wanting to change. But in a few short months Dr. Bishop seems to have succumbed to the malady so prevalent among crusaders and televangelists. He exaggerates, he dramatizes, he manipulates. He creates monsters out of homosexuals, then presents himself as the one to drive a wooden stake through their possessed hearts. The crowds applaud, as crowds will do for any great performer (and Dr. Bishop has proven himself to be nothing if not a virtuoso), and the money flows in from grateful donors. But we're left wondering what worthy goals the doctor has fulfilled, what future goals he and his organization have, and, whatever they are, how he supposes showmanship of this sort will accomplish them.

The Vine
Orange County's Premier
Lesbian and Gay Newspaper
Thursday, April 14, 1992
Page A-1

Dr. Bishop's Traveling Homophobe Show

If you're bored with the same, tired parade of over-weight bald homophobes shaking their fists at you on Sunday morning television, you just might check your listings for the next appearance of Dr. Gregory Bishop, Orange County's golden boy of the Religious Right. He's a cross between Billy Sunday and Charlton Heston—a moderately cute psychotic fresh off the mountaintop, belching out a creative mix of stories, lies, and hellfire. And he's coming soon to your neighborhood.

He may have already been there, in fact. Did your local church just sponsor an antigay pep rally? Did parishioners in your area just circulate a petition to have the nearest gay bar removed for decency's sake? Or was your local bar recently surrounded by funda-mentalists threatening to burn it down with you in it? Then you've been Bishopped.

Oh, and were you assaulted recently? Silly me, I forgot—that's a sign of being Bishopped, too. It seems every time some nasty gay says anything unkind to the doc, some other nasty gay gets his head bashed in.

Funny. I thought the doc wanted to hate the sin but love the sinner. Been loved lately? If so, wouldn't you like to return the favor? I know it's unfashionable to sound like BRAVO, but I'm beginning to see their point of view. Who knows—if they ever start up again I might just don a black T-shirt and sign up. And a lot of people I know would join me. Not because we agree with everything they do, but because we're so sick of the Greg Bishops that keep popping up like weeds.

Dr. Bishop is, you'll recall, the man responsible for the treatment center for gays that was discontinued after the church hosting it was burned down, which was perhaps the only good thing you'll remember about that night. (AB101—need I say more?) After the fire and the accidental death of Dr. Bishop's patient in that same blaze, Dr. Bishop took his act to the road. He now heads Citizens United, a group dedicated to "educating the public" about gays.

—Continued on A-17

Berean Community Church
1703 Mesa Blvd.
Newport Beach, California 92643
Rev. Michael Cain, Senior Pastor

April 16, 1992

Gregory Bishop
12702 Black Spruce Ave.
Garden Grove, CA 92704

Dear Greg:

I'm writing you about official church business, but I'm also writing to you as a friend. One who's baffled and, frankly, a little hurt. I've left messages on your machine which I assume you've been getting, and I've written two notes over the past month just to see how you're getting on. You've been unable or unwilling to return my calls or notes, which is forgivable. I know how hard messages can be to return. But you know, I'm sure, that I and many others here at Berean are hearing about you constantly in the news, and you must know we're concerned. Yet you've cut all communication with us and, according to Christine, virtually all communication with her. She's given me permission to put it to you that way. What's happening to you, Greg? And why am I suddenly expelled from your life? I'm confused.

When you requested an extension of your sabbatical, we granted it. I must tell you that several of us wondered what your intentions were at the time. You stated your need to form an organization combating the gay agenda, and while we agreed in principle with your goals, many of us—especially me—had reservations about your motives. You seemed a little too eager to fight and far too reluctant to forgive and heal.

Seeing your television interviews and reading about your church appearances confirms my worst fears along those lines. I know you've become extremely popular lately, Greg. You've amassed considerable support for your organization. The public, at least many segments of it, are seeing you as a hero. But some of us are seeing something else. Please hear me, Greg, when I tell you, with tears, that the Greg Bishop I see on television is not the man I've known and admired. It's a stranger doing a parody of Greg Bishop, saying things he doesn't really believe and acting out a role that doesn't suit him at all. Your displays reek of the sensationalism you and I used to scoff at. What happened, Greg? I want to believe the best about you, but it's hard not to see your whole crusade as a childish, destructive way of working out your anger over Robbie and the way the gays treated you. I don't begrudge your anger; only your way of venting it. And I fear where it may lead you and Christine.

Greg, God will not bless theatrics. He won't honor half-truths and grandstanding. If you're really called to fight the gays, then do so by all means. But do so fairly—in a way that honors, not embarrasses, our Lord. If you were only rebuking their sin and encouraging people to resist their tactics but love them as people, then I would be right there cheering you on. But you've strayed so far from the balanced, sincere approach you had last year that I barely recognize you anymore.

Which brings me to the official part of this letter. Unless you're willing to come in to a special meeting of the board of elders to explain the behavior we've seen and heard about these past months, your position with the Berean Community Counseling Center as clinical director will be terminated. While we've appreciated the fact that you've never brought Berean's name into your crusades, the fact remains that you are still on our staff and do, therefore, represent us whether you want to or not.

Is it too much to ask you to call me, Greg? I won't push myself on you again, but will wait to hear some word indicating you've received this letter and letting me and the board know what your plans are. If I've sounded harsh, please forgive me. But there's a harshness building up in you too, Greg, and it will reap you a bitter harvest if you don't prayerfully deal with it.

You know I'm here when you're ready to do that. I remain your friend and brother in Christ, always.

Love,

Michael

"And good afternoon. I'm Calvin Blanchard and this is 'Open Heart,' coming to you weekdays at three on KLVE Orange County. I'll be with you till five o'clock sharing thoughts and conversations, and I hope you'll share a few thoughts of your own when our phone lines open up."

He used to love opening the show. Now the words came mechanically. But today's commentary was the first he'd delivered in weeks with any real feeling. It might get him in trouble, but who cares? It was time somebody in the Christian media commented on Greg Bishop.

"But before we get to today's guest, let me share some concerns I've had for some time but have been reluctant to address. And those concerns center on the group Citizens United and the way they're presenting the Christian viewpoint of homosexuality."

The engineer looked at Calvin through the glass partition and crossed himself in mock anxiety. Calvin grinned and continued.

"Now some of you, I know, are supporters of Citizens United. You consider Dr. Bishop one of the few men strong enough to stand up to the gays and you admire him for the work he did at the Berean Counseling Center. He is, after all, the man the late Robbie Carlton credited for helping him through his own struggle with homosexuality. And for that he deserves some applause."

Calvin wished Greg would have returned his calls. It seemed unfair to comment on him publicly without giving him a chance to respond, but his behavior warranted some comment. And maybe this would get a reaction from Greg, finally. Any reaction was better than none.

"But since he formed Citizens United, I've begun to wonder if Dr. Bishop isn't adopting some of the same tactics Christians condemn when gays use them. Let's take the tactic of dishonesty, for example. Gay advocates have certainly been willing to employ that one. Look how long they promoted the myth that ten percent of the population was homosexual. Some of them still cling to it in spite of numerous studies proving it to be false. And how about their claims that people are born gay? A few studies suggesting varying brain structures in *some* homosexuals have now been taken by gay spokesmen and presented as though homosexuality has been proven to be inborn. And, of course, comparing the so-called plight of gays to that of blacks has been one of their most dishonest, inappropriate tactics. A quick study of the income and political clout of gays shows a breach between their 'plight' and that of African-Americans that's as wide as the Atlantic."

Calvin sipped some water and continued.

"Okay, so they're not always honest. Maybe we shouldn't expect honesty from secular movements. But from Christian leaders we expect higher standards. And in Dr. Bishop's case, I'm sad to say, I'm disappointed. When he warns us about gay terrorism and encourages us to get active politically to fight the gay rights movement, I say, "Go for it, Greg." But now he's saying more, and much of what he's saying is every bit as untrue as the myths gays have been peddling.

"I daresay Dr. Bishop knows that not all gays are child molesters, yet he freely lumps them together in that category when he speaks in public. As a psychologist and as an intelligent man he knows that demon possession is not a sufficient explanation for the cause of homosexuality, but at times he'd have us believe that all gays are candidates for the local exorcist.

"My question to Dr. Bishop, then, is this: If something is a sin, why not just call it that? Why all the fancy exaggerations? What purpose, besides causing people to become violently angry at homosexuals, is being pursued by Citizens United? Those are hard questions, but when an organization is in the throes of white-hot popularity, as Citizens United certainly is these days, it serves them well to ask themselves the hard questions and not get carried away with the arrogance of success. That arrogance, and the carelessness that goes with it, can be the beginning of the end.

"That's something to think about, anyway."

Lisa turned the kitchen radio off and laughed.

"What's so funny?" Roxanne asked from the living room.

"Oh, this guy is great. This Calvin Blanchard on KLVE? He just did an editorial on Greg Bishop."

Roxanne and Lisa were regular KLVE listeners. In spite of their constant, mutual reassurances that leaving the Baptist church and joining the gay church had been the right move, they missed the good Bible teaching they'd become accustomed to. The doctrine at their new church tended to be weak; admonitions against sin of any kind were rare, and it was unclear where the church officially stood on a number of doctrinal issues both women felt were foundational. Christian radio provided them the sort of teaching they hungered for.

It also provided them a chance to hear at least one Christian radio personality they related to: Calvin Blanchard. He seemed so authentic, gentle, balanced. And his voice sounded more than a bit like their friend Jeremy's, which was, of course, coincidental.

"What did he say?"

"He really put Bishop in his place!" Lisa called back from the kitchen. She was straightening up after a late lunch while Roxanne thumbed magazines in her easy chair. Lisa was again between clerical jobs; Roxanne's schedule was light today. "He said he's being dishonest when he talks about us."

"Well! That took some guts."

Just as her lover returned to her reading, Lisa felt the discomfort rise again. Slowly, as always. She inhaled deeply.

Focus, she commanded herself. *The discomfort comes because you're full of doubts. You're doubting basic things that should have been settled long ago. God loves you just as you are. You're doing what's best for yourself, so it has to be right. You're a lesbian and there's nothing you can do about it. He made you this way. Now relax and focus.*

But the Bible so clearly says—

Forget it. You've been so programmed with the wrong interpretation of the Bible that it's hard for you to shake it.

Lisa closed her eyes, thought of praying, then decided against it.

The vague uneasiness had been growing, not diminishing as she thought it would, ever since she had officially come out. Only Roxanne knew, and she brushed it aside the first time Lisa confided in her. "You're just having the usual doubts, babe," Roxanne assured her. "They'll go away after a while. Be patient."

Lisa had been patient, and nothing had changed. So she entered therapy five months ago, working with a woman who encouraged her to accept herself and recognize her doubts as internalized homophobia. She had taught her the deep-breathing techniques she was now using to get past them.

"And," her therapist had recommended, "you should write your mother at times like that. Those are the times you need her warmth."

Lisa took three more deep breaths, stood up, opened her eyes slowly, and looked for a writing pad.

Dear Mom,

Now, I know how you worry, so let me set your mind at ease about what's been happening with me. Remember when I told you about Robbie Carlton and our plans for him? And remember when I wrote that we might be staging some pretty outrageous demonstrations in the near future? Well, I suppose you put two and two together when you heard he was killed in the fire at that church. Yes, Mom, we set it. But we never intended anyone to be hurt.

When Governor Wilson killed our chance to live where we please and work without being afraid, can you imagine how betrayed we felt? BRAVO happened to be meeting that night, and when we heard what he'd done we were outraged! Yelsom said we had to make a statement, and where better to make it than Berean Community Church?

Not everyone at the meeting went. But those of us who did planned only to paint some messages and set a small fire. Don't laugh, Mom. I know you're thinking, *Small fire . . . is this girl crazy?* But I swear we didn't know anyone was in the building. We ran away as soon as it was set, so we didn't even see how big a fire it became.

The next day we were all horrified to read that someone had died in the building, but what can I say? We didn't know, and our intentions were good.

Last November, Roxanne and I and the rest of BRAVO decided not to back down, in spite of this. It's upsetting, because so many people in our community don't understand us. I'm sure someday they'll see we were right.

Roxanne and I have been making new friends at the church. It's taken some time getting used to a church where you can be lesbian and Christian and nobody has a problem with it. I'll have to admit I still have some reservations about certain Bible verses, but I try not to dwell on them. Roxanne and I are happy, and we know God loves us.

We tried to explain that to our new friend Jeremy. He's with BRAVO, not the church. We invited him to church, but he says there's no way he could reconcile Christianity with homosexuality. He pulled out all the Scriptures saying it's wrong, and we pulled out all our arguments, and the three of us never got anywhere so we called a truce. But I really like Jeremy. He says he was raised in the church but left it when he discovered he was gay. How sad.

Did you make any New Year's resolutions? I made only one: to not be afraid anymore. Roxanne and I are committed to each other and to human rights. (In that order!) I've finally found a person *and* a cause I can believe in, which makes all the hurt worthwhile.

Well, I gotta go. Thanks for letting me prattle away and for always being there. My therapist says our relationship is one of the most important ones in my life right now. I agree.

Roxanne sends her love.

Love,

Lisa

THIRTY-SIX

*C*alvin's phone jarred him awake at 1:30 A.M.

He knew the time because he checked and double-checked the digital clock by his bed before picking up the receiver. Who on earth...?

"Get this drunk freak outta here!" a man barked before Calvin could even say hello.

"What?"

"You Jeremy? Or Junior?" the man asked none-too-patiently.

"This is Calv—oh! Jeremy? Yeah, yeah, that's me!"

"This is Mike at The Shaft. Pretty boy here says you're his partner."

Calvin blinked. Partner?

"So you can either come down here and partner him outta this place or we'll let the cops do it."

Calvin cleared his head, sensing opportunity.

"What's Yelsom done?"

"He's drunk and he's making a scene. Making threats, too. And calling people names. And he just picked a fight with two customers and we don't put up with that. So he's permanently eighty-sixed. Got it? After tonight I don't want to see him here again."

Calvin's breath came hard and fast.

Yelsom is drunk. Which means he needs someone to pick him up. Which means he needs a ride home.

"Please don't let him leave. I'll be right down."

The Shaft was a fifteen-minute drive from his apartment. He made it in less than seven.

It was near closing time; most of the customers had cleared out. The few left were standing around the back corner. They were gathered around something, snickering, gesturing.

"Can't stand the guy," one of them was saying. "It's a good cause but he's such a mouthy jerk."

Calvin jogged across the wooden floor. It had to be Yelsom.

"Where's Junior?" a raspy voice demanded to know.

"Here!" Calvin shouted before he reached the group. They parted to reveal Yelsom, hunched on the floor holding his stomach, enraged.

"You stupid little twit!" he lashed out. Drunk and helpless, Yelsom looked more like a wounded dog than the impressive warrior he fancied himself to be. "Why have I had to wait with these faggots staring at me?"

"I punched him," a man Calvin recognized as the bartender explained, "and I *never* hit customers. But this guy went too far tonight. Came in here a little blitzed already, then really put it away. I cut him off after two rounds, but I guess he hustled up drinks from other customers. He's ripped to the gills, man. Started calling us all a bunch of worthless faggots. Then he starting picking on two people who were just sitting there minding their own business. He said that's his calling—picking off stupid fruits. That's when I'd had it."

Yelsom glared at Calvin while the man spoke. "Get me outta this scumhole, Junior. *Now!*"

"I'm sorry," Calvin said to the bartender and the others in the group. "We're going. Come on, Yelsom, work with me."

Calvin knelt and slipped his arm around Yelsom's waist, hoisting the uncooperative man onto his feet and supporting him across the bar to the exit.

"Thanks for getting him," the bartender said. He was friendlier now that the pest was leaving. "I didn't really plan to call the cops, but I couldn't let him drive home in that shape. I didn't want him walking home, either. Three guys have been jumped in the alley back here recently." He pointed at the back of The Shaft, where an alley ran the length of the street. "Gay-bashing is up again, you know."

Calvin knew.

The bartender shook his head at Calvin. "I didn't want another incident outside my bar, even if it did involve a customer I don't like. How did you ever wind up with a guy like that?"

They were nearly out the door; Yelsom was incoherent, so Calvin spoke freely:

"It was a mistake. I didn't know what I was getting into. But I'll be dumping him soon."

Then he remembered.

"Hey, if he brings this up next time he sees you, would you mind not telling him that I took him home?"

"He won't be seeing me. I'm not letting him in here again, remember?"

"Yeah, right," Calvin nodded. Yelsom was getting heavier by the second. "But just in case, please don't mention any of this, okay?"

"You got it."

His car was parked a block away; Yelsom was dead weight, but in his excitement Calvin barely noticed.

He unlocked the passenger door, deposited his "partner" into the seat, locked the door again, and quickly walked around the car to the driver's side, his shoes clicking and echoing in the early-morning air.

He jumped inside and locked his door. It was pitch-black. No one on the sidewalk. No traffic. Silence.

Yelsom broke the quiet with heavy breathing that turned quickly into snoring.

Calvin waited, petrified to be alone in his car with this drunk maniac, but excited to finally get his chance.

The second hand on the Mazda clock clicked softly. Two minutes before 2:00 A.M.

Yelsom's snores grew deeper, more regular.

Calvin looked around the street again. Nothing.

Touch the monster, get the info. Now or never.

His right hand, shaking, reached across the seat toward BRAVO's leader and felt his back pocket. Yelsom stirred minutely; Calvin left his hand in place, frozen. Yelsom settled again. Calvin reached again, felt, and pulled in a quick, smooth motion.

The thin wallet slid out easily. He held it aloft, never taking his eyes off Yelsom. He wasn't wearing his jacket tonight; only a thin, tight T-shirt. Calvin noticed, not for the first time, how thick his arm muscles were.

If he wakes up, I'm history.

He waited another full minute, flipped the wallet open, kept it in his right hand, then peered across the seat at Yelsom one more time.

Yelsom was dead to the world. Calvin bent down to examine the wallet by the dashboard's muted lights.

He bypassed three credit cards and found the driver's license and checked the personal data. The name wasn't Yelsom—

Bishop had said he used an alias—but it was the address Calvin was interested in: 223 East Hale, apartment 3, in Santa Ana.

Calvin didn't have a pen. No matter; he would remember the address.

"Two twenty-three East Hale, number three," he whispered aloud, still reading the license. "Two twenty-three."

A huge hand slapped onto his right wrist and clutched it, then shook it like a shark thrashing its prey. Heat shot up Calvin's arm and spiked into his brain, nearly forcing a scream.

"Whaddya doin'?" Yelsom growled.

The open wallet dropped to the floor.

"Whaddaya *doin'*?"

Yelsom's voice cut into Calvin, who turned, afraid to face him, but compelled to. Still clutching his wrist, Yelsom was turning slowly toward him, his head lolling back and forth. Drunk, brutal eyes fixed themselves on their prey. Yelsom, still glaring murderously, let his head roll back then suddenly thrust it forward, snarling as if to bite into Calvin's face.

"Faaaaag. *FAAAAAAG!*"

Hot, putrid breath assaulted Calvin, who closed his eyes and flinched, backing as far away in his seat as he could.

Yelsom's teeth missed his face and snapped shut in the air like a steel trap. His head then landed somewhere near the bottom of Calvin's right pectoral muscle, where it lodged itself as Yelsom crashed back into a drunken stupor.

The terrified man in the driver's seat could not have been paid to move one millimeter.

They remained locked in that position for five minutes until Calvin finally regained his breath, disengaged his arm from Yelsom's death grip, pushed Yelsom's head away, fished the wallet off the floor, and redeposited it in his passenger's right pocket.

His hand still shook as he turned on the ignition and started toward Santa Ana.

He knew the city well. Hale wouldn't take long to find. If memory served him correctly, it was in the lower-rent district.

Memory served. Calvin found it in less than 30 minutes, during which time his terrifying passenger remained motionless. He drove up to the tiny apartment building and parked; the change in motion stirred Yelsom.

"Whaa—what's happening?" He looked at Calvin and was suddenly alert. Drunk, but alert.

"I brought you home, Yelsom. Let's go on inside," he offered, starting to get out of his side of the car.

"Stay put." The authority was back in Yelsom's voice. "I don't want company."

And with that he shoved the door open and staggered off toward the building. Calvin drove off the second the door slammed shut, anxious to leave without further incident.

But he would have no trouble returning when the opportunity came.

THIRTY-SEVEN

May 9

Hi, Mom.

It's Friday night and I'm alone. Surprise! Me saying I'm alone is like an otter saying he's wet. What else would he be?

Christine's pizza sat, greasy and half-eaten, next to her notepad. She picked up a cold slice, chewed, and deliberated over the paragraph she'd just written. It was a bleak opening, but what use was there in trying to sound perky? Mom would see right through it; she always did.

She continued.

Greg's speaking somewhere in Westminster tonight, I think (yeah, *think*, because it's tough keeping track of his celebrity schedule these days). Then he's off to New York next week for a taping of "The Melanie Stone Show." That makes four of the five major talk shows in just a few months. Not bad for someone who just hit the lecture circuit. I guess we have Alexandra Chappel to thank for that.

At the thought of Alexandra she slapped her pen down, chomped into the rest of the pizza violently, swallowed, and wiped her hand.

"Thank for what?" she asked, looking around the empty house. She was writing at the breakfast table while the kitchen darkened in the May twilight. "Another night of solitary confinement?"

That wasn't quite fair, of course. She could accompany Greg anytime she chose; Alexandra encouraged it. ("You play such an important role, dear! A speaker gains credibility when his wife is on his arm.") But the public Mrs. Bishop, pretending to applaud her husband's new flamboyant style, was her least favorite role. So she was alone by choice. Still, it was Alexandra's influence, by opening so many doors for Greg to walk through, that narrowed Christine's options. She could make the rounds with Greg to his speaking engagements, or stay home and wonder about what was happening to what had been a darned good marriage. Writing to her mother was a way of formulating—or trying to, at least—an answer.

She picked her pen up again.

> But I'm not too anxious to thank her. True, this Citizens United business has pumped Greg up. He's nothing but high energy these days, and I guess that's better than the depression he sank into last fall. But there's so much distance between us these days I don't know if we'll ever bridge it.

Distance. That's the word she'd been looking for these past weeks when trying to define the problem. Not hostility; no arguments or flare-ups. And Greg couldn't be accused of inconsideration—not in the technical sense, anyway. He'd been polite, if not attentive, helping with household chores and handling the budget as he always had. But he was in another world now, where homosexuals were the root of all evil and he was the anointed exorcist weeding them out. She couldn't join him there, or even pretend to approve. He sensed it; she was not a part of his adoring public, and for that she was banished from his inner life. Alexandra, acclaim, the chance to be a hero, and hatred for the gays who'd killed Robbie (and thereby killed his hopes to free himself from an old hurt) were his constant preoccupations. There was no room for his wife.

Predictably, their love life had fizzled. Greg didn't seem to mind, and Christine flat refused to ask for physical attention as if it were a favor. So they'd settled in, by mutual silent agreement, to a routine of polite coexistence. Greg worked on speeches and public-relations ideas for Citizens United by day, then spent evenings either traveling to speak or meeting to discuss strategy with Alexandra and Tom Wooding, or reading alone in his tiny den while Christine watched television. And the distance between them grew to be as wide as the gap between the man she'd married and the self-absorbed crusader she now simply lived with.

> Actually, I don't know if I want to bridge it. You can be lonely for someone you enjoy being with, but how can you miss someone you've lost respect for? And don't think I'm being harsh, because I'm not the only one whose opinion of Greg has changed. Most of our friends are uncomfortable with the direction he's taken, and they're keeping their distance. Pastor Mike sure isn't impressed, either. Ditto for Greg's own mother and relatives. Some people really think he's wonderful and say that a lot of what he does is right. But plenty of others discern a kind of overkill in the way he does it. Yes, he's popular in some circles. But not everywhere. Some churches flat refuse to have him speak because they're turned off by his theatrics. He's turned into one of those people you love or loathe— there is no middle ground.

So where does that leave me? she thought, leaning back to rest her eyes. The question distracted her; she mulled it over, decided to think about it later, then suddenly lost interest in writing the letter. She dropped her pen on the table, wrapped the rest of her pizza in foil, and put it in the refrigerator. Maybe she'd finish the letter tomorrow, or maybe she'd just give Mom a call over the weekend instead of writing.

Maybe, maybe. Everything was so vague these days. She sighed and checked the clock on the stove. It was 7:45 already.

Where'd the time go? We must do this again soon.

She laughed.

Don't worry, we will.

Some herbal tea to wash out the taste of pizza sounded good. She got up to put a kettle on. She'd rented a couple of movies to watch; that would fill up the rest of the evening. Maybe Greg would be home by nine, or maybe this would be a late night for him.

So many maybes, so little time.

She said it out loud while filling the kettle with water and turning the stove on. It would make a good bumper sticker; she was designing it in her mind when the teakettle started to hiss and the phone rang at the same time. She yanked the receiver off the wall and turned the burner off with her free hand while she answered.

"Mrs. Bishop? Christine Bishop?"

She'd never heard the woman's voice before.

"Yes?"

"My name's Celeste Bolton. I work for Dr. Alex Crawford, and I'm an old classmate of Greg's. I don't know if he's mentioned me before?"

The woman sounded hesitant, almost guilty. Christine couldn't help being suspicious.

"I don't think so," she said stiffly. "Can I help you?"

"Actually, yes. I've been trying to reach Greg for weeks. I paged him a few times and never got a response. I know he's on sabbatical, but his secretary told me he is still carrying his beeper."

"Yes, he is," Christine answered, omitting the fact that Greg had gotten into the habit of flicking it off when he was busy or preoccupied. Few calls came in from the counseling center these days, anyway.

"Dr. Crawford has asked me to forward some materials to Greg. He says it's urgent. But I don't have your home address and I didn't think he would get them if I sent them to his office."

"That's fine. Our address is—"

"And Dr. Crawford just called me again."

"Oh?"

"He was, uh, agitated." Celeste's voice was tight with strain. "He's been anxious for me to get this stuff to Greg. Pushy about it, in fact. He just called and asked if I'd sent it, and when I said I needed your home address, he gave me your phone number and said to call you up right now and get it. He said he couldn't leave until he was sure Greg had gotten it."

"I don't understand."

"Me neither. But Dr. Alex is planning a long trip. Don't ask me where, 'cause he's not telling. He's leaving either tonight or early tomorrow. He says he needs a long, private retreat where he can't be bothered, but I think there's more to it than that."

Christine was beyond jealousy now; the fear in this woman's voice was contagious.

"I work part-time for Dr. Crawford now," Celeste went on. "Remember the heart attack he had last spring? He was just getting back on his feet when he had a relapse. A bad one. Did you know that?"

"No!" Greg hadn't mentioned it. He probably didn't know either; he'd lost touch with Alex. "Is it serious?"

"Very." She paused. "It happened after they set fire to your church."

Christine's stomach dropped. Something was wrong—very wrong.

"When Dr. Alex heard about it he keeled right over. All alone, too. He barely made it to the phone. No hospitalization this time—just the emergency room. But afterward, he told me he was through with his practice and he wanted me to stay part-time to help him close things out."

"Why hasn't Greg been told about this?"

"Because that's the way Dr. Alex wanted it. He was very adamant about it. I must have heard, 'Don't tell Greg' a thousand times."

Christine was unnerved. "Why? Alex is our friend; that doesn't make sense!"

"He wanted to let Greg know later," Celeste explained, "after he had gotten this other information together. 'Things have gone too far,' he said. He didn't even want to see Greg until then. He's completely isolated himself."

"What information?"

"That's what I'm telling you. He started having me go to the UCI Library, doing the weirdest research. He gave me a few names and subjects and said to photocopy every article I could get my hands on pertaining to these—*subjects*."

This was wearing thin; Christine wished the girl would get to the point. "Exactly what are these subjects? Are they the things you're supposed to mail to Greg?"

"Yes. I have them right here."

"So what are they?"

"Do you know anything about The Covenant?"

"The *Covenant?* Never heard of it."

"Reverend Willard Manchester?"

"No."

"Alexandra Chappel?"

Christine waited to catch her breath, then tried to sound casual.

"Yes. Yes, we do know Mrs. Chappel. Why?"

"Well, she's, uh, she's mentioned in here, in a way."

Christine wanted to scream. Was this girl incapable of giving a straight answer?

"Look," she said, fighting for calm, "why don't I just give you our address and you can send this stuff to Greg, okay?"

"Right. I'm sorry if I sound rattled, but I'm worried about Alex. When I couldn't get hold of Greg, I thought he'd go through the roof! He's losing it, you know."

"Losing it?"

"Obsessed. With this stuff, and with Greg. And acting as if he is fighting guilt, come to think of it. He comes in the office once a week for an hour or so to sign papers, clean files, whatever. And he saves news clippings. Whole stacks of them. About Greg."

"*What?*"

"He saves clippings—whenever Greg's been interviewed. Anytime he makes the news, Alex saves the paper. And then... oh, it's weird, but it's probably nothing."

"Celeste, *please!*"

"Right. Well, he shakes his head at the clippings and sometimes I hear him mutter, 'I'm so sorry, I'm so sorry.'"

Christine poured water from the kettle into her cup. It was lukewarm by now, but she needed it; her mouth had gone dry.

"Celeste, instead of mailing this stuff to Greg, can you fax it?"

"I don't see why not. When?"

"Now?"

"Oh! Sure, okay, my husband and I have a fax machine here. What's your number?"

Christine gave it, thanking God she had insisted on getting a fax machine when she started up her small business.

"There are eleven pages total," Celeste warned her. "Dr. Alex underlined certain parts. And there is a cover letter from Alex to Greg. I read it; it's creepy."

"So he's seen these materials?"

"Sure. He took the photocopies he thought were most important and stapled them together. Made little notes in the margins and highlighted some sentences, too. They might not come out too clearly on the fax, but you'll get the idea."

"Thanks. And Celeste? Maybe we should keep this between us."

For whatever reason, Christine was afraid of this getting out.

"Sure. Let me know if you need anything else, okay?"

"Will do. I'll wait for the fax."

She thanked Celeste again, hung up, then poured more tea and waited.

After five minutes the fax still hadn't come. Christine imagined Celeste as the sort of woman who fumbles through routine actions like sending a fax—breaking her nails and fretting.

Come on, lady, this is killing me! she thought to herself. As if in response, the fax machine nestled in the corner of the kitchen beeped and whirred to life.

Christine watched the sheet protrude, lengthen, roll onto the kitchen floor toward her, and finally stop.

She hesitated long enough to consider leaving the fax message until Greg got home and letting him deal with it.

No way, girl; you're in this, too.

She crossed the linoleum floor, picked up the long, thin sheet, and ripped it off the machine.

It was flimsy and unmanageable. Before reading it she decided to cut it into eleven separate pages and, having done so, she sat down at the kitchen table, placed the papers over her mother's letter, and set her tea carefully to the side.

The cover letter from Alex wasn't dated. But it was, as Celeste said, creepy:

> I should have told you all of this last spring, but couldn't. They had me by the throat, but they promised me that you and Christine wouldn't be harmed in any way. But you've already been harmed, probably more than you know. I have to take an extended leave, but this should explain things. Disengage yourself from Alexandra Chappel immediately. Nothing she is offering you can be worth your soul.
>
> I love you deeply, Gregory. Let your better self direct your decisions. We'll talk again, but not for some time.
>
> Alex

The letter was incoherent enough to dismiss as a sick man's ramblings, and lucid enough to take as a concerned friend's warning. Christine wasn't sure which interpretation to choose.

Page two featured the cover of *The Journal of Aberrational Cults and Sects*, dated September 1986. Several topics were listed; one had been underlined.

"The Survival and Resurgence of White Supremacy as an American Religion."

The article was by Eunice Gibbs, Ph.D. Eight pages of it were included in the fax. Christine read the introductory paragraph:

> Groups holding to a philosophy of white supremacy continue to thrive and recruit new members throughout the United States with the beguilement of elitism, for to belong to such a group, one is told, is to claim one's true identity as an heir to divine appointment. Racist religions, whether their label be the Ku Klux Klan, Aryan Nation, or The Covenant, appeal not only to prejudice but to ego—a fact often overlooked in the analysis of these groups. For it is not only the hatred of blacks, Jews, and other "non-Aryans" that unifies them, but a conviction that they are a chosen people, set apart by God to establish order in a chaotic, morally bankrupt culture.

"The Covenant" had been underlined; "Alexandra Chappel" was written in the margin.

She reached for her tea and sipped thoughtfully.

Alexandra Chappel associated with a white supremacist group?

That wasn't exactly news; on the tape, Ferguson had alluded to her father's ties with the Klan. But Alex probably didn't know about that. So was this a warning? No doubt he'd learned Alexandra was supporting Greg and Citizens United. Had he done a background check on his favorite student's new patroness, found out about her father, and become alarmed?

That would explain things. Maybe.

She read on.

But the allure of elitism and an excuse to indulge racial prejudice are not the only attractions to supremacist cults. A third selling point holds tremendous appeal, and accounts for a resurgence in converts among otherwise moderate conservatives.

Christine shuddered. Not at the printed words, but at Alex's notations.

"Otherwise moderate conservatives" was underlined; "Greg?" was jotted next to it in the margin.

A few drops of tea spilled across the page before she noticed her hand was visibly shaking.

Stop it.

She said it aloud before turning back to the article.

Frustrated with their diminishing influence in American culture, some conservatives find themselves attracted to and aligned with racist groups because of the moral ideologies they set forth and their obvious zeal to promote them. All supremacist organizations denounce abortion, homosexuality, and drug abuse, for example, often staging impressive rallies against these perceived social ills without revealing their own true identity and agenda.

"Impressive rallies" was underlined; even if it hadn't been, she would have gotten the point.

Although many supremacist groups, such as neo-Nazis and the KKK, flaunt their racism, other groups conduct business more secretively. Presenting themselves as nothing more than reactionary zealots, they appeal to undiscerning mainstream supporters who applaud them without scrutinizing their backgrounds. Thus social conservatives, religious and nonreligious alike, are often duped into supporting supremacist organizations with their finances and participation.

The first page of the article ended there. Christine flipped to the second page, where the third paragraph, subtitled "Doctrine and Calling," was heavily underlined.

> A running theme in racist theology is a belief in the inferiority of all non-Aryans and in the divine commission of true Christians to reinstate Aryan rule.

"Oh, come on, Alex!" she groaned. Much as she disliked Alexandra and the Citizens United bunch, she couldn't imagine anyone taking such nonsense seriously—not even them. And, come to think of it, she had never heard a racial slur from any of them. Not even Greg.

She caught herself. Not *even* Greg? *Especially* not Greg! In all their years together he had never ... why, some of their friends, *good* friends, mind you, were ... Oh, it was too ridiculous to think about!

You ARE sick, Alex.

She read on.

> A lesser-known group with roots going back to the 1930s named The Covenant, for example, holds to theories of the inferiority of non-Aryans. The Covenant's teachings are linked back to the Old Testament book of Genesis, in which satanic beings are presumed to have had intercourse with humans. According to supremacists, Genesis 6:1-13 describes supernatural entities cohabiting with females, producing monstrous offspring and offending God. This monstrous offspring is described as a degenerate race setting itself at odds with the true seed of Adam and Abraham. Thus a battle between the seed of Abraham and the offspring of Satan, most brutally illustrated when the "demonic" Jews crucified God's Son, is thought to continue to this day. Some supremacists view the 1960s struggle for civil rights as a lost battle between "purists" and the degenerate race. Others consider the Jew the great enemy and fear America's infiltration by Jewish forces now classifies her as a "Zionist Occupied Government."

"The Covenant" was circled. "Today, in Orange County and elsewhere" was written in the margin with an arrow pointing to the entire paragraph.

"Give me a break," Christine sighed.

She flipped the page over and considered putting the sheets aside. Alex wasn't himself; hadn't Celeste said as much? He'd had a relapse, and his mind was affected. She pushed her chair back and got up for more tea. Enough of this, she decided; let's watch a movie. Let Greg deal with it, call Alex, whatever. This wasn't her business anyway—

Just then her gaze fell on the fourth sheet and stayed riveted.

Two black-and-white photos were shown with the caption "Chronicles of Hate" printed above them. It was the people in the photos—no, their eyes—that commanded her attention. Cold, intelligent, malicious eyes, staring into Christine. Challenging her.

The photos were clipped from a feature story in another magazine, which described them as family pictures of white supremacists from the South and the East Coast. Evidently a journalist had gained the trust of these families, then gotten them to speak for the record, even persuading them to pose in their natural environment.

One photo showed a middle-aged, muscular, black-haired man posing in front of an unfurled American flag. A table littered with pistols and boxes of ammunition stood to his left; above it, a stained-glass window suggested the picture was taken in a sanctuary. Dressed in khakis and a dark sweater, head erect and eyes blazing , his left hand rested on the shoulder of a boy no more than twelve who was obviously his son. His father's arrogance, or at least a good imitation of it, was mirrored in the young face, and his stocky build suggested a similarity to the older man's physique in the near future.

A Bible was tucked under the boy's left arm. A tiny smile played at the corners of his mouth. His right arm supported a rifle aimed directly at the camera. The caption beneath identified the subjects:

> Mr. Alexander Wooding, a self-proclaimed "purist," insists he wouldn't dream of raising a son who wasn't adept with firearms.

"Alexander Wooding" was underlined heavily; the boy's face was circled.

Christine double-checked the article's date.

October 25, 1959.

The boy would be in his mid-forties by now. Just like Tom Wooding, who was a burly gym manager with arms the size of tree trunks. Greg adored him; next to Rick Mosley, he'd become a favored companion.

When had Greg insisted on buying a gun?

Oh, hold it!

She'd actually risen from her seat in panic, then calmed herself.

Greg bought the gun because he was worried about Bennie coming over here, remember? It was only out of concern for you, dumbo, not some quirky Aryan nonsense.

Still, there was Alexander Wooding, in black and white, passing on his hatred to young Tom (possibly young Tom—she couldn't be sure since the article didn't name the boy). And here was Tom Wooding, in 1992, heading up a conservative (fascist?) organization. And Greg was rubbing elbows with him.

And speaking for them.

She scanned the next photo.

Another family scene, but the reporter clearly hadn't photographed this one. It was much older; Christine guessed it to have been taken in the mid-1930s judging by the clothes. Perhaps the subjects had given it to the journalist?

The husband was a cleric, dressed in traditional garb: black suit, black shirt, starched white collar. He was strikingly handsome, with high cheekbones and thick black curls framing jet-black eyes and a square jaw. Not a man to be trifled with; everything in his posture and expression showed it. He stood behind his wife, a petite woman seated on a high-backed chair. Trim and pretty, but sad-looking, somehow. Next to her stood a child.

A daughter.

Five, maybe six years old, at most. Strong and serene-looking, lovely and self-possessed. Christine knew before reading the caption:

Reverend Willard Manchester, pictured with wife Doria and daughter Alexandra in 1937, is one of the earliest members of The Covenant. He preaches a mixture of the Bible, sophisticated ideologies, and traditional Ku Klux Klan tactics.

The girl's face, like the boy's in the other photo, had been heavily circled by Alex. "Alexandra Chappel" was written in the margin; "sophisticated ideologies and traditional Ku Klux Klan tactics" was also underlined.

Today. In Orange County and elsewhere.

Christine read the rest of the article, which went into more detail on the goals, history, and allure of groups like The Covenant, then went back to the page titled "Doctrine and Calling," reread the beliefs of The Covenant, then turned back to the photos.

She stared long and hard at them, trying to organize her thoughts while fighting the flood of shock that made organized thinking so hard.

You have evidence, not proof.

She held the thought; it offered some comfort. *Proof* means you *know* someone's guilty; *evidence* points to the *possibility* or *likelihood* of guilt. The difference was subtle but vital; she kept it in mind while she tried to argue herself out of needless worry.

The *evidence* suggested both Alexandra and Tom Wooding were raised by lunatics. It was possible this was all a case of mistaken identity, but not likely—the age factors, Josh Ferguson's remarks about Alexandra's family, the names, and the physical similarities between the photos and the grown subjects were too much to dismiss as coincidence. But that didn't *prove* Alexandra and Tom were carrying the family tradition into the 1990s.

But impressive rallies, conservative social action, recruiting—what does that say about them?

That they're conservative activists, so what? Was it so absurd to believe they had both rejected their parents' racism without rejecting conservative beliefs? The two aren't the same!

But there was more to Alexandra Chappel than conservative fund-raising, and Alma Ferguson had known it. "She's a viper," she said, remember? And what are vipers, if not subtle, vicious, and lethal?

That didn't explain Greg's participation, though. Even if those two were as crazy—

Dangerous, Christine, not crazy. Stop writing this stuff off as though it's an eccentric habit!

Okay, as *dangerous* as their fathers, how could they possibly convert Greg to racist beliefs?

Who says they did? Read "Doctrine and Calling" again:

> *...they appeal to undiscerning mainstream supporters who applaud them without scrutinizing their backgrounds.*

"Without scrutinizing their backgrounds"—Greg could work right alongside them and have no idea? But wouldn't it have come out, sooner or later, as they got to know each other? Some slip of the tongue, maybe, or some racial insult?

Look again: "Others conduct business more secretly." Secrecy is their business; they're too smart to blow their cover with a slip of the tongue.

Unless, of course, they did plan to reveal themselves to Greg. Maybe later, once they had gained his trust, or made him so dependent on them he would *have* to go along with whatever their plans were.

Which was probably the plan all along: to align Greg with The Covenant unwittingly by making him head speaker for Citizens United, which was probably just a cover for The Covenant. Then, when the time was right, they would reveal who they *really* were. By then he'd be so wrapped up in them, not to mention dependent on them for a job, that he would have to go along with their plans.

The thought shot Christine out of her chair again with a frightened gasp. She stood in the center of the kitchen, took a few deep breaths, then went to the sink for a glass of water.

Then to the living room, water in hand, away from the crazy papers and the effect they seemed to have on her thoughts. *Focus,* she ordered herself, settling onto the couch. *And think about what you're proposing.*

Could Citizens United, a well-known, widely supported organization, get away with being a cover for a group as aberrant as The Covenant? Regular Christian people belonged to it, as well as professional types, teachers, lawyers. Good grief, she'd even seen some people from Berean Community Church at that first meeting. Did she really think they were Nazis or Klan members or whatever?

Impossible. A conspiracy of that size would have some leaks, some defectors. It just couldn't be pulled off, especially in an area as sophisticated as Orange County. And even if it could be pulled off, exactly what would their "plans" be? White and colored restrooms in Southern California? School segregation? Get real; they'd be laughed out of the state.

Alexandra and Tom might be racists—they'd been bred for the disease, certainly—but could even they, two intelligent adults with fairly normal lives, be so paranoid as to believe in a Zionist occupied government? Or so pathetic as to think their race was "chosen"? Could they have ever been successful, socially or in business, if they were that demented?

Again, impossible.

And there was something else—something more pertinent, something which blew the whole theory out of the water.

Greg. He was still Greg Bishop, her husband. And she knew him.

He was successful long before he met these people, so forget the nonsense about his becoming dependent on them. He was a licensed psychologist, a darned good one, and he could make a living on his own without any help from Alexandra Chappel. And, come to think of it, his very nature—independent, maverick, even—would rebel at the idea of becoming dependent on any person or group, legitimate or not. So what could they possibly offer him that would convince him to join a racist group, if indeed they were even involved in one themselves, which was still questionable?

Nothing. They had nothing to buy him with.

"There," she said, then drained her glass. "That's the end of it." She propped her feet on the small table in front of the couch, sighed, and let her body relax. Nothing to worry about; Greg's just gotten carried away.

Then why did Alex go to the trouble of collecting the information on The Covenant?

It was a tiny thought—unobtrusive at first, then irritating like a pebble in a shoe. You try to ignore the pebble, but finally have to deal with it. Christine blocked the thought, or tried to, but it persisted, demanding attention.

Why did Alex go to the trouble of—

"All right, all right." She sat up to consider the question, which to her dismay opened up a flood of others.

Alex wasn't crazy. Sick, but only physically. Something rational drove him to collect this data; something *real* had him so worried he insisted on Greg getting it immediately. And something frightening had him muttering "I'm so sorry" whenever he saw news clippings about Greg.

They promised me nobody would harm you or Christine in any way.

She had skimmed over Alex's message on the fax earlier, ignoring its implications. Now it stood out.

They.

Who are *they?*

The people he was warning Greg about, of course. He knew them. And if he knew them, he was qualified to say they were dangerous, which is what his warning amounted to, wasn't it?

Nothing is worth whatever you're getting from this.

Alex wasn't crazy. He was afraid.

And yes, intelligent people like Alexandra and Tom *could* be a part of something as evil as The Covenant. Weren't there professional, intelligent women and men who joined up with Jim Jones in the seventies? Smart people can do stupid things; rational people can hold monstrous beliefs.

Come to think of it, had she ever felt anything but uneasy in the presence of Alexandra Chappel? Their personalities clashed, yes, but it was more than that. From day one Christine had felt a chill whenever she was with the woman, and she hadn't felt much warmer toward Tom Wooding or Rick Mosley. They sensed it, too; they must have. Hadn't they always seemed to come between her and Greg, shutting her out, minimizing her influence with her husband so they could exert their own?

And what about their influence? "Ye shall know them by their fruits," Jesus said, and the fruit of Greg's relationship with Alexandra, Tom, and Rick spoke for itself: aloofness, extremism, phoniness, obsession.

She drew her legs off the table and tucked them under her, then wrapped her arms around herself. It was cold suddenly.

They had been waiting for him all along.

Christine shivered.

Out of the blue, Rick Mosley shows up at the gym wanting to work out with Greg. Coincidence? Mosley—the man who'd enjoyed beating up a homosexual—wasn't he just the sort to hang out with a bunch like The Covenant? And wasn't he the one who got Greg hooked up with Tom Wooding in the first place?

Then, the very night Citizens United voted Greg in, Alexandra was on the phone, congratulating him. And since that night she'd gradually moved into his life, pretending to be his patroness but becoming, in fact, his owner. No, the people of Citizens United couldn't all be racists; most of them probably didn't know what The Covenant was. But Alexandra and Tom did; she was sure of it. And someday, somehow, they were grooming Greg to join them.

"Greg?" she asked aloud. "Bigoted? Hateful?"

Racially bigoted, no. But hateful? Definitely, toward one group, anyway. Alexandra had given him a vent for his bitterness toward gays; Citizens United, with the best of intentions, had legitimized it.

And, for all his strong points, he was also vulnerable to acclaim. He had power and popularity—a tough combination for any man to handle. Alexandra had given that to him as well; for that, he was indebted to her.

But indebted enough to join her cult? Surely, once Christine showed him this material, he would end their association immediately, even take public action against these people.

Wouldn't he?

That she even had to ask was perhaps the most terrifying thought she'd had so far.

Christine huddled on the couch in the darkened living room for the rest of the evening, waiting for her husband to come home.

THIRTY-EIGHT

Yelsom had a new toy.

It was ivory, shaped in a slight curve, with a tiny button near the top, where the forefinger rested.

Click!

The six-inch, double-edged blade snapped to attention out of the innocent-looking handle. It caught the light brilliantly.

Click! Click!

He lay on the bed, flicking it open again and again, transfixed.

Heck of a way to spend a Friday evening, he thought, but he was content. The bars had become a bore. Since the incident at The Shaft he'd felt like a pariah when he went out; bartenders were slow to serve him, managers snubbed him, and formerly friendly customers ignored him. It was unfair overkill, of course; he wasn't the first patron to make a drunken scene in a gay bar. But the general resentment the community felt toward him and BRAVO had festered for months, and his behavior that night gave them an excuse to express it.

But who needed them, anyway? His own company was fine for now; drinking alone didn't bother him a bit, and there was still BRAVO's next phase to think about. He had already called Jeremy and ordered him to round the kids up for a 5:00 P.M. meeting on Monday at the old theater basement. Jeremy (wimp that he was!) begged off attending with some nonsense about schoolwork, but Yelsom didn't want him there anyway. Loyal as the kid was, he doubted Jeremy had the stomach for phase three.

Phase three. Good stuff. And none of the victims would press charges, so no one in BRAVO had to worry about being arrested.

Click!

Pretty toy.

He rolled across the bed to grab the half-empty beer can he'd been nursing, then snagged a pack of cigarettes and lit up when the phone rang.

East Coast. He'd been expecting the call.

"Yeah, everything's set," he muttered.

He listened, then frowned.

"No, no! Bring all of them. We need the East Coast people." He took a puff and flicked the ashes. "Well, the core group, anyway. The committed ones. These people out here are getting soft. They need to mix with some real fighters."

He sipped some beer, then laughed.

"Right, and there's also Greg Bishop to deal with. Soon? I'd say so." Pause. "Definitely, for sure."

He nodded and smiled.

"Nice! Okay, Monday evening at 10:00. Got the address?"

He lay back onto the bed, discarded the beer and cigarette, and picked up the switchblade with his left hand while holding the phone in his right.

"Yeah, but that's not *his* address. Oh, didn't I tell you? We should start where the *money* is. And the influence. It isn't really with him; it's with her. She's the power behind the scenes."

He held the handle up to the light.

"Alexandra Chappel."

Click!

Christine jumped off the couch and ran to the entryway the moment she heard Greg's key in the lock; he nearly collided with her coming through the door.

"Hey!" He backed up, then stepped forward to kiss her forehead—a mechanical action he had adopted in lieu of the longer embraces he used to give her.

"Celeste Bolton called."

Greg froze guiltily, a reflex reaction to having Celeste on his mind so many months ago.

"Who is she?"

Neither of them had moved from the doorway. "A college friend," Greg said as casually as he could manage. The way Christine was searching his face made him increasingly uncomfortable. "She works for Alex now; I'm sure I've mentioned her to you before."

She shook her head. "And who is she to *you?*"

Greg sighed, stepped around Christine into the living room, and started to peel his jacket off. "Who *was* she to me, you mean.

We went together in school. She dumped me." He threw the jacket onto the couch and flopped down next to it. "We hadn't spoken in years, then out of the blue I find she's working for Alex. We talked the day I got the tape, remember?"

Christine, still in the doorway, pivoted to keep facing him as he spoke. "And?" she asked.

"And?"

"She almost sounded guilty calling here. At first, anyway. And as soon as I said her name you acted like you'd been caught red-handed."

"Nothing to catch."

"Did you have an affair with her?"

She may as well have slapped him; his astonishment was genuine, and she knew it. "Unbelievable, Christine! Where did that come from?"

She folded her arms and threw her head back, close to tears. "Just answer the question! I've had too many surprises lately, so just be straight with me."

This was the last response Greg expected when he came through the door. "I've never had an affair with anyone and you know that," he said firmly. "But," he sighed, "if you want a straight answer, I did have her on my mind quite a bit last year, and over the phone we got flirtatious a couple of times. I nipped it in the bud, and I never saw any reason to talk about it. I wish you hadn't asked, but there's your answer. Satisfied?"

"Fine." The strained expression she'd greeted him with barely changed as she crossed the living room, snapped on the lamp beside the couch, then went into the kitchen.

"So is that what you're upset about?" he called after her.

She returned with a handful of papers. "I wish." She slapped the fax sheets down on the coffee table in front of Greg, then sat on the couch next to him. "This is what Celeste called about. She faxed this over."

The cover sheet was on top. Greg recognized Alex's handwriting immediately, read his message, and scowled.

"What's this supposed to mean?"

"Alex thinks you're in trouble. So do I."

"Trouble?"

"Just read it. All of it. I'll wait till you're finished."

He began reading, slowly at first, then scanned the papers faster, his breathing keeping pace. Christine measured the effect the pages had on him by the steady widening of his eyes. When he got to the photographs, he put them on the coffee table, then hunched over with his chin in his hands, staring helplessly at the future leaders of Citizens United.

"Alex had Celeste look these up," Christine finally said. "He had another heart attack. Did you know that?"

His head jerked up. "Alex? No! When?"

"Last October. She said it might have had something to do with the fire at the church. He's going away for a while, but he wanted Celeste to get this stuff to you before he went."

Christine couldn't remember when she had last seen Greg so vulnerable. His shock was turning to dread, and something in his frightened expression brought out a tenderness she hadn't felt for some time.

"Honey?" she began gently. "He saves news clippings about you. Celeste says he's gotten obsessive about what you've been doing lately. Something is so wrong here, with you, Alexandra, even with us. He's warning you that you're being used. So are a lot of other people in Citizens United, probably."

Greg recovered a bit of composure. "But what's to warn? Alexandra and Tom aren't necessarily like their fathers." He flicked the pages. "In fact, these might not even be their fathers."

"Don't count on it. Do you know Alexandra's maiden name?"

"Now, how would I know that?"

"Dollars to doughnuts it's Manchester. It all adds up. Look at the dates."

"Even so," Greg mused, "it doesn't mean *they're* into all this stuff. They've never talked about race or taking over the world or anything like that."

"If they had, would you ever have joined them?"

"Of course not!"

"There you go. They keep it under wraps."

"But why? What would they want with me, anyway, or with the Citizens United group?" Greg sounded half-convinced Christine was right and half-incredulous, much as she'd been earlier. She appealed to the first half.

"I've thought it all out." She spoke rapidly to keep him from interrupting. "Restore the kingdom, that's their agenda. No, don't laugh! Just because we think it's ridiculous doesn't mean they aren't committed to it. They get support from conservatives, just like the article says. People like you who don't know who they really are. And they're using you; you give them a legitimate public front. Look at how many people love you now! They raised you up, you put Citizens United on the map, and The Covenant reaps the benefits!"

"What benefits?"

"Who knows? Finances, maybe. Maybe the funds you bring in are funneled into The Covenant. Or maybe they actually think you can help them take over the world. I don't know. Who can figure out what these crazy people are plotting?"

Greg gave a quick laugh. "Weak argument, counselor. Show me specifically why they would go to the trouble of using me that way and maybe I'll buy it. But you're wrong about who did what for whom. *They* put *me* on the map, not vice versa. And they've never even hinted that they wanted anything more out of me than to fight the gay agenda. No kingdom restoring, no cross-burning, nothing."

"Not yet, anyway," she persisted. "Read Alex's note. He says you've been harmed already, and to get out now before any worse damage is done."

"You know I wouldn't let that happen to us."

"*Us?*" Christine leapt off the couch and glared at him. "What's *us?* There hasn't been an *us* since I don't know when!"

"Christine—"

"And there never will be until you break away from them. If you really care about us, think! Is there any future in what you're doing? Even if there is no Covenant, how long do you think you can make a living this way?"

"Alexandra says in five years she'll have made me one of the top conservative speakers in America."

Now it was Christine's turn to feel slapped. She stared at him, sputtering until she found her voice.

"*What did you say? Five more years of this? That's what you're planning?*"

She had never, in seven years of their marriage, screamed at her husband so loudly. The blast threw him back into the couch.

"I should have said something," he offered weakly. "The time just didn't seem right."

The look on her face! Greg fished for anything to say that would change it.

"Look, you're shook up over some crazy stuff Alex sent you, and it shakes me up, too, but I don't really think—"

"Prove it." Her voice turned steely and firm.

"Huh?"

"Prove it's crazy. Call Alex. Now."

He hesitated. "Well, it's kind of late to be calling."

"It's important; he'll understand."

"Not *that* important."

"Then why did he send it?"

"I don't know!"

"Then find out. Call him."

"He's overprotective, you know. Moody, too. He might have latched onto this stuff and just drawn some conclusions."

"Ask him."

"We'll all feel stupid when this is over, Christine."

"There's the phone."

She hadn't budged from her spot next to the couch, where she stood frozen with her hand pointing toward the kitchen phone. Greg, knowing she wasn't about to let him off the hook, plucked the phone off the wall unit and dialed.

"This is Alex," the recorded message said. "I'll be out of town for a few weeks, but leave your name and number and I'll call you as soon as I'm back."

Greg hung up without leaving a message. "He's already gone."

Undeterred, Christine threw out a new challenge.

"Then try Alexandra. Tell her what Alex sent you and see what she has to say."

Refusing would have been an admission, Greg knew, so he dialed Alexandra's number, keeping his eyes on Christine. She stood in the living room and watched, arms folded, expectant.

"Alexandra? It's Greg. Look, I'm sorry to call so late. Recently I got a hold of some intriguing information sent to me by a fellow psychologist, Alex Crawford. I believe it may have to do with Citizens United, and I was wondering—"

Christine's expression caught Greg's eye, alerting him to rethink his choice of words.

"—*Christine* and I, in fact, were wondering if you could just answer a couple of questions."

Christine could see he was uncomfortable questioning Alexandra about anything.

"Okay, just a couple of things. First, was your maiden name Manchester?"

Long pause; either Alexandra was taking a long time to answer, Christine figured, or she was giving a long answer. Greg glanced at her and nodded, furrowing his eyebrows.

"Well, the information Alex sent me suggested it was. In fact, he sent me a detailed description of a group called The Covenant, and said you were a member of it. Do you know of any such group?"

Another long pause. Greg looked more and more worried.

"Well," he finally said, "that would be fine, if you don't want to talk about it over the phone." Christine started to protest but he held his hand up to stop her. "Monday at your house, then. Oh, about eight, I guess. Does that sound okay? I'll see you then."

He hung up, stunned. Christine moved toward him.

"Well?"

"She couldn't give me a straight answer. She wants to explain everything over a late dinner on Monday."

"That's as good as admitting it's all true."

Greg stepped back to the couch and dropped himself onto it. The photos sat on the table in front of him. Christine watched him silently.

"What was that you said about us?" he asked dully. "There is no 'us' anymore?"

"Not really."

"Hmm. Figures."

"Why?"

He looked at the photos again. "Because I don't even know if there's a me anymore."

THIRTY-NINE

Calvin unlocked the door to apartment 3 on Monday evening at 6:45, while it was still light. It was a twenty-minute drive from his home to Yelsom's Santa Ana dwelling, but it had taken months to get here.

Tonight's meeting provided the first real opportunity since he'd had the keys made. Yelsom insisted he attend the prior meetings; no excuse would have been accepted. But somehow tonight was different. The man barely argued when Calvin said he had finals to study for. "Be sure you get everyone else rounded up" was his only response, which surprised Calvin. He knew the meeting had to be fairly important; Yelsom had remarked that tonight's gathering was "the beginning of the end." Calvin agreed, but silently, and for different reasons.

Tonight he would finally break in, seize the tape (if Yelsom had it, which was likely but not guaranteed), and Jeremy would disappear forever, taking the evidence with him. To Greg, or the police, or someone.

He moved quickly. The same key opened the deadbolt and doorknob. He knew the occupant would already be on his way to the theater in Newport Beach where BRAVO met, but his story ("Yelsom! Thought I'd drop by so we could drive to the meeting together") was ready in case the man was still here and saw Calvin lurking around his building.

He entered quickly and decided not to turn on any lights. Plenty of sunlight was available; he worried about suspicious neighbors who might have seen Yelsom leave and wonder what Calvin was doing there.

The place was tiny and sparsely furnished: a small living room with a brown love seat, a wooden box for a coffee table, two cheap lamps on even cheaper end tables, a decent sound system, and a folding chair. The kitchen stood to the right; a bedroom tinier than the living area was to the left. Half-filled ashtrays and beer cans were the only decorations. No plants, pictures, or knickknacks to be found. With nothing even hinting at the personality of whoever lived there, the place had all the charm of a fluorescent light.

Calvin started with the sound system, sifting through tapes and CDs. No videos. An old Rolling Stones cassette sat in the player; nothing else seemed to have been used for a while.

The kitchen took less than a minute to poke around in; as expected, nothing of interest was there. (Though Yelsom's culinary tastes might have been worth noting—beer, beef jerky, and cheese filled the refrigerator.)

The bedroom had more to offer. An open book sat next to the pillow on the unmade bed, with a yellow legal pad next to it. Calvin picked up both, looking first at the book.

The Night of the Broken Glass.

He skimmed the table of contents: an overview of the darkest events in modern history. *Typical of Yelsom to enjoy reading stuff like this,* he thought, tossing it back on the bed. Then he turned to the yellow pad.

Notes from the book, no doubt. Phrases like "systematic coercion" and "politics of fear" were jotted down. Names, dates, and times were listed, too. The first one caught his eye.

Chappel, 5/12, 10:00.

Tonight. The beginning of the end.

Be sure you get everyone else rounded up.

Keep moving.

A television stood on a tiny metal stand at the foot of the double bed; on top of it was a VCR. Videotapes sat in a box under the stand. Calvin dug in.

Classic movies, war stories, horror films (lots of those), and documentaries on World War II. And one noncommercial tape at the bottom.

Eureka.

He pushed it into the player, sat at the foot of Yelsom's bed, and watched.

The introduction from Ferguson to Greg unnerved him. Poor Bishop; no wonder this had become an obsession to him. Then came the sequence of interviews—informative, but hardly worth all this trouble.

Then another subject was introduced. A strange one, a twist. Then another interview, conducted more secretly, with the last person Calvin expected to see on this tape.

Saying the last thing he had ever expected to hear.

"No," he moaned when it finished. "No way."

He rewound the tape to the beginning of the last interview, watched it again, then checked his watch.

7:30.

He grabbed the phone next to Yelsom's bed while he pulled out his wallet out to find Greg Bishop's business card. He looked up the number on the card and dialed. Christine answered.

"It's Calvin, Christine. Emergency. Let me talk to Greg."

"Calvin? My gosh, how are you—hey, emergency? What kind?"

"I need Greg. I've got the tape. The Ferguson tape. Where's Greg?"

"On the freeway, I guess. He's on his way to Alexandra Chappel's house in Corona del Mar."

"*No!*"

"Calvin, what's the matter?"

"Does he still carry a pager?"

"Yes, but—"

"Beep him. Now! Tell him *not* to go to Alexandra's! Greg doesn't know what he's walking into!"

"Then let me know so I can tell him!"

"No time! I'll come by with the tape. You'll see. Just get Greg, now! Tell him to come home. I'll be right over."

He slammed the phone down, hit the eject button on the VCR, yanked the tape out, grabbed the box it came in, and headed for the door. It would take about fifteen minutes to get to the Bishops' home in Garden Grove, where they could sort out the best way to handle this. Just the three of them.

Wait.

He stopped in the doorway, remembering. There were other people involved, people he cared about. They were sitting in the meeting right now, thinking they were going to do one thing, when in fact they were—

Roxanne and Lisa deserved to know. He would have to tell them now, and in so doing he would also have to tell them about himself. It was time.

He was out of the apartment and screeching through the parking lot in less than a minute.

At 7:35 Greg slowed to a near stop on the Newport freeway at the Seventeenth Street off-ramp. At first only the traffic in the right lane had come to a halt. But then the second lane became clogged, then the third, and now even the carpool lane was at a standstill.

He peered through the windshield, trying to see past the cars lined up in front of him, but the stopped traffic stretched out for miles ahead. Whatever caused it couldn't be seen. An accident, probably; slow traffic on this freeway after 7:00 was unusual.

He'd be late for dinner, but that didn't bother him. It was answers, not food, that he was anxious to get. He hit the radio knob; oldies filled the car.

Greg had been unsettled since Friday night, scared of being duped into some bizarre scheme, but equally afraid to give up the speaking and publicity he had come to enjoy. But no matter; if what Christine suspected was true, he and Alexandra were finished. He'd return to work, put more effort into his marriage, and try living normally again. If Christine was wrong, no harm was done. Alex's fax warranted some kind of explanation, anyway, and there was nothing wrong in asking Alexandra to furnish one. He was eager to hear what she would have to say.

But more than anything else, he was tired and frazzled. Too many emotional upheavals, too many unknowns, too much water (and pain) under the bridge. He looked forward to sleeping tonight; he'd done little else all weekend.

Greg's thoughts drifted to the television show scheduled for next week. Melanie Stone. He yawned; televised interviews were already losing their glamour. Besides, he was slightly miffed that Yelsom (Bennie) had already been interviewed by Melanie.

The thought of Bennie made him glance toward the bottom of his seat, where he kept the revolver.

Ever since he had purchased it last spring, the Magnum .357 had been kept at the house, where it belonged, and which was the only place he was licensed to have it. But as his speaking engagements drew more protests, both Tom Wooding and Rick Mosley had persuaded him to keep it under his car seat.

"They're more likely to attack you in your car than they are to come to your home," Wooding had reasoned. Greg consented— not because he thought he needed a pistol under his car seat, but because it felt so darned fun, and dangerous, to have it there.

The Supremes were on. He cranked up the volume as his car edged its way, at less than five miles per hour, along the 55 freeway toward Corona del Mar.

His pager, clipped onto his belt, was silent. If he had remembered to turn it on, it would be beeping now, letting him know that his wife was frantically trying to reach him.

FORTY

Calvin pulled onto Calybourne, one of the narrow one-way streets near the shore at Newport Beach, and looked for a space. The Blackwood Theater had a parking lot, but Calvin knew it was filled to capacity most nights. Not by theatergoers, since the place had closed down years ago, but by whoever couldn't find any other place to park. And, of course, by BRAVO members.

A gay man sympathetic to their cause owned the building and had let them use its basement for meetings since early 1990. In its heyday the theater had been a stomping ground for foreign and cult film lovers. Movies that other theaters refused to show were regular fare at the Blackwood, and the *Rocky Horror Picture Show* was a weekly event, shown at midnight every Saturday from 1978 to the last weekend the theater did business.

Calvin circled the block three times before finding a space. He maneuvered in, parked, got out, then remembered the tape. It was sitting on the passenger seat; he didn't feel comfortable leaving it there. He stuffed it down the front of his shirt, wrapped his denim jacket closer around him, then jogged the remaining two blocks to the meeting.

He wasn't quite up to the task; he staggered up to the back door of the Blackwood and pulled it open, breathless and panting.

He went down the metal stairs, entered the long hall leading to the main basement area, and cautiously walked up to the closed double doors.

Yelsom's voice could be heard issuing final instructions and directions. Even through the doors Calvin could sense the tension inside. There was no shouting or celebrating; the fun had gone out of these meetings months ago.

Suddenly the doors were thrown open, and Calvin had to jump back out of the way. BRAVO members—not too many, these days—made their way past him quickly, nervously. A few said a brief hello; nobody stopped to chat. They had other things on their minds.

Lisa and Roxanne were among the last to emerge; Yelsom was far enough behind them not to see Calvin (he hoped) when he grabbed Roxanne's arm, put a finger to his lips, and pulled her aside.

"This way," he hissed, guiding her away from the metal stairs and further into the building, where a carpeted stairway with a rope thrown across it led to the theater's balcony. "We've got to talk alone."

Lisa and Roxanne, startled but willing to trust Jeremy, followed him up two flights of stairs into the dark, musty, and heavily draped balcony area. Calvin picked a seat in the first row and hunched into it, motioning them to do the same.

"What are you *doing?*" Roxanne whispered. She and Lisa regarded him with consternation.

"Please listen. Please!" His urgency scared them into cooperating. "What was the meeting about tonight?"

The girls looked at each other, then Lisa spoke. "It's gotten worse. Yelsom's gone over the edge this time, so we're quitting. We just decided that before you came in. It doesn't matter what he thinks anymore; we're out."

"Why?"

"He's meeting everyone over at Alexandra Chappel's house tonight. You know who Chappel is?"

He nodded.

"We're all supposed to be there at ten in front of her place. He's going there alone, first, to break in and restrain her, maybe even beat her up. Then we're all supposed to go in with him and tear her house apart."

"*Why?*"

"He says it's the third phase," Roxanne said, and the loudness of her voice cut the air. They all winced. "And," she whispered, "he's getting the inspiration for it from Nazi Germany."

"Uh-huh," Calvin said thoughtfully.

"You don't look surprised."

"Nothing surprises me these days."

"He says some gay groups are using Nazi tactics for inspiration. Isn't that sick? And he's using this one thing they did as a model in an effort to scare the homophobes."

"*The Night of the Broken Glass?*"

That visibly shocked them. "Has he told you about this already?" Lisa asked.

"In a way. It's the night the Nazis—well, not the Nazis, but their collaborators—marched through Berlin and broke into Jewish shops and homes, trashed them, and attacked whoever was in them. Right?"

"Right!" Roxanne said, again too loudly. Calvin cautioned her with a finger to his lips. "He's brought it up before," she continued more quietly, "but I didn't think he would actually want to do it! He says this is the final step in silencing the church. We've gone to their meeting places, he says, but now we have to follow them home."

"Incredible."

"And this is just the beginning. He has a long list of people we're supposed to do this to! He's backing down on his word, Jeremy. That's why we're leaving. Remember when he promised no one would get hurt?"

"Sure."

"We don't trust him."

Calvin took both of their hands and leaned closer. "With good reason. There is more to this than meets the eye. I need to show you something. Now. Tonight. Will you come with me?"

"Where?"

"To Greg Bishop's home." He handed Lisa a card with Greg's address on it. "Meet me there. We'll leave now."

"Greg Bishop?" Roxanne yelled. "Why would I want to go to his home?"

"And why would you, Jeremy?" Lisa asked suspiciously.

"Because he's—"

Roxanne cut him off. "Jeremy! He's the one who says all those horrible things about us and you're going to his home? And you want us to come?"

Lisa stared closely at him. "Why?" she repeated softly.

"Because he's a friend."

Roxanne's mouth dropped open. "Someone who calls us demonic perverts is a friend of yours?"

"I've called him on that stuff, Roxanne."

"I heard you do it," Lisa responded slowly.

"What?" Roxanne asked her. "When?"

"On the radio," she said, then turned to Calvin. "Right, Calvin? Calvin Blanchard, our favorite Christian radio talk show host?"

All three sat in silence, looking at each other, looking for words.

"I've got so much to tell you," Calvin finally said. "Hate me, scream at me, but first let me show you what I've found."

He opened his jacket and pulled the tape from under his shirt. "You stole this from Bishop's office, remember?" he whispered. "I've just seen it. You need to see what's on it, too. Then you decide whether or not you ever want to speak to me again."

"I'm not sure I want to speak to you now!" Roxanne insisted.

"See the tape first!" he almost yelled. "I was just in his apartment and saw the whole thing. You've got to believe me."

"Who wouldn't believe a nice guy like you, Junior?"

Yelsom's voice settled on them like ice water.

"School out early tonight?"

He was standing just out of their view, midway down the stairs, audible but not visible.

"Yeah," Calvin said weakly.

"Good. I need you." They heard him take a few more steps; the girls froze while Calvin considered bolting.

Please, he mouthed, handing them the tape. Roxanne didn't move; they heard Yelsom coming closer.

"Jeremy? Let's go."

Lisa quietly took the video and dropped it into her purse just as Yelsom appeared on the landing. "Private conference?"

"Rehearsal for Romeo and Juliet," Lisa returned, getting out of her seat and heading past him.

"Ah!" Yelsom smiled. "And who's playing Juliet?"

The girls walked out without answering.

"Come on, Jeremy. Let's go to The Shaft."

Calvin got up uncertainly. "I thought The Shaft was off-limits to you."

"Not anymore. Another couple of guys got jumped in the alley behind the bar. The manager wants to meet with us and talk about BRAVO volunteering some security, you know? I like the idea." He pulled Calvin out of his seat. "It'll help mend fences between us and the community."

"But what about going to Alexandra Chappel's house?"

"The Shaft will take only a minute."

It didn't make a bit of sense, but Calvin complied, walking down the stairs ahead of Yelsom. As soon as they got to The

Shaft, he would head for the exit. His days as BRAVO's secretary were over.

By now the theater was empty. They locked the back door and walked into the parking lot.

"Over here," Yelsom ordered, gesturing toward a brown Ford Bronco. To Calvin's surprise, he opened the passenger door for him.

"Didn't take me for a gentleman, did you, Jeremy?"

Calvin got in. Yelsom hit the door lock switch.

Lisa knew the Garden Grove area fairly well, but she still made a wrong turn on Harbor Boulevard, landing them a few miles south of the Bishops' home. After searching the area and finally checking with a gas station attendant, they found the street and the number. They parked directly across from the house.

"Wait."

Roxanne, seated on the passenger side, put her hand out to stop Lisa from opening her door.

"Do we really want to do this?"

Lisa considered. "Yeah," she nodded, taking the tape from her purse. "If for no other reason than *this*."

They walked across the street, up the Bishops' driveway, then stood together nervously on the porch and rang the door-bell.

A beautiful brunette with wide, friendly eyes answered.

"Is Dr. Bishop in?" Roxanne asked.

"No. He's out for the evening. Can I help you?"

They hesitated; Lisa jumped in.

"I'm Lisa, this is Roxanne."

"I'm Christine Bishop."

"We know. We're from BRAVO."

FORTY-ONE

Look, we feel as weird about this as you do!"

Christine had backed into the doorway wall, wide-eyed and tense. Lisa understood; Roxanne was less gentle. "We didn't come here out of the blue, you know! A friend of yours sent us."

"Calvin Blanchard," Lisa added.

"Calvin?" Christine thought a moment, then remembered Calvin had been an infiltrator at BRAVO. It would make sense for him to know these women, but why would he invite them over here?

"He was going to join us, but he got sidetracked by Yelsom."

"So is he still coming over?" Christine asked.

"We hope so. He gave us a videotape we stole from your husband's office," Lisa went on. She noticed Christine's reaction. "Yeah, that was us. Yelsom wanted it. He's the head of BRAVO. Anyway, Calvin retrieved it from him and he watched it, I guess. We've never seen it, but he's anxious for us to. And for your husband to, as well."

They could tell Christine was dubious; Lisa could hardly blame her.

"Calvin has already told us who he really is. I guess he's been doing some kind of undercover work—but he's still our friend."

"Maybe," Roxanne added.

"Please, can we come in?"

Christine opened the door wider.

"The videoplayer is in here," she said, leading the way.

The three of them stepped into the living room.

Parking spaces around The Shaft were scant, so Yelsom had to park the Bronco three blocks away. Calvin thought of sprinting off as soon as the car stopped, but reconsidered. If Yelsom meant him any harm, he would have driven to some remote spot. Instead, here they were in the middle of a main street. Better to find out what this guy was up to. He had come this far; he might as well finish the job.

They walked the three blocks in silence.

Just as they approached the last block Yelsom grabbed Calvin's arm and jerked him to the left.

"Back entrance. Bob doesn't want us discussing this in front of the patrons, so he'll meet us in the back."

Yelsom's arm was a vise. Calvin wasn't used to making quick decisions, and was clueless when it came to protecting himself physically. Before he could answer, Yelsom had propelled him toward the alley behind The Shaft.

Where so many gay men had been found beaten.

He couldn't think. Yelsom's grip tightened. It was already dark—by 8:45, even in summer, the streets needed lighting—but in the alley it went from dark to black.

"The door is over there," Calvin heard Yelsom say. His left arm was still in the man's clutch. "Go ahead."

Yelsom suddenly released him. To his right, some twenty yards ahead, light spilled under a door and rock music could be heard. Calvin walked toward it slowly and (he hoped) casually.

He glanced to his left. No Yelsom.

"Yelsom?"

No answer. He walked more quickly. Just a few yards more.

"Junior."

It came from Calvin's right, a few steps ahead of him.

"Oh, Junior?"

That came from behind him. He froze.

Something stirred to his left; he couldn't see a thing.

"Pssst."

Directly in front of him.

"Seen any good movies lately?"

"Yelsom?"

Click!

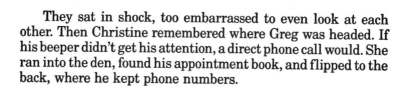

They sat in shock, too embarrassed to even look at each other. Then Christine remembered where Greg was headed. If his beeper didn't get his attention, a direct phone call would. She ran into the den, found his appointment book, and flipped to the back, where he kept phone numbers.

Back in the kitchen she dialed Alexandra's number. Lisa and Roxanne stayed in the living room, silent. The tape had devastated all of them.

Christine got a busy signal. She dialed again; still busy. She walked back into the living room to join her guests.

"I'll never get over this," Lisa said, on the verge of tears. "Never."

Roxanne looked at Christine. "I don't expect you to believe this, but all along we thought we were doing the right thing. We couldn't have known."

"Never!" Lisa added.

Christine seated herself on the couch facing them. "How could you have known? How could any of us, for that matter?" She felt a wave of nausea. "I think I might be sick." She headed for the kitchen.

"You can't get through to Chappel?" Roxanne called after her.

"Line's busy." Christine found some bicarbonate in the cupboard by the kitchen table. "I'll keep trying, though, if I have to get an operator to cut in!" She poured the powder into a glass, mixed in some water, and stirred. Just then her eyes fell on the discarded letter she'd begun writing to her mother on Friday.

She returned to the living room. "Boy, now is a time I'd sure like my mother here."

Roxanne, who had been talking softly to Lisa, looked up. "What's that?"

"I was just noticing a letter I'd been writing to my mother. I could use her presence right now."

Lisa looked at her, tears starting to fill her eyes. "I write to my mother all the time. It helps."

Roxanne looked uncomfortable. Christine said nothing.

"She's such a comfort. So accepting, you know?"

"Yeah, that's nice to have," Christine offered, a little confused by Lisa's reaction to the subject of letter-writing.

"Whenever I'm down, I just sit at the table...and I...I write down—"

She broke into sobs. Christine looked at Roxanne.

"Her mother won't speak to her. Hasn't spoken to her for years," Roxanne explained.

"What on earth—"

"When Lisa told her mother she was lesbian, her mother said she'd rather have a dead daughter than a perverted one. She doesn't even know where Lisa is anymore. But Lisa's therapist has her write to a sort of pretend 'good mother.' It's supposed to have a healing effect."

Lisa looked up at Christine. "Sometimes," she whispered through tears, "I feel like that's all I've got."

Christine forgot everything else for the moment but the pain written on the young woman's face. She stood up, hesitated, then knelt down in front of the couch where Lisa sat, and gathered her up in her arms. Lisa wept loud, noisy wails, clutching Christine.

Roxanne watched, uncertain and afraid.

After nearly an hour of stop-and-go traffic, Greg had finally inched past the source of the freeway congestion: a five-car pileup in Santa Ana just off the MacArthur Boulevard off ramp. By the time he pulled up to Aqua Marine Drive it was almost nine o'clock—an hour later than he was expected. Steeling himself for a lecture, he parked in front of Alexandra's two-story Spanish-style home and walked up the driveway.

Wait, he said to himself, slowing his pace. What was wrong with this picture?

Too dark, that's what. Not a single light in or around the house was on. Alexandra expected him; lights should have shone through her huge picture windows or from the bedroom upstairs. Not even the porch light was on.

He jogged up the walk to the door and started to knock, then noticed it was open a crack.

"Alexandra?"

No response; just a dark living room yawning in front of him.

He stepped in and felt glass crunch under his left shoe. Opening the door wider, some light from the street illuminated the living room, where glasses had been shattered, furniture overturned, and a telephone receiver, yanked off the hook, sat beeping.

BRAVO was scrawled on the wall.

"Alexandra, it's Greg!" he yelled.

He heard a scurrying sound upstairs and a voice saying, "Sssh! It's him."

He leapt backward, out the door, then stood on the walkway. *Think quick. Consider.*

Consider what? Was there anything else to do but go in and face it?

He jogged back to the car and groped under the seat for his revolver. He gripped the gun, walked as quietly as he could back to the house, and entered.

More sound from upstairs. A man. Two men? Two, at least. Whispering.

Feet shuffled above Greg's head. He turned left at the stairway. A portrait of Alexandra Chappel and her late husband greeted him.

He froze again and listened. Nothing.

"Alexandra?"

Two footsteps answered.

"I'm coming up, whoever you are. I'm armed. I don't want anyone hurt, but I don't have any reservations about using this baby." He took the steps as he spoke; the staircase wound up and to the right. "We can talk—we can hash things out—without getting crazy, okay?"

After a few more steps, Greg called out, "I'm almost at the top."

"Gregory."

Alexandra's voice was weak; frightened.

"Alexandra? Are you all right?"

"Yes, yes. Please drop the gun. No trouble, please. Everything's going to be all right."

He stepped toward her bedroom. "Alexandra!" He rounded the corner and strode through her doorway. "Are you—hey!"

Five men stood in a semicircle around Alexandra Chappel, who was seated, head bowed, in a high-back chair. She was dressed in a blue pantsuit with a scarf arranged around her neck.

Ropes were wrapped around her waist, binding her to the chair. Her hands were tied behind her back. She looked up at Greg.

"Gregory, be careful."

Her face was bruised; welts were rising on her left cheek and forehead, and a pencil-thin line of blood ran from one of her nostrils onto her scarf.

"Freeze, all of you! Now!"

Greg raised the gun in his right arm and supported it with his left.

"Put your hands on your heads. Do it!"

He hadn't taken the time in the semidarkness to identify the men, all of whom now lifted their hands obediently. All but one.

"Greg?" Yelsom said, dressed in his traditional outfit.

"Shut up, Bennie! Or Yelsom, or whatever you call yourself. Hands on your head. Now!"

He still didn't watch the others, except to see that they were complying. His eyes were fixed on Yelsom.

"Okay, okay, but first, just let me—"

"I swear, Bennie, I'll use this if you don't put your hands on your head now!"

Greg was screaming, hysterical, furious.

"Careful, Gregory, *please!*" Alexandra pleaded.

"Put them on your head, Bennie!" Greg's right arm trembled violently; the gun wavered. "Do it! Now! *Now!*"

Yelsom's hands went to his head and rested on snow-white hair. "Okay, okay, they're up. Now allow me—"

"I said freeze!"

"—just one more thing." And with that, Yelsom yanked his hair off. And Greg, so shocked he dropped the gun, realized that Yelsom had looked so familiar because he was, indeed, an old friend.

Another old friend.

"Take it easy, Greg," Rick Mosley said, holding his blond wig in his left hand. "Everything's gonna be all right."

FORTY-TWO

*Y*ou need a drink, Greg."

Somehow they'd gotten into the living room.

Rick Mosley had scooped the gun off the bedroom carpet while Greg, shocked into a near stupor, stood motionless. Rick and Tom Wooding (whom Greg hadn't recognized at first) then guided Greg by his shoulders down the stairs and into the living room, seating him in one of the few undamaged chairs. The others followed, and now Alexandra, untied and definitely not in danger, repeated herself.

"You need a drink." She stood at the bar, mixing and stirring. Blood still streaked from her nose; Mosley saw Greg staring at it and laughed. "Makeup, that's all. Pretty real, huh?"

The other three men stood silently behind the couch, facing Greg. They watched him closely, like bouncers eyeing a troublemaker. Mosley tucked the pistol under his belt and sat on the couch. Tom stood by the bar.

Greg brushed Alexandra's offer aside and kept his eyes on Mosley.

"Trust me, you need one," Alexandra said. She crossed the carpet, drink in hand. "Here." She handed him a glass of ice with a thin amber liquid poured over it. "Scotch and soda. Sip it."

He nudged her hand away without looking at her.

She set the glass on the table next to him. "I'll just leave it here."

Greg didn't respond. He could only stare at Rick Mosley.

Without the wig, he was uglier than Yelsom had ever been. His painted face, startling but at least consistent with a wild hairpiece, was now capped by normal, short brown curls, and the contrast was awful.

"Have some, Greg," he said gently.

Greg took a sip of scotch—the first alcohol he'd touched since boyhood. It buzzed through him, dulling the shock. Barely.

Alexandra seated herself next to Mosley on the couch.

Greg scanned the room. Alexandra Chappel. Rick Mosley (Yelsom), Tom Wooding the gym manager, and three strangers.

A nightmare with no interpretation.

Mosley broke the silence. "I'll explain."

Alexandra nodded at him, and Greg recognized, in their exchanged glances, some sort of partnership.

We created monsters, Greg. Our monsters have come back.

"My God," Greg moaned.

"I expected you at eight," Alexandra said. "I was going to explain everything before they got here. When you didn't show up we figured you weren't coming, and we had work to do."

"The house had to be messed up like there had been a struggle, and I had to get her into her makeup," Mosley added. "And her ropes."

Alexandra rubbed her arms. "By the way, Richard, they do hurt. Not so tight next time."

"Sorry."

"We never meant any harm," Alexandra said to Greg earnestly. Mosley nodded, and Tom spoke up.

"That's true, Greg. We're your friends. Try to believe that."

The others murmured in agreement.

Greg raised both hands, perplexed, then looked at the three men standing behind the couch. Alexandra seemed to remember her manners.

"Oh, yes. Greg, let me introduce you to Martin Lassiter, Jack Romano, and Leonard Adkins."

The three nodded politely.

"They comprise part of our enforcers," she explained.

"We look better in ski masks," Romano said dryly.

"They work the streets," Alexandra added.

Mosley took over. "I know you must be—" he trailed off. "Gosh, I can't even imagine what you're thinking! You must have a thousand questions."

Only one came to mind.

"Why?"

Mosley cocked his head thoughtfully, then shook it.

"No, no," he began. "Let's start with *who* and *what*, then work our way to *why*."

"Believe me, Gregory," Alexandra added, "that's the only way this will make sense to you."

"So we'll start with *who*," Mosley announced, then slipped

into his Bronx accent. "I'm Yelsom, obviously, activist extraordinaire and head of the Orange County chapter of BRAVO."

"How?" Greg gasped. "How did you do it?"

"President of the Cal State Drama Club of '69, don't you remember?"

"But all this time," Greg stammered, "all this time I was sure you were—"

"I know who you thought I was."

"Then he's...not here? Bennie's not in California?"

Mosley, Alexandra, and Tom exchanged looks.

"He's here. But first things first, Greg."

"Yelsom." Greg couldn't get over it. "You're Yelsom." He took another sip, a larger one this time.

Mosley pointed playfully. "I had you, didn't I? You never guessed it!" he gloated. "I'll never get a part like that again. An actor's dream!"

"Don't start that again," Tom broke in.

"Right. But seriously, Greg, didn't you ever wonder why you and I—you and *Yelsom*—were never close enough to get a good look at each other?"

"I thought you were Bennie and you were avoiding me or something like that."

"No, I just couldn't let you blow my cover. If you had gotten close enough to recognize me, that would have brought an end to everything. But, hey, didn't the name *Yelsom* ever make you think?"

Greg blinked. "Should it have?"

"Yelsom, Mosley. Mosley, Yelsom. Same name spelled backwards."

Greg spelled it out, then groaned.

"Don't you like it? I even made up that bit about his parents saying, 'He sure yells some,' and spread it around. I've had some good laughs over it, let me tell you."

"I always thought it was ridiculous myself," Alexandra said crisply. A chime sounded; she looked at a small Seiko clock on the mantel. "We don't have a lot of time, Richard."

"Right." He reached into his pocket, pulled out a cigarette, and lit it. (*Mosley smokes?* Greg wondered.) Then Rick leaned forward and began. "Remember when we were pledging the Argonauts?"

Greg nodded.

"Of course you do. Remember the way you ran away like a scared little girl?"

His voice turned cold and level.

"Don't run out on me again. It'll be more serious this time." He took a drag from his cigarette, then puffed angrily. "I've waited twenty years to ride you for that."

Greg's mind raced. Mosley finished exhaling and his tone lightened. "But that's okay. 'Cause I took your turn for you."

Ten punches each.

Greg was nauseated.

"I jumped in and finished the job. He was dog meat by the time I was through."

The voice was Mosley's, but the icy, cruel eyes were Yelsom's.

No, Mosley's. They'd been Mosley's all along.

"And I found my calling that night."

Alexandra, who had been listening approvingly, smiled. Tom nodded; the thugs behind the couch did the same.

Greg sank further into the chair, appalled. "That's disgusting."

"Oh, come off it!" Mosley snapped, clapping his hands together and jolting Greg upright. "You hate them as much as I do. Tell me you don't!"

Greg was silent.

"What did Ferguson say to you? *Stop them?* Have you done it?"

No answer.

"Then who *is* going to stop them, Greg?" He arched his back. "Who's going to take the responsibility?"

"You can't do it alone," Alexandra declared.

"Neither can we," Tom said.

"It takes more than prayers," Jack Romano offered from behind them. "It takes work."

"United effort!" Alexandra enthused.

"And like-minded people," Tom added, "who can solve the homosexual problem and prove we were the ones to handle the *other* problems all along!"

"And," Mosley concluded, "you're our man."

Greg started to protest but Alexandra stopped him.

"Oh, you are. Yes."

"Never."

"You're the beginning of a plan that's going to set in motion the strongest move toward purity this country has seen in decades!"

Who's crazy, Greg wondered, *them or me?*

Mosley leaned forward again and stamped out his cigarette on a crystal ashtray in front of him. "The Argonauts were child's play; this is the real thing. No running this time."

Greg couldn't have been more confused; Mosley sensed it. "You'll understand," he said, then looked almost pleadingly at Alexandra. "He'll *have* to understand!"

She nodded. Rick closed his eyes and considered where to begin. Then he nodded, looked directly at Greg, and announced: "I hate them."

He breathed deeply. Everyone was silent.

"Faggots. Sickos. *Freaks.* Their blood oughta be splashed all over this stinking county."

"You hate them," Greg repeated. "So? That's nothing new."

Greg's mildly sarcastic tone seemed to amuse Mosley. "Ah, I'm horrible and hateful, yes? But hatred always has a beginning. Care to hear mine?"

Greg had, to his surprise, finished his drink. He held the empty glass in both hands and waited.

"I spent half my childhood," Mosley began softly, "running away from the old man. I escaped to the movies. That's where I learned to act. I also hung out at The Pike. Remember?"

The Pike was an old amusement park on Ocean Boulevard. Greg had been there once or twice.

"*They* were there. They hung out like a bunch of vultures, waiting for kids like me who were alone. Kids who were confused. Kids they could...talk into...doing *things!*"

The last word came out in a sob. Alexandra put her left hand over Mosley's right one and squeezed it.

"Kids who needed money," he went on bitterly. "Money to pay for the groceries they would have had if the animal they lived with hadn't drained the family budget on booze."

The Yelsom rage was on display again, and it was no act.

"They *used* me."

It was clear to Greg what *used* meant and how it had affected Mosley.

He thought back to Rick's expression that night on the beach. Anticipation.

Me first.

"It made me sick!" he went on. "And I didn't know what it all meant. Did it mean I was one of them? Was I a pervert, too? I hated them. I hate them. *I hate them!*"

His shaking was as violent as his tone. Alexandra patted his shoulder.

"Do you know what it's like wondering whether or not you're normal, Greg? Do you?"

His voice had risen to a hysterical pitch. Greg looked at him helplessly.

"That's when I knew they should all be shot." He jumped from the couch and started pacing, breathless, energized as the story progressed. "That's why I was so excited that night, can't you see? When we found your little friend on the beach, I finally had a chance to make a statement. Bash!"

Mosley exploded, pounding his right fist into his left palm, stalking back and forth, eyes shining.

"'That's for all your friends who made me feel like a freak,' I said when I hit him. And bash!" he yelled, repeating the pounding gesture over and over. "'That's for being a sick punk freak,' and *bash!* 'That's for coming out here to spread your perversion.' Bash! Bash! Bash!"

Greg looked to Alexandra for some human response, something in her that might appeal to Mosley and tell him this was wrong. But no; her face radiated approval.

Mosley stopped pacing. "We went back to that spot a few times. Me and Desmond and a few other guys from the club. We made statements. Lots of 'em." And with that he slammed his fist into his open palm again and resumed his pacing. "Bash!" Pounding and bellowing, stalking, then pounding again. "Bash! Bash! Bash!"

Alexandra's enjoyment of the performance was clear, but when she caught Greg watching her, she pulled herself up and adopted a more serious expression.

"But then I got busted," Mosley said, stopping to catch his breath. "Police were out one night patrolling the beach. You'd think they'd have awarded me for helping them keep the city safe, but no. The others got away. I wasn't quick enough. I was sentenced to a few years' probation. Ha! Probation? No way—not this kid."

He was getting excited again, catching a second wind.

"But everybody else in the Argonauts decided I'd gone too far, that I'd put the others up to it. Hypocrites! They're the ones who got it all started! The club couldn't have a guy who had been arrested, they said." He waved his hand in disgust. "They dumped me. They said I needed help—that *I* had a problem. That's when I realized that my old man was right about one thing. The majority of the pure ones are too cowardly to fight."

"The pure ones?" Greg mumbled. *"The pure ones?"*

"He was a trashy drunk, but he was right. He said Martin Luther King was the beginning of the end—that once he was finished all kinds of other crazies would start hollering for *their* rights, too." He went back to the couch and sat beside Alexandra. "But nobody believed him. They all said *he* had a problem. Maybe that's what drove him to drink. Maybe he was ahead of his time."

Greg protested. "That's sick. You're—"

Mosley ignored him. "I hated him, but I'll say this much: He stood by me when he heard I'd beaten up a few queers. He handed me some cash and said to hightail it out of Long Beach and find a big city where I could disappear for a while. So I scraped up a few more bucks, kissed Mom good-bye, and landed in New York. Dad told me I'd find like-minded people if I looked hard enough."

"That's where I came in," Alexandra interjected.

Our monsters, Greg. Our monsters are coming—

"In the summer of '89," she began, "I saw Richard and some other young men protesting the gay parade in New York City. I was there visiting friends. We were trying to catch a cab, but the area was crawling with those *people.*"

She shivered at the memory.

"And then I spotted them. A few brave men carrying signs, taking a stand. I was impressed, especially by this one," she said, indicating Mosley. "He was obviously the leader. I walked right up and asked what group he represented. And he told me he wasn't with any one group—that he had tried a few of them but none were too well organized. I invited him out to dinner on the spot. I saw an opportunity, Greg, because for years a good idea had been coming together in my mind. When I met Richard, I felt hope."

Greg was finding it hard to listen or even to stay awake. Twice his eyelids started to droop. He took the glass from his lap and dropped it on the table.

"Another drink?" Alexandra asked.

"Uh, no."

"All right, then, let's get to the heart of the matter. Who," she posed, "are the two main groups fighting the homosexual movement in America?"

"Dunno," he slurred.

"Traditional religious groups, and groups like ours."

Like ours. Greg understood. *The pure ones.*

"How many people in America call themselves Christians?"

"Uh, I dunno."

"Millions. If millions of Americans call themselves Christians, and Christians are against homosexuality, how on earth has the gay rights movement gotten so far?"

"I give up."

"That's the problem. Most people do that. Most of you pray, a few of you speak up, none of you fight. You give up."

"And the Bible says not to give up," Mosley declared, taking the floor again. "God's people fought His enemies in the Old Testament. True, Greg?"

Mosley invoking the name of God was the ultimate obscenity.

"True," Greg admitted.

"And they fought to the death. To the death! True?"

Greg knew where this was going. "To the death," he repeated.

"Right!" Tom bellowed, clapping his hands. Lassiter and Romano were also showing some kind of zeal. Even stone-faced Adkins looked moved.

"'Do not I hate them, O LORD, that hate thee?' King David said in the Psalms. Didn't he? Greg!"

He was starting to droop again; Mosley's voice brought him back.

"Didn't he say that?"

"You want—" Greg's voice slurred. He giggled, then tried again. "You want permission to hate, Rick?"

Mosley abandoned his earlier, wilder role and played the

instructor again. Hands on hips, he stood over Greg and hissed: "I'm not looking for permission to hate. I've *got* it."

Alexandra interrupted. "Let me tell it."

Mosley stopped himself and sat down obediently. Alexandra leaned forward.

"There are so many of us, Greg," she said earnestly. "Intelligent, concerned citizens—not just funny little men in white sheets and swastikas. You know us."

Us. And Greg knew what he had been hoping never to know.

Alexandra Chappel. Rick Mosley. Tom Wooding.

The Covenant. Meeting under the guise of Citizens United. With Greg Bishop representing them to an unknowing public.

You're our man.

His heart caved in.

"We have a plan, Greg," she continued. "And it can't fail."

Mosley lit another cigarette. Alexandra spoke more rapidly. "I mapped it out with Richard in New York."

"The Covenant," Greg quavered. "Restore the kingdom."

She didn't even hear him. "When the blacks got their laws passed in the sixties," she said, "and became respectable, the whole country went over to their side. We lost that battle."

"No." Greg was sick, literally. "No, no, no."

"And twenty years earlier, when the Jews spread their lies about the Holocaust, the country went to *their* side, too." Refined as she was, Alexandra Chappel was having a hard time containing her hatred. Her voice turned coarse, brittle.

"And if the gays become respectable, we'll lose our battle with *them*, too. As long as they act like animals, marching in their parades and rioting every time somebody says 'boo' to them, they look terrible to the public. But they'll catch on. They'll do just like the blacks did and put an all-American face on their sick lifestyle. They're doing it now. They're in government, education, law, everywhere!"

"Blacks and gays," Greg stammered, "aren't in the same class. You know that. This isn't the same thing—"

Alexandra ignored him, her fury rising.

"Nice, respectable *perverts!* And when they're nice, people will sympathize with them. *We can't let them be nice!*"

The living room reverberated as Alexandra, Mosley, Tom, and BRAVO's street thugs Romano, Lassiter and Adkins—

responsible, no doubt, for the wave of violence against gays last fall—added "Amen!" "Yes!" and "Go for it!" with holy fervor.

Greg couldn't take anymore. It was time to leave and to tell. Tell everyone.

He tried to rise but was too dizzy. He thought of attacking them, beating them down, but his body wasn't taking orders from his brain. Nothing worked. Speech was his last defense.

"Pure ones?" he said. "There's nothing pure about you. You're filthy. You *hate*. That's your calling."

Even speaking was hard now. *A nondrinker should never have tried hard scotch*, he thought.

The pure ones watched him, unmoved.

"Hear us out," Alexandra said. "Then, if you still feel that way, so be it."

"So be it," Mosley agreed.

Alexandra resumed her speech.

"We can't let them be nice. But we knew that, sooner or later, they would adopt a more respectable approach. So we infiltrated them."

"Yours truly gets the Academy Award as best infiltrator of 1991!" Mosley declared.

"He's been wonderful," Alexandra agreed. "He told me he could act."

"I'm a born mimic. Show me a movie once and I'll act out the starring role for you better than the star himself did."

"So we came up with a plan."

"Act like them! Then infiltrate their ranks."

"I sent him out to the gay bars."

"What an education! I learned their mannerisms," he said, puffing his cigarette in an effeminate way, "and the gay lingo. And all the gay arguments. Remember me on TV? I had it all down. I even changed my name. I had to, of course."

"When he was ready, we started looking for an activist group for him to join. One that was radical, one he could encourage to do the worst things imaginable—things that would make even the most open-minded people sick."

"We decided on BRAVO. And I met their founder. Guess who?"

Your friend—the one who they assaulted on the beach? He moved to New York and became one of the city's foremost gay activists.

Mosley could tell Greg had guessed.

"Bennie Hudson ran away from home after our encounter," he continued. "He met this rich older guy on one of those gay cruise lines and they paired up. But in '88 the older guy came down with AIDS. That's a mercy, if you ask me. Puts them out of their misery."

Nothing Mosley said surprised Greg at this point.

"When he died, Bennie was sitting on a nice inheritance. That's when he founded BRAVO. He was one angry kid, believe me. He's got AIDS himself, you know. He's on his last leg."

"You know Bennie?" Greg barely got the words out.

"Of course I know him! But he never recognized me," Mosley laughed. "But then, how could he? We'd only met once, in the dark, and that was many years ago. I'd perfected my look by then. I worked my way up the ranks of BRAVO."

"Richard rises to the top wherever he goes," Alexandra beamed.

"And I talked Bennie—the idiot!—into sending me to California. What with AB101 coming up and all, I told him the Orange County chapter of BRAVO needed me. I checked it out. The other guy heading it up wasn't strong enough. Bennie finally gave me the go-ahead."

"But we had plans ourselves, Greg," Alexandra commented, "which included Orange County. And Dr. Crawford. And, eventually, you. Orange County is a testing ground. If it works here, we're taking it around the country."

"So I moved out here in the fall of 1990." Rick reached for the ashtray again. "Alexandra sponsored me."

She took over while he put out the cigarette stub. "I already knew Tom. He's a long-standing member, as both our fathers were. His father is my namesake, in fact. So I shared my ideas with Tom and we organized in no time."

"Citizens United," Greg said. "Are they all—"

"Of course not," Tom answered. "Most of them couldn't handle it. Only a few of them even know about The Covenant."

"Meanwhile," Alexandra continued, "Richard won the Orange County gays over—"

"Which wasn't easy! I had to go to a different bar every other night just to make myself known! I deserve a medal for sitting in those cesspools."

"Then," Alexandra said, "we had to find a conservative leader to fight the gays. One who had credibility with the community, who people would follow, and who wasn't publicly associated with *us*. We're still working for more credibility."

"More's the pity," Mosley complained.

"Most of us in The Covenant have too much history on record," Alexandra added. "Mr. Wooding, here, for example"— she pointed at Tom—"has had his hands slapped for arson, armed robbery, and an occasional assault. If he'd been our spokesman, there's no question the media would have followed his paper trail right to the county courthouse!"

Wooding blushed and ducked his head.

"And our boys over here?"

The thugs smiled; one winked.

"Hardly the sort Orange County conservatives would follow, don't you think? Then there's Richard, who's marvelous at fooling homosexuals but not so refined as to win the general population over. We need someone like you, who'll fight the gays and win the support of the public. Someone who will work for us without anyone knowing it. Without knowing it himself, if need be."

"Someone," Mosley reflected, "who could start off as a gentleman—who could win respect for his ability to articulate the right view without coming off like a right-winger."

"Someone," Wooding added, "who people would rally around. Conservatives—especially Christian conservatives—are so glad to hear a public figure stand for morality that they'll usually follow him with a passion. Especially if that person is angry about the way things are going downhill in this country."

"And you're angry, Greg," Mosley insisted. "That's one reason people are following you."

"And you've been doing so well!" Alexandra leaned forward and emphasized. "People love you, Greg. You've got popularity now, and *power!*"

She noticed his disgusted expression. "Oh, don't turn your nose up at power. It's like money. The only people who say they're too good for it are the ones who can't get any."

Mosley continued. "We needed someone we could sponsor, then gradually, hopefully, persuade to join us all the way."

"And you would have, Greg." Alexandra sounded so confident. "Given just a bit more time, you would have come to your senses and embraced The Covenant. It's what made you what you are today."

Of every evil thing he'd heard so far, that was the most horrible.

"Our leader—you, Greg—would stir the public up against the gays. And our infiltrator—Richard, of course—would stir gays up against the public. The Christian public, especially. Civil war is only a breath away."

"Then we step in," Wooding said proudly.

"With our spokesman leading the troops," Alexandra said, pointing at Greg. "We'll show them how to handle gays. Our street troops knock 'em down when they act up. Our leaders—like you, Greg—expose their filthy ways to the public, just as you've done."

"And done very well," Romano affirmed.

Alexandra drew a breath. "And finally, not this year, perhaps, and not next year, but finally, finally! Finally we'll take off the mask and show it was The Covenant, not Citizens United, who solved the homosexual problem. Finally, when we've won enough popularity so nothing could knock us down, we'll reveal ourselves as the one group capable of cleaning the dirt off the streets! And finally we'll regain the ground we lost!"

"And finally," Mosley gushed, "we'll regain respect in the public's eyes. Then we'll really get to work."

In his dazed state Greg envisioned The Covenant at work reclaiming America and redefining the kingdom of God: a place where nobody unacceptable to them would be allowed to exist.

All in consummation of a plan set in motion with the seduction and manipulation of one man.

One man—

They had me by the throat.

"Alex Crawford," Greg managed to say. "Was he your first choice?"

"He would have been perfect," Alexandra remarked sadly. "He had already done battle with the gays by the time we met him. I was sure he would work out."

"He would have, too, if it weren't for Josh Ferguson."

Josh Ferguson? What on earth—

"At first he was doing so well! He needed money, so I approached him about supporting him financially whenever he traveled to speak. People were following him; everything was progressing just fine. But one day, during his counseling session with Joshua, he mentioned my name."

"We had no idea Ferguson was one of his patients," Mosley said.

"But when Alex told Joshua I was sponsoring him, Joshua told *him* what *he* knew about me. He mentioned our affair, if you could call it that, and the unfortunate way it ended."

Only Alexandra Chappel, Greg observed, *would call arson and murder "unfortunate."*

"And he warned Dr. Crawford about me. That I was dangerous. That I'd burned his silly church down when he was a boy, as if I could do a thing like that!"

"But your father could," Greg answered.

"Perhaps." She dripped arrogance. "Anyway, that's when we lost the good doctor. He asked me if I was the monster Joshua made me out to be, and I saw no reason to mince words. He'd been attacked by the gays himself! He should have appreciated our plan. I was certain he would, so I laid my cards on the table. But he balked."

Mosley looked annoyed. "Lily whites. They say they're with you one minute, and the next minute they're turning on you."

"He ran off tattling to Joshua, and they came up with a cozy plan. Joshua videotaped Dr. Crawford explaining everything we were trying to do, and tacked it onto that silly report he was doing. Then Joshua called me and said we had to meet immediately. I hadn't heard from him for years, but of course I knew about his career. And I suppose he knew about mine."

She's a viper, Greg. Stay away from her. If my husband were alive he would tell you the same.

"Joshua came to my home with a hidden camera in his coat. He sat right where you are, Greg! And he told me he knew what we were planning and that if we didn't stop, he would expose me publicly in a report he was doing. I told him there were good reasons for my actions and that I wasn't ashamed of them. I explained everything to him. No reason not to, since Crawford had already done as much."

Alexandra looked at the couch to the left of Greg, as though she were looking directly at Ferguson when he had sat there.

"He threatened me again, but I wasn't intimidated." She assumed the meanest smile Greg had ever seen.

"I knew I could hurt him more than he could hurt me."

Greg asked how.

"He'd been stupid enough to admit he was seeing Dr. Crawford!"

Greg blinked, not getting it.

"Don't you see?"

"No."

"Why did men go to Dr. Crawford?"

"Oh."

"By telling me he was one of Dr. Crawford's patients, he admitted he was gay. And how many Southern Californians would have been interested to hear their own Mr. Limelight was a closet homosexual?"

She laughed eerily.

"I had that man in my pocket and he didn't even know it! All I needed was proof that he was a homosexual in treatment with Alex Crawford."

Mosley grinned. Greg wet his lips, trying to keep up with the story. "How did you know Josh had a hidden camera when he talked to you?"

"I saw the whole video, Greg, remember?" Mosley answered for her. "Her conversation with him that night is on it. That's why we couldn't let it get into the wrong hands."

"And that's why we decided to get a hold of his records—so we would have proof that he was gay. First we sent those girls to apply for a job at his office. That would have been the easiest way to get the files on Joshua. But neither of the girls got the job."

They almost had better luck at my place, Greg remembered with a chill.

"So we conceived the idea of a break-in. Why not? It was just the sort of thing BRAVO would do. We got Joshua's file, plus a few bonus points."

"Robbie Carlton's name, for one thing," Greg said miserably, wishing for the strength to tear them all to shreds. Why were his arms so heavy?

"That helped. Outing him stirred up animosity against BRAVO, which was important, but that wasn't the real prize. The real prize was what we found on Crawford himself, not his patients."

"You found something on *Alex?*"

"Ha!" Mosley cried. "Did we! I found it myself, in fact, when I was looking through the files of people on the 'out' list. Are you ready for this, Greg?"

He waited.

"Insurance fraud."

"*Alex?*"

"The billings on his patients' files didn't match the ones sent to their insurance companies. He kept both sets of bills in the files, so it was easy to catch. He would see a patient twice in a month but bill the insurance company for four, maybe five visits that same month. He made as much money *not* seeing patients as he made seeing them!"

Greg was about to argue that Crawford's patients would have noticed if he was ripping their insurance companies off. Someone would surely have blown the whistle on him, he started to say. Then he remembered.

I charge them very low rates, Gregory. They'd never afford me otherwise. And they're all grateful. And cooperative.

But Alex didn't need to cheat, did he? He could earn good money.

Earn it, but not keep it. *I'm terrible with money, Greg. It will be the death of me yet.*

Poor Alex.

Alexandra watched him. "The wheels are spinning, aren't they, Gregory? Figured it out? After BRAVO sent that letter to Joshua, I called him and said I could stop BRAVO from exposing him *if* he cooperated. But he wouldn't. He told me he'd rather die."

My situation is quite hopeless, as you'll see—

"Which he did."

She said it as though she felt nothing. In all probability that was the case.

"Then I visited Dr. Crawford in the hospital. It was the day after you saw him, I believe."

Hadn't Crawford's attitude changed that same week?

"I told him what we'd found in his files. I was kind, Greg, I want you to know that," she said. "I offered to pick up the tab for his medical bills if he cooperated by telling us everything he knew about Joshua's report."

And he accepted. He must have. That's why he seemed so guilty afterward.

"We didn't know if Ferguson left 'Unforgiven Sins' at the studio," Mosley said, "or if it was ever scheduled to be shown."

"I told him he had a choice. Help us, and his bills would be paid and no one would be the wiser. If not, he could look forward to an angry judge lecturing him on ethics." Her voice became almost girlish. "He accepted the offer most graciously."

They had me by the throat.

Mosley took the ball again. "He knew about the tape. You told him about it when you visited him, remember? And he told us you had the only copy."

Greg let that sink in.

They promised me nobody would harm you or Christine in any way.

"And then it was so clear to me," Alexandra sang out, "that you, not that idiot Crawford, were the one we were looking for all along. You, Gregory! A man who started off as a gentleman. Who won the public's respect."

Dr. Bishop, you're the first man I've heard so far with a truly balanced approach to this issue.

"A man the gays could push until he got mad and the public got mad with him."

We're on your side now. Stand tall.

"I asked you myself if you'd be interested," Alexandra said, "that night at the Five Crowns. Of course, you hardly knew me then, so why should you have said yes? But Richard and Tom had already started working on you, so we decided to let them do the recruiting."

"We knew you'd like us once you got to know us," Tom added.

Mosley jumped in. "So we gathered a bunch of good fighters to band together with you to show that The Covenant can solve this problem. And we're solving it! Can't you see? Can't you see we're turning the tide?"

"People are angry now," Tom enthused.

"Furious! They're on your side! You're winning. *We're* winning!" Mosley said, standing tall.

"And not just us, Greg," Tom added. "Think about it! Right now there is a Greg Bishop in cities around the country, and there is also a Yelsom right there to help raise him up!"

"Along with a bunch of loyal followers to support him!" Mosley yelled, pointing at the three smiling men behind him.

"Once the public sees we can handle this problem, they'll love us!" Alexandra exulted.

"Not once they know what you really are."

"Don't count on it," she answered serenely. "We'll gain their trust. It may take years, but when we've won enough of these battles, they'll see we're the *only* group that can restore moral order to America."

"Then they'll know," Mosley added, "that we were right about other problems as well."

"Racial problems," she recited. "Immigration. Affirmative action. Political correctness. People are sick of it all!"

"And angry!" Mosley thundered. "There's a backlash coming."

"They'll look to us to offer solutions to those other problems once they see how well we solved this one. And they'll finally see we were right!" She was standing now, lost in her vision of a pure America.

Mosley stood at her side and pointed emphatically at Greg. "We warned them what happens when a Zionist occupied government gets a foothold, and they'll finally believe us. They'll finally see who gave our jobs to the foreigners, who let the blacks get preferred treatment, and who let the queers stampede over normal citizens."

"Not all of them," Greg offered, "have done that. Not all of the gays are like—"

"They're evil!" Mosley boomed.

"You helped make them that way," Greg whimpered, knowing he had been duped into doing the same.

"No!" Mosley argued. "I just helped bring out what was already in their hearts. I gave them a platform to do exactly what they wanted to do all along. I didn't make them crazy; they were that way already."

"And people will see," Alexandra said grandly, "that we can put down the crazies everyone else was afraid to fight! That's how they'll come to love us."

Greg wondered how two intelligent adults could believe anyone would go along with such a plan.

Then he answered his own question.

When Hitler was in power, the trains ran on time.

Something else was occurring to him, though. Something infinitely worse.

Robbie.

Murderous feelings rose and churned.

Robbie was outed by BRAVO. By Yelsom.

By Mosley.

Who, for the sake of stirring up hatred against gays, incited BRAVO to set the Berean Community Church on fire.

Leaving Robbie Carlton—scared, talented young Robbie Carlton—dead.

Because of the pure ones in front of him.

"Robbie!"

Greg lunged out at them and fell onto the carpet, spread out like a drunk, his legs turned to rubber.

Mosley reached down and put his hand under Greg's chin to pull it up. Then Mosley crouched in front of him.

"I'm sorry about Robbie. I never meant for him to be hurt. We had no idea anyone was in the church," he said solemnly. "I never thought Ferguson would kill himself, either. That wasn't the plan; I swear it."

He picked Greg up, then dropped him back into the easy chair. "But don't get too holy on me, Greg. You've used that kid's story to dazzle crowds all over the place. You've gotten a lot of mileage out of Robbie Carlton and the fire, my man. It's a crowd-pleaser."

The motion of being dropped made Greg dizzier than ever, and now the room began spinning. He heard another chime.

Then he heard Alexandra, somewhere to his left, telling Mosley that time was running out.

The men stepped forward from behind the couch. Alexandra and Tom stood beside them.

"Greg?" Mosley asked sharply.

His head dropped forward. He was nodding off.

Mosley shouted his name again.

He opened his eyes and saw nothing. "I'm drunk," he mumbled. "The booze was too much."

"So was the Amitrex," Alexandra said. "You've had about 90 milligrams."

"No," he whispered.

"I should know. I mixed it with your scotch. You didn't think," she asked primly, "that I'd take a chance on you running out of here, did you?"

He tried to speak but couldn't, then tried to guess their intentions but couldn't do that, either.

"Bennie is on his way over here," Mosley said slowly and loudly.

"He's coming with BRAVO. The East Coast chapter, that is. They play hardball, Greg. Tonight's a big night. We've been planning it for weeks. They're going to trash this house. It's the beginning of a whole new battle."

"Alexandra's house first," Tom explained, "and of course, she won't press charges or identify anyone, so no one gets arrested. Your house is next, so we hope you will be with us by then. Then Crawford's place. We've got him where we want him; he has no choice but to cooperate."

"So none of the victims will say they actually saw their assailants. Get it?" Mosley laughed. "BRAVO won't know why, of course, but I've assured them there won't be any legal troubles."

"And," Tom said, "after three break-ins like that, everyone will fear—and hate—BRAVO more than ever!"

No wonder Alex is leaving, Greg thought.

"They don't expect to find you here," Mosley said, "but I told Bennie that someday soon I'd hand you over to him."

Greg heard but couldn't respond.

"I don't want to, Greg! But I will if I have to. We talk on the phone a lot, and he is always asking about you. If he gets his hands on you, you're history. He has waited a long time, and he's crazy."

Greg moaned.

Alexandra stepped forward and leaned over him. "If you come with us and promise to cooperate, we won't let BRAVO touch you. You don't have to do anything more than what you've been doing all along—just keep cooperating. You have a good future, Gregory. Don't ruin it."

He shook his head, and when he did the room appeared to spin wildly.

"Greg!" Mosley shouted. "Don't blow it again!"

He gave one more small shake of his head.

"No?" Alexandra asked. "Are you sure?"

His eyelids fluttered; his lips formed but couldn't say no.

"Greg!" Mosley yelled. "Come on!" He was shaking Greg by the shoulders; Greg barely felt it.

Alexandra stopped him and delivered her verdict.

"It's over."

Mosley sighed and let Greg's shoulders drop.

"Stay here to meet Bennie and the others, Richard," Alexandra ordered, her voice suddenly brisk and businesslike. "Tom, Martin, the rest of you—do whatever else you need to do to the house, leave me tied up in the bedroom, then go before BRAVO gets here."

The men jumped into action.

"Richard?"

Mosley turned away from Greg to face her.

"Let them see me tied up, but make sure they don't touch me! Then disappear. They'll find that boy in the alley any minute now, so you need to lay low for a while. Explain that to Bennie."

"But if he sees Greg here, that gives Greg a chance to tell him about me!"

Alexandra regarded Greg for a moment. "I don't think so," she pronounced. "I don't think he will say much of anything. He can barely speak now."

Mosley stepped away from him. Alexandra leaned close to Greg and spoke loudly into his ear.

"Richard will give you to Bennie with BRAVO's compliments. He will say that he found us both here: me, the lady of the house, and you, my dinner guest. He'll make it a reunion."

Greg was sinking; her voice sounded more and more distant.

"A reunion between you and someone with plans for you."

She was miles away now.

"Someone who is dying to see you."

He felt her breath on his mouth now.

"I had such plans for you, Gregory. You could have been great. But you'll still be great. You'll be more of a martyr than Robbie Carlton ever was. And when people see what our enemies have done to you, they'll hate them more than ever."

Mosley stood next to her. "Alexandra? The guys upstairs are ready for you."

"Good-bye, Gregory."

He opened one eye to see Alexandra Chappel leaning closer, wetting her lips to plant a kiss on him.

His eye closed and he slipped away, but not before he summoned up all his remaining strength to spit in her face.

FORTY-THREE

Voices rose and fell, faces surrounded Greg, and he slipped in and out of dreams.

He was back in high school, glad to be so young again, but something unsettling was happening. A group of people—he supposed they were the Argonauts—had gathered around his chair, trying to decide what to do. They dressed strangely for the occasion but it was, after all, Black Tuesday, so their black T-shirts were appropriate.

"So I'm gonna leave him here for you," Mosley was telling another man whose back was to Greg. (*Probably one of the pledgemasters*, he thought. *Ramsey or Boswell. They were so cruel.*)

"But you're a pledge just like me!" Greg wanted to say to Rick. "You can't call the shots!" But his mouth wasn't working. He could only listen.

"I've got to split. Heat's on, you know? Listen, show these people"—Mosley gestured to a group of men and women somewhat familiar to Greg—"how to do it right, okay?"

"You said nobody gets hurt!" one of the women said.

"I lied," Mosley laughed. "Timid souls, you may now leave if the going is getting too tough."

The scene around Greg began to seem real. "Am I dreaming?" Greg slurred, but no one seemed to hear.

Mosley was gone; someone else was talking excitedly.

"Bennie knows where he wants to take him!"

"Then let's go!"

Greg's head rolled back as strong arms hoisted him out of the chair and carried him through the door.

"Quiet, quiet!" someone whispered.

Greg saw trees, stars, then the open door of a van in front of him. He flew through it and crashed into the darkness.

Laughter floated in the blackness, and the air around him smelled of booze. People were drinking beer, he noticed, and thus he assumed he was still with the fraternity. Someone offered him a can, but he knew better than to accept. Pledges weren't allowed to drink with members. Besides, he didn't want any more booze, anyway.

The van lurched forward, his head rolled back, and he was asleep.

Christine and he were walking along the beach, laughing, remembering the nightmare they had been through in 1992 and how glad they were to have put it all in the past. A little boy toddled along beside them; he had Greg's eyes and Christine's hair, and he was deliriously happy.

Greg bent down to pick him up and had nearly grabbed him around his little waist when an excited voice jerked him out of the dream.

"We're almost there!"

Another voice, a familiar one, said, "Hey, bring him up front."

Two sets of arms grabbed Greg's shoulders and heaved him forward from the rear of the van to the back of the passenger's seat. His head swam and it took several seconds to open his eyes and refocus.

The passenger turned to face him.

Greg tried to scream.

Death was seated before him, grinning at him. He wore a black hood over his skeleton face; cheekbones jutted through his thin skin, accenting his bright, fiery eyes and diabolical smile.

"You awake, Greg?" Death asked.

"I will be," Greg mumbled. "I've had nightmares before. Christine will shake me out of this."

Death giggled. "What'll we play?" It pulled out a knife. "Blood brothers?"

It teased Greg with the knife, moving it in slow circles in front of his drunken, drugged face.

"Or shall we sneak cigarettes from your dad?" It inserted a cigarette butt into its mouth. Someone produced a lighter and clicked it. Half of Death's face was horribly lit up, showing bright purple splotches zigzagging across its cheeks and forehead. It inhaled, then put the cigarette in front of Greg's eyes and laughed when he flinched.

"No, I've got a better game. One you were always good at. You'll love it."

The van jerked left as it exited the freeway and turned onto Ocean Boulevard. It slowly began to dawn on Greg that Christine wouldn't shake him out of this.

"I'm not dreaming."

The van rocked with laughter.

"And these aren't the Argonauts."

He took in the smell of smoke, the male and female faces around him, the sound of hard rock blaring from the front.

"I'm not dreaming!"

The cry was muffled by the carpeted walls of the dark green van speeding down the cliffs of Cherry Beach.

The van descended, idled, then shut off. No one spoke.

They waited in the parking lot. "See anyone?" someone whispered.

Whispered. That meant they wanted to go unheard, unseen. Or else someone might stop them.

It was worth a shot.

"Please, somebody help me—"

Two hands pulled Greg's shoulders from behind and pinned him to the van's floor while another hand forced a wad of cloth into his mouth. He gagged and tried to get away, but was no match for whoever was holding him.

Minutes passed. Then someone said it was clear, and the doors at the back of the van swung open.

A salty night breeze hit him first, then the sound of sand crunching under him, then another sound—the stuff of memories and bad dreams.

Waves. Crashing waves.

Someone stood Greg upright, then two people—one on each side—grabbed his arms and yanked him forward. His head stayed down; he could only see his feet try to keep up with his abductors.

They were running now, dragging him along while his useless legs etched lines in the sand.

"Stay low!" someone hissed. "Keep out of the light."

The waves were closer now; the air colder. Dry sand gave way to cool shoreline. They stopped suddenly and let his arms go. He lurched forward and flopped, belly first, onto the wet ground.

Greg moaned, sick and despairing. In his desperation to catch his breath, he inhaled sand. Someone grabbed his left arm and flipped him onto his back.

The water swelled and crashed right up to his ears; he was near the edge of it. Black summer sky loomed over him. He shut his eyes, opened them again, and saw a tribunal of nearly twenty cold, smirking faces. They gathered in a circle looking down at him.

Death was one of them; the others deferred to him. And Death was no stranger to Greg.

Death smiled and sang in a gravel-like, thin voice: "It seems we've stood and talked like this before. We looked at each other in the same way then, but I can't remember where or when."

Greg nodded and was relieved to finally understand where he was, who had him, and why.

"Bennie," he sighed.

Bennie, wrapped in a black pullover sweatshirt with a hood to protect him against the cold, nodded. He was shockingly thin. "Finally got my name right? Last time we saw each other you didn't seem to remember me."

Greg looked at the others, strangers all. But they knew him; he could tell. And they hated him.

Bennie stepped forward to put one foot on his chest. "This," he said to the others, "is Dr. Greg Bishop. He cures homosexuals."

That set off a frenzy. The members of the group shrieked, then began doing grotesque imitations of paralytics and cripples. They threw themselves ferociously into the parodies, kneeling next to Greg, beseeching him, jabbing his torso.

"Oh, doctor," a woman begged, "this darned homosexuality is acting up again and it's only a week before my daughter's wedding! I'd hate to show up queer. Can you get me straightened out before Sunday?"

"Doc, the whole left side of my face has gone gay, see?" a man mocked, twitching his cheek. "If I can but touch the hem of your garment, I just know I'll be healed." He touched Greg's chest as though it was a hot iron.

"Yeow!" he cheered. "I feel the power. Glory be! Where's a woman? I'm healed, I'm healed!"

Two of them, a man and a woman, touched Greg then paired off, smooching and clutching each other. "Hallelujah! Look at us! We're so straight we can't keep our hands off each other!"

Bennie's laughter could be heard above it all. Greg, barely able to move, watched the scene indifferently. Drugs and shock had numbed him.

The chaos played out, and Bennie took over while the group again circled Greg.

"Oh, but he started curing homosexuals years ago. I should know. He offered quite a cure to me, didn't you, doc? That was in the days of aversion therapy."

Now Greg was afraid. Not of Bennie or his cohorts, but of the story he knew was coming.

"See, first they lure you into their treatment facility. It looked a lot like this one, come to think of it. Then the doctor enters and looks you over to decide if you need treatment. All he has to do is say four little words for treatment to commence."

Greg would have plugged his ears if only his hands would move.

"'I ... don't ... know ... him.' Amazing what those words can ignite, huh, Greg? As soon as the doctor says, 'I don't know him,' his assistants step in and take over. They do the actual work, you know, but isn't that the way it is these days? Doctors only give you a few minutes while the assistants do all the grunt work."

Greg closed his eyes, trying to drift back into his drug-induced stupor. But he was far too awake now.

"Oh, and what tedious grunt work!" he heard Bennie say. "They lay hands on you, rub you down, give you an adjustment. You name it, they do it!"

Bennie's tone went from sarcastic to sinister.

"But the doctor didn't see it. He must have had other patients to attend to, so he had to run."

Greg opened his eyes again to see Bennie staring down at him with unspeakable contempt.

"You were so good to provide a cure for me. It took. I've never been the same since."

He knelt down and spoke into Greg's face. "Say, Greg, you're looking under the weather yourself. Need a cure?"

"He sure does," the group murmured in agreement. "Looks like a cure is in order ... yup."

Bennie nodded at Greg, watching his eyes closely to monitor his reaction. "We'll make a game of it, okay? The one you were always the best at."

Bennie glanced behind Greg. The waves lapped closer. He felt the edge of them on his scalp.

"Who's the champ at holding his breath underwater?"

Bennie delivered the question as a judge would prescribe a method of capital punishment. Two BRAVO members ripped Greg's shirt open and yanked it off his back.

Greg expected to be more frightened; instead, he wondered, with a kind of detachment, how long it would take.

"Oh, but I can't join you!" Bennie said with mock sadness. "No swimming for me. I've been under the weather too, see?"

He pointed to the lesions on his face.

"God zapped me."

A young man gave a pair of handcuffs to Bennie. Two others grabbed Greg's arms and pulled him down the damp slope, which got cold, colder, then ice-cold.

Salt water splashed and flowed over his shoulders and down his stomach, then over his head as he was dragged further. The wave receded. Bennie ordered them to turn Greg around and sit him up so that he faced the ocean, which now splashed over his lap. Bennie stood behind him and prepared his hands to be cuffed.

Random thoughts hit Greg: He hoped Christine wouldn't have to identify his body. Maybe he would merely sink if they took him out far enough. Was his wallet still in his pocket?

"Of course, I'd never let anybody do this to someone I knew," Bennie whispered harshly from behind Greg's ear. "Maybe, if I know you, this can all be prevented."

Greg drew no hope from the cat-and-mouse remark and returned to his own thoughts.

No, his body wouldn't sink—of course not. It would wash up within hours, most likely. How long would the morgue take to figure out who he was?

BRAVO stood in a semicircle around Greg and Bennie, who dangled the cuffs indecisively. "Do I know this guy?" he asked out loud.

"Beats me," someone said.

"He's a stranger," a woman mocked. "Looks strange to me."

"Oh, I've seen him on television," another man said. "He was so informative! He said I'm a child molester by nature, and that as soon as I've satisfied my appetite for strange flesh I'll turn to children. My brother has two kids who I'm no longer allowed to see, thanks to Dr. Bishop's educational series."

Cold water settled into Greg's lap, making his pants heavy. His teeth chattered.

"I've seen him on TV, too!" a woman chimed in. "He said I have the spirit of Sodom—a strange, violent spirit that violates and attacks."

"Well," Bennie considered, "let's not make a liar out of him, shall we?"

"Oh, no, let's not!" they said in unison.

A strong wave hit Greg's chest. Salt water sprayed upward and drenched him. Bennie's voice became deadly soft.

"I told Yelsom we would kill you if he turned you over to us. Of course, he believed it and was all too anxious to deliver you. But I've always found Yelsom a bit flamboyant, haven't you? Still, we could make him happy and do it, couldn't we?"

"Bennie," Greg stammered, "you've got to know something about Yel—"

"Of course, we've never killed anyone before. But, hey, everyone starts somewhere. And what have I got to lose? I haven't got much time left anyway."

"Let me talk. Just for a moment—"

Bennie slapped his face, hard. The cuffs jangled.

"You've talked enough for one lifetime."

Greg gave up. Somehow it all seemed useless. They would never believe him if he tried to tell them; he could scarcely believe it himself. He would die and nothing would change, nothing would matter. Christine was right, Alex was right, they had all been right. He'd blown it; time to pay up.

"The question remains," Bennie said. "Do I know this guy? If I do, we'll just call it a night and go home. After all, I'm not a savage. I kill strangers, not friends."

He pulled Greg's hair hard, forcing his head to snap backward with his face tilted toward Bennie, who peered at his victim.

"Have we met? The face is familiar, but... hmmm."

Everyone waited.

Bennie's head shook slowly.

"Nope. Doesn't ring a bell."

He stood up.

"I don't know him."

The others moved in for the kill.

"But, hey, don't take it personally," Bennie laughed as the handcuffs snapped over Greg's wrists. "I'm just awful about remembering people. It'll be the death of my social life!"

Hands cuffed under him, Greg was dragged by his feet into the surf, where he floated, then tilted, head backward, into the water. He held his breath.

Further out, then down. Three sets of arms pushed his chest underwater. He plunged under, descended, hit bottom. Feet stomped his chest and legs, then held him to the ocean floor while dizziness set in.

His mind tried to tell his body it was over—no use fighting. Give up. But his body would have none of it and his legs kicked harder and his torso thrashed wildly and refused to stop—even as his lungs filled and his head grew lighter, even as his mouth tried to form one last protest, and even as a hand came from nowhere and grabbed his hair and pulled him up and held his head above the water and someone screamed at him to breathe. Even then he thrashed.

Bennie slapped him.

"Greg!"

He jerked and kicked.

"Stop it!"

Bennie backhanded him at least five times before he stood still, waist-deep in water, hands cuffed, and chest heaving.

Bennie held him as though he was a baptismal candidate, whispering urgently into his face.

"It's incredible, isn't it? The feeling of another person having the power of life and death over you! Feel your heart! It's about to burst out of your chest, right? One word from me and it's over. These people want your blood, and all I have to do is look away and let them have it."

Greg gasped and heaved.

"But it's not over yet."

Greg could only wheeze in response.

"I got a life sentence when you left me here that night. Why should you get off with anything less?"

Greg sucked air gratefully and looked at Bennie, who stepped back into shallower water. The other BRAVO members had left the water and were now watching from the shoreline. Greg stayed put.

The waves were swelling, getting bigger, crashing louder.

"I wasn't too important to you that night, was I?" Bennie shouted. "Just another faggot getting what he deserves, right?"

Greg shook his head but found no voice to answer with.

"Who won, Greg? You or me? I could kill you, but that would make you a martyr and you're not martyr material. Besides, there are worse things than death. There is hell. Hell's eternal, right? Then let me send you there."

Then slowly, dramatically, but in dead earnest, Bennie lifted one hand to the sky and pointed at Greg with the other. His hood fell back, showing his entire skull, which seemed lit from within. Greg's shivering was violent now, as his old friend, former victim, and current enemy invoked the darkest curse he could muster:

"You had power over me twenty years ago and showed me no mercy. You—a normal, heterosexual male—the model of virtue. Then you went and made a career for yourself telling the world what monsters people like me are. Now one of those monsters has power over you. And do you know what he is going to do?"

He laughed shrilly. "The cruelest of all things. He is going to spare you. You watched your friends surround me to attack and you didn't have the decency to lift a finger. I saw my people surround you to attack and I stopped them. So who is the monster? You can't atone for what you did to me, Bishop. Now live with it!"

His face glowed; his voice was ecstatic, triumphant, eerie.

"Live with it when you face your wife and tell her what happened tonight. Live with it when you tell your adoring public about what horrible perverts we are. Live with the knowledge that a pervert showed more class, more mercy, more humanity than you did!"

Greg cowered under the words, which hurt more than punches or slaps ever could have.

"A two-bit faggot spared you."

Greg stepped toward Bennie and tried to speak and failed again.

"So you can never again pretend you're better than me. You can never again feel superior."

Bennie caught his breath and delivered one last blow.

"You've been outclassed, outdone, by one of *them!*"

Greg finally found his voice.

"Bennie."

Bennie turned and waded to shore.

"Bennie!"

Greg stayed put, hands still cuffed, desperate for Bennie to look at him.

"Bennie, listen! Bennie!"

The surf crashed, receded, gathered momentum, and crashed again.

A man from BRAVO handed Bennie a towel, offered him his jacket, and walked him, along with the others, back toward the cliffs.

"Bennie! Bennie!" Greg screamed.

Bennie broke from the group, turned to Greg, and called softly.

"It's amazing to scream for help at the beach, isn't it? No one hears you."

FORTY-FOUR

*Q*uiet please."

Nobody moved.

"Five, four, three, two—"

Upbeat music filled the room. A prerecorded voice announced "Melanie Stone Live." The hostess faced the camera and began.

"Good evening. I'm Melanie Stone; thank you for joining us."

The teleprompter flickered as she read from it. Her two guests followed along.

"Many Americans welcome the advances made by the gay rights movement. This June marks the twenty-third anniversary of the Stonewall riot, a turning point in gay history commemorated in parades and rallies across the country. Some public school districts now celebrate Gay and Lesbian Pride week, and some political candidates have already met with gay leaders and pledged them their support if elected."

Anticipation buzzed throughout the studio. Tonight would be the show to end all shows; most of the production crew knew it, and Melanie looked forward to a huge boost in ratings.

"But other citizens," she continued, "question the validity of the gay rights movement as strongly as they question the normalcy of homosexuality itself. Two such people are my guests tonight, who are here to discuss their concerns about the growing acceptance of homosexuality."

Camera Two did a close-up of the guests as each was introduced.

"First, Alexandra Chappel," Melanie said, "who is the wife of the late Senator Raymond Chappel of Georgia, and has been an active spokeswoman for conservative causes. She claims she was recently vandalized and assaulted by militant homosexuals. And with her is Richard Mosley, who describes himself as a concerned citizen and spokesman for Citizens United, a Southern California group Mrs. Chappel helped organize earlier this year."

Mosley, dressed handsomely in a dark-gray suit, smiled at Camera Two. Alexandra had done likewise, smoothing her navy knit dress while nodding toward the lens. Television suited them both.

"Mrs. Chappel, let's begin with you," Melanie said. "What exactly is Citizens United, and what are its goals?"

"Citizens United is a coalition of people who are concerned, as you said, about the indoctrination of the public by the gays."

"That's not quite what I said," Melanie interrupted.

"Not in so many words, no," Alexandra returned smoothly. She was far too seasoned to let an interviewer ruffle her. "'The growing acceptance of homosexuality' is how you put it, Melanie, and that spells indoctrination. There is a propaganda campaign being run in our public schools, our courts, and our city councils. It's a well-orchestrated attempt to indoctrinate the public with a radical redefinition of the family."

The sentences flowed easily from her; she'd repeated them often enough.

Melanie's dislike for her guests was contained but discernible. "So," she continued, "you oppose this indoctrination, as you call it. At other times your organization has referred to gay terrorism. Is that the same thing?"

"No, and I'm glad you asked that," Alexandra said eagerly. "It began as indoctrination, but now it has turned into terrorism."

"Explain, please."

"Years ago, gays said all they wanted was equality, so they pushed for nondiscrimination laws, civil rights, and so forth. That was first on the agenda."

"Surely," Melanie asked, "you're not saying they've achieved all those things?"

Mosley, who had been quietly deferring to Alexandra, glared at Melanie.

"No, they haven't," Alexandra agreed, "although they've certainly won a round of applause from the media and the government. But they still haven't won over the general public. That's the next goal, and they'll take whatever steps are necessary to achieve it."

"You know that yourself, Melanie," Mosley added. "You had one of their leaders on your show last year, remember? He admitted his group would do anything to silence their enemies. He was proud of it, in fact."

"Indeed," Melanie said.

"We've got a horrible problem in Orange County," Alexandra continued. "As you mentioned, my home was decimated by the gays last week, and I'm afraid that's just a taste of what we can expect in the near future."

"Did they know it was your home?"

"Certainly! I was targeted, don't you see? It's all part of the plan."

"Describe the plan, please."

"It started last spring. Gays started blackmailing key public figures into admitting *they* were gay. Then gay groups started riots in front of the local churches."

"People were terrified to go to church—can you imagine?" Mosley asked indignantly.

"But even that wasn't enough. They turned violent when Governor Wilson vetoed a gay rights bill in California. They can't take no for an answer. They set a church on fire while a young man was inside."

"Robbie Carlton," Melanie said. "We're familiar with the story."

"After that we were all fed up," Mosley huffed, shifting his position in his chair and recrossing his legs. Alexandra sat demurely.

"So that's where Citizens United came in," she said to Melanie. "We've tapped into the dissatisfaction that many people feel over the gays' behavior."

"Not just dissatisfaction," Mosley added. "Anger."

"Let's talk about that anger for a moment, shall we?" Melanie asked them both. "Isn't it true that, along with the gay demonstrations you've mentioned, there has also been a rash of assaults committed against gays in Orange County?"

"Some assaults, yes," Alexandra conceded.

Melanie checked a notepad she held in her hand. "Over twenty assaults since October of last year, Mrs. Chappel. That's more than some."

"We can't keep people from getting angry!" Mosley burst out.

"But," Alexandra interjected, "we don't condone violence against anyone."

"Oh, no," Mosley agreed.

Melanie rechecked her notepad. "And yet violent acts have occurred at your rallies and at demonstrations sponsored by your organization," she pressed.

"But again," Alexandra said with some strain, "we don't condone violence or claim responsibility for it when we're not the ones committing it. Our speakers educate the public and mobilize support for our viewpoint, which is a legitimate activity."

"And is Greg Bishop," Melanie said directly to Alexandra, "one of your speakers?"

The question stopped them both cold. Alexandra looked at Mosley, who picked up the ball. "He is, yes, and a darned good one."

Darned absent, too, Mosley thought. He hadn't heard from Bennie since that night; he could only imagine what he—what *they*—had done to poor Bishop.

"Yes," Melanie nodded. "Well, others share your concern over the activities of gay radicals." She turned to point at a monitor. "We have some clips tonight from a documentary on the subject, which we'll show now."

The guests hadn't been told about this. Mosley's brow furrowed; Alexandra showed only slight surprise.

"This is just the final portion of the film. I'd like to get your comments on it afterward," she added.

"Certainly," Alexandra said crisply.

The studio lights dimmed. All three looked at the monitor.

Hundreds of gays were shown gathered in front of a cathedral, carrying signs and shouting, "Stop the church!" Police lined the entryway to the building, clearing an entrance for people wanting to go inside. Several did, somewhat timidly, and several other people stood outside watching the demonstration. The weather was clearly cold—protesters and spectators alike wore thick overcoats and gloves, and steam rose from the protesters' mouths as they chanted and screamed.

Mosley recognized the scene. He reared his head back, stunned and furious, then checked to see if a camera was on him. Seeing there wasn't, he decided on a quick exit, then noticed security guards at both doors.

They hadn't been there when the interview started.

"Can I use the bathroom while the tape runs?" he whispered to Melanie, who kept her eyes on the monitor and pretended not to hear.

Alexandra caught Mosley's tension and looked at him questioningly.

"It's the tape," he murmured.

He started to rise out of his seat when Alexandra grabbed his hand.

"Don't. We won't run. They'll take it as an admission."

Her hand was ice-cold.

Joshua Ferguson's voice narrated the scene.

"So if the laws against homosexuality can be challenged, and the American Psychiatric Association can be persuaded to change its position, the organized church remains the last obstacle toward the legitimizing of homosexuality. And that obstacle, gay activists say, is the target of the gay nineties."

Bennie appeared, in a black T-shirt with the BRAVO logo, seated on a park bench. His face was full, and large biceps strained his short sleeves. The virus, if present when this interview was taped, hadn't yet begun its work.

"The organized church has committed unforgivable and unforgiven sins against us," he said into the camera. "Unforgivable in that they cannot be excused, and unforgiven in that we will hold the church accountable for every one of them."

Joshua's narration overrode Bennie's voice.

"This is Bennie Hudson, the founder of BRAVO—Bent on Removing All Vestiges of Oppression. Bennie lives in New York City, where he and his former lover, now deceased from AIDS, first became involved in gay politics. His lover's death, Bennie says, was the galvanizing force behind BRAVO's creation.

Again, Bennie's voice was heard.

"—and when Malcolm died, his family allowed their minister to condemn him and his so-called lifestyle at his own funeral service! They were all good Christian folks, you know. And I began to realize, after the funeral, how much I hated these people—all of them—and how much they hated me. That's when my interest in forming a group to fight them was born."

"But," Ferguson's narration continued, "Bennie also learned a way to channel that interest into a strategy he feels will neutralize the church's influence in America."

"Humiliation, intimidation, silence," Bennie recited. "That's our strategy, and we're enacting it state by state. We'll start by humiliating every closet case we learn about."

"And," Ferguson's off-camera voice asked, "can you elaborate on closet cases—what they are and what you plan to do with them?"

"Easy. A closet case is a queer—we use that word now, by the way, so don't look so shocked when I say it!—a queer who pretends he's not a queer. And there are plenty of closet cases in the church. The reason they're so crucial is this: If we can prove that lots of 'good Christian people' are queer, then we'll make it even harder for the Religious Right to say homosexuality is a sin when it's right in their own backyard."

"And how do you expose these closet cases?"

"We warn them first, because it looks better if they come out on their own. It encourages other people to do the same thing. But if they're still unwilling to do it themselves, we do it for them."

"And you're already doing this?"

"In some cities, yes."

"And the rest of your strategy?"

"Intimidation. We protest at churches with pastors who preach hatred toward us from the pulpit—"

"What constitutes 'hatred toward us?'"

"Oh, you know, saying that we're sinning, that what we do is an abomination, that we're all going to hell, stuff like that."

"Isn't that a basic Christian belief, though? That homosexuality is a sin?"

"It's a basic Christian belief that's bigoted, that's what it is! They have the right to believe it, but we'll make it harder for them to teach it. And finally"—Bennie paused for effect—"we'll silence them. In every area we take over, we'll make it so rough on them that they'll either have the good sense to quit persecuting us with their diabolical, archaic doctrines, or we'll find other ways to shut them up."

"You're talking terrorism now."

Bennie smiled at the camera. "Well, you know what they say: One man's terrorist is another man's freedom fighter."

Joshua took up the narration again. "But this form of freedom fighting, as Mr. Hudson calls it, may actually have the opposite of the desired effect. Pastor Carl Watkins of Emmanuel Lutheran Church in Connecticut had his church services picketed after he refused to perform a wedding ceremony for two gay men in his congregation."

A thin, middle-aged cleric was shown sitting in his church's sanctuary.

"They blew whistles and shouted names and made such a disturbance we couldn't possibly hold services that day. Were we scared? A little. But *mad* is a better word. Ironically, when I asked my people to pray for those gay demonstrators the next Sunday, one of the men in the congregation stood up and said, 'Well, pastor, I'll *prey* on them gladly, but I sure won't *pray* for them!' And the entire assembly applauded. That's about all they accomplished, you know. They just made people hate them all the more."

"Which is just what some people are banking on," Joshua said, appearing on camera and walking toward a familiar-looking house.

Alexandra stiffened.

"He must have taped that when I wasn't home."

Mosley stood up. Alexandra sat, regal and frozen.

Ferguson gestured toward the house. "This is the home of Alexandra Chappel, a woman known for her fund-raising skills and expertise on the lecture circuit." He stopped in front of the brick walkway. "The widow of a Georgia senator, Mrs. Chappel has enjoyed a good name among religious and political conservatives."

Ferguson's eyes twinkled.

"But they, and you, might be surprised to learn of some of her other skills."

On the monitor appeared a close-up of Alexandra sitting in her dimly lit living room, leaning forward. The camera angle was a bit low, centered on her chest and throat, and the sound was fuzzy. But the subject and her words were unmistakable.

"We're everywhere, Joshua, face it. And we're not backwoods, sheet-wearing bubbas anymore. We're smarter and more well-heeled than ever."

"The *we* Mrs. Chappel refers to," Josh explained, "is a movement known as The Covenant, a white supremacist organization believing they are God's chosen, the true Israel, the rightful heirs to the covenant promises between Jehovah and His chosen people in the Old Testament. Their mission is to restore moral order to America and other Aryan nations, and their first step is to restore credibility to the white supremacist movement."

Back to Alexandra.

"The religious types who say how awful we are would be the first to agree with most of our goals. We're antiabortion, antigay, anti-big government, profamily. It's the racial issue people stumble over—usually because of the misconceptions they have about us. So now we're letting them get to know us as social conservatives first."

"Dr. Alex Crawford," Josh continued, "is one of those who got to know Mrs. Chappel that way. He was once, in fact, sponsored by Mrs. Chappel as a spokesman against gay rights, but has since renounced her goals and tactics. He fears that others will be led to believe, as he was, that they're doing the right thing by aligning themselves with her."

Alex appeared in his office talking with Joshua.

"Mrs. Chappel is organizing a group called Citizens United. It will be billed as a grass-roots effort to fight the gay rights movement, but in actuality it will be a recruiting ground for white supremacists. Their plan is to raise up legitimate conservative leaders who'll rally people around them to fight the gays."

"When you say 'legitimate conservative leaders,' you mean leaders who aren't with The Covenant?" Joshua asked.

"Correct. But these leaders will attract all types. Some people will join them because they sincerely oppose homosexuality, but others will join simply because they hate gays. And The Covenant will be able to tell which is which."

"So it will be a mixed group?"

"It will. They used me, I'm afraid. They were trying to raise me up as their spokesman to gain credibility for themselves. They financed my lectures and made it worth my while to say rather extravagant things about gays which, in retrospect, I now regret saying. Mind you, I still oppose homosexuality in any form. But this group truly encouraged me to slander the gays in ways even they don't deserve."

"Our hidden camera," Joshua narrated, "captured a recent conversation with Mrs. Chappel in her Corona del Mar home, where she discussed the goals of The Covenant, an organization she supports financially and actively."

She reappeared on the screen.

"We lost our battles over segregation in the sixties because the image of the Negro was so sanitized. Martin Luther King accomplished that; so did others. The public swallows television images so easily without checking the facts. So when blacks started putting on suits and marching peacefully, we were suddenly the bad guys. You know the power of a camera. We lost our credibility when the news programs showed them looking so noble then showed clips of us burning crosses and shaking our fists."

Ferguson's voice broke in. "Mrs. Chappel's group believes, among other things, that blacks, Jews, and other races have usurped true Israel—an Aryan Israel, mind you—and are gradually putting a stranglehold on white Christian Americans and their ability to raise their families in peace."

Alexandra continued. Her unguarded cynicism on this tape contrasted with the gentler approach she used when she knew the cameras were rolling.

"Of course, things were looking up during the Chicago and the Watts riots, when Negroes showed their true colors so boldly the media *couldn't* ignore it. But they'd wised up by then, and knew they would never get away with their natural behavior for long—not if they wanted civil rights and all that."

"And now," Ferguson announced, "we get to the role Mrs. Chappel hopes The Covenant will play in the 1990s."

Still seated on her couch, Alexandra was shown laughing sarcastically.

"Fags? There's no easier group to manipulate. What do you think we've gone to all this trouble for?"

"Exactly what trouble," Ferguson asked off-camera, "have you gone to?"

"We've got our people in every major city infiltrating homosexual political groups, getting a foothold, and hopefully rising to leadership positions. In fact, one of our most promising young men, Richard, is currently leading the BRAVO group in Orange County. Homosexuals live to throw tantrums. Haven't you noticed? Every time they don't get what they want they throw a fit. The only thing they love more than sex and drugs is a television camera to act up in front of. And we're right there with them to make sure they never stop throwing fits. We want them to throw even bigger ones, because once they're absolutely drunk with power—and that'll be soon, by the way—they'll do things so outrageous and offensive that even the most die-hard liberals won't be willing to defend them. Then we'll step in. Our groups will slap the gays back in line. People will cheer us for it. Then we'll regain the credibility you've tried so hard to take from us."

She pointed her long index finger at the person she was talking to. Bright red polish flashed across the screen.

"We'll ride to respectability right on their deviant little backs. And you won't interfere. I loved you, Joshua, then I hated you. You've occupied an important place in my heart, but I'll never let you interfere."

On tape, Alexandra Chappel looked far more triumphant than her counterpoint in the studio, who watched, trembling, while her own ghastly image vanished from the screen.

Ferguson replaced her for some final words.

"Militant gays hope to silence the Christian viewpoint on homosexuality. Angry Christians, pushed to the limits of the charity they espouse, may grow weary of turning the other cheek. Some may even be tempted to react with violence, not silence. And The Covenant, whose goals would disgust both gays and Christians, eggs both groups on and waits to gather the spoils."

He paused.

"Let the millions of Americans calling themselves evangelical Christians take note. Homosexuality is, like it or not, a social issue that cannot be ignored. If organized Christianity finds itself unwilling or unable to tackle it, there are those waiting in the wings who are more than anxious to tackle it for them."

Blackout.

The studio lights came back on to reveal Melanie Stone and her two ashen-faced, disoriented guests. An assistant brought a third chair onto the set. Alexandra stared straight ahead impassively. Mosley gripped the arms of his chair, furious but controlled.

"Mrs. Chappel?" Melanie's voice seemed to awaken her. "There is quite a difference in the goals you've described tonight and those you mention on this tape. Can you comment on that?"

Silence.

"This tape was made by the late Joshua Ferguson, with whom you were well acquainted, weren't you? In fact, wasn't it Mr. Ferguson you were speaking to on the tape?"

Nothing.

"Mr. Mosley, I'm told you're the promising young man Mrs. Chappel refers to in the tape. I'm informed that you yourself are the one who started the fire at the Berean Community Church, which killed Mr. Carlton, and that you may be implicated in a recent assault on a young radio announcer. Is that the case?"

If looks could kill, Melanie Stone would have been massacred.

"You didn't mention The Covenant earlier this evening. Would you care to tell us about it? Is it connected with Citizens United, or is Citizens United simply a front for The Covenant?"

Mosley's chest was heaving. His arms and legs twitched and jerked as if he were tied to his chair.

And still nothing from Alexandra, who seemed suddenly removed from the scene, as if she was above all this nonsense. She wouldn't even deign to acknowledge it.

Melanie waited again. "Well, then, perhaps our next guest can shed more light on these questions. He is well-acquainted with your work and describes himself as somewhat of an expert on both of you."

Footsteps clapped loudly on the studio floor; Mosley heard someone approaching from behind the set partition.

"Welcome, Dr. Bishop."

Melanie stood and extended her hand. Greg Bishop strode onto the set, smiled at the three of them graciously, shook Melanie's hand, and seated himself between Alexandra and Mosley.

For a moment nobody spoke.

Melanie broke the ice. "Doctor, you were initially scheduled to be tonight's main guest, representing Citizens United. Yet you contacted our offices earlier this week and suggested we have Mrs. Chappel and Mr. Mosley on as well, although, of course, they weren't aware you would be with us tonight."

"They weren't aware I'd be alive tonight," Greg said politely.

"And you provided us with the tape, for which we thank you."

"It deserved a wide audience, and I couldn't think of a better way to present it."

Melanie smiled. "You've been associated with both my guests in the past—is that correct?"

Greg looked at both of them and nodded.

"More than associated. We were a team. And we're full of surprises—"

A scream—deep, male, but oddly effeminate and wild—cut the air. Mosley leapt from the set and collided with Camera Two while he barreled his way toward the exit.

"Catch it! All of it!" Melanie yelled at the camera operators.

Camera One picked up the rest of the action, showing Mosley throw himself into the mammoth security guard at the main exit and push him back several feet with little effort. The second guard was seen joining in, then the camera panned back to include two policemen who scurried forward with handcuffs and orders to Mosley. Microphones picked up curses, screams, and the sound of scuffling while Mosley was restrained but not subdued.

Panning further back, Camera One caught Melanie Stone and Greg Bishop, who had grabbed her off the set and into a corner of the studio for safety's sake. And finally, whether by accident or the camera operator's sense of the aesthetic, the camera panned in closer to the lone, graceful figure of Alexandra Chappel, still in her seat, serene and unmoved by pandemonium. Untouched, untouchable.

She sensed the camera's nearness and looked directly into it, speaking to someone who wasn't there.

"To Satan. For the destruction of the flesh."

She closed her eyes and a tight smile thinned her lips.

"Oh, Joshua. You finally finished your statement."

FORTY-FIVE

Los Angeles Times
Saturday, May 17, 1992
Page A-1

Orange County Terrorist Group Uncovered

WASHINGTON, D.C.—An extraordinary confrontation on live television has exposed the existence of a terrorist group which may be responsible for the death of gospel singer Robbie Carlton. As cameras rolled on CNN's "Melanie Stone Show" at 9:00 P.M. last night, a video report produced by the late investigative reporter Joshua Ferguson was shown, revealing the program's two guests to hold leadership positions within The Covenant, an underground white supremacist organization with branches throughout the country. It has been learned that The Covenant, which investigators believe has a branch in Orange County, may also be linked to a series of assaults on gays, plus attempted manslaughter, arson, blackmail, and conspiracy.

The videotaped report, titled "Unforgiven Sins" and originally intended for viewing on Ferguson's "Limelight" program before his suicide last year, chronicled the escalating conflict between religious conservatives and gay radicals. It also documented clandestine conversations, revealing an attempt by The Covenant to masquerade as militant gays and antagonize religious groups, creating an atmosphere of hostility between conservatives and gays, and giving The Covenant credibility with conservatives by offering a rigid, sometimes violent "solution" to the "homosexual problem."

"They capitalized on the tension between Christians and gays," said Melanie Stone, "creating an even bigger problem than the existing one. Then they offered themselves as the answer. And it seems to have almost worked." Stone denied any knowledge of the group's involvement in violent activities, but confirmed that she had been tipped off to their agenda by Dr. Greg Bishop, an Orange County psychologist who forwarded the tape to her last week, and who suggested the on-air unmasking of Mrs. Alexandra Chappel and her protégé, Richard Mosley. Bishop also participated in the program, making a surprise entrance after the video had been shown.

The on-air confrontation began when Alexandra Chappel, wife of the late Senator Raymond Chappel and a renowned political activist, was asked to comment on taped conversations shown between her and Ferguson. After a brief verbal confrontation precipitated by Bishop's presence on the set, Mosley attempted to flee the studio, where he was apprehended by security guards and police who'd been advised of a potential altercation. Both Chappel and Mosley were arrested without incident.

—Continued on A-17

The Orange County Register
Saturday, May 17, 1992
Editorial Section

So What Did We Learn?

The relieved sigh you're hearing is that of an exhausted public hoping to believe that a devastating chapter in Orange County history has finally closed. Of course, last night's CNN debacle evokes emotions other than relief—outrage, perhaps, or any variations of indignation. But if allegations raised last night are true, then relief is the emotion of choice.

From Joshua Ferguson's merciless "outing" to Greg Bishop's ravings, we've viewed the attacks and counterattacks between radical gays and their right-wing enemies as we would a freeway accident: compelling and repulsive, commanding us to turn away while ordering us to look closer. It was intriguing when it began, unsettling as it progressed, anguishing when it climaxed. As BRAVO, Citizens United, Robbie Carlton, Greg Bishop, et al played out their tragedy, we felt, with each development, like children who had entered a haunted house for a lark and discovered a series of inexplicable, all-too-real ghosts. It stopped being fun; we got scared and wanted to go home. And now, with fingers crossed, we think we might just be there.

If The Covenant is responsible for the arson, assaults, and general destruction they stand accused of, and *if* they inflamed the already-angry ranks of BRAVO to commit heinous actions, and *if* last year's "outings" were part of a grander plan, then the exposure of The Covenant means the game is up and we are home free. But, like Dorothy nestled back in Kansas, we need to reflect. What did we learn?

First, we have learned that neither side is going away. There will always be homosexuals, and there will always be people—religious and nonreligious—who believe homosexuality is wrong. A uniform opinion on the subject is a pipe dream which should be abandoned by both groups. The subject calls for extended debate, yes, but not the sort which attempts to silence its opposition and tolerate only its own position. And that—the attempt to silence one's opponent by intimidation or any other like means—must in the future be seen by us, the public, as a lack of integrity and credibility. If we give no audience to modern McCarthyites, be they gay or conservative, we'll frustrate their tactics.

Second, we have learned to appeal to our religious bodies for a more responsive, dynamic approach to the vexing subject of homosexuality. Most religions frown on homosexuality and, if polls can be believed, so do most Americans. So in light of the burgeoning gay rights movement, we look to our spiritual leaders for guidance. And, frankly, so far they've disappointed us.

Some in the clergy have watered down their beliefs to accommodate culture, assuming society should influence the church, not vice versa. If these revisionists think their stand will enhance their popularity, they might well ask themselves if popularity is a noble quest for a man of the cloth. They might also consider an old axiom: People neither trust nor respect a man who compromises his views for their sake.

Others have simply been intimidated by the politically correct mandate to shun those naughty Bible references about sex and morality. Weak shepherds indeed, one wonders how ably they will guard their flock in times of true crises if a gay rights demonstration outside their church is enough to silence them on this issue.

Equally guilty are the pulpit-banging hate-mongers—a vocal minority who snarl and foam over homosexuality while winking at any number of other vices. They, more than the others, played beautifully into The Covenant's agenda.

And somewhere in the middle, the majority of the religious population—overlooked, as usual—wants to effectively respond to gays while compromising neither compassion nor conviction. To them a request is posed: Find a way. Because in spite of the break we may be getting from extremist groups, their members will always be with us, hatred and zeal intact. How to keep from their clutches remains a pertinent question. Let the church be the first to produce answers.

"And good afternoon. I'm Calvin Blanchard and this is 'Open Heart,' coming to you weekdays at three on KLVE Orange County. I'll be with you till five o'clock this beautiful June day, sharing thoughts and conversations, and I hope you'll share a few thoughts of your own."

The studio was plastered with cards, ribbons, balloons. Management had gone out of its way to provide a gracious send-off. Today's broadcast was preceded by a two-hour office party; a private dinner had been held the night before at the general manager's home. And letters of goodwill had flowed in for two weeks since Calvin Blanchard announced his resignation from "Open Heart."

"This is, as you know, my last broadcast with KLVE. It caps off an incredible stream of adventures."

Like pretending to be a gay radical, breaking and entering, stealing, and running errands for a maniac.

Then being left bleeding in a dark alley. He couldn't remember feeling the knife go into his chest or hitting the ground head-first, which had knocked him unconscious. Nor could he fathom why Yelsom had fled the scene without first ascertaining that his victim was silenced once and for all. Somehow, whether through carelessness on Yelsom's part or intervention on God's, Calvin had been left for dead. But the knife that was aimed at his heart had missed its target by mere fractions of an inch. Though the wound was severe, it had not killed him. If a drunken patron of The Shaft hadn't wandered out the back door and stumbled over what he thought was another gay-bashing casualty, the story might have ended differently. The paramedics were almost too late in getting there. But not quite.

All of this took volumes of explaining to his pastor, old friends at Gateway, detectives, family, and KLVE's owners and managers—in that order.

They had taken it pretty well, all things considered. Friends and family were shocked, and plenty of Christians questioned the ethics of his activities. But the professional community responded more kindly. So kindly, in fact, that a book deal had just been finalized and an ample advance was in the mail. Evidently people thought he had quite a story to tell.

But Calvin needed time for himself, and with the book advance—enough savings to see him through a full year to finish the manuscript—Calvin decided, with difficulty, to leave broadcasting.

"Believe me, my decision to leave KLVE was reached after a considerable amount of agonizing. I've had a family here and I have no illusions about ever being able to replace them. Let me say unequivocally that I've received more support and valuable experience here than I'd ever hope to find anywhere else. And in spite of the controversy I involved myself in, apart from anyone's knowledge here at KLVE, I've been asked to stay. But I'm at a crossroads now. I need a break."

And rest. Pastor Cox all but commanded him to. There were relationships to rebuild at his church, friendships to renew, explanations to make. Once the smoke had cleared, Calvin was appalled to realize how many people he had neglected for so long. He'd had to; living a lie made intimacy impossible. There was a lesson in there somewhere.

It was a lesson Alexandra Chappel and Rick Mosley had yet to learn. Calvin wasn't surprised to hear that upon their arrests they were defiant, unrepentant. Nor was he surprised when, having been released on a $100,000 bond raised by supporters, Mosley jumped bail and disappeared. Alexandra claimed no knowledge of his whereabouts. Ever the gracious lady, she awaited her own trial with confidence in her vindication. She told the press as much.

Tom Wooding was reported to be less confident; no bail was raised for him as there had been for Alexandra and Mosley. In addition, Wooding's prior record left him in a precarious legal position. And no one knew where Lassiter, Romano, and Adkins— The Covenant's three henchmen—had disappeared, though warrants had been issued for each.

Citizens United had, predictably, disbanded. Each member received a lengthy letter of explanation and apology from Greg Bishop.

BRAVO had, by all accounts, likewise disbanded. But to Calvin's surprise, Greg had refused to press charges against or even identify his assailants. Calvin assumed he had his reasons.

"I want to thank you for the encouragement you've sent me through your letters," Calvin went on. "Bear with me, please, because I intend to answer them all. Some of you expressed sympathy to me for the ordeal I've been through. Some of you have quite sincerely taken me to task for living a double life and for not letting the proper authorities handle things when they got too hot. And I intend to answer your concerns, too. But let me clarify one point on air: I do not apologize for fighting the gay agenda. I made mistakes while fighting it, sure, and in my efforts to understand what really caused the death of my dear friend Josh Ferguson—"

We got them, Josh, he thought, pausing. *Just like you told Greg to. But at what price?*

"—I accidentally aligned myself with a group whose goals were every bit as horrible as any the gays have. Still, I've learned firsthand that a gay agenda *does* exist, an aggressive and dangerous one, and I can't say I was wrong for having tried to oppose it. So I hope the extremes of groups like The Covenant won't discourage the rest of us from standing our ground. I certainly don't intend to shy away from fighting the good fight."

The engineer gave Calvin a grin and a thumbs-up from behind the glass.

"The most common message I've gotten from you all," Calvin continued, "has come in the form of a question: What now?"

He smiled at his engineer, who, like thousands of others, was anxious to hear the answer. And, like thousands of others, the engineer was disappointed but curious at Calvin's reply:

"I have absolutely no idea. I've got a book to write. After that, I'd like to put all the lessons I've learned this year into practice. How? I can't say yet, folks. Meanwhile, I'm open to suggestions. When the phone lines open up, maybe you'll have a few for me."

FORTY-SIX

*C*hristine sewed new sofa cushions while Greg read aloud from the book in his lap.

"Jerome. Jordan."

Plenty of time to lounge around the house. No appointments, no chores. The late afternoon June breeze was perfect. Christine had opened all the windows to catch it.

"These will brighten things." She held up her work. "See?"

"Hmm. Nice." He thumbed a few more pages.

He would be returning to his post as clinical director of Berean Counseling in July. Everyone on the board wanted him back; Pastor Mike went out of his way to call and say so. Greg's sorrow over his recklessness as Citizens United's leader was genuine; his life was again in order. It was generally understood among Berean's leadership that if Greg Bishop could be an example of how to go off the deep end, he could also be an example of how not to drown once you've gone there.

Even Pastor Ruben had extended a welcome-back phone call, though he couldn't resist throwing a few jabs in the process.

"So, Greg," he'd said over the phone, "I guess you won."

"Meaning?"

"The board is considering another try at starting a ministry to gays. Or repentant gays, or whatever you call them."

"*Repentant* will do."

"I don't get it. After all they put you through, you still want them coming to our church?"

"More than ever."

"Well, the compassionate approach isn't without merit; I'll give you that. But what about the other gays? The ones who still want to take over?"

"What about them?"

"They're still gaining power."

Greg wouldn't let himself think about that.

But he *was* ready for work, hungry to solve problems and empathize with people who had them.

Christine had one of her own—a problem, that is. It reappeared every morning. He hated to see her sick but loved the cause of it.

"Justin?" he asked, fingering a page.

"Justin Allen Bishop," she replied, then shook her head. "Too formal."

"When did we decide on 'Allen'?"

"It's a great middle name. Fits between any first and last name just right."

"Assuming it's a boy. What did you think of Jerome?"

"Not bad, not so great." Christine looked up from her sewing. "If it *is* a boy, I still don't see what's wrong with Gregory, Jr."

Greg shook his head stubbornly. "One is enough."

"Oh, you!" She punched the cushion she was working on. "I hate it when you belittle yourself. He could do a lot worse than be like his daddy. A whole lot worse."

"And a whole lot better. You really want to see him turn out like me? Think about it."

She stopped sewing and cocked her head, considering. "Probably." Then, more firmly, "Yes. Definitely."

"Because?"

"Because I don't want my son or my husband to be the best saint or the worst sinner. You're a perfect balance. Haven't I told you that? You're way too godly to be the sort of man Christian women should avoid, but you're way too earthy to be anyone's idea of a monk. You're just right. I want my son's wife to say the same about him."

Nothing could have suited Greg more. He put the book down, scooted toward her, and put his hand over the pillow she was working on. "Can this wait for a minute?"

"Or an hour, if you prefer."

"Just a few minutes. I want to hold you."

They snuggled contentedly. Without conversation in the room, the radio, which had been playing all along, was more audible. A Bible teacher was expounding on grace.

"Hold onto your own sin, and you can't experience true forgiveness, because you're denying there is anything to forgive. That's a sure way to live a graceless life. An even surer way, though, is to hold onto someone else's sin by remembering it, conjuring it up, and refusing to forgive it. You know, Jesus doesn't command us to forgive just to lay down some kind of a moral imperative. He commands us to forgive because unforgiveness is too heavy a weight for anyone to bear."

"That's it," Christine murmured into Greg's cheek.

"Hmmm?"

"Weren't you listening?" She drew herself away for a moment to turn the radio off, then lay next to Greg again.

"Unforgiveness. Bennie never forgave you; you never forgave yourself. Alexandra never forgave Joshua Ferguson, and your friend Rick Mosley never forgave anyone in his life, I suppose."

Greg jerked slightly and looked out the window, a reflex reaction to hearing Mosley's name.

"No," he said, gazing across the yard into the street. "He doesn't have it in him to forgive."

Christine stroked his shoulder. "You still don't think he will come for you, though?"

"No. Not for harm, anyway. But maybe for fun and games he'll come back later."

"Fun and *games?*"

Greg looked back at her and nodded. "That's how he sees it. The more I think about it, the more I get the feeling he loved every minute of it. He's a beast at bay for now, but he loves the chase. He'll be back."

Christine felt a momentary chill and decided not to let it spoil the mood. "At least," she mused, "we got another chance. This thing nearly ruined us."

"Especially me. I still can't believe some of the things I said."

"And did. It brought out the worst in you."

"Like you said it would."

She put both arms around him and held on. Tight.

"But things are a hundred times better. Between us, and you and Pastor Mike."

"And Calvin and everybody."

"And Lisa, I think."

"Lisa?"

"Of Lisa and Roxanne. We're having lunch this week. She wants to talk. I think she's having some doubts."

"About what?"

Christine laughed and hugged. "Honey. Can't you see the obvious?"

"Ah. Good." He was quiet for a moment, lost in thought.

Christine nudged his arm. "So. We had a happy ending, right?"

"Basically."

"Everyone's okay?"

The question hung, and Christine knew where his thoughts had drifted. Both of them knew; she finally said it.

"You need to find him. And go to him."

FORTY-SEVEN
==================

*F*inding Bennie was easy; going to him was the hard part.

Greg called information for the number of Roger and Claire Hudson in Long Beach and was told there was only a Claire Hudson. He jotted the number down, figuring Bennie's father was by now deceased or divorced.

His hand quavered when he dialed; not having spoken with Bennie's mother for twenty-five years, he could only guess what she was going through. And how she felt about him.

Claire Hudson's voice was soft and defeated, but instantly recognizable.

"Mrs. Claire Hudson? Bennie Hudson's mother?"

"Yes?"

"This is Greg Bishop."

He heard a gasp, then dead silence, as though she had put the phone down or against her chest.

"Mrs. Hudson, are you there?"

Another gasp, a clearing of the throat, then a dry laugh. "You've become quite the crusader, Greg, keeping our children safe from gays and all."

Greg took the sarcasm in stride. It was hardly unexpected. "Mrs. Hudson," he said patiently, "could you please let me know how to reach Bennie?"

"Are you sure you have time for someone as immoral as Bennie?"

"I have time for an old friend—"

"You pathetic *fraud!*"

Greg pulled the receiver away and rubbed his ear.

"Time for an old *friend?* What right do you have calling him that?"

"Maybe none; I don't know."

"Do you have any idea what you did to him?"

"More than you could imagine. It's no comfort, I'm sure, but there is nothing you could say to me that I haven't already said to myself."

"You played right here, right here in my yard. You slept in this house and ate my food, and I drove you and Bennie to school every week."

"I haven't forgotten—"

"And you left him there like a dog!" Greg knew she had waited two decades to say it. "A dog to be kicked around by your friends, your...I wish I'd taken a photo of him after they dragged him off the beach. I'd smear it in your face every day till your death. Do you know what it feels like seeing you on television talking morality? Do you know what a sick joke you are? *Do you?*"

He could let her go on, uninterrupted, for another half hour, or he could adopt a more professional tone and take control. He opted for control.

"Mrs. Hudson, you've got every right to get angry at me for that. We could get together soon and you could say all you need to say, and I promise I'll listen. But for now, there's Bennie."

She quieted.

"I know he is very sick, and there are things I need to say to him. Believe me, he'll be better off if he and I make peace. Don't you agree?"

Mrs. Hudson sighed. "He's gone way downhill. He may not even recognize you."

"I'll be brief. And sensitive."

More silence while Mrs. Bishop considered.

"St. Mary's."

"Pardon?"

"St. Mary's Medical Center. Room 317."

He scribbled it down. "Thank you." She didn't respond but wanted to; he could sense it, so he stayed on the line.

"I can't sing to him anymore," she finally said, as though to herself. "He likes love songs and show tunes. Hymns, too. But my voice gets so tired I've had to stop. I can't rub him down anymore, either. He's too sore. And he can't talk. But he still likes to be touched. Lightly. He's just a baby now."

Greg listened, waited. But her voice had trailed off and there was clearly nothing left to say, so he thanked her again and said good-bye.

Then came the hard part.

Driving from Garden Grove to St. Mary's took twenty minutes; he kept his mind clear. The most important discussion he had ever faced was waiting, but for once Greg Bishop wouldn't rehearse or even consider how he would handle it. Whatever he said to Bennie had to be genuine, uninhibited. They would both know if it wasn't.

"Room 317," he told the woman at the nurses' station.

"Are you a family member?"

"Old friend."

She pointed the way. He walked quickly past a waiting area and down the hall. Bennie's room was the second one on the left. Greg stood in the doorway, looked inside, and felt himself go numb.

The skeleton on the lone bed was alive and gowned. His eyes were bright, sunken, wide open, and vacant. A respirator mouthpiece covered most of his lower face; tubes ran into and around his limbs, linking him to machines that pumped and hissed while the chest cavity heaved then stopped, then heaved and stopped again.

Greg rechecked the number on the door. A nurse passed in the hall.

"Bennie Hudson?" he asked, pointing.

She glanced inside, nodded, and walked on; she'd seen this reaction hundreds of times. Greg stepped toward the bed, then backed away to the wall, still staring at Bennie.

Know what G.A.Y.S. stands for?

What?

Got AIDS yet, sucker?

Pretty good, Bishop!

Greg moaned at the recollection.

"Bennie."

Too soft, no response.

He moved closer to the foot of the bed. Through the sheet Greg saw a pitiful outline of knees, ankles, and feet. The skin covering them was thinner than the sheet covering the skin.

Bennie stared at the ceiling, or into space. Greg moved to the left of the bed, took three steps, and brought his face down. He smelled a foul, unidentifiable odor. *But who cares*, he thought, leaning closer still.

Recognition flickered across Bennie's face.

"Yeah, Bennie. It's me."

Something in the eyes responded.

"So here we are."

He pulled a wooden chair from the wall and leaned as close to Bennie as he could.

"Can you hear me?"

Greg wondered where to begin, then reminded himself to speak freely.

"Here we are and nobody won."

Bennie's eyes stayed wide and glazed.

"I didn't win. Neither did you. We thought we would change things, didn't we? You thought you'd make people mad at Christians and I thought I'd make them hate gays. We flopped."

Remembering what Mrs. Hudson had said, Greg reached over to stroke the mat of hair on Bennie's scalp.

"Can I touch you here?" he asked, stroking lightly and knowing his friend couldn't respond.

He grazed Bennie's hairline with two fingers.

"Your mom said you like to be touched." He kept stroking with his left hand and reached his right hand down to touch Bennie's. The contrast between their hands—thick and sinewy versus frail and bird-like—was appalling. Their fingers brushed lightly.

Like blood brothers.

"Ah, Bennie!"

He pulled his hands away, straightened up, and felt a sharp urge to cry. Only then did he realize that, through all the turmoil the past months had brought, he hadn't cried once. Not one drop.

He turned back to Bennie.

"I want to make peace. And I want to tell you something. You were only half-right. You got a life sentence that night, but so did I."

He slowed his speech down to make sure Bennie heard every word.

"I was as obsessed with you as you were with me. Every time I heard someone talk about gays I'd remember a bloodied kid on the beach. Every time I saw two little kids acting like buddies I'd hear you screaming. Every time I got a degree or an award and thought I was hot stuff, I'd see your eyes. Pitying me. You've been a thorn in my side that I couldn't rip out. Maybe you think that you were not important to me. Bennie, I've lain awake hating you because you were *too* important to me!"

Bennie moved for the first time. Greg barely noticed, then saw that he was making a trembling effort to raise his right hand.

Greg took the hand and held it lightly in his own. "You're hearing me? Squeeze if you understand what I'm saying."

He felt a light pressure in his palm.

"Good. Bennie?"

He brought his face close to Bennie's again.

"You see me okay?"

Squeeze.

"Then look real close," he whispered. "See that I'm sorry. I've been sorry all my life and I can't do a thing about it. But know it. Know how sorry I've always been."

Another squeeze. Greg returned it, and their hands stayed locked. He breathed deep, deeper than ever, and felt incredibly light. Was there anything more to say?

The respirator whirred and hissed; otherwise, the room was still.

Unusually still, Greg thought. Almost thick with silence. And then, suddenly, with peace.

A wave of it—or something like it, something wonderfully familiar—swelled over him. *Here*, Greg thought, *while a man's life ebbed? Peace in a place like this?*

Another wave hit him, stronger than the first, and he knew. *He's here.*

Greg's back shivered. He withdrew his hand, held it in mid-air, and closed his eyes. *And He brought His peace.*

Greg opened his eyes again, saw Bennie's emaciated form, and finally knew what should have been obvious from the start. There *was* something more to say.

"You're leaving."

The words flowed without forethought. His voice returned full force, and Greg realized the authority coming from him was no longer his own.

"And you'll see God, either as a friend or an enemy. What'll it be? You had a lot of accusations against me, and they're all true. But what about God? Have you ever thought He might have a few accusations against you?"

Bennie's eyes registered something; Greg guessed what it meant.

"Not just by being gay. Homosexuality is wrong, for sure, but it's just the tip of the iceberg. You've sinned millions of ways. We all have. And every sin made its mark somewhere. Someone's got to pay. Who will it be? You?"

Greg paused.

"You can't appease God any more than I could appease you. 'You can't atone, Bishop, so live with it.' Remember saying that? If you felt that way about me, think how He feels about you! And all of us, for that matter. We've all sinned. Anything less than perfection is a sin, so we're all guilty. And if I couldn't pay for my sins against you, you sure can't pay for your sins against God."

Greg prayed mentally as the words came tumbling out of him. Closer still, he was speaking into Bennie's ear.

"But Jesus paid. That's what the cross was about. He was punished because someone had to be, and He didn't want it to be you. Remember Sunday school? 'God so loved that world, that He gave His Son.' For you. So you wouldn't have to pay, and nothing would stand between the two of you. So you could belong to Him. So you could have what you've been looking for all your life."

Bennie's hand trembled.

"Perfect love."

His eyes widened slightly.

"He wants you. Do you want Him?"

Squeeze.

"Talk to Him. In your mind, repeat what I'm saying, but say it to Him. Tell Him you want Him. Like this."

Without thinking, Greg closed his eyes and combined every altar call he had ever heard.

"Jesus, I want to be forgiven for everything—everything I've done, every sin, every shortcoming. I believe You took the punishment for me. That was Your gift to me, and I accept it now. Save me. Come to me now; come into my heart like You said You would. Make me Yours."

Greg's breath ran out. He opened his eyes.

"Bennie, did you pray with me just then?"

Squeeze.

"Did you believe what you were saying?"

Squeeze.

"And do you know He's with you now? Inside you, even?"

Grip. Hard and solid.

Greg exhaled. Bennie's grip loosened only slightly; Greg wouldn't have considered releasing it. And his eyes, like his hands, locked into Bennie's one last time.

There was nothing more to say—no final blessing, no perfect finish. It was over, and it was good; trying to say more would have been futile. So with that in mind, Greg drew another breath, found his voice, and started to sing.

FORTY-EIGHT

*G*reg walked down the hall, found a bench by the nurses' station, sat down, and wept. Freely, loudly, indifferent to anyone who might have seen him.

When he was finished he made his way to the parking lot and shielded his eyes against the afternoon glare. There was still time for a drive.

Without planning to, he wandered down Ocean Boulevard, cruising in the right lane and marveling at the changes that had taken place along the coast—mammoth hotels, the International Trade Center, clusters of restaurants.

And the beach at Cherry Avenue coming up on the right.

Greg coasted down the hill, past the cliffs, and into the parking lot where he sat, idling the motor and scanning the beach.

Early summer. A light breeze, and a smattering of cars parked throughout the long strip. Strollers on the sand, mostly elderly, and a few swimmers. The oil islands, prettier at night when they were lit up, deceptive in their appearance of being close enough to swim to. Sea gulls, of course, and the lull of small waves lapping a hundred yards ahead.

Still a pleasant spot, but he wouldn't return. He had come to say good-bye. It took less than five minutes.

Heading back home to see Christine was an agreeable thought. He held onto it while he turned off Ocean Boulevard onto the freeway. His mind couldn't handle any more for now; just Christine, and home. Plenty of time later to sort out the rest.

What a job that will be, he thought as he entered the on ramp. *Sorting it all out.*

But he knew, already, how it would work. Events and people—some horrible, all incredible—would become memories; memories would become lessons. All of them, eventually, would be studied, categorized, and recorded forever.

Doubts would come; some were already forming—especially about Bennie. Had he really understood, really accepted Greg's apology, really prayed from the heart?

But as quick as the doubts came, so also came reassurance as Greg remembered that the squeeze of Bennie's hand, like the presence of God in Room 317, had been very strong indeed.

AUTHOR'S NOTES

California Assembly Bill 101 (which granted sexual orientation the protections afforded to race, gender, and religion) passed the State Legislature yet was vetoed September 29, 1991, by Governor Pete Wilson. Statewide demonstrations followed, and acts of vandalism did occur. But to the author's knowledge, no churches or private properties were damaged, and no one was injured or killed in connection with these protests.

The organizations BRAVO, Citizens United, and The Covenant are fictitious, but such groups do exist. Certain militant gay organizations adopt tactics similar to those used in the story by BRAVO; to the author's knowledge, physical assaults have not yet had a part in these tactics, but at times verbal threats of violence have been made. White supremacist groups continue to flourish, often under the guise of Christianity, and their beliefs and goals are similar to those ascribed to The Covenant.

There are no such drugs as Amitrex or Phynothal.

Gateway Ministries (also a fictitious group) is based on the work of Exodus International, which for twenty years has provided counsel and support to people overcoming homosexuality. Exodus International-sponsored ministries can be found throughout America and Europe. For more information, contact Exodus International, P.O. Box 2121, San Rafael, CA 94912.

ACKNOWLEDGMENTS

The title *Unforgiven Sins* was conceived by Bill Jensen of Harvest House Publishers. Eileen Mason, also of Harvest House, offered great help in nurturing the book along. Dr. Ken Williams provided advice on medical details; Raymond Jones, M.Div., MFCC, gave counsel on ethics in the psychiatric profession. The details of Assembly Bill 101 were provided courtesy of the staff of California Assemblyman Terry Friedman. The staff at the Christian Research Institute of Irvine, California, supplied information about white supremacist groups.

Editor Steve Miller served as an invaluable source of support and guidance. *Unforgiven Sins* would surely have been abandoned but for his patience, expertise, and faith in the project.

Grateful acknowledgment is made to each.

*Real Hope for Those Who
Struggle with Homosexuality*

Desires in Conflict

by **Joe Dallas**

doesn't offer any quick fixes. What you will find
is effective help for restoring sexual wholeness
and moving ahead in the Christian life.

Desires in Conflict will help not only those who
struggle with their sexual identity, but provide
real understanding and information to anyone
who cares about a family member or friend who
struggles with homosexuality.

CONTEMPORARY FICTION
FROM HARVEST HOUSE

THE RECKONING
by *James Byron Huggins*

In a world ruled by the purest survivors, the fiercest warriors, Gage was the strongest—an American executing his country's darkest missions with legendary cunning and skill. Until—wounded and dying—he found mercy at the hands of an aging priest. Separating from the secret world he once dominated, he chose a life of solitary faith. But the murder of his mentor and the theft of an ancient manuscript force him to emerge and face his greatest battle. From the streets of New York to the inner recesses of the Vatican, Gage challenges the awesome might of an ageless evil.

A WOLF STORY
by *James Byron Huggins*

Long ago, the inhabitants of the deep woods were given a difficult choice: to follow the Silver Wolf and his Lord, the Lightmaker, or join the secretive forces of the Dark Council. A war rages across the harsh wilderness, and the Dark Council is on the threshold of victory—only a lone wolf, Aramus, stands in their way.

This fast-paced novel portrays the struggle between good and evil—which is more than strength against strength, more than wit against wit. It is a path of endurance and faith....

RUMORS OF ANGELS
by *John Vincent Coniglio*

The world's greatest legal mind was finally getting the trial he had spent his life preparing for. Will stood ready to challenge the reality of Christ's resurrection—and brand it forever as a myth. A final warning that he was violating sacred ground fell on deaf ears—"The God whose logic you question is the God of the universe.... If I were in your shoes, I would bend a heedful ear to the proclamation of the angels in the tomb that morning."

Startling and unpredictable, *Rumors of Angels* is a search for evidence...a search for facts...and ultimately, a search for truth.